BRIGHT
LIGHTS
&
SUMMER
NIGHTS

KAT SINGLETON

Copyright © 2024 by Kat Singleton

All rights reserved.

This book, or parts thereof, may not be reproduced in any form without the express written permission of the author, except for the use of brief quotations in a book review.

Printed in the United States of America.

ISBN: 978-1-958292-14-3

This is a work of fiction. The names, characters, and incidents portrayed in the novel are either products of the author's imagination or used fictitiously.

Cover Design and Interior Images by Ashlee O'Brien with Ashes & Vellichor

Cover Photo by Katie Welter with Cadwallader Photography

Cover Models: Joshua Alwran and Katie Welter

Developmental Edit by Salma R

Edited by Sandra Dee with One Love Editing

For my girlies that are still figuring life out. Here's to getting a little lost before being found. I hope you find your very own grumpy billionaire with a dirty mouth along the way. Until then, have the best time with Preston Rhodes.

PLAYLIST

When Emma Falls in Love - Taylor Swift
Stolen - Dashboard Confessional
peace - Taylor Swift
Summer Love - One Direction
The Prophecy - Taylor Swift
Mess is Mine - Vance Joy
Espresso - Sabrina Carpenter
The Alchemy - Taylor Swift
Confident - We Three, M Humlie, B Zimmerman
sex - EDEN
So High School - Taylor Swift
Paradise - Bazzi
National Anthem - Lana Del Ray
Daydreamin' - Ariana Grande
Sun to Me - Zach Bryan
Best Friends - 5 Seconds of Summer
Someone to You - BANNERS

AUTHOR'S NOTE

Bright Lights and Summer Nights is a billionaire, sports, fake dating, age gap romance. It is full of banter, sweet moments, and scenes that'll have you blushing. I hope that you love Emma and Preston as much as I do. This is the third and final book in a series of interconnected stand-alones set in the Black Tie Billionaires Series.

Bright Lights and Summer Nights contains mature content that may not be suitable for all audiences. Please go to authorkatsingleton.com/content-warnings for a list of content warnings for the book.

1
Emma

"I WOULD SAY I'M SHOCKED, BUT I'M ACTUALLY NOT SURPRISED AT all," my best friend, Winnie, tells me, her eyes narrowed on me from across the small café table.

My nose scrunches as I try to decide if I'm offended by her comment. "Listen. I know I don't have the best history with jobs, but that one was even more terrible than most. My boss was pushing sixty and kept asking me to do *private* work at his house." I take a long drink of my iced coffee, remembering the creepy looks he was always giving me. "Private work at his house can't be good, Winnie."

She shrugs, nodding as she realizes I have a point. "I could always see if we could get you a job at Bishop-Moore." Her voice is sweet, and I know she's just trying to be nice by offering a job at the hotel dynasty she runs with her husband, Archer Moore, but working another job that I don't have a passion for is the last thing I want to do.

With a groan, I sit back in the padded chair of the fancy restaurant she'd invited me to. "That's nice of you, Win, but I think I need to figure out what I want to do with the rest of my life instead of just jumping from one job to the next." I sigh, wishing that all of my friends didn't feel the need to offer me jobs.

"Maybe you just need to take a break for a moment. You

could take a step back and decide what you want to do—think of it like a gap year. Yours would just be a little later than most."

I shake my head. I know she means well because there isn't a mean bone in Winnie's body. She's probably the sweetest person I've ever met, but her words sting a little because I'm tired of being the only one in my friend group who has no idea what they're doing with their life. Winnie married Archer, and the two of them have created an empire together. Margo married Beckham Sinclair, the two of them becoming a power couple themselves with him running a cybersecurity empire and her becoming one of the most sought-after artists. And then there's Camden, who is like a brother to me, but even he keeps offering me jobs at his art galleries when I should never be trusted with expensive art. Even Camden's girlfriend, Pippa, who has become one of my best friends, has tried to convince me to move to Colorado and work at her bakery with her.

"I feel like my *entire* life after college has been a gap year. I followed you and Margo to California. I followed you both back to New York. All I do is *follow*." I try not to let the sadness seep through the tone of my voice, but I'm twenty-five and lost. I don't want to feel like I'm pitiful, but it's hard not to when everyone has their lives completely figured out. I meet her eyes as I try to appear more confident than I feel. "I have no idea what to do with my life now that following you isn't an option."

Winnie thinks over my words for a minute, just staring at me with a look that I'm all too familiar with. She's probably the only person in the world whom I can sit in comfortable silence with. I know when she's ready to talk, she will; it might just take a moment.

Finally, she clears her throat as she neatly runs her hand over the white tablecloth of the table. "Why don't you get away? Travel somewhere? You've always loved posting about our girls' trips. You could make a blog about finding yourself."

I scoff, my eyes wide as I look at her. "*One*, blogs don't exist anymore, and *two*, I'm not starting a blog founded on me having no idea what to do with my life. That seems pathetic."

She waves her hand in the air, completely undeterred by me shutting her idea down completely. "Then forget about blogging and get away for a little bit. Find yourself...and maybe in doing that, you'll find what you want to do. I know it's cheesy, but life *can* be a little cheesy sometimes, Emma. If you want, you can stay at our Hamptons house. It's already been two months since we closed, but a lot of the things I ordered were on backorder and are only now arriving. You could do me a favor and stay there and sign for the deliveries."

"Winnie, you can hire anyone to do that. You don't have to offer it to me because you feel bad for me."

She shakes her head. "I'm not hiring you to do anything. It isn't a job. It's a free place to stay while you figure out your next steps."

I stare at my best friend, wondering if I should take her up on her offer or not. Now that I've quit another job, I don't have any obligations in New York right now. I could go wherever I wanted. The Hamptons doesn't sound so bad. We've been a few times as a friend group, and it was a blast. I'm sure going during summer is even more fun because it's the busy season.

"I can tell you want to say yes," Winnie adds, a smile forming on her lips because she knows she's right.

I roll my eyes, leaning forward and putting my elbows on the table. "It seems irresponsible of me to say yes. Shouldn't I be interviewing for a new job or something? Isn't that what *adults* do?"

It's Winnie's turn to roll her eyes—something I don't see her do often. "Screw being an adult, Em. It's one summer and a chance to figure yourself out. Prioritizing yourself might be one of the most adult things you've ever done."

I laugh, raising an eyebrow at her. "Did getting married make you a poet? Damn, Winnie, that was deep."

She throws a linen napkin at me, her cheeks getting red with embarrassment. "I'm just trying to make a point. You're still young—and *seriously* hot—you have so much time to discover what you want to do with your life. Maybe a summer in the Hamptons *will* change your life in ways you aren't expecting."

I'm quiet for a moment, really thinking her words through. I hope she's right. I've always been the fun, single friend who lived life day to day. But I'm ready to start making plans—I want to settle down and find what I want to do with the rest of my life.

The idea of forever has always been scary for me, but now as everyone around me has found their own version of it, I realize I might want that too. Maybe a couple of months in the Hamptons will be *exactly* what I need.

2
Emma

My grip is tight on the handle of my suitcase as I stop in the driveway of Winnie's Hamptons home. My lips twitch as I look up, a wide smile spreading over my face.

"This will do," I mutter under my breath, gazing at my home for the summer until the Uber driver interrupts me from my thoughts.

"Having a party?" he asks, handing me a tote bag with three bottles of wine.

I shrug. "Those are for me."

The man quirks an eyebrow, staring me down with a speculative look on his face.

I blow out some air, trying to ease the awkward tension. "Don't judge me, Simon. It *was* Simon, right?" I add on, worrying that I may have messed up his name.

"Yes, it's Simon." He turns around to get the rest of my luggage from the back of his sedan.

Simon hasn't been my biggest fan since the moment he picked me up from the airport. I had a luggage carrier spilling over with suitcases as I waited on the curb for my ride. I was supposed to arrive in Long Island hours ago, but due to my flight being delayed twice, I'm arriving as the sun sets.

I won't let the late arrival time and fussy driver burst my bubble, though. I've got three bottles of wine I spent way too much money on and a big empty house all to myself. *Nothing can rain on my parade.*

"I hear Pembroke is having a lavish, exclusive party tonight," he notes, grunting as he drops my suitcase to the ground.

"Really?" I ask, intrigued. I've visited Pembroke Hills—one of the most expensive country clubs in the country—multiple times with my friends, but I've never gone alone. I don't think I'd even be able to get in, but it would be a fun time...

"Yes," Simon answers. "My wife loves to tell me where all of the events are taking place each night, even if she never wants to get out of the house to actually go to them."

"There's nothing wrong with staying in," I say, taking my last piece of luggage from him. I hadn't thought about getting all of these inside Winnie's place on my own, but I know it might be too big of an ask to have Simon help me.

"Not at all," he responds. "But you're young and should be attending all the fun parties. If my wife, Trina, was here, she'd insist you go."

I cock my head to the side. "It's been a long travel day. Plus, I wasn't invited."

Simon closes his trunk with a loud *thud.* "Something tells me you'll figure it out." His eyes travel to my large pile of luggage I'll have to lug inside. "Maybe try packing lighter next time?" He winks, softening his comment just a little.

Maybe I was wrong about Simon.

"It's not in my personality to pack light," I quip with a shrug. I must have an outfit for every situation, and I like to have options. I will always be the person who adds additional bags to my flight registration and will still manage to pay an overweight bag fee.

Simon shakes his head at me. "Have a good night. Stay safe." Before I can answer, he slides into the car and drives away, leaving me and my collection of luggage alone.

WINNIE

Hope you made it to the house safely. Let us know when you're settled!

MARGO

Em, that's Winnie's way of telling you she's worried about you.

WINNIE

Me? Worried? Never ;)

EMMA

You always worry.

Made it to the house and enjoying a glass of wine. Thank you again for helping me with my quarter-life crisis, Win!

WINNIE

Let me know if you need anything. Make sure to go out and enjoy yourself!

MARGO

This is where Winnie types a long speech about finding yourself...

WINNIE

Had to delete everything I just typed so I could prove you wrong.

I take a drink of my wine, staring at my phone as I wait for their next text. The house is a little empty without my friends here with me. Every other time I've visited the Hamptons, it's been with them.

Any other time, you'd find Beck, Camden, and Archer seated at the breakfast nook, talking about boring business stuff that I didn't care to pay attention to. Margo and Winnie would be hunched over interior design magazines, planning the next thing they'd decorate together. And Pippa would either be drinking straight from the wine bottle with me, or she'd be in the kitchen baking something new while she forced all of us to taste test.

Taking a deep breath, I place my phone face down on the counter and try to push away the feeling of loneliness. I think part of this summer in the Hamptons is me needing to be okay with being alone and learning who I am. There's nothing like hitting rock bottom only to realize you have no idea who you are —and what you'll do with the rest of your life.

My phone vibrates against the counter, but I leave it face down. Maybe the start of this summer of self-discovery will be less of me depending on my friends. Winnie and Margo are the best friends I could ever ask for. I met them in college when I desperately needed to find people who accepted me and showed me what it was like to be loved and cared for. I've allowed myself to let their choices dictate the path of my life. I followed both of them to LA after college and then moved back to New York when they decided it was time for them to come home.

This summer, I want to figure out where *I* want to be—*who* I want to be. I want to learn to love myself. And I want the start of that to be tonight.

Looking at the half-empty bottle of wine, I grab it by the neck and press the top to my lips. In a few easy gulps, I've emptied the entire bottle. "Ah," I say, wiping my lips with the back of my hand.

I slide my phone off the counter, opening up the camera app and turning it to face me. It's not the cutest I've ever looked in my life, but I feel inspired—and maybe Winnie was right about documenting it.

Letting out a nervous breath, I smile at the camera. "This might be the silliest thing I've ever done," I mutter, tucking a strand of my blonde hair behind my ear. "But doing new things is all about making yourself uncomfortable, right?"

I pause, waiting for an answer before I realize that I'm talking to a screen—no one is going to answer me. Laughing, I shake my head. "My name is Emma, and I'm *kind of* a mess." I take a break, tilting my head to the side as I look away from the camera for a minute. "Well, it's more than kind of. I'm a huge mess. But I'm trying to get my life together, and I figured I'd document it. I'm going to use these videos as a diary of some sort. That way, when I look back—when, hopefully, I have my life together—I can see how far I've come."

For the next ten minutes, I ramble on about my life story and everything I want to do this summer. I'm more open about things than I feel like I may be while sober, but it's refreshing to voice all my fears out loud and address them by saying everything I want to accomplish before I leave the Hamptons.

By the end of it, I feel lighter than ever. I still have no idea what my future holds, but at least I'm doing something about it. I feel so good that I decide I actually am going to go out tonight. Do I have any idea if I'll even be able to get into this fancy, exclusive party at the club? *No*. But it doesn't hurt to try.

I film one last video telling my audience of no one but myself that I've decided to go out tonight and that I'll keep them posted. I leave my phone on the counter and run to the room I'll be staying in to get ready.

I have no idea where the night will take me, but I want an outfit that makes me feel hot as hell—and one that gives the illusion that I belong somewhere as fancy as Pembroke Hills Country Club.

And I think I know *just* the outfit I want.

Tonight is the first night of an amazing—hopefully life-changing—summer. And I'm ready to get it started.

3
Preston

"You could at least *pretend* to be enjoying the welcome party for my wedding," my sister, Peyton, jabs before taking a sip of her dirty martini.

I grunt, my fingers tightening around the beer I've been nursing for the past hour. "I'm sorry, P. I'm enjoying it. You know me and parties—they aren't my thing."

"I remember hearing all about your legendary parties in college," she quips.

Cheers erupt in the corner of the busy bar as her future husband is coerced into taking another shot. She looks at Jackson lovingly, as if he can do no wrong, even though it takes him about five tries to finish off taking a shot instead of swallowing it down in one gulp.

Personally, I think my baby sister could do better than a man who wears a collared shirt even to the beach, but she's madly in love. So, my opinion doesn't matter. He loves her dearly, and she loves him.

I don't hate the guy; I just don't love the fact that the next week will be filled with one party after another before their wedding day on Saturday. It isn't Peyton's fault—although, she does love a party—it's more our parents. Their only daughter is getting married, and since I have zero plans to walk down the aisle anytime soon, they've spared no expense for the festivities.

Not like they ever would anyway. P and I grew up surrounded by money—the richest of the rich. Weddings are a big deal, no matter how much I loathe them.

"Dreaming of your party days?" Peyton asks, interrupting me from my thoughts.

I take a drink of my lukewarm beer, rolling my eyes. "Those days are over. Almost lost the chance to be drafted because of those party days, remember?"

It's her turn to roll her eyes. "You were *the* best quarterback anyone had seen in years. A few drunk videos of you running through the press weren't going to ruin that."

I smile. "It was almost enough for Mom and Dad to disown me, though."

We both look to our parents on the other side of the room. They're deep in conversation with a couple that Mom talks shit about constantly.

"I think it was the sleeve of tattoos that almost got you disinherited," Peyton offers, pointing to my arm.

In the freshly pressed suit, you'd have no idea that tattoos run along both my arms.

"They *were* pretty pissed about the tattoos," I note, fighting back a smile. I have good parents. They were great growing up, but I was a rebel despite their best attempts to make me into the perfect, clean-cut son they wanted me to be.

They wanted me to play soccer, so I chose football. They said I should go to school for finance; I went to college for marketing. They expected me to take over the family business; I opted for going into the draft and using my first rookie check to invest in my college roommate's start-up. The tattoos were just icing on the cake for going against exactly who they wanted me to be and becoming who I desired to be.

Plus, there was no reason for me to try and be the perfect child. The moment P was born when I was eleven, I knew she'd be the favorite. I was okay with that because as soon as my parents brought her home, *I* knew she was perfect.

"Peyton, dear, come mingle with our guests!" Jackson shouts across the crowded space, holding his arm out for her.

She looks at me with an apologetic smile. "Turns out I'm supposed to go *mingle*." She emphasizes the last word playfully. "Try not to look too bored tonight, okay? It's the off-season. I've given strict orders to Ryan to leave you alone until next week, so live a little." She winks before backing up and heading to her fiancé.

I fight the urge to grab my phone from my pocket and see if I've heard anything from Ryan, who's been my agent since I was a rookie. He's been hounding me on signing an extension with the Manhattan Mambas, and since I'm at the peak of my career, they're offering me a stupid amount of money for five more years.

Problem is, I don't want to sign it. I want the upcoming season to be my last one, and I fear my agent might have a heart attack when I tell him that.

With a loud sigh, I drink the rest of my beer and set it on the bar. I push off the counter, wanting to find water and get some fresh air. People in the crowd try to stop me to talk, but I pretend I don't hear them as I squeeze through the bodies. I'll come back and talk to people because I know that's what P and my parents want, but first, I need ten minutes of calm.

I finally find the back door of the space, and the moment the salty beach air hits my face, I'm able to take a deep breath. I grew up frequenting the Hamptons with my family, and there really is nothing like the air here.

I walk around the building, trying to hide from view if someone were to open the back door. No one should come looking for me, at least if I don't stay out here too long, but I want to make sure I'm allowed at least a few minutes of peace.

But it only lasts a couple of minutes before a heel comes flying over the large metal gate, almost hitting me in the face.

"What the fuck." I take a step back, trying to see into the dark to find out where it came from.

"Is someone there?" a voice hesitantly asks from above.

Before I can answer, another heel comes flying at me.

"Yes!" I yell, rubbing my chest where a particularly pointy heel just hit me. "Someone is definitely here."

"Shit," the voice on the other side of the fence says under their breath. "Could you maybe just…go away for a minute?" they ask, their voice louder this time.

My lips twitch. Her voice is sweet but sultry, going up a little bit in pitch at the end as if she's nervous.

"Why? So you can stop assaulting me with heels?"

The woman nervously laughs. "*No.* So I can climb this fence without someone watching me undoubtedly land on my ass."

"You want me to walk away from you breaking into a private party?" I ask, taking a step closer to the direction of her voice.

There's nothing but silence for a few minutes until she finally speaks again. "Basically. You can go back inside and pretend I was never here—and I'm spared the embarrassment of you watching me land on my ass. When I walk in, we'll both pretend I belong at this party. Sound good?"

"*Or,*" I begin, stopping at the gate and looking up. It's so dark I still can't see her, but she's piqued my interest. There's no way I'm going inside until my eyes land on the little trespasser. "You can climb the fence, and I can help you down so there's no injuries involved."

"You promise you won't rat me out?" she asks cautiously. She's so close, close enough that if the trees weren't so thick and if the moon were full, I might actually be able to get a glimpse of the face behind the voice.

"It depends," I answer, tucking my hands into the pockets of my pants. "Do you promise not to cause any trouble at the event?"

"Are you security?" she asks, her voice tight with unease.

I laugh, the sound vibrating my chest. "Not quite."

It's silent for long enough I begin to wonder if she decided to leave. For some reason, my stomach sinks slightly at the idea of never seeing the face that goes with the voice. I clear my throat. "You comin' down now?"

She groans, and relief floods my body with the knowledge she didn't go. "I guess I have no choice. Those shoes cost me an entire paycheck."

My eyes flick to the shoes for a moment before my attention returns to the top of the fence.

A few grunts and curses come from the other side before finally, a tan thigh and a bare foot appear at the top.

She's blonde, her hair barely hitting the tops of her collarbones, but because of the dark, I can't fully see her face.

I squint, trying to make out her features. "On the count of three, jump down and I'll catch you."

Her hair blows in the wind as she nods her head. "Okay," she says tentatively.

"One…" I begin, lifting my hands in the air to help her down. "Two…"

"Wait!" she yells, shifting her weight slightly at the top. "How do I know you won't let me face-plant?"

"Guess you're just going to have to trust me," I counter, wiggling my fingers, even though I'm unaware if she can see them or not.

She laughs sarcastically, the sound echoing off the trees. "Trust a total stranger who is witnessing me commit a felony? You really have reached rock bottom, Emma…"

Emma.

I play with the name in my head, surprisingly wanting to immediately know everything about her.

"Well, *Emma*," I begin, lowering my voice slightly. "You have two choices. You can trust me to catch you and attend the party you've worked so hard to break into, or you can jump back down and return home wondering what would've happened if you just trusted a handsome stranger in the dark."

"Very bold of you to call yourself handsome."

This makes me laugh. A loud one that comes from deep

inside my chest. Now isn't the time to tell her that just last year, I was announced as the sexiest man alive. My publicist forced me to do a photoshoot and a media tour for the entire thing. It isn't my favorite accolade I've been awarded, but I'm confident enough to know most view me as handsome.

"Why don't you jump down and you can tell me yourself?" I fire back, desperate for her to take the bait and jump.

I wait for her to respond, but instead of answering, she does the last thing I was expecting. She launches herself from the top of the fence without any sort of warning.

She yelps, her body catapulting into mine.

"Fuck," I mutter, my hands grabbing her hips as my feet plant into the grass to try and stop the both of us from falling to the ground.

The stranger—Emma—grips my arms like she's holding on for dear life. Her arms wrap around my neck as her shaking body molds to mine.

"What happened to counting down?" I ask, my voice tight.

She laughs under her breath. "Counting down makes it worse. I had to go for it."

Before I can respond, she pulls away. I let her feet hit the ground, confident she's safe now. I want to give her some sort of witty remark, but I'm too thrown off by the sheer beauty of the woman standing in front of me to speak.

4
Emma

A LOUD LAUGH BUBBLES FROM MY THROAT AS I TAKE IN THE stranger staring at me with an unreadable look on his face. "Wow. It turns out you *weren't* lying," I mutter, wondering if I said it for his benefit or for mine.

He cocks his head to the side, his sharp jawline now illuminated by the moon. "Lying about what?"

"You are *stupidly* handsome," I answer, wishing it wasn't the truth.

His lips twitch. It isn't a full smile, but even though I barely know this man, I could guess that a full smile is hard to earn from him. "You say that like it's a bad thing."

My hands find my hips as I take another step back, the grass soft beneath my feet. "It's a terrible thing. The more handsome a man is, the more of an asshole he is, too. It's a proven fact."

One of his dark eyebrows rises as he watches me closely. God, does he have to be *so* attractive? His blue eyes are almost piercing, feeling like they're staring me down right to my soul as he thinks something over.

I use the silence to my advantage, my eyes roaming over him so I can drink him in. His dark hair is buzzed short on the sides and slightly longer at the top, but not by a lot. The haircut suits him, bringing attention to all the sharp lines of his chiseled features.

"I'm going to pretend you didn't just assume that I'm an asshole," he notes, turning around and reaching down to grab each of my discarded heels.

I smile. "Don't take it too personally. Like I said, it's a proven fact. Men who know they're unimaginably handsome are walking red flags."

He ignores me, instead choosing to hold both my heels in one hand and branding the other one out between us.

My eyes narrow as I watch him carefully. I look from his outstretched hand to the one holding my shoes.

"I'll take those. Thank you." I reach to grab them, but he lifts them into the air and out of my reach. Without my heels on, he's got quite a bit of height on me. I have to crane my neck to look up at him.

"Handsome and trying to steal my shoes?" I fire, jumping to try and snatch the shoes anyway.

"I don't want your shoes, Emma."

My spine stiffens at the way he says my name. It has never sounded so good as it does coming from his lips. "Then hand them over," I demand, needing to get out of this man's presence before I do something stupid like ask him if we should just break the tension by sleeping together.

He holds out his hand again. "Let me help steady you," he offers, holding out the shoes.

I watch him for a moment, wondering if it's a trap. Deciding he might actually want to help and not be a total asshole, I place my hand in his. It takes everything in me to stay composed and keep my face straight as I shift my weight to one leg to slip the heel on. His skin against mine is electrifying. My entire body heats with just the smallest touch of our skin.

His grip is firm, even as I shift again to slide on the other shoe. After both are on and I'm steady on my feet, he keeps his fingers wrapped strongly around mine for a moment too long.

He stares at me, and the longer it stays silent between us, the thicker the tension gets. It finally gets so thick that I have to speak up in an attempt to break it.

"You know my name. It's only fair I know yours." My voice comes out weird, far deeper and breathier than I'd like.

"Preston," he answers immediately, as if he was just waiting for me to ask.

"Preston," I repeat. His name's sexy. *He's* sexy. He's so attractive I'm wondering if part of my self-discovery this summer should be discovering *him* a bit more.

"Come get a drink with me inside, Emma?" he asks.

God.

I have a generic name. It isn't anything special or groundbreaking—but coming from his lips, it sounds like the greatest name someone could ever be given.

"What's the catch?" I ask, waiting to follow him inside. I like how confident he is, how he turns around and begins walking to the door like he already knows I'll follow him.

Preston looks over his shoulder. "No catch. One drink. If I'm too boring for you—or too much of an asshole—you're free to explore the party you snuck into alone."

"One drink?" I repeat, wondering why it feels mildly disappointing imagining myself exploring the party without him.

"One drink. No strings attached. It's an open bar, and I heard the hosts of the party spared no expense when it comes to this celebration."

I pick up my pace, awkwardly running until I catch up to him. "You should've led with 'an open bar.'"

"There's no way in hell you're getting me to take a shot that's called a Blow Job," Preston argues, a deep line appearing across his forehead. We've been talking for over an hour, and after a few drinks, one thing I've learned about him is that you have to really work to get a reaction out of this man.

I lean over the bar, trying to flag down the bartender to absolutely order two Blow Job shots. When I still can't catch the attention of the bartender, I look back at my grumpy company. "The shot is delicious, I promise."

"Not happening," he responds, his voice void of any humor.

I bite my bottom lip, even though I know I'm probably ruining the red lipstick I'd worked so hard on applying. "You don't strike me as the kind of man who doesn't enjoy blow jobs."

Preston rubs his hand over his face, desperately trying to hide the slight blush on his chiseled cheeks. "Do you just say whatever comes to your mind, no matter what?"

Before I can answer, the bartender walks by, and I finally get the chance to order. "Two Blow Job shots," I request, holding up two fingers and winking at Preston, who still has the ghost of a smile on his lips.

The bartender looks between Preston and me as if he isn't sure if I'm serious or not. Preston finally lets out a long sigh before giving one curt nod of his head.

I frown, wishing the bartender would've listened without Preston having to give the green light, but I don't let it bother me for long.

As we wait for the bartender to bring us our shots, I take a step closer to Preston. He's got one elbow on the bar, his fingers wrapped around a beer glass. For some reason, I find it hot that he's drinking a beer. Everyone else in this bar is walking around with expensive crystal glasses of bourbon or scotch.

He looks out of place drinking a beer, but I love it. And it's the only thing about him that looks out of place. The way he holds himself, his ridiculous chiseled features, and the way he can command the room with little effort tells me that he belongs in this world. He has money—and I'd bet the small dollar amount I have to my name he grew up surrounded by money.

"So, are you going to tell me what you have against blow jobs?" I tease, taking a step toward him. I'm well aware my tone has gotten flirtier with each drink and the more time I spend with him. I can't help it. I'm incredibly attracted to this man. Maybe I also enjoy getting a reaction out of him.

His jaw clenches, muscles along his cheeks feathering with the movement. "Nothing against blow jobs when it involves my cock. I'm just not a man who enjoys taking shots—especially ones with a name like *Blow Job*. I'm too old for that."

He doesn't move. Even when I take another step closer to him, completely invading his personal space. In fact, he stares right at me, as if daring me to get even closer.

I don't. He's the most attractive man I've ever seen, which means he's *exactly* what I don't need this summer. It doesn't stop me from at least enjoying the flirting tonight. My head may feel a little fuzzier than normal, but I'm still fully in control of my actions. I won't let anything more happen between us aside from the innocent flirting.

"Is bringing up my cock the way to get you to stop talking?" Preston pushes, giving me a smile that doesn't reach his eyes.

God. He's the *good* kind of asshole, the kind that has me squeezing my thighs together. Or maybe it's the mention of his…*cock* and the way the word sounds coming from his lips.

"You'll have to work harder than that to get me to shut up," I counter, feeling my cheeks heat. I'm not someone who ever blushes—but oh my god, he's doing a good job at making me do just that.

Preston leans back a little, his eyes roaming down my body. He takes a large drink of his beer, and I try not to stare at the muscles in his throat as he swallows slowly. Finally, he looks back at me with one raised dark eyebrow. "Don't tempt me, rebel."

Before I can comment on the nickname, a girl with dark hair is squeezing right between Preston and me.

"Preston," she says, her voice high-pitched. "I was hoping you'd be here."

He looks over her head right at me, his shoulders tight as he answers her. "You knew I would be."

She laughs, looking back at me as if I'm an outsider to their inside joke. Hell, maybe I am. "Preston is just *so* funny, isn't he?" she marvels. "He's *always* been this funny."

I don't miss how she emphasizes the word *always*. She's doing everything she can to make it clear the two of them have known each other for a long time.

The woman reaches out and runs her hand down his chest, making one of my eyebrows shoot up.

To Preston's credit, he immediately pushes her hand off him, but she doesn't seem to understand he isn't interested. I stand there, not wanting to get involved in whatever this is.

"Funny," I muse, taking the shots from the bartender. "The last thing I ever expected to call Preston was funny. His personality seems a little dry."

The woman looks at me as if I just committed a crime. Surely, she can't really think Preston is all that funny. I've known him for not even two hours, and nothing about him screams comedian. I guess you could confuse his dryness with humor, but I don't think anything that comes out of his mouth is intentionally funny.

"Would you like a Blow Job?" I ask her, holding up the shot that was supposed to be Preston's.

"That's my Blow Job," Preston counters, taking it from my hand. The whipped cream at the top jiggles with his rushed movement.

"Thought you weren't into blow jobs," I counter, trying to hide my grin. This is far too entertaining. I don't know whose eyes get wider—hers or his.

"What's your name again?" the girl asks, narrowing her eyes like she hates me without even knowing a thing about me.

"You never asked in the first place," I answer with a sweet smile. "But it's Emma."

"You're Preston's..." She lets the words hang in the air for a moment.

Before I can answer, Preston distracts me by holding the shot to his lips and taking it in one easy gulp. He slaps the empty shot glass on the counter and looks at me with a genuine smile. "She's my girlfriend."

5
Preston

"*GIRLFRIEND*?" EMMA REPEATS, HER VOICE TIGHT AS SHE LOOKS intensely at me.

"I didn't know you had a girlfriend," Marsha whines, her lips jutting out in a pout, which is comical because I've never shown her a shred of interest in the countless years she's been friends with Peyton.

"I'm entitled to keeping my private life private," I answer, reaching out for Emma. I take her hand and pull her closer. She narrowly avoids spilling her shot all over Marsha in the process. I look down at Emma with affection. "My Emma really likes to keep things private. Don't you, sweetie?"

Emma, to her own credit, doesn't move away from my touch. If anything, she leans a little closer, allowing me to wrap my arm around her.

"You know me," she says through gritted teeth. "I *never* share my personal details."

My lips twitch as I fight a smile. I don't know her well, but in the conversation we've had tonight, I've learned that she's an open book.

"Is this new?" Marsha asks, her eyes bouncing between Emma and me.

"Yes," Emma answers immediately.

"Not really," I say at the same time.

Emma looks up at me with her eyebrows drawn. As if she's just remembering she still hasn't taken her shot, she lifts it to her lips and drinks it completely. She sets the glass on the bar and wraps her other arm around my middle.

Leaning in, she gets as close to my ear as possible. "I'm going to kill you," she whispers, looking at Marsha with a smile. "I'm not your freaking girlfriend."

I pretend to not hear her. It wasn't my intention to say that to Marsha, but the last thing I want is to have her hanging over me all weekend. A little white lie and a few minutes of pretending we're dating would deter Marsha for the week. I'll make sure to thank Emma for going along with it later.

"It's time we go visit the other party guests," I announce, grabbing Emma by the arm. I hold her tight enough in hopes that she won't move but loose enough that if she wanted to get away from me, she easily could. "I'd love to introduce my girlfriend to the other guests, so we'll be going."

"*Girlfriend?*" I hear my sister shout from across the bar.

"Oh fuck," I mumble, realizing this tiny lie just got a whole lot bigger with the beaming smile on P's face.

"Who is that?" Emma asks in concern, watching Marsha walk away.

My teeth grind together as I turn around and stop directly in front of Emma. She yelps. Her hands falling to my chest are the only reason she doesn't walk right into me.

"Here's the thing," I begin, glancing over my shoulder to see my sister doing her best to get to us despite guests trying to steal her attention. "I'm going to need you to pretend to be my girlfriend. Just for tonight. Can you do that for me?"

"No," Emma answers immediately. Her eyes are wide as they scan my face. She's looking at me like I've completely lost my mind, and I'm not sure I blame her.

I look up at the ceiling for a minute before looking back at her. I hope she can see the vulnerability in my features. I don't ask favors from people often—certainly not from strangers—but the giddy look on my sister's face is not something I want to wipe away the week of her wedding. "*Please?*" I ask, knowing that any second now, Peyton is going to come barreling into us.

"I don't know you," she whispers, even though it isn't necessary. Peyton has been stopped by friends of my parents, buying us a little more time. "I can't just pretend to be your girlfriend."

"Just for tonight. Do it for me and I won't tell anyone that the real reason you're here is because you snuck into my sister's wedding arrival party."

Emma gasps, and before I can apologize for the cheap shot, Peyton makes it to us.

"Preston," Peyton says through a bright smile. "Who do we have here? Have you been hiding a girlfriend from me?" Peyton's eyes giddily bounce between Emma and me as she waits for me to answer.

Emma pinches my arm, clearly not happy with how this is playing out.

I ignore it, hoping my sister will make this quick. I stifle a groan, knowing that Peyton has begged for me to bring a girlfriend around her for years. Something tells me she's about to want to spend all night speaking with Emma instead of enjoying her own party.

"Peyton, this is my girlfriend, Emma." I put my arm around Emma once again, letting out a sigh of relief when she doesn't run. Her posture is stiff, letting me know that while she hasn't completely ratted me out for my lie, she's clearly not loving this whole experience either.

Peyton's entire face lights up. Emma awkwardly holds her hand out to shake Peyton's, but Peyton completely ignores it and instead rips her from my grasp and wraps her arms around her neck.

"Oh my god. I've always wanted a sister," my sister admits, keeping her arms pinned around Emma.

"Great," Emma responds, her voice tight.

Fuck. What have I gotten her into?

"P, let her breathe," I demand.

Peyton looks at me from over Emma's shoulder. "You've never introduced someone to the family, Pres. I'm sorry for being a *little* excited about it." Despite her argument, she does pull away and let Emma go. Although I want to take a step closer to Emma and make sure she doesn't run for the hills, I don't. I stay where I'm at. She probably thinks I'm some creep just randomly pulling her into being my fake girlfriend for the night. The least I can do is give her some space.

"So nice to meet you." To Emma's credit, she keeps her voice composed. She even gives Peyton a warm smile, making the tension in my muscles soften slightly.

"I cannot believe you brought a date to the wedding and didn't tell me." Peyton points a finger at me before poking my chest.

"Oh, don't worry. I'm just here for the night," Emma lies. Or maybe it isn't a lie. I don't miss how my stomach drops slightly at the thought of not seeing her again after tonight.

"Nonsense. You have to come to the wedding. You have to come to *all* the celebrations," Peyton demands, leaving no room for argument with her tone.

"She's just here to keep me company tonight. Don't worry about adjusting anything for the week. I know how carefully you planned it out," I add, realizing I didn't think this through at all when I lied about Emma being my girlfriend.

Peyton waves her hand dismissively. "Are you kidding me? I'll be upset if she doesn't come to the wedding week events." She turns her attention to Emma, grabbing her hands and holding them close to her. "You'll come. Right?"

"Ummm…" Emma looks at me with fear.

I give her an apologetic look, hoping she knows none of this was my intention.

Maybe I should just tell Peyton it was a misunderstanding. She knows how clingy Marsha can be. If I just admit that I lied about Emma being my girlfriend because I was trying to get Marsha off my case, I think my sister would understand.

"Gram! Come meet Preston's new girlfriend!" Peyton shouts, getting the attention of someone I'd really prefer not to lie to.

"Oh shit," Emma says under her breath. Unfortunately, it was just loud enough that Peyton heard it.

Peyton gives Emma a reassuring look. "Gram is amazing. You'll love her."

Emma looks over at me, her eyes wide. "*Honey,*" she begins, emphasizing the word *honey* a little too much. "Don't you think it's a little early to meet *Gram*?"

"There she is!" I say, looking over at Gram, who is closing in on our little circle. My grandmother is easily one of my favorite humans on the planet, if not my favorite. She's always so effortlessly cool—and takes shit from no one. She helped shape me into the man I am today, and I do feel a twinge of guilt that I'm going to lie to sweet, old Gram.

Gram barely spares me a second glance. She shoos me away with a wave of her hand and goes right for Emma. "You're too beautiful for him," Gram says immediately before even introducing herself.

Emma's jaw drops. Apparently, Gram's quick wit is enough to stun Emma speechless. She tilts her head and purses her lips. Before she can find a response to Gram's words, Gram beats her to it.

"I thought I'd die before ever seeing Preston bring home a woman for us to meet."

6

Emma

I CAN'T DO THIS. I ABSOLUTELY CANNOT DO THIS. PRESTON'S GRAM looks exactly like Betty White, and no one—and I mean absolutely no one—can lie to a woman who looks like the angel that is *the* Betty White.

"Hi," I manage to get out, despite the feeling of my throat swelling up from nerves. "I'm Emma."

Grammy's cold hands wrap around mine. She seems so frail as her fingertips dig into mine. "It's so nice to meet you, Emma. I'm Lois, but you can call me Gram."

All I can do is nod. I think I want to kill Preston. I was having a great time with him—I even pondered if maybe I should allow myself just *one* night of fun with him because he seemed like he'd be absolutely mind-blowing in bed. Now, I've found myself sucked into some charade for his family as I pretend to be his girlfriend. I've always wondered what it'd be like to role-play, but I envisioned it happening in the bedroom to spice things up, not at a family event where I'm getting the hopes up of a sweet old lady.

Was Preston's sister's friend really *that* bad? The moment I get him alone, I want to ask him what stage clinger we're talking about for him to go to these great lengths to keep her away.

I realize that I've been internally panicking for too long as his grandma watches me closely, waiting for me to answer. "Oh, Gram seems special. I'm good with Lois."

She scrunches her nose as if I just said the most ridiculous thing ever. "If you call me Lois, I'll be upset. I know it must be serious for Preston to bring you to Peyton's wedding. You're *family* now."

Family?

I can't be part of his family. Fuck, I barely had my own family growing up. It was just me and my aunt, nobody else. I don't know how to be a part of a family, and I don't particularly want to learn by pretending either.

I should run. I wore the worst heels possible to ever run in, but I should make it work and run for the damn hills.

"Mind if I have a moment with Emma alone?" Preston asks, cutting in. His large, warm hand moves to the small of my back. It almost feels possessive, and I try not to focus on the fact that I don't hate it. I would've loved the feeling of the warmth of his palm through the thin fabric of my dress if I didn't have to lie to his family about being his girlfriend.

Gram smiles wide. She winks before giving a nod of approval. "I remember those days. Your grandfather used to be *very* eager to get me alone as well."

I blush, and I'm fairly confident Preston blushes, too. Peyton is the only one seemingly unbothered by Gram's crude words.

Preston clears his throat, his fingers twitching against my back uncomfortably. "Oh, it's *just* to talk, Gram. Promise."

"You don't have to lie to me about funny business. I get it," she quips. I'd find her absolutely hilarious if I wasn't being roped into lying to her.

Before I can say anything, Preston is leading me out of the large room. His fingers are strong around my wrist as he tries to find us somewhere private to talk. Eventually, he leads us into what seems to be a coat closet, but one that isn't in use due to the warm weather outside.

As soon as the door shuts, my hands find my hips. "Preston, I want out of this lie. *Now.*"

He nods, threading his fingers together and placing them behind his neck. "I know. I'm sorry. I didn't mean to drag you into this."

"Then let me out. I'll just sneak out the back door—you can tell everyone we got in a fight, and I won't have to look your grandmother in the eye again and pretend to be in love with you."

He narrows his eyes on me, his biceps tightening. *Is that a tattoo on his wrist?* I want to take a step closer to see if I'm imagining it because I've always been a sucker for a man with tattoos. He didn't strike me as someone who'd have them, but I swear there's something peeking out from underneath his fancy watch.

"No," he states calmly, breaking me from my concentration on trying to figure out if he's got tattoos or not.

"Yes," I counter. He can't force me to stay. He's lucky that I even went along with his silly plan to begin with.

"My family would never believe me if I told them we got in a fight and you left."

"Why? They don't even know me."

"What plans do you have this week?" he asks, completely ignoring my question.

I take a step back, wanting as much space between us as possible because the tension in the air is thick, and right now, I'm really annoyed with him. "Plans that do not involve other people. I want to be alone."

He frowns. "Who comes to the Hamptons to be alone?"

I huff, folding my arms across my chest. "If you must know, people who have no idea what they're doing with their life and are in the midst of a quarter-life crisis."

This makes him smile. He tries to hide it by turning his head, but he fails miserably. "So, it sounds like you don't have any plans at all, then. *Perfect.* You now have plans with me."

My jaw flies open. The audacity of this man. I'm not sure if his arrogance is extremely attractive or a blaring red flag. Maybe it's a little bit of both.

"I do *not* have plans with you. I have plans with myself."

"How long are you here for?" he prods.

I purse my lips, annoyed he keeps asking me questions instead of letting me out of this whole charade. "It doesn't matter. After tonight, you won't see me again."

"Answer the question, Emma."

I swallow, trying not to give him a reaction to the demanding tone of his voice. *God, why is it so sexy?*

"I'm here for the summer. No set timeline. Until I have to find a new job or figure out what I want to do with my life."

"You have the rest of this summer to figure your life out. Spend this week pretending to be my girlfriend, and then we'll go our separate ways. You can discover yourself, and I can tell my family my schedule got too busy and we didn't work out."

"Too busy to have a girlfriend?" I ask sarcastically.

He lifts a shoulder. "Something like that."

I want to ask him what he could possibly do for his family to think he's too busy for a relationship, but I bite my tongue. It doesn't matter. As hot and charming as Preston is, I still don't want to spend my week pretending to be his girlfriend.

"Is she an ex-girlfriend?" I ask, voicing the first question that pops into my mind.

A wrinkle appears on his forehead. "*Marsha?*" he asks incredulously. "Absolutely not."

"You sure? Are you trying to make her jealous? Or did she get too clingy after the two of you had a fling?"

Preston takes a step closer to me, his jaw flexing in anger. "Try again."

I take another step backward, not wanting to be too close to him. He's frustrating to no end, but I can't deny that there's some attraction between us. I can fight it and still recognize it's there.

"You broke her heart?" I offer, my shoulders hitting the wall.

He shakes his head, tucking his hands into his pockets. "She's been interested for years. I've never given her the time of day—and I don't intend to."

I roll my eyes. *Men.* I'd bet money he's given her mixed signals, giving her just enough attention for her to think he's interested before he ghosted her. "Oh, so you're just too cool to give any woman attention? Is that it?" I don't know why I'm arguing with him. It doesn't matter. Whatever reason he has for starting this whole debacle doesn't matter in the slightest because I want out.

"That isn't true."

A sarcastic laugh bubbles from my throat. "*Okay.*"

"The moment your heel came flying at me, I knew I wanted to give you as much attention as you'd let me."

My mouth snaps shut. *Oh shit.* He's good. I should've known he'd know exactly what to say to make me pause. "Is that just a line you're using so I won't bail?"

"It's a line I'm using because I must admit, all night, the only person capable of capturing my attention has been *you*."

I narrow my eyes, trying to figure out if he's being sincere or not. We've been wrapped in our own little bubble since the moment we walked into the party. People tried to talk to him, but he brushed them off. We'd stood at the bar, lost in conversation and oblivious to everything else going on for a long time before Marsha came up and ripped us from it. He'd been nothing but attentive—which is impressive, considering I now know this is his sister's wedding event, and I'm sure he knows almost every single person in attendance.

"Talk to me," Preston pushes. "I know you have something to say, so just say it."

For a moment, I refuse to meet his eyes as I try to gather my thoughts. I was having a great time with him. I even remember thinking to myself I was so grateful for the driver who encouraged me to go out tonight because it'd led me to this charming, handsome man who I could flirt with for a night. But I wanted tonight to be just that—one night of fun. We'd share some laughs —probably a few too many drinks—and I'd go home alone and wonder for the rest of my life if I should've let the smooth-talking man in the Hamptons take me home for the night.

Never did I think I'd find him asking me to be his pretend girlfriend for a week to appease his family. Never did I think I might actually consider it.

"Tell me what this next week would involve," I finally offer. My lip feels raw from chewing on it.

"To be honest, I don't remember everything on the agenda. Basically, it'll be one fancy party after another, some in the form of brunch, some as afternoon socials, and others at night. I promise, they will all be adventures."

"You're really trying to sell me on this being an adventure, aren't you?" I fold my arms across my chest, trying to decide if this is what I want to do with my week.

He rubs his lips together, giving me a coy smile. "Is it working?"

I let out an exasperated sigh. "I don't know," I answer honestly. "I'm all for an adventure, but you're basically a stranger to me. I'm not sure I want to spend a week pretending to be your girlfriend. My entire reason for coming here this summer was to be alone and find myself—not pretend to be someone else."

Preston shakes his head. "I'm not asking you to be anyone but exactly who you are, Emma. All I'm asking is for you to pretend to like me enough to be my girlfriend." His expression is so sincere, chipping away at my resolve to keep saying no to him. "Hopefully, that isn't too hard."

"It might be the hardest thing I'll ever do," I tease.

He lifts an eyebrow. "Is that a yes?"

I shrug. "I'm still thinking about it."

"And when will you have your answer?" His voice is rough, the sound of it sending shivers down my spine.

"I guess you'll have to wait to find out. Let's go back out to your sister's party. I have to test-drive the situation a little longer before I make my decision." I open the door, leaving him waiting behind me.

I don't look back to see if he follows or not. I know he will. What I don't know is if I'm going to agree to this crazy idea. One thing I know about myself is I love crazy ideas, and what I love even more is a wild story. What's wilder than agreeing to pretend to be the fake girlfriend of this super hot guy who clearly is rich as fuck? Not much.

Preston doesn't need to know this, but I think I already know my answer. I'll tell him yes because I don't want to live with the what-if of telling him no for the rest of my life.

7
Preston

"COME ON, LET'S GET YOU HOME," I TELL EMMA, CAREFULLY LAYING my hand on the small of her back.

Emma glares at me, adorably sticking her tongue out to show her displeasure. "Oh, but *honey*, I just got started telling everyone about our first date."

"We can save the rest of the story for another time," I assure her. Emma had just started telling my family about the first date we never had. Her story was getting a little too elaborate to seem believable, so I had to cut in. If she agrees to be my girlfriend for this week—which I hope she does—we're going to have to go over a few things first. The first thing being how we met and some details about how we first started dating.

I might also have to tell her who I am and what I do for a living. She doesn't seem to have a clue, but I feel bad leaving her in the dark, although it is refreshing for her to treat me like a normal human.

"Do you really have to go?" Peyton asks, her words slurring slightly. She adjusts her body in Jackson's lap as she watches us both with sad eyes.

"Do we really have to go?" Emma whines, leaning into me and batting her eyelashes in my direction.

"Yes," I clip, wrapping my arm around her waist to keep her next to me.

"Is it because it's past your bedtime?" Emma teases, sharing a conspiratorial look with Peyton and Gram. "Are you about to get even grumpier?"

Gram laughs, throwing her head back and clapping her hands together. "Oh, Preston, I love her already!"

Even my mom presses a hand to her mouth as she tries to hide her smile.

Emma looks at me. Her cheeks are flushed from the drinks she's had, and her lipstick has worn off, leaving a red ring on the outside of her lips. She's absolutely breathtaking, but I keep that to myself. I've probably weirded her out enough by asking her to pretend to be my girlfriend. The last thing she needs from me is to throw unwanted compliments her way.

"*Preston.*" Emma draws out my name slowly. "Let's just stay for two more minutes."

I shake my head, guiding her forward. Leaning in, I place my lips to her ear, making sure none of my family can hear what I'm about to say. "We need to get a story straight before you tell them anything else."

Her lips part, but she doesn't say anything. All she does is nod, allowing me to guide her toward the exit.

"See you tomorrow!" Peyton calls, jumping off Jackson's lap and throwing her arms around Emma's neck. Emma steps backward once, attempting to stay steady on her feet as Peyton puts most of her body weight against her.

I keep a good grip on Emma, making sure the two of them don't tumble to the ground.

"Will I see you tomorrow?" Peyton asks, focusing on Emma instead of me.

Emma turns around to look at me. "I think so," she answers, watching me carefully.

I don't say anything, hoping that's true. Partly because I feel like it was a great idea to bring a fake girlfriend to the wedding festivities so everyone else will leave me alone but also because I think it'll be fun to spend more time with her.

"Good night, everyone," I call, hoping to actually make it out the door before someone else can stop us.

I'd rather go out the back door so we aren't seen by anyone else at the club not attending the private party, but I'd foolishly parked in the front. As we walk down the hallway to the sound of voices drifting from one of the swanky club restaurants, I try not to think about how many people might still be there.

It's almost two in the morning—surely it can't be that busy. People here don't recognize me the way they do back in Manhattan. Still, my publicist will have my ass if I'm seen escorting a tipsy woman to my car.

Keeping my head down, I quickly lead us through the halls of Pembroke Hills Country Club. A couple of times, Emma asks me to slow down, but I don't listen to her until we're at my car with no one around.

"This is your car?" she asks, looking at the convertible in front of us.

"It's my rental for this week, so yes."

Emma runs her hand along the cream-colored paint. "Is it fast?" she asks. Her blue eyes meet mine, and I have to look away, scared of getting lost in them if I allow myself to stare.

"You could say that," I answer. The car is incredibly fast, but I haven't had the chance to really put it to use—yet.

I reach for the door handle, opening the passenger door for her. Before she slides in, she turns around. "Are you sure you're okay to drive?"

"Yes. I'd never risk it," I assure her.

She pauses for a minute, looking me up and down as if she's trying to decide if I'm sober or not. I let out an annoyed sigh, trying to point for her to get in. "Emma, I'd never get behind a wheel if I felt like I wasn't in the right mind to drive. I'm not stupid. I promise."

"Okay," she finally relents, falling into the front seat rather ungracefully.

Leaning down, I grab the seat belt and pull it out, making

sure my fingers don't brush against her chest as I pull it across her body.

"I can do it," she whispers, trying to take it from me.

"No," I snap. "I want to make sure it's done properly. Just let me do it."

"Just let me do it," she mocks, trying her best to lower her voice to match mine. She's terrible at it, but I keep that opinion to myself. She's kind of cute trying.

I snap the seat belt into the buckle, pulling on the part that rests against her chest to make sure it's tight.

"It's choking me," she argues, her lips turning up into a smirk.

My jaw tightens. "You'll be fine. It needs to be tight to work." We're too close in this position. I should move, but I'm frozen.

"I'm going to have to figure you out, Preston," she mumbles, reaching out and tapping the tip of my nose like I'm a child.

"And why's that?" I ask, my voice tight.

"Because you're grouchy and moody but also sweet and protective." Her eyes travel to where my hand rests on the seat belt, my knuckles just barely brushing over her skin.

I quickly pull my hand away. I hadn't even realized I'd been touching her and that our faces were so close, but I know I need space from her. Before she can call me out on something else, I shut the door and round the car. I'd left the top down on the convertible because of the beautiful summer weather.

Should I ask her if she'd rather put the top up?

She's quiet as I turn the car on. Her head falls backward against the headrest, and her eyes flutter shut. She keeps them shut even as I pull out of the parking lot.

"Where are you staying?" I ask, realizing I have no idea where I'm taking her.

Her eyes pop open as she comes to the same realization. "I'm staying at a friend's. Keep going straight, and I'll tell you when to turn."

I risk a glance over at her. I'm not sure I want to trust her navigating when she's had a few too many drinks. "Could you tell me an address?" I push, wanting to make sure I take her to the right place.

"Nope. I don't do addresses. You'll turn by that cute little ice cream stand. I know how to get us there."

My fingers tap against the steering wheel. "Could you at least tell me who your friend is? I might know the house depending on that."

She laughs. "I doubt you know my friends. Well..." Her words pause, and I have to look over at her to try and find out why she stopped. "Maybe you would know them. My best friend is Winnie Bishop—married to Archer Moore."

My eyes widen. "You know Archer?"

She folds her arms across her chest as she shifts her body in the seat so she faces me. "*You* know Archer?" she asks, throwing my question back at me accusingly.

"Archer and I played football together what seems like a lifetime ago."

"If I told him your name, would he recognize it?" she prods. Her lips press into a thin line. I wonder if she's trying to figure out if I'm telling the truth or not.

"Archer would definitely recognize my name." Archer and I talk enough. I'd almost forgotten that he'd recently bought a place out here, but I know exactly where it is. As much as people like to pretend the Hamptons is large and private, everyone knows everything about everyone here. It's just how it is. Mostly because we all come from Manhattan.

"I'm going to ask him, then," she quips, turning her body to face the windshield once again as I start driving and turn at the ice cream stand.

Peyton told me all about it—turns out Archer bought a place a couple blocks away from the house Peyton and Jackson are renovating right now.

The rest of the car ride is quiet as we head to Moore's place. It's pretty coincidental that the woman I roped into being my fake girlfriend for my sister's wedding is friends with Moore's wife. Emma and I are really going to have to make sure our stories are straight for the week. This will include more people than I imagined when I first came up with the lie.

"This one," Emma instructs, seconds after I've already turned into the long driveway.

The moment I put the car in park, she's trying to get the door open, even though it's locked.

"Let me walk you in," I demand, already getting out of the car.

Emma continues to struggle with the door handle, not understanding that her efforts are futile unless she unlocks it.

Making it to the passenger side, I reach over and pull the lock up. Her lips part in annoyance, as if she's mad at herself for not thinking of that in the first place.

"I don't need you to walk me in," she protests as I swing the car door open.

"Don't remember saying you needed me to," I clip, reaching out for her hand. She ignores it, sliding out of the car—almost falling on her face in the process and steadying herself on her feet at the last minute. With a loud groan, she rips one heel off and then the other before walking to the front door.

"You can leave now, Preston," she calls over her shoulder. I make sure to stare at the back of her head, trying my hardest not to look at the way her hips sway with every step she takes.

"Once you're safe inside, I will."

"Pretty sure I'm safe. We're in the Hamptons." She looks around, spreading her arms out wide as she does a spin. "Nothing's going to happen to me."

My teeth clench as I get annoyed that she doesn't take her safety seriously. Nowhere is safe. She's in an unfamiliar place; it'd be smart for her to be more aware of that. "Don't say that," I bark, realizing my tone might be harsher than it needs to be.

Emma stops at the bottom of the stairs of the two-story Hamptons house. It's larger than some of the other places I've been to here, but it still holds a lot of charm. There's a small side-walk to the left that leads right to a white picket fence. Behind it, you can see the smallest glimpse of a pool and a guesthouse tucked into the backyard.

This is a really nice place, and I haven't even seen the inside yet.

"Look, I'm all safe and sound now. No one's jumping from the bushes to murder me. You can go back to wherever you're staying knowing I'm *totally* fine." Emma's entire face lights up as she looks at me with the biggest smile, as if she finds her words hilarious even though I'm not laughing at all.

"Make sure you lock the door once you're inside," I demand, watching her type a code into the keypad of the door.

"Thank you, grumpy Captain Obvious," she mumbles under her breath, a small giggle escaping from her lips after.

The door swings open. It's my time to go, but for some reason, I want to find another excuse to just spend a few more minutes with her. I don't, instead deciding to back away and head back to my car.

"It was wonderful to meet you tonight, Emma," I tell her, tucking my hands in my pockets.

She stands in the doorway, her body perfectly illuminated by the lights she'd left on in the house. "It was unexpected meeting you tonight, Preston," she responds, leaning her shoulder against the door frame.

"A good unexpected or bad unexpected?" I press, hoping she doesn't already regret how the night transpired.

She shrugs. "I guess we'll see how this week goes. I could have major regrets."

"Or it could be the best week of your life," I counter, hoping she doesn't leave this with regrets.

"Best week of my life? That'd be hard to accomplish."

"I guess I've got my work cut out for me, then," I respond, my lips turning up in the smallest of smiles.

"You should do that more," Emma offers, changing the subject.

"Do what?"

"Smile. Not be so stiff."

"You just met me. How do you know I don't smile a ton?"

She laughs, her head falling backward with the motion. "Oh, I knew it after ten minutes of talking with you. Good night, Preston."

Before she can close the door, I speak up, needing to hear her say that she isn't going to run this week. "So I'll see you later, then?"

Emma lets out a long sigh. "Yes. I can't say no to an adventure—especially when it's a week full of rich people things. Count me in—but you won't see me before noon because part of my self-discovery is sleeping in."

I nod, trying not to let her see the way my shoulders fall with a relieved sigh. "Understood. See you later, rebel."

8
Emma

MY HEAD IS POUNDING. IT'S LIKE THERE'S A TINY LITTLE GUY WITH A hammer sitting between my temples, beating both sides of my skull.

I groan, realizing that my phone is vibrating on the pillow next to me. Pulling my own pillow over my head, I try to ignore it. My head is making it obvious I had a little too much to drink last night, and the last thing I want to do is talk to someone. All I want to do is go back to sleep and hopefully wake up without this excruciating headache.

My phone stops vibrating for not even a minute when it starts back up again. Another loud groan escapes me as I push the top half of my body and reach for it. Winnie's picture pops up on the screen.

I slide to answer, trying to clear my dry throat. Maybe she needs me to meet a delivery driver or something for the house. "Hello," I answer, realizing my voice sounds scratchier than normal.

"Emma!" Winnie excitedly says on the other end of the line. "I've been trying to call you all morning."

"What time is it?" I ask, letting my cheek fall into my pillow.

"It's almost one in the afternoon," she answers. "Were you sleeping?"

"Maybe," I tell her, not wanting to admit I've slept that long.

In my defense, it was early this morning when I even made it to bed to begin with.

Winnie sighs nervously. "So you haven't seen any of my texts? Or the ones in the group chat?"

I pull my phone away from my ear for a minute, tempted to look at them because of her nervous tone. "No," I answer, pressing the phone to my cheek. "What'd I miss?"

"Well...two things. Do you want the good news or bad news first?"

"Good news," I respond immediately, far too hungover to get the bad news first.

She laughs. "I thought you'd say bad news first."

"I had a little too much to drink at that fancy club last night. It was a great time, but oh my god, I'm paying for it today."

"I know," Winnie tells me.

"*You know*?" I ask, wondering if I called her last night. I thought I remembered most of the night, but now that I think of it, after Preston dropped me off, I don't really remember going to bed.

"You've gone viral," Winnie explains, her voice a little cautious as if she doesn't know if the good news she's telling me is actually good news.

I shoot up in bed, my heart racing. "What do you mean I've gone viral?"

"I told Margo I loved the video you posted early this morning. I think a lot of people our age can really resonate with it."

"What did I post?" I ask, my heart racing in panic. I tug the phone away from my ear and put Winnie on speaker, anxiously opening up my profile. My eyes widen at the number on top.

"*Seventy thousand followers*?" I scream, blinking to see if it's my eyes playing tricks on me. I went to bed with *maybe* nine hundred followers—and that might even be guessing a high number.

"Your video got twenty million views overnight," Winnie points out. "I think that number is only going to grow, Em."

I groan, focusing on the tiny thumbnail of my face for my most recent video. "Win, before I watch this, how drunk do I seem? Do I make a complete fool of myself?"

My stomach turns at the amount of people who've already watched it. If Winnie tells me I make a fool of myself in this video, I might just permanently go into hiding here in the Hamptons. Everyone here is in large sun hats and oversized sunglasses. I could totally go incognito and pretend I never put my face on the internet—not that I think anyone here would recognize me from one silly viral video anyway. I'm just being dramatic and having to think of possible backup plans in case I watch this video of myself and am completely mortified.

"You don't make a fool of yourself at all," Winnie reassures me, her voice easing a little bit of my nerves with how confident she sounds. "You can definitely tell you've had something to drink—but it isn't messy at all. It's relatable. Margo and I spent an hour on the phone today just reading all of the comments. People want more, Em. You don't have to watch the video with me on the phone, but I'll be here if you need me. Before we do that, I still have the bad news..."

I close my eyes, completely forgetting that she thought my drunk video going viral was considered good news. "I don't know if I want to know."

"It isn't terrible, I promise," Winnie rushes to say.

"What is it?"

"Well..." Winnie sighs. "One of Archer's friends needs a place to stay. He's in the NFL, and he had some rabid fans find out where he was staying, and they don't want it to get out of control. I thought it'd be fine if he stayed in the guesthouse. Archer's assured me you won't even know he's there."

I take a relieved breath. She and I might have to have a chat about what we consider good news and bad news. Because me complaining about my life being a mess to the internet and it going viral doesn't really seem like good news to me, and having someone stay at a guesthouse that is fully furnished and at the corner of the lot doesn't exactly seem like bad news.

Plus, there's not much I could say even if it did bother me. Archer and Winnie are graciously letting me stay at their new place; if they want to help out another friend at the same time as me, that's up to them.

"NFL?" I ask, knowing absolutely nothing about football but feeling fairly confident that those letters have something to do with the sport. "That's fine. I don't know how much I'll be here this week anyway."

Winnie laughs. "You mention that in the video. Or, to quote you exactly, *'I may not know what I'm doing for the rest of my life, but this week, I'll be living the life of luxury with an incredibly hot man as my tour guide.'*"

"That's an exact quote?" I squeak, regretting all the drinks I had last night—and that isn't even including the fact I have a major headache from them.

"Yes. Watch it. I *promise* it isn't as bad as you think! You were built for this. Lean into it."

"If I watch this video and it's embarrassing, I'm going to be *so* pissed at you for lying to me."

"I'd never lie to you. I bet your password is still jellyfish1234 —if I thought it was too embarrassing, I would've logged into your account and deleted it for you."

"That's what friends are for," I tease, hoping she's right.

"Love you, Em. I'll talk to you later, but I'll go ahead and tell Archer his friend is good to go to the guesthouse whenever. You shouldn't even know he's there."

"Love you, Win." I anxiously wait for her to hang up so I can witness what I posted with my own eyes and not trust Winnie to tell me whether it was bad or not.

My heart hammers in my chest as I click the video and turn my phone volume up to full blast. The video starts with me before I ever went to Pembroke Hills. The beginning is fine. All I do is talk about getting my life together and finding myself. It's when the phone camera shakes for a minute and it's me hours later from earlier this morning that makes my stomach turn from nerves.

"Hi again," I begin, a wide smile on my face. "So you could say tonight turned out far different than I expected." A small giggle escapes my chest. "I may not know what I'm doing for the rest of my life, but this week, I'll be living the life of luxury with an incredibly hot man as my tour guide. Can you believe it?" I pause for a moment in the video, looking at something out of the camera view before focusing my attention back on the screen. "I don't really believe it myself. Maybe I'll wake up tomorrow and find out that I imagined the whole scenario, but I know I didn't. You know when you just have this feeling that you should say yes to something? That your gut is just screaming at you to take a chance? That's what I did. I may not find myself this next week, but I'm allowing myself the chance to live a little. We're told too many times in life not to make mistakes, to be too cautious, and I'm over it."

A loud hiccup escapes my throat as I adjust my position in the video. So far, the video isn't as bad as I feared, but it isn't over yet, so I watch to make sure it doesn't get worse. "I'm over being scared of making mistakes. I want to make all of the mistakes; that way, I don't have any regrets. This week could turn into nothing. It probably *will* be nothing, but I'll have fun and maybe discover a little about myself. And I think we could all use some time to figure out who we are and who we want to be. I'll keep you posted on my adventures—and mistakes—this next week. I have a lot to learn, like is there really a difference in forks while eating?" I shrug, giving the camera a wide smile. "Now I need to go to bed before I say something embarrassing like I'm spending the week with the hottest—and grumpiest— man I've ever seen. You can discover yourself while someone else…discovers you, right?" Another giggle comes from my throat. "Kidding. Good night, fellow adventurers! I'll be back tomorrow." I blow the camera a kiss and end the video.

I stare at the still picture of me on my phone. I would be a lot happier with the viral video if I hadn't made the last comment, but there's nothing I can do about that. It could be worse—but could be better as well.

I bring my legs into my body and get comfortable, clicking on the comment section so I can see what people are saying. For the next twenty minutes, I comb through the thousands of comments that inspire me to keep being transparent. It feels validating to know there are so many people my age out there who feel stuck, and despite the hangover wreaking havoc on my body, I feel completely content for the first time in forever. Like I actually did something right.

I smile, reading a comment where a girl asks me to describe the hot guy I'll be spending the week with.

I'm excited about today—and it feels good to finally be excited about something in my life.

9
Preston

I sit in the driveway, my thumbs tapping against my steering wheel as my agent's voice trails from the speaker of my phone.

"Everyone in the front office is wanting an answer, Preston," Ryan says, his voice tight. I know I'm making his life far more complicated than necessary right now, but it's my right to do so. I've given my all to football for years. My heart isn't in it anymore. I don't want to completely trash my body, and as I get older, I realize that I want to be known for things other than my stats as a quarterback.

"If the front office wants an answer today, then I don't think they'll like the one I give them," I answer angrily, knowing it's not fair to take out my frustration on Ryan.

He sighs, staying quiet on the other end of the line for a moment while he gathers his thoughts. "I'll tell them you haven't decided, then." It isn't hard to hear the disappointment laced in every single one of his words.

"Ryan, I really think this is going to be my last year." I look at the house in front of me, trying not to let the rush of sadness completely envelop me. There's a part of me that wants to keep playing for another five years, but the larger part of me is tired.

Football was never my biggest dream—it was just something I was good at. The closer we get to the next season, the more I believe I want one final year to say goodbye to the sport I've played for as long as I can remember. And then I want to be done—for good. It's time for me to move on and enjoy life outside of football. I want to invest in more companies and actually have time to have a say in the inner workings of those businesses. I want to take a vacation and not worry about what I can and can't do according to my contract.

I'm just ready for the football phase of my life to be complete.

"You're saying that because last year was hard. That was a tough loss in the Super Bowl. What if you get back out this year and realize you still have more years left in you?"

"Even if we won last year—or we win this year—I think I'm done, Ryan. You can keep putting off telling them that, but I don't see my decision changing."

I can feel him rolling his eyes on the other end of the line. I've had so many tough conversations with him over the years that I've memorized the way he reacts when he doesn't like my answer. I'm sure he's sitting in his office, facing the windows with his knuckles pressed to his lips.

Finally, he speaks up again. "Okay. I'll tell them you need more time. Have you made new arrangements for a place to stay this week? Somewhere more private—and secure," he adds at the end. "I don't need Savannah calling me worrying about a PR nightmare."

I'd called both Ryan and Savannah, my publicist, first thing this morning to tell them I'd be staying somewhere different. The small bed-and-breakfast my family rented out for the wedding party was too public. Before things got out of control and too many people were told where I'm staying, I opted to find somewhere a bit more private. I didn't want people trying to get to me to overshadow Peyton's big day.

"Preston?" Ryan pushes.

"Yes," I answer, sitting up in the driver's seat. I lean forward, looking at the large, pristine house in front of me. "I've found somewhere far more private."

"And secure?" Ryan prods.

I laugh. I don't know if the house would necessarily count as secure, but no one will find me here. So in that case, I guess we could call it secure. "Yes, Ryan. I'll be fine."

"Call me if you need anything," he tells me before hanging up the phone.

I slide it into my pocket before getting out of the car. My bags are stuffed in the trunk, but I want to check out the place before bringing them in. I tell myself the reason I'm hurriedly walking to the front door of the main house has nothing to do with Emma and everything to do with me wanting to make sure she's okay with me staying in the guesthouse.

I knock, my hands finding my pockets as I wait for her to answer. I stare at the wood door that seems to be freshly painted a deep navy blue. Music pours from inside the house, making me wonder if Emma would even hear me knocking. I knock again, this time louder in hopes that she'll hear me.

The music doesn't stop. I'm about to knock for a third time when the door swings open. Emma stands in the opening, a T-shirt way too big for her hanging down to her thighs as she stares at me with a small wrinkle across her forehead.

"If you're here to take me to some kind of wedding event, I need at *least* an hour to get ready. I'm still recovering from last night."

I lift a shoulder. "I did try and get you to drink water. You kept telling me you didn't need it."

She groans, her fingers clutching the door to keep her upright. "It's all your fault. You could've pushed a little harder for your *girlfriend* to drink water." The way she says the word *girlfriend* makes my pulse spike.

I swallow. "I did push for you to drink water. You called me the hydration police."

She nods in understanding. "Because of your delivery. You shoved water in my face and basically growled the word *drink*."

I don't argue with her, knowing it'll get me nowhere. Instead,

I opt to straighten my spine a little and look into the house behind her. "You going to let me in?"

Her face scrunches up. "No. You can come in when you pick me up for our fake date of the day. What time do we need to be there?"

"In about an hour," I answer, taking one small step closer.

"A simple text or phone call to give me more of a heads-up would've been nice."

"I didn't get your number." If I wanted to get it from Archer, I probably could have. But that takes the fun out of it. If—or more like *when*—I get her number, I want it to be because she decided to give it to me. Besides, if Archer finds out about us, it wouldn't make sense for me not to have my girlfriend's phone number.

"So you showed up where I'm staying? Very old-school of you."

"How are you feeling today?" I ask, counting the number of drinks she had last night in my head. Maybe I should've tried a little harder to get her to drink water and eat something.

"I feel hungover. But I'll be fine. Come back in an hour, and I'll be ready for…" She pauses, her gaze traveling to the sky in thought. "Could you remind me what we're doing today?"

"We've got a garden party," I inform her.

She purses her lips as she nods in understanding. It's quiet for a moment as she repeats the movement over and over until eventually her eyes meet mine. "And what *exactly* is a garden party?"

We both burst out in laughter. I can't help it. Not many people have made me clutch my stomach with laughter, but she's managed to do it.

"Ugh," Emma says, pressing her palm to her forehead. "Don't make me laugh. My head hurts."

I take a breath, trying to wipe the smile from my face. "I'm sorry," I apologize, my hand wiping over my mouth. "I just realized how ridiculous a garden party sounded once you asked what it was."

Emma leans against the door, a hint of a smile still on her full lips. I focus on keeping my eyes on hers so I'm not tempted to sneak a glimpse at the bare skin of the tops of her thighs. "What is one supposed to wear to a garden party?"

My resolve breaks for a fraction of a second as my eyes roam her body. "Something with pants."

Emma gasps, looking down. The fabric bunches in her hand as she lifts it up, showing off a pair of small boxer shorts. "I *am* wearing pants, thank you very much," she informs me, rolling her eyes as if the fact I thought she wasn't wearing pants was the most ridiculous idea ever.

I lift my hands in surrender. "Excuse me for thinking otherwise."

She keeps her eyes trained on me for a minute. I want to ask what's running through her head as she watches me closely, but I don't. It doesn't really matter what she thinks of me—at least, I tell myself that.

"Is that what you're wearing to a nice, ritzy garden party?" She lifts an eyebrow as her eyes travel over my collared T-shirt and khaki shorts.

"No," I answer, looking at the outfit I'd quickly thrown on early this morning before breakfast with my family. "I'm going to change at my place into something a bit nicer."

She nods, straightening her spine and taking a step back. "Then I'll get back inside and get ready for our day, and you can go back to your place and change. Meet me back here in two hours?"

"I'll see you in *one* hour," I correct, sliding my sunglasses from my forehead and over my eyes. "And I am at my place." I point in the direction of the guesthouse. "Or at least close to it."

"Shut up," Emma hurriedly says, her jaw hanging open. "*You're* the NFL player?"

10
Emma

I WISH PRESTON WASN'T WEARING SUNGLASSES SO I COULD SEE MORE of his expression. Instead, he stands on the front doorstep with his lips pressed into a thin line.

"I do play for the NFL," he answers coolly, as if it's a totally normal job.

"That's football, right?" I question, knowing little to nothing about the sport. My aunt raised me, and since it was just me and her, and because she wasn't a fan of sports, I couldn't tell you anything about it. "Are you any good?" I push, suddenly even more intrigued by the man standing in front of me.

A small laugh rumbles deep inside his chest. It's different from the full laugh he let out just a few minutes ago after my comment about the garden party, but it's still one I cherish. He seems to be serious so much of the time that getting any kind of reaction from him seems like a small win.

"Yes, I play professional football. I guess you could say I'm good."

"Would Google tell me the same thing?" If he wasn't standing in front of me, I'd already have my phone out and be looking up his name to find out just how good he is.

"Does my answer matter? I bet the moment I go back to the guesthouse, you're going to do an extensive search of my name."

I nod, it just now occurring to me that along with the news that he plays professional football and doesn't run a hedge fund or something like that, he'll be staying here at Winnie and Archer's. "Wait a second," I say, my arms crossing over my chest. "I had a momentary lapse in judgment. You're the friend Winnie called about? You'll be staying in the guesthouse?"

His lips twitch. "Yes, for privacy reasons. Is that a problem?"

Yes. It *absolutely* is a problem. "No," I lie. For some reason, my heart rate increases with the lie—or what I think is a lie. It shouldn't bother me that we're going to be so close, but it does. I've already told him I'll spend every day with him this week doing wedding events; I don't know why I'm nervous having him so close even when wedding events aren't taking place.

Preston cocks his head to the side. He watches me closely, his blue eyes trailing over my face. I wonder if he can see right through my lie. I don't ask him if he can. My body heats with the intense stare, but I lie and tell myself it's because of the sun beating down on us.

"I'm going to get ready now," I declare, shifting on the balls of my feet.

"One hour, Emma," he says, holding up one thick finger. "I'll meet you back here then."

Before I can argue with him, he's turning around and walking down the long sidewalk that leads to the driveway. I watch him for a minute, wondering what I've signed myself up for this week.

I'm slipping into what seems like the twentieth dress I've tried on when the smell of coffee wafts into the room I'm staying in. I pause, holding the straps of the halter dress as I try to figure out where that delicious smell could be coming from.

I'd opened some windows when I woke up to let in the ocean

breeze throughout the house. Maybe the smell is coming from a nearby house—or even Preston's guesthouse. I close my eyes for a minute, relishing in how good it smells, even if I won't have any.

Ignoring the delicious aroma surrounding me, I look at myself in the mirror. My fingers hurriedly work at tying the two straps of the halter dress into a neat bow at the nape of my neck. If Winnie were here, she'd help me pick out an outfit that would probably be more appropriate for a garden party, but I'm working with the options I brought.

The cream-colored dress has little blue flower details all over the fabric that complement my eyes. I was hesitant at first to choose this dress because of the way the ruched fabric hugs my body. It's formfitting, but it reaches all the way to my mid-calf, so even though it clings to the small curves of my body, it still seems fairly modest.

If I had more time, I would've carefully curled my hair and put a little more effort into it. Knowing I didn't have long to get ready, I opted to pull my hair into a slicked-back bun and spend more time on my makeup. Considering Preston's sister was the person who kept handing me drinks while we mingled at the party, I have no doubt his entire family will know I'm not feeling my best today. But despite the hangover, I want to look my best.

I take one final glance at myself in the mirror, knowing this will have to do. I don't have time to overanalyze every dress I brought, and since I'm not well-versed in knowing what one is supposed to wear to a garden party, I'm just going to go with something I feel good in.

And I know even with the hangover I'm still dealing with, I look good.

I grab the Chanel purse Winnie and Margo got me for my birthday last year off my nightstand. I stuff all the things I think I'll need for the day in the purse and swipe a layer of lip gloss over my lips before tossing it into the bag as well.

Standing at my nightstand for a minute, I debate pulling my phone out of my purse and recording something to go up on my profile. This morning's video has only gone more viral as each hour has passed. I was embarrassed about it for five minutes before I let Winnie's words change my mind.

It's okay to be a bit of a mess, and if my experience is resonating with anyone else, then I want to be the one to tell them it'll all be okay. And if it isn't okay, then there's still so much adventure left that'll lead to everything working out—at least, I hope that's the case.

I pull my phone out, plastering a smile on my face, even though it feels a little silly to talk to myself through a camera.

"Hello again," I tell everyone, keeping my voice low, even though Preston's in a totally different house than me right now. "I'm terrible with words and might embarrass myself even more if I spend too long talking to myself, but I wanted to say thank you to everyone who saw my *slightly* tipsy video from last night and decided to follow me. This summer is all about self-discovery and self-love, and I'm excited to take you on the journey with me." I smile, flipping the camera around so you can see my entire body in the mirror. "On today's episode of *Emma has no idea what she's doing with her life*, I'll be attending a garden party for the first time."

I take a step closer to the mirror, panning to the outfit I'd thrown together, hoping that I'll blend in with everyone else with what I picked out. "So please tell me this outfit is acceptable for a *garden party*." I do a mock British accent, even though not a single person I met last night was actually British. "Actually, don't tell me if it isn't because by the time I post this, I'll already be there, and your opinion won't matter. I'll check back in with all of you later to tell you about my first official garden party experience."

Taking a deep breath, I flip the camera around so it's back on my face. I smile, trying not to show the nerves that are taking over. "Wish me luck," I say confidently, pretending that I'm not suddenly incredibly nervous. I blow the camera a kiss before stopping the video.

I walk out of the room, following the scent down the hallway until I stop in my tracks, finding Preston standing in the kitchen, his back to me as he searches through the refrigerator.

11
Preston

I DON'T KNOW WHAT REACTION I EXPECTED FROM EMMA WHEN I decided to sneak into the main house after getting ready, but it wasn't the one I'm getting right now. She stares at me, her blonde eyebrows slightly drawn in on her forehead.

"I don't remember inviting you inside," she says, folding her arms across her chest. The movement brings my attention to the dress she's wearing—and how it molds perfectly to her body. The hint of a smile on her painted lips tells me that she isn't upset about finding me here.

"You took longer than an hour to get ready." I shut the refrigerator doors, finding nothing useful in there.

"I told you I would," she responds. "What are you doing here?"

"I figured instead of waiting alone at the guesthouse that I'd come here and make you some food to help with the hangover." I point to the two coffees I have sitting on the counter. "I also made coffee. I wasn't sure if you liked hot coffee or iced coffee, so I made both."

Her eyes narrow on me as if she's trying to figure out if I have ulterior motives for the coffee. I don't—I just know when I used to be hungover almost every weekend that a coffee always helped. She doesn't move, opting instead to just stare at me suspiciously.

"Do you not like coffee?" I question, the thought just now occurring to me that maybe coffee isn't the answer to her hangover.

"I love coffee," she answers, still not moving from her spot.

I keep my focus on her face, although the urge to let my eyes wander down her body is strong. The dress she chose for this party might be the death of me. She looks too fucking good. I already know that all of Jackson's fraternity brothers are going to be dying to steal her attention, and as her fake boyfriend, it'll be my duty to keep them away.

Letting out a long sigh, I pick both coffees up, careful not to spill the hot coffee that is filled to the brim of the mug. "Hot or cold?"

"Your personality? A little bit of both."

My lips pull down into a frown. "I meant how you like your coffee."

She smiles, clearly proud of her joke, as she makes her way to me. The closer she gets, the more the sweet scent of her perfume surrounds me. It smells like orange blossom and jasmine, reminding me of the different scents you'd find in my grand-mother's greenhouse growing up.

"You really made both, not knowing how I took my coffee?" Emma asks, stopping right in front of me as she focuses on the drinks in my hand.

I clear my throat, wondering why she's looking at me like I went above and beyond just by making coffee. "I'll drink anything," I answer, trying to not make this a big deal. "I figured whichever one you didn't want, I'd drink." I've already had two cups of coffee today, so I definitely don't need another, but she doesn't need to know that.

Emma reaches for the iced coffee, her finger brushing against mine in the process. "I'll take my caffeine any way I can get it," she jokes. "IV is probably my preferred method, but after that, iced coffee is typically my go-to."

"Do you want cream?" I ask.

Emma quirks an eyebrow. "Preston," she scolds. "That sounded a little dirty."

My ears heat. I didn't mean for it to be dirty at all, but now my mind is going places it absolutely shouldn't be going. I blink, trying to rid my memory of the way she said the word *dirty*. Turns out, her saying it sent very filthy thoughts to my head.

I swallow, trying to play it cool. I don't know what it is about this woman, but she gets to me more than anyone I've ever met. I'm known on the field—and to the world—as a stone-cold quarterback. No one can get to me, but she makes a dirty joke and I'm blushing like a child.

This is bad. But I don't care—it's not going to stop me from bringing her to my sister's wedding party today and surely making things even worse. She'll undoubtedly get me to blush more because of the way she doesn't hold back with every thought that comes to her mind.

"Preston," Emma calls, playfully hitting my arm.

I shake my head, focusing on her once again.

"I lost you there for a minute," she teases, her lips wrapping around the glass straw in her coffee.

"Turns out I might need this coffee more than I thought," I lie, carefully lifting the mug to my lips and blowing on the hot liquid for a second before taking a sip.

It's quiet between us for a moment. We both look at one another, our eyes roaming the other's face. I want to look away, to hide my face and hope she doesn't see the slight color that is covering my skin because of her.

"Thank you, by the way." Emma's words break me from my thoughts.

"For what?"

"For the coffee. It's much needed."

I shrug. "It's no big deal, really."

Emma cocks her head to the side, watching me intently. "Small things matter, too. It's still sweet you thought of me."

A sarcastic laugh comes from deep in my throat. "No one's ever called me sweet."

It's her turn to laugh. She laughs so effortlessly, her head thrown back and her eyes closed. "Oh, I didn't call you sweet," she corrects. "I just called the *gesture* sweet."

I hold my free hand up in defense. "My mistake."

Emma drops the conversation, instead taking a step away from me and looking behind me. "Did you decide to raid the pantry while looking for coffee?" she asks, pointing to the array of food lined up on the counter.

I let out a long exhale. "I wanted to make you some food to help cure the hangover, but it turns out you have nothing here to eat but stale Pop-Tarts and an abundance of boxes of noodles."

"My flight got in late last night," she tells me, picking up the box of Pop-Tarts and inspecting the expiration date. "I didn't have time to get groceries."

I nod, setting my coffee down on the kitchen island and tucking my hands into my pockets. "That's right, you were too busy breaking and entering."

Her free hand falls to her chest. "Low blow, Preston Rhodes. Plus, if I hadn't broken into the party, you wouldn't have a fake girlfriend preventing all your sister's friends from flocking to you at the wedding."

I drop the topic, surprisingly grateful she decided to crash the party. Despite her propensity to catch me off guard and even make me blush, I've enjoyed the little time I've spent with her so far. I've enjoyed it so much that I'm ready for more of it.

"Rhodes, huh?" I prod, changing the subject. "Seems to me you did some research instead of getting ready."

She told me she was going to do so, and her beaming smile tells me she doesn't care at all that I know about her looking me up, that her doing that is probably the reason we're running late to this party.

"I had to know everything about you before I spent the next week being your girlfriend."

I can't help but roll my eyes. "You can't know everything about me from the internet."

She lifts an eyebrow. "Your family is in investment banking—I basically called that, by the way," she adds with a smug look in her eyes.

"That's a very safe guess," I point out.

She waves at the air dismissively, not caring about my comment at all. "Your dad could've owned a law firm, been a brain surgeon, or even funded a start-up. Instead, he took over investment banking just like your grandfather and grandfather's father and so forth."

"You were right about my family." I keep my tone soft, wanting her to know I'm not upset about her looking us up. It was nice when she didn't know who I was, but she was bound to find out eventually.

Emma takes a drink of her coffee, but her eyes stay focused on me. I want to know what she's thinking. Does she think differently of me now that she's looked me up? It doesn't seem like she does, but I can't be completely sure.

"As much as I like to brag about myself, I don't think I was right about *you*. You screamed investment banker...not one of the best quarterbacks in the NFL." Her eyes drift to my arms. I'd opted for a short-sleeved polo and a pair of slacks, knowing that's how Peyton would want me to dress. My mother will be furious that my tattoos are exposed, but I know Peyton won't care as long as I'm dressed well. "I also wouldn't have guessed you'd be hiding those tattoos either. You seemed so prim and proper. Kind of stiff."

She laughs, and I don't know if she's laughing at herself or at my reaction to her comment. Either way, she covers her mouth with her hand in an adorable motion.

I rub the back of my neck, waiting for her laughter to die down before speaking. "I'm not stiff."

She lifts a shoulder. "You kind of are, but it isn't bad. It's just your personality."

She must take my silence as displeasure because she keeps talking, not waiting for me to respond. "Don't worry, there's a lot of endearing qualities about you that make you mysterious. The tattoos, the football, even though I could guess your family was very against that. The fact you did actually help fund a start-up that is now one of the leading apps in the world."

"You don't need to rattle off everything the internet told you," I say, pushing off the counter and heading for the front door. I'm surprised Peyton hasn't already called me asking where I'm at, but I know she's probably busy entertaining guests. "We should probably get going," I tell her as I reach the front door.

"What about my coffee?" Emma asks, sticking the straw in her mouth and beginning to suck. My own coffee is abandoned on the kitchen counter, but I didn't need the caffeine to begin with. I'll clean it up when we get back from the party.

"You can bring it in the car," I tell her, opening the front door. I want her to be comfortable and not rush to drink her coffee.

Surprising me, Emma follows without any arguments. She grabs a purse I hadn't noticed she'd placed on the counter and follows me out the front door—her lips still wrapped around that damn straw as she sucks down her coffee.

"You don't have to drink it all before we get in the car." I stand behind her, watching her type in the code to lock the house.

She turns, looking at me and holding up her near empty cup. "My aunt knew nothing about cars, so I know nothing about cars, but I know enough to know my iced coffee doesn't belong in a car that nice."

I'm quiet for a moment, fighting the urge to ask more about how she grew up. It's the second time she's mentioned it being just her and her aunt, and I want to know more about that. No matter how badly I want to ask for more details, I keep my mouth shut. If she wants to tell me, she will. It's clear she's very comfortable sharing at least some details about her life. Until then, I'll be left wondering.

"I would've let you drink it in the car," I note, walking to the passenger side and opening the door for her.

She gives me a warm smile. I like the way she's wearing her hair today, all of it pulled away from her face so I can see every radiant inch of it. "I know. But you got all tense when you said to bring it in the car—more tense than you already are."

"So now you can read my body language?" I shut the door behind her, wanting to fasten her seat belt for her again to make sure it's done properly but knowing she's in far better shape this afternoon than she was early this morning. If I tried to do it now, it might just make me look like a control freak. Which I kind of am, but she doesn't need to know that. It'll just give her more ammunition to tease me.

Emma waits to respond until I slide into the driver's seat. She leans back in her seat, tilting her face to the sun with a wide smile. "When your body language is that obvious, yes, I can read it," Emma finally answers. She keeps her eyes shut as she lets the sunshine beat down on her skin.

"I'll play more coy next time," I say, making an attempt at a joke.

It must work because she laughs. "Or you could just let me figure you out, Preston Rhodes."

I shift the car into drive and pull out of the driveway, mulling her words over for a minute.

"We'll have to see about that, rebel."

12
Emma

"I THINK IN ANOTHER LIFE, I WAS SUPPOSED TO BE RICH," I comment, sitting forward in the seat as Preston drives up a long driveway with trees lining both sides of it. "This is so nice."

We've only been in the car together for ten minutes, and all of the tension I'd felt talking to him last night is back. Finding out he was a professional athlete should've made him less attractive —a professional at any sport screams one red flag after another —but I'm afraid the pictures I found of him playing football only made him hotter.

"Wait until the actual wedding day," Preston responds.

I laugh, staring at the massive fountain at the end of the driveway. I don't even know if I should call it a fountain—it seems more like a freaking pool.

"My friend Margo married Beckham Sinclair, and they had a huge wedding reception in Manhattan. I think most of New York was there. Will this top that?"

Preston pulls up to a valet stand.

I didn't know there were valets at houses, but apparently, here in the Hamptons, anything goes.

Before getting out of the car, he looks over at me. "I know Beck. I was there at the wedding reception—although I didn't stay long." He looks at his hands on the steering wheel, his thumbs tapping against it nervously. "Parties aren't really my thing."

I'm quiet for a moment, wondering how I missed him at their reception. It was a busy day as Winnie and I worked hard to make sure Margo had the reception of her dreams. It still shocks me that I didn't see him there, but then again, there were so many people in attendance it wasn't possible to notice every single person.

"You say parties aren't your thing," I begin, looking at the massive house in front of us. "But they definitely seem to be your sister's."

This gets him to laugh. He nods, following my line of sight. "That's very true. Peyton has always loved a party. She's been preparing for her wedding day since she was about three years old. I was a teenager, and she was begging me to attend her teddy bear weddings."

"I really do love your sister," I state, getting excited to see her again. She was so much fun last night—and incredibly cool. I know she has to be so busy, but I do hope to spend some time with her.

The valet steps up to the car, letting out a low whistle. "This is a beauty," he notes, eagerly taking the keys from Preston's hand.

"Be careful with her," Preston responds, getting out of the car. "It's a rental."

The guy nods, rushing over to open the door for me. Preston beats him to it, aiming a dirty look in his direction for even attempting to be the one to open my door instead of him.

I give the valet driver an apologetic smile. Hopefully, he doesn't take Preston's grumpiness personally. I'm about to tell him that Preston's face is almost always turned down in a scowl when the valet attendant gasps.

"Are you Preston Rhodes?" he asks in amazement. I look to Preston, finding that he's pulled his sunglasses off.

Preston presses his hand to the small of my back, gently

guiding me away from the attendant and putting himself between us.

"I am," Preston answers cooly, showing no emotion in his face as he looks at the guy. "But we've got to get going."

He begins to push me along a stone path that leads to the side of the house. I try to stop, but his hand is firm as he continues to guide me where he wants me.

I look over my shoulder, finding the valet attendant still staring at us with his mouth hanging open. "You aren't even going to offer an autograph or a photo?"

A low growl comes from Preston's throat as he grabs my hand and pulls me into a tucked-away terrace on the side of the house.

I yelp, focusing on not stumbling in my heels. "Preston," I scold, looking up to meet his eyes.

He lets go of my hand the moment he knows I'm steady. His hands find his pockets immediately as he stares at me with his cobalt-blue eyes. "If I offered him a photo or signature, it would turn into more people asking me for one, and then I would become the focus instead of it being on my sister and Jackson. I refuse to take anything away from her this week."

His voice is rough and gravelly, sending weird tingles down my body. I like it, his determination to not let his fame take away from Peyton's big week. "Maybe you're sweeter than you think," I tease, trying to break the tension. I'm just realizing how secluded we are on this little terrace. There's a small table and chairs on the stone, with ivy hanging all around us.

"We must have varying definitions of sweet. Not wanting to steal attention from my sister's big day shouldn't be considered sweet. It should be considered normal."

I nod, suddenly needing to get away from him. Even in the bright sunlight without the buzz of alcohol, my attraction toward him is still very much there. There's a reason I followed him into the party last night without knowing anything about him, but wanting to give in to the budding tension between us might make pretending to be his girlfriend more complicated than it's worth.

Looking at the sharp cut of his jaw and the way his tattoos stick out against the pale blue hue of his shirt make me think complicated wouldn't be so bad. It's just one week of pretending before I'll never see him again. I'm about to ask him if he feels it, too, but he speaks up first.

"Before we get to the party, we need to talk about our story," Preston interrupts me from my thoughts.

"Our story?"

He rubs a hand along his mouth in frustration. "Yes. Our story. How we started dating, how we met, all of it."

My mouth snaps shut because I hadn't thought too hard about what we would tell people. I vaguely remember beginning a story last night when talking to Peyton, but I do remember Preston cutting me off before I could divulge too much about how he and I supposedly met.

I nod my head. "Right. What exactly did I say last night?" Some things are fuzzy, although I do remember his Gram talking about her sex life with Preston's late grandfather for what felt like an eternity, so I didn't forget *all* of the conversations I had last night, even if some I kind of wish I did.

"You said...and I quote, 'Preston took one look at me and was a goner.'"

I shrug, my lips twitching with a budding smile. "I mean...is that even a lie?"

He stares at me with a blank expression, not giving me any indication of what he's thinking. "I took one look at you and wondered why you'd scaled a fence in a pair of heels."

"I really should be given more credit for doing that in a pair of stilettos," I offer, my mind going back to how difficult that was. "You're an athlete, but really, I am, too, for that," I tease. I grew up doing cheerleading, but my small high school wasn't that great. Not much came out of it after I graduated because I wasn't good enough. Now, the only physical activity I get is my daily hot girl walks and the occasional spin class with Margo and Winnie.

I thought for sure that comment would get Preston to smile, but he stares right at me with not the smallest hint of one on his face.

"My next thought may have been you were far too stunning, and I was far too intrigued by you, to prevent you from breaking into my sister's welcome party."

My heart rate picks up. "Aw, Preston, did you just call me stunning?"

Finally, I get a reaction from him. His eyebrows draw in before he rolls his eyes. "You're breathtaking, and you know it. Don't try to pretend you don't."

I fold my arms across my chest, trying to hide my developing satisfied smile. "I know, but I still wanted to hear you say it."

Preston shakes his head. I think he might be flirting—and I love it.

"So," he begins, straightening his spine. "Back to our story. How are we going to tell them we met?"

"We could lie and say Archer introduced us," I offer.

Preston runs his fingers along his chin, deep in thought. It brings my attention to the veins on the top of his hands. Damn, I always thought I was a thigh girl—which he seems to have beautiful ones—but maybe I'm a hand and arm girl too because, holy shit, the way the muscles of his arms ripple and the definition of the veins all the way down to his fingers are hot as hell.

"Are Archer and Winnie not coming to the wedding? Or Beck and his wife?"

I panic for a moment, wondering if I'm going to have to lie to my friends about Preston and me. I hadn't thought about them being at the wedding, but their Manhattan social circle is close-knit. There's a good chance either—or both—of my best friends could show up and see right through our charade.

"Well," Preston prods, "are they?"

"Winnie and Archer have been so busy with the company

merger recently. I need to double-check with her, but I'm pretty sure they're traveling this weekend."

He nods. "And Beck?"

"Margo is very pregnant. He barely lets her leave the house. I doubt they'll be coming out here."

"Probably should still avoid saying they introduced us just in case one of them shows up."

I sigh, hoping neither one of them show up. I'm a terrible liar and far too honest to be able to look them in the eye and say I just happened to start dating Preston Rhodes. I could try and pull it off, but I'd rather wait and see them another time this summer when pretending to be Preston's girlfriend for a week is just a distant memory no one else has to know about.

"Can't we just say we met somewhere in New York? I live there, you live there, we just stumbled across one another."

Preston stares at me. I don't know if he's thinking about my idea or if he hates it. Finally, he clears his throat before his eyes meet mine again.

"I don't go out much anymore, but we can keep it vague."

"There were tons of videos of you out at parties on the internet," I point out, thinking of the vast array of photos of him leaving different places with a model or an actress holding his hand. There were tons. Even more photos of him in the back seat of SUVs and cars with his eyes appearing red and not seeming sober in the slightest.

Preston swallows slowly. "I used to go out a lot until it almost cost me my career. I'm almost thirty-seven—it seems odd to still be out partying. Staying in is much better for both my physical and mental health."

My eyes trace over the defined muscles of his arms again. It's obvious how much work he puts into his body...almost too obvious.

"We met at a nice dinner spot...Alexander's, maybe? It's popular but not one of the main places people spend time. Not the nightclub vibe, quiet, and could even be romantic."

One of the corners of his lips picks up. "I love Alexander's."

I smile, twisting my hands together in front of me because the intense way he looks at me right now makes me nervous. "Alexander's is great," I get out, wondering if the sun is too hot on my skin—even though technically we're in the shade—or if it's because of the look in his beautiful blue eyes.

"So, we met at Alexander's. You saw me and immediately knew you needed my number."

"I don't even have your number now," he responds.

Is he flirting? I think he is. I *hope* he is.

"You haven't asked for it."

"Emma, since you're my girlfriend, can I have your number?"

"Only if you say it's because you want it and not because I'm pretending to be your girlfriend. You're living on the same property as me; you don't need my number."

I look down at my feet, needing a break from his intense gaze for just a moment.

He doesn't give me long. His pointer finger and thumb find my chin, coaxing me to look at him once again. "I want it," he says, his voice deep and casual, doing funny things to my body.

"Okay," I respond, unable to come up with some witty remark.

Preston nods, letting his fingers linger on my chin for a few more seconds before dropping his hand. "We met at Alexander's a little over a month ago. We've been spending time together since—keeping it low-key so the press doesn't find out."

I nod, thinking about the articles I stumbled upon of the women Preston had been seen with years ago. The comments—and even the articles—were harsh on the women he was with. I'd like to think I have thick skin, but I don't think I'd ever want to open myself to that much scrutiny. The handful of hateful comments I got from people made me realize I may not want to have strangers hating on me on the internet.

In less than five minutes, I was able to locate the workplaces of five of the people who were nasty in my comments. It took all of me not to send over the rude things they were saying to their boss.

I can't imagine the scale of what it's like for Preston—and the women he's seen with. I'll stick to playing his girlfriend at a private event where the worst thing that can happen is having his grandma divulge facts about her sex life.

"You still with me?" Preston asks, bringing attention to the fact I'd spaced out for a moment.

I blink, trying to clear my head. "Yes. That sounds good to me. I'll keep it vague today and gear the conversation away from us."

This finally gets Preston to smile—an actual one. He even shows the slightest amount of his perfectly straight, white teeth. "It's like you've been through media training."

I laugh—not a cute, sexy giggle, but a full-blown laugh where I'm horrified to admit that even a snort comes out. "I'm the furthest thing from being media trained...*trust me*," I add, thinking about the video of me circulating right now where I'm admitting how much of a mess I am. "But I promise not to spill your lie to your family. I'll do my job of keeping Marsha—and any of the other women that flock to you—away."

Preston keeps the smile on his face as he cocks his head to the exit. "Good girl. Now, let's go."

13
Preston

"AM I UNDERDRESSED?" EMMA ASKS FROM MY SIDE. SHE LOOPS HER arm through mine, giving everyone who looks in our direction a small smile.

My jaw flexes, annoyed by anyone who's looked at her and given the indication that she looks anything but perfect. "Not at all," I say through gritted teeth.

I feel her gaze against mine. "Good. I know I look hot in this dress, but it's hard not to think about the fact the dress I'm wearing is off a clearance rack when everyone else's here…" She pauses for a moment, her eyes moving from me to travel over the different groups of people. "Well, when everyone else's here doesn't look like that at all."

I stop, tugging on Emma's arm slightly so she'll turn to face me.

"Why are we stopping?" she asks.

"Because I want to tell you something," I get out, running a hand against my mouth. "You look beautiful." I try to keep my words slow and steady, not wanting her to know that my heart pounds with that admission. It isn't the first time I've called a woman beautiful, but something is different about Emma. Something I don't want to think too deeply about.

She presses her fingers to her upturned lips. "Thank you," she responds under her breath. It's quiet for a few beats before she fake tosses her hair over her shoulder. "But I didn't question that. I just questioned if I was underdressed."

"And I'm telling you it doesn't matter—and that you aren't."

Her smile gets even wider. It's the first time I've noticed she has one dimple on her right cheek. It's adorable. "Thanks for the pep talk."

"Was it a pep talk, or was it you fishing for compliments?" I tease.

One of her hands flies to her chest as her mouth falls open. "I'd never fish for compliments."

My head cocks to the side, and I lift an eyebrow. "Are you sure about that?"

Emma pulls her lips between her teeth, doing her best to hide her smug smile but failing at it. "Yes," she answers confidently, pushing her shoulders back. "I shouldn't have to fish for compliments. I should just be given them."

I can't help but laugh. This woman. Her boldness is both incredibly sexy and absolutely adorable at the same time. "Should we go look for my sister?" I ask. Even though we're late to the party, I haven't seen Peyton yet. I know she's got to be here somewhere. I'm hoping she's been so busy she doesn't even notice our late arrival.

Emma nods, her eyes traveling to the stones at our feet. "Wait!" she says, bending down and messing with something from the ground.

She stands up and meets my eyes. She points to our feet. "It's a penny," she explains, as if that should tell me enough.

"We can leave it," I tell her, taking a step toward the largest group of people.

Emma doesn't move. She looks between the penny and me as if walking away from it is the worst possible thing I could do.

"Preston," she scolds, pointing to the penny. "The penny is heads up. It's a lucky penny. You have to pick it up."

"I can leave it for the next person," I offer, not believing that a coin will bring me good luck.

"No, it's a heads-up penny for *you*. I turned it for you and everything. It's something my aunt and I used to do." The way her voice slows a little at the end makes me want to ask why. It's not the first time she's mentioned her aunt, but this time, it's said almost sadly. It isn't my place to push her to tell me more, but I find myself wanting to. She picks up the penny with a huff, clearly unamused by me not being the one to do it.

I walk back to her, reaching out between us and giving her my hand. My palm faces up, waiting for her to hand me the penny I'm sure I'll end up losing on accident.

She doesn't hand it to me right away. Instead, she narrows her eyes on me, turning the penny over between her fingers.

"Can I have the penny?" I ask, trying to keep the skepticism from my tone. I've never been a superstitious person—although many men throughout my time playing sports have been. But it seems important to her to give me this penny she found, so I play along with it.

"Promise you'll keep it," she says, her tone accusing, as if she knows I have no plans on keeping the penny.

I swallow, wondering why it means so much to her. Her skin is warm against mine as she carefully places it against my palm. She slowly wraps her fingers around mine, forcing me to close mine around the coin. We stay locked in that position for a moment, the two of us staring at one another.

"I promise," I tell her, my voice cracking because of the intensity in which she looks at me.

Emma blinks a few times, a smile popping up on her face. I'm learning she's almost always smiling, but they're all different smiles. She has one when she knows she said something witty, one she gives you when you compliment her, and there's even one she gives with her eyes narrowed while she's just waiting to call you on your bullshit. I've only known her a day, but I've already seen so many. And am ready to witness—and learn—even more of them.

Her eyes look to our hands, where her fingers still rest

against mine. "Better hold on tight to that penny. It'll be the only way you get lucky this week." She gives me another one of her smiles—the satisfied, smug one before she waltzes away, her eyes landing on my sister.

I stare for a moment, the penny tucked neatly against my skin, as I watch her hips sway with every step she takes away from me. She's continually surprising me, and I can't help but shake my head, a small smile on my lips because of her comment.

Pulling out my wallet from my back pocket, I slide the penny safely into one of the openings, trying to keep my promise to Emma.

For a moment, I don't move, instead choosing to watch the interaction between Emma and Peyton. My sister runs up to Emma, almost tackling her with how quickly she runs right at her.

"You came!" Peyton yells, wrapping her arms around Emma's neck.

I can't hear Emma's response from my spot, but whatever she says makes Peyton laugh and look right at me.

"I'm not shocked," Peyton responds, still looking at me. Whatever Emma responded with must've had something to do with me because now they both look my way with knowing smiles.

With a sigh, I tuck my wallet back into my pocket and close the distance to them. "Do I want to know what you're saying about me?" I drawl, pinning them both with an accusing glare.

They glance at one another conspiratorially before breaking out in giggles. "Probably not," Emma answers honestly, her eyes flicking to my hand for a moment before looking back at me.

I fight the urge to tell her I'd kept the penny; I'd just put it somewhere safe instead of deciding to hold onto it any longer and risk losing it.

"Preston, I know I told you this last night—at least I think I did; everything is a little fuzzy because of the drinks—but I love

Emma, and you must keep her. Deal?" Her pitch goes up an octave at the end, as if she's leaving me no room for discussion.

Both Emma and I are quiet for a moment, both of us knowing the show we're putting on for Peyton.

Emma loops her arm through Peyton's, pulling her close. "Who says I want to be kept?" She looks over at me and winks, as if she believes her comment will be a relief to me. It isn't. For some reason, I actually hate the answer.

"Plus," Emma begins, pulling Peyton toward a bar that's set up not too far from us, "who says I want to keep Preston? I'm undecided if I can put up with his constant grumpiness," she teases, her tone not serious at all.

Peyton laughs, gladly following Emma to the bar but looking over her shoulder to give me an apologetic smile. "I promise he's not that bad. He's a total softie—almost a teddy bear, really— underneath that reformed bad-boy attitude and football star muscles. He's just terrible at letting anyone in."

Emma's only response is to laugh, and I don't know if that laugh is a good thing or a bad thing.

Before I can ask, they stop at the bar that is draped in a sheer white fabric. The material blows in the wind with the soft breeze, and it makes me stop and really take a look at the event happening around us.

Flowers have been brought in and placed everywhere. Paired with the flowing, sheer, white fabric they have on every table and draped along arches, it really is a beautiful sight. It all looks perfect for Peyton. I hope today—and all the festivities for the week—are everything she's dreamed of when it comes to her wedding.

"Everything looks great," I tell my sister, wrapping my arm around her as she waits for a drink. I pull her into my side, resisting the urge to mess up her hair the way I always used to when she was a child.

Peyton nods her head, looking around at the busy event. There are definitely more people here than there were at the event last night, but there's far more space for people to spread out.

I look around at all of the faces, only vaguely recognizing some of them. "How many of these are Mom and Dad's friends?" I ask, watching Emma take a tentative drink of the champagne Peyton handed to her.

Peyton follows suit in looking around at the party. A small sigh escapes her lips as she focuses on the group of people surrounding our mom. "A lot of them," she confesses with a groan. "I couldn't say no as they kept adding more and more people to the list. Plus, I felt bad. They're paying for the wedding. Shouldn't I let them invite whomever they want?"

I'm quiet for a moment, not wanting to give my opinion on it. She's got to be getting a ton of different ones with everything going on; she doesn't need mine as well.

"I'm sure it means more wedding gifts," Emma pipes up.

This makes Peyton laugh. She waves her champagne in Emma's direction. "That is *very* true. I had to keep adding useless things to our registry because everything was purchased, and Mom kept telling me to add more. I now have enough dishes to host twenty people if needed."

"Are you a good cook?" Emma asks, staring at Peyton with a small crease along her forehead.

Peyton gasps, shaking her head. "Not at all. Jackson doesn't even allow me in the kitchen. I almost burnt the entire town-house down once when I was trying to make garlic bread."

The garlic bread incident happened years ago, and it's still funny to hear about. It's true that Peyton was never really good at cooking, but she also wasn't ever interested either. She was too busy to stay in one place. She'd help in the kitchen for five minutes before she was ready to move on to something else in the house.

"Plus, I don't think it's my fault," Peyton continues. "Preston got all the good cooking genes and left none for me." She nudges me with her shoulder and a smile before looking over at Emma. "Be honest. Was it his cooking skills that sold you?"

Emma looks at me for a moment, an unreadable look on her face. "He's truly full of surprises," she finally answers, avoiding the question by not really answering it at all.

Peyton's eyes light up when she notices Jackson walking our way. He's really gone for it today with his outfit. He's wearing a polo and a sweater vest—completing the outfit with a visor with the word GROOM etched across the front.

"I've got to go see my groom," Peyton says excitedly, pushing away from the bar and practically skipping. She twirls to face us, a knowing smile on her lips. "You two enjoy some time to yourselves, okay? We'll catch up more later!"

As soon as Peyton joins Jackson and is out of earshot, Emma looks at me with wide eyes.

"You're a hot quarterback in the NFL and can cook? Is that even fair?" she asks accusingly, as if it's the worst thing in the world that I'm all of those.

14
Emma

"EMMA, DARLING, TELL US MORE ABOUT YOUR FAMILY," GRAM softly demands from across the table.

My stomach sinks a little as I try not to pay attention to the number of eyes on me. We've been at the event for a little over an hour, giving me the opportunity to meet the guests at the same table as us. We're under a tent, giving us a small reprieve from the hot rays of the summer sun.

"Um," I respond. My leg taps underneath the table as I try to think about how much I want to divulge to the people looking at me. They seem nice for the most part—except Marsha, who has been staring daggers at me the entire time I've been here.

A large, warm hand finds my leg. Preston's fingertips burn through the thin fabric of my dress as he digs them into my thigh, forcing me to stop with the anxious tapping. "Gram, why don't we *not* interrogate my girlfriend over hors d'oeuvres?"

A shiver runs down my spine at the possessive way he says girlfriend. I've only heard it come from his mouth a few times, and it's something I don't know if I could ever get used to.

Gram gives me an apologetic smile before taking a drink of her whiskey. It's something I love about her. The server stopped by to try and hand her a champagne with cotton candy placed on top, and she immediately shot the server down. She was polite about it, but it didn't take long for her to request something a little stronger—something certainly with more of a kick.

"I'm sorry, Emma. I don't mean anything wrong by the question. I'm just so intrigued by the woman who finally locked down Preston's heart."

My cheeks heat with her comment. I fight the urge to correct her that I absolutely haven't locked down Preston's heart. I wait for Preston to do it, but he doesn't. Braving a look over at him, I find him already watching me. He seems deep in thought, two tiny lines appearing right between his dark eyebrows.

His eyes rip from mine, as if he just realized that I was staring back at him. "The fact that she's captivated my attention should tell you all you need to know."

My body jolts at his words—at the directness of them. The delivery leaves no room for questions. He squeezes my thigh, reminding me that his hand never left in the first place.

Gram smiles and even aims a wink in my direction. "Your reaction tells me a lot," she offers.

It doesn't happen a lot, but I'm too stunned to even respond right away. The possessive way Preston speaks about me, the way he reassuringly keeps his hand placed on my thigh, it really feels like he's a boyfriend sticking up for me.

I have to remind myself that he and I only met last night. After speaking with him for five minutes, it felt like we'd known each other for much longer. We just clicked like that.

I clear my throat, trying to ignore all of the people staring at me. Even Peyton, who was deep in conversation with Jackson and someone else, has focused her attention on me.

"Growing up, it was just me and my aunt Vanessa. My mom got into an accident when I was a baby and passed away before my first birthday. My grandparents had both passed, and my mom never told my aunt who my father was. My aunt was young, but she raised me as her own. It's just been me and Aunt V my entire life. She's my best friend, and I owe everything to her. She pushed me to leave Illinois and go to school in New York, even though I'd never known anything but her."

"That's beautiful," Gram responds, holding her glass of whiskey to her lips.

I shrug. I'll never stop shouting from the rooftops about how much Aunt V means to me. She didn't have to become a mother to me at twenty-one, but she did anyway. She put her entire life on pause for me, and now that I haven't lived in Illinois for years, it worries me that she never gave herself time to fall in love.

She lives alone, and I'm constantly at war with wanting to return home to be with her. All I can do is really try to get my life together this summer and make her proud—and make sure that I visit home every now and then.

Preston's hand strokes along my thigh. I'm thankful I didn't wear one of my shorter dresses because I'm not sure what I'd do if I felt his skin against mine right there. When agreeing to be his fake girlfriend, I didn't take into account the fact that I was already incredibly attracted to him and what might happen as we continue to play the part.

He leans in close, his lips brushing against the shell of my ear. "You hadn't told me any of that." His voice is low with a hint of a growl to it. Is he mad that I told everyone here before I told him?

I turn my head to the side, trying to keep my response discreet. If our cover is blown, it won't be because of me. This new position puts his lips incredibly close to mine. His breath is hot against my cheek. I stare down so I don't look into his eyes. I don't know if we've been this close this whole time, and I don't trust myself when I stare into his eyes.

"You didn't ask." I keep my voice below a whisper. "It's not like we've had all the time in the world to share our stories."

It's only because his mouth is right next to me that I'm able to hear the rumble of disapproval from low in his throat. He shifts his body, making sure to keep his hand on my thigh, even though there's absolutely no reason for it to be there.

Preston pretends as if no one else is here. He lifts my chin with one strong finger, and I love the small scrape of a callus I feel against my tender skin with the movement. I'm worried he might actually be upset with me by the intense set of his shoulders and the hard press of his jaw.

"You good?" he says, asking the question as if there aren't countless pairs of eyes aimed right at us.

I nod, giving him a smile. I don't know anything different than my mom not being with us anymore and being raised by my aunt. I'm proud to share the story of how much Aunt V sacrificed to raise me. I have never minded sharing it; it was always the way people looked at me after that I hated.

Preston doesn't seem convinced. He narrows his eyes, his dark thick eyelashes almost dusting his sharp cheekbones with how much they've turned into slits. Whatever he's thinking, he doesn't voice anything else.

I have to look away, my eyes finding his sister's to try and escape the intensity of her brother.

She rests her chin in between her hands with her elbows propped on the table. Her eyelids flutter as she stares at me with her mouth hanging open. "Oh my god," she mouths at me, shaking her head slightly.

"Anyway," I say with an anxious laugh. I look down to my plate, where my crab cake still sits. Trying to ignore the weight of Preston's hand on my leg, I pick up my fork and take the largest bite possible. I almost force the entire thing into my mouth because I'm so anxious with everyone's eyes on me—Preston's especially.

I chew a few times, immediately regretting ungracefully shoving almost an entire crab cake into my face. "This crab cake is immaculate," I manage to get out despite my mouth full of food.

This gets Gram to laugh, and soon, the rest of the table joins in as well. "Oh, Emma, you're such a hoot," Gram drawls. "You must stay for the family dinner later."

I look over at Preston, my eyes wide with fear. I don't know if I'm prepared for the small family dinner—I'm folding at one simple garden party with him.

"I'd love to," I lie, my words coming out jumbled because of all the food in my mouth.

Preston stays silent, making me wonder if he wants me to stay tonight or if he's ready to end the charade for the day. I try to shift in my chair to get his hand to move, but he doesn't let me. His fingertips stay digging into the fabric of my dress for the rest of the meal.

And not for the first time in the last twenty-four hours, I ask myself what the hell I've gotten myself into.

15
Preston

"So, how serious are things between you and the chick you brought?" Holt Carmichal asks me as we wait for our drinks at one of the pop-up bars on the property.

My head whips in his direction as I try to figure out if I just heard him correctly. I loathe small talk—hate it, really. I was spacing out as he was striking up casual conversation and trying to get details from me about next season. I'd checked out of the conversation so I'm not sure I heard him correctly with the last question. "Excuse me?" I ask, not bothering to hide the annoyed tone to my voice.

"The chick you brought…" Holt begins, pointing the head of his beer bottle in Emma's direction. I look where he points, finding Emma deep in conversation with my sister and grand-mother. The three of them appear to be gossiping like they're in high school. "Are things serious between the two of you?" Holt pushes. "Or when you move on to the next one, would you be okay with me shooting my shot?"

I've had opposing team players trash-talk me, and I've been able to keep completely cool.

I've had fans from our biggest rival team shout obscene and horrible things to me, and it didn't faze me.

But for some reason, the thought of Holt Carmichal having anything to do with Emma has my blood boiling. I'm pretty sure

I see red—and it's been a long time since I haven't been able to keep my cool just because of something someone said to me.

I used to be a hothead; that was all part of my twenties—until now.

My fingers tighten around my own beer bottle. The look I give him must be scathing because he holds his hands up defensively before my anger subsides enough to even get words out.

"She has a name," I manage to get out through gritted teeth. "And to be frank with you, Holt, the fact you had the nerve to even say that to me has me wanting to smash your face in."

A choking sound comes from Holt's throat at my words. His mouth flops open and shut like a dead fish.

An angry laugh rumbles through my chest. "Don't worry. You're safe today, Carmichal. It's my sister's wedding week, and I'm not trying to create a PR nightmare. But know my kindness can only go so far. Talk about my girlfriend like that again, and I don't give a fuck what brand deals I lose and what repercussions I'll face. You got that?"

The asshole can't even come up with a response. What a fucking loser. I'm well aware that I grew up with a silver spoon in my mouth, but I've spent my entire adulthood trying to make a name for myself that has nothing to do with my parents' fortune. Holt can't say the same. He has a title at his father's law firm but barely practices law because of the cases he's fucked up. I have no idea why Jackson is even friends with him, but it's none of my business.

Holt was really none of my fucking business until he decided to try and insult Emma by not even learning her name.

"Sorry, bro." Holt takes a few steps away from me as if he isn't quite confident that I won't risk it and aim a right hook his way. I'm tempted to, not caring at all about my reputation or what it could do to my throwing hand.

I take a deep breath, attempting to center myself. Emma's loud laugh from across the yard is a welcome distraction. But hearing her beautiful laugh—so happy and carefree—while a man wanting her attention can't even remember her name just pisses me off more.

My hand flexes at my side. "Get out of my sight," I seethe, wishing I didn't have to see him for the rest of the week—or ever again, really. "And next time, don't ask a man about having a turn with his woman. It's rude and tacky as hell."

"Got it," Holt responds, his voice breathy with fear.

He begins to scurry away, joining all of his loafer-loving friends, but I have one more thing I have to say.

"And you shouldn't need to know this because you shouldn't plan on talking to her at all, but her name is Emma. Get it right."

Holt at least has enough common sense to not say anything back to me. He hurries away, not even looking back as he makes his way to his friends.

"Well, that was entertaining," the bartender says from behind me. My body tenses, not realizing we had an audience for the exchange.

I turn around, finding a kid probably barely legal to drink smiling at me. I groan, wondering if he really caught that entire conversation.

The kid—Davis, if his name tag is correct—gives me a knowing grin. "Don't worry, dude. Jealousy happens to the best of us. Your secret's safe with me. Huge Manhattan Mambas fan."

My muscles tense at his comment. "I wasn't jealous. The guy was just being a dick."

This makes Davis laugh. Without any prompting or explanation, he begins to make a cocktail. "The guy was a total dick. If you weren't going to threaten him, I was going to. But I know jealousy when I see it, my man, and that was pure jealousy."

I stare at him, blinking a few times as I try to come up with a response. "It wasn't jealousy," I demand, trying to keep my tone firm. "He was being disrespectful to me by even asking and, more importantly, by not even using her name."

"Want me to kick his ass?" Davis asks. His tone is joking, and it actually breaks the tension, making a small laugh escape me.

"No. He's actually harmless."

My eyes find Holt, who is watching me with a cautious expression. Maybe he really is scared I'm going to say to hell with my morals and march my way over to him. I won't, but I lift my beer in a tiny salute to him just to make him nervous.

"For what it's worth, and I mean this in the most respectful way possible, I get it," Davis pipes up, putting two cherries in a drink that's a soft pink.

"Get what?" I ask, turning around and resting my forearms against the bar.

"I get why you'd be jealous. Your date…she's magnetic. As a bartender, I get paid to watch people. I've noticed how everyone is drawn to her today. It makes sense why you'd be jealous of someone else wanting her."

I drag my knuckle along my bottom lip, thinking his words through. *Was I jealous?* Surely not. I've never been a jealous man. But is it that I'm not a jealous person or that I wasn't interested enough in anyone to make me that way?

Clearing my throat, I straighten my spine and finish off the last of my beer. I'm not jealous; I just don't like Holt being disrespectful.

But what if you are *jealous?* an annoying voice chimes in from the back of my head. I don't listen to it any further. I've known her for a day—there's no way she's already making me jealous.

Davis has the nerve to laugh at me. He shakes his head, gently sliding the pink drink across the bar top to me. "You can go ahead and take this to her. Something tells me she'll love it."

I look down at the drink. "What is it?"

"A new recipe I'm messing with. Today, I'm thinking about calling it 'The Wingman.' What do you think?"

I roll my eyes at the kid. I like him, which is saying something because I barely tolerate anyone outside of my usual inner circle.

"I don't need a wingman," I declare, still taking the drink.

He lifts a shoulder. "Of course, you don't. You're Preston Fucking Rhodes. Just let me pretend I was one for a legend."

This gets me to laugh. "It takes a lot to become a legend. Not sure I earned that title." My eyes roam to where Emma still stands locked in conversation with Gram and Peyton. "Plus, the sport I play means nothing to her."

Davis hums in surprise. "Is that refreshing?"

I look at him suspiciously, wondering why he seems to have such a read on both Emma and me. Are bartenders always this intuitive, or is it just him?

I sigh. "To be determined, Davis."

Leaving the drink on the bar, I reach into my pocket and grab my wallet. I pull out a hundred-dollar bill and slide it across to him. "Thank you for the advice, even though I didn't ask for it."

"The tip isn't necessary," he responds, looking at it as if he's not sure if he should take it or not.

I slide it even further toward him. "Doesn't matter, take it." I look around, making sure no one is watching us. "If you have a pen, I'll sign something for you, too. Just don't tell anyone."

A squeaking noise comes from his throat. "Are you kidding?"

"I'm not really known for being funny," I admit.

Davis hurriedly reaches into his pockets, finally finding a pen. He looks around, picking up a napkin and placing it carefully in front of me. "Thank you for doing this, man. I know it must get annoying when people ask you to sign something."

I sign the napkin for him and hand it over. He laughs at what I signed.

DAVIS,
LET ME KNOW WHEN YOU NEED A WINGMAN. I OWE YOU ONE.
PRESTON RHODES

"Good talking to you. Hopefully, she likes the drink."

"Taking it to her now," I answer before making my way to Emma.

The moment her eyes meet mine and she gives me a bright smile, I wonder if maybe Davis was right. Is she getting to me more than I thought?

Even if she is, I'm not going to do something about it. I get her for the rest of this week, and I'm going to savor every moment.

16
Emma

"I REALLY WISH YOUR GRANDFATHER WAS HERE FOR THIS," GRAM notes from my side, looking at the people gathered around the small, intimate table with a longing look in her eyes. She looks to Peyton, her eyes slightly misting over as she smiles.

Peyton blows her a kiss, placing a hand over her heart. "I really wish he was here, too. He would've been the life of the party."

Dinner has been nice—and not at all as intimidating as I thought it'd be. When Gram said it was intimate, I didn't imagine it only being immediate family. We're sitting under the stars, twinkling lights strung around us at a circular table that's low to the ground. Pillows of different shades of white and blue circle the table, making the dinner seem far more casual than the party earlier.

Gram stays quiet for a moment, her mind clearly elsewhere.

Preston is the one to break the silence from my other side. He reaches across my front, his forearm brushing against my breasts, as he takes his grandmother's hand. "You should tell Emma about the night you and Grandpa met."

Peyton excitedly claps her hands, pushing off where she rests against Jackson's chest for a moment. "Yes, please do, Gram. You know it's one of my favorites." Peyton's eyes meet mine, a soft smile on her lips. "Something tells me you're a romantic, Emma. You'll just *love* this story."

"Just a little bit of one," I answer, holding up my thumb and index finger and creating the smallest amount of space between them. I'd like to think of myself as a romantic, but I think a large part of that is because I've never really had a steady boyfriend. I've never had someone do big gestures for me—or even little ones—and I'll continue to wait, and hope, for the person who does.

"You have to tell it, Gram," Peyton prods.

"It really is a special story," Preston's mom chimes in.

Gram pulls her shawl closer to her shoulders. Her eyes roam over her family members seated around the table. "Are you sure all of you want to hear it again?"

Everyone nods as I lean in close to her and nudge her with my shoulder. "I'd love to hear it if you're willing to share."

Gram sighs, looking to the sky for a moment before looking back at me.

"I was eighteen and was visiting the Hamptons with my family for the summer. I'd never had a boyfriend—and I didn't want one either, despite my parents' wishes to marry me off."

Everyone is quiet as she looks off into the distance, as if she's picturing that day in her head. "There was a bonfire on the beach one night. Everyone who was in for the summer attended. It was a big deal, and my sister had to drag me to it."

"You didn't want to go?" I ask. I only met her yesterday, but Gram seems to love a party. I'm a little surprised she wouldn't want to go to one.

Gram swats at the air. "Of course, I didn't want to go, darling. I wanted to stay home and read a book."

"But you went, and tell her what happened next," Peyton demands, leaning forward even more.

Gram raises an eyebrow at her granddaughter. "Am *I* telling this story, or are *you*?"

My teeth rake against my bottom lip as I try to hide my smile. I like her sass.

"Sorry, Gram," Peyton apologizes, leaning back and letting Jackson wrap his arms around her once again. "I just *love* love, and I absolutely adore this story."

"Then let me tell it, child," Gram remarks, winking at Peyton to soften her words.

I sigh, loving the banter between this family. I never knew what it was like to have big family dinners or events. We didn't have family Christmas, weddings, funerals, or any of it. Holidays were spent with just Aunt V and me. On some occasions, she had to work, so I'd spend Christmas watching Hallmark movies or trying—and failing—to make Christmas cookies.

"I went to the party so my sister would stop pestering me about it. I was sitting right next to the pier, completely minding my own business…still reading my book, of course."

I laugh. "You're an icon for going to the party and still bringing the book."

"It was a mystery novel, and I had to know if my theories were correct. You can imagine how annoyed I was when Joseph walked right up to me and asked if I wanted to dance."

"What did you say?" I ask, fully invested in the story.

"This is the best part," Preston responds, leaning close to speak right into my ear. I don't know why he feels the need to do it. His comment can be heard by everyone; it's not like it's a secret.

"I ignored him, of course," Gram responds with a careless shrug. "My book was more important, and I didn't even think he was talking to me. But then he had the audacity to snatch it from my lap when I didn't answer him."

I gasp. "No, he didn't."

She nods. "Oh, he sure did. I ripped my novel from his hands and smacked him right atop the head with it."

"And he didn't run?" I ask, trying to imagine a young Gram completely taking out a potential suitor with a book.

She lets out an annoyed sigh. "No. He was persistent. I'll give him that."

"Grandpa used to swear the moment she hit him with that book, he fell in love with her," Preston remarks.

I turn to look at him for a moment, loving the way he speaks about his grandparents. I've learned more and more about him throughout the day, and I'm scared to admit that there's nothing I've discovered that I don't like.

He tips his chin up, gesturing for me to keep listening to Gram. I follow his direction, looking at her once again and waiting for her to keep telling the story.

She stays quiet for a moment, a serene smile on her face before she speaks up again. "Preston is right. He used to say that —although I don't know how much I believed him. Either way, I hit him upside the head with that book, and it didn't deter him for a second. He asked me to dance again, and I told him there was no music."

"Very bold of him to ask you to dance if there wasn't any music," I note, taking a drink of some fruity cocktail that's one of the best drinks I've ever had. I'm on my second one, and I'm trying not to drink them too quickly so I don't end up tipsy like last night—and have to deal with a hangover tomorrow. But it's hard to not want to drink it all at once with how great it tastes.

"If Joseph was anything, it was bold. He didn't care that there wasn't any music. He said we'd make our own, and then he held his hand out to me."

I'm quiet and shift my position, eager to hear what happens next. Luckily, she doesn't make me wait long.

"I don't know what compelled me to take it, but I did. He pulled me up onto that pier, and we danced."

"Without any music?" I ask, trying to imagine a young Gram being swept off her feet by a handsome stranger. It's incredibly romantic.

"Without any music," she responds. "And I didn't admit it to myself for a very long time, but I fell in love with him on that pier. The way he hummed my favorite song as we danced, even though he had no way of knowing it was my favorite. The way he asked about my book, sat on the pier with me, our feet hanging over the edge, and listened for twenty minutes as I told him the entire plot of the novel. It was…" She pauses, looking up at the stars and closing her eyes for a moment. You can feel the love she had for her husband radiating off her—the love she still holds for him, even though he's left this world.

"Romantic?" I finish for her, my voice full of awe. I've slowly watched my friends fall in love, and it's something I crave—something I want to experience. Looking at Gram, I wonder what it's like to have such fond memories of someone decades later and still hold so much love for him.

Gram opens her misty eyes and looks right at me. "Yes," she manages to get out. She reaches over and grabs my hand. Her cold fingers wrap around mine, holding tightly as she gives them a firm squeeze. "It was romantic. He was a romantic. And it was the easiest decision I ever made to say yes to his proposal a month later."

My eyes widen. "A month?" I look around the table to see if anyone is as shocked as me about how quick their romance was, but their faces tell me all I need to know. They've heard this story before and aren't shocked at all about how quickly their love story unfolded.

Gram smiles, squeezing my hand again. "If we're being honest, it was more like three weeks, but I always thought saying a month sounded better. When you know, you know. There isn't a one-size-fits-all time limit for love." She looks at Preston over my shoulder for a moment. "Right, Preston?" she prods, raising a thin eyebrow.

Preston coughs. I choke on my own spit. The two of us create a symphony of different noises at Gram's words.

"Lord have mercy," Gram barks, rubbing my back.

Preston and I pull it together under the scrutinizing stares of his family.

"Sorry to ruin the story," I comment, taking a drink of my water. My throat burns from coughing, but the ice water helps to soothe it.

Gram swats at the air. "It's fine. I've told it a million times."

"Thank you for telling it to me. It's beautiful. The two of you seemed really lucky to meet and share a life together."

This gets Gram to smile so big her entire face lights up. "We were the luckiest. I'd give anything to dance on the pier with him again."

No one speaks, letting her words hang in the air around us. My eyes roam the table, looking at the elegant flower arrangements expertly placed along the table. Lit candlesticks also line the table, the gold sticking out against the white tablecloth.

An idea pops into my head. In one quick motion, I'm pushing off the pillow on the ground and leaning over the table. One by one, I begin to blow out the candles.

"What are you doing?" Preston's mom asks. All I do is briefly look up and give her an apologetic smile. I don't care what she thinks of my idea; all I care about at the moment is Gram.

Once I've made my way around the table and blown out every single candle, I spin to look at Gram with a hesitant smile. We don't have a pier, but we have a table, which will have to do. I hold my hand out, waiting for her to take it. I do a deep bow, trying to make the moment as dramatic as possible. "Dance with me?"

17
Preston

"Darling, you don't have to ask me to dance," Gram responds to Emma, staring at her outstretched hand.

"I know I don't have to. But I never say no to dancing, and the table is kind of like a pier. Right?" Emma smiles cautiously. She chews on her bottom lip as if she's worried that Gram might not take her up on her offer.

I watch Gram anxiously, not sure what she'll do. Emma's idea is certainly out of the box, but it makes me admire her even more. Her determination to recreate a memory for a woman she just met yesterday makes an unfamiliar feeling run through me. I try to shake it off, but the feeling only intensifies when Gram takes her hand and allows Emma to pull her off the pillow.

"Peyton, dance with us?" Emma asks, looking over to my sister with a more confident smile this time.

Peyton eagerly jumps out of Jackson's arms and steps onto the table.

"Everyone, grab your drinks!" Emma demands, picking her drink up and taking a sip.

Surprising me, both Mom and Dad follow Emma's direction. They each pick up their drink, allowing more room for Gram, Peyton, and Emma to have room to dance.

Gram laughs nervously, holding on to Emma for support. "We don't have any music."

"You're in luck—kind of." She giggles, taking off one of her heels and then the other. She throws them both at me, reminding me of last night when I first met her. "I'm a terrible singer," Emma continues. "But my mind is like a vault of song lyrics. Hope you like One Direction."

Peyton lets out an excited scream. "Oh my god, were you a Directioner, too?"

"Huge," Emma responds immediately.

"Two Direction who?" Gram asks, standing between Emma and Peyton, looking completely lost.

This makes both Emma and Peyton bust out in a fit of laughter.

Sliding my phone from my pocket, I hold it up. "I know this isn't technically the same thing, but we have new and improved technology now. What if I just play a song?" I offer.

"I think that's Preston's way of nicely telling us he doesn't want to hear us sing," Emma chirps, wrapping her arm around Gram.

"Or his way of ensuring I don't have to listen to Two Direction," Gram quips.

I chuckle, thumbing through the music on my phone to try and find something Gram would like. "Any requests, Gram?"

Gram shakes her head.

As a joke, I land on "Cotton Eye Joe," expecting all of them to whine. Instead, Emma's mouth drops open with excitement. "Oh, don't threaten me with a good time." She holds her drink in one hand and takes Gram in the other. "Peyton, grab Gram's other hand. We're getting down right now."

In a fit of laughter, the three of them begin to dance in a circle around the table, knocking down flowers and candles in the process. The mess they're creating doesn't stop them at all. The laughs get deeper, their movements get quicker, and soon, the three of them are doing twirls on the table while belting out the lyrics to "Cotton Eye Joe."

I stare at Emma, completely in awe of her. I can't do anything but focus on every single one of her movements. She's breath-taking, and I'm starting to wonder if Davis did have a point earlier. He was right about one thing: she's absolutely magnetic, pulling every single one of my family members in—myself included.

My mom—who has never been known as the life of the party and has always preferred standing on the outskirts—pulls up her dress and climbs onto the table to join them. Soon, the four of them are spinning one another on the table, completely oblivious to the fact the song has changed to a slow one I don't even recognize.

I lean in closer, halfway wishing I was up there holding Emma's hand and spinning her around the makeshift pier instead of my sister.

Emma throws her head back, laughing at something Gram says. I can't hear whatever comment Gram made, but I still watch Emma closely, wondering if I could ever get her to laugh like that for me.

She opens her eyes, straightening her neck, and her eyes immediately land on mine.

I'm mesmerized.

She lights up the room with everything she does. Her bright smile. Her carefree laugh. The small gesture of asking Gram to dance to try and give her a piece of her past back. The effortless way she brings my mom out of her shell.

All I know is that I can't look away from her.

I don't know how many songs go by with the four of them just dancing on top of the table. It's as if not a single one of them has a care in the world. My dad and I smile and laugh right along with them. Even Jackson joins in.

I can't tell you the last time I remember laughing with my family the way we have tonight. It may have been years since we all let go like this and just enjoyed ourselves.

And it's all because of the woman dancing in front of me. She lifts her arm, letting her fingers dangle in the air and waits for

Peyton to take them. She does, and Emma begins to spin Peyton around like she's a ballerina.

"I might get dizzy," Peyton gets out between fits of laughter.

Emma straightens one of her arms in front of her and takes a step back, accidentally knocking down one of the vases of flowers still standing. Peyton copies the same movement until both their arms are completely outstretched.

Peyton pulls Emma in, twirling her all the way until Peyton's arms are wrapped around Emma's middle. They rock back and forth together before Emma spins out of the embrace. The music playing from my phone comes to a stop at the perfect time.

All of their chests heave from the dancing—or maybe it's the laughter.

"What a show!" Jackson claps, staring at my sister with so much love and adoration that it makes me feel a little guilty about hating on some of his outfit choices.

Gram pulls Emma into a huge hug, wrapping her thin arms around Emma and holding tight. They stand right in front of me, allowing me to hear what's said.

"Thank you for that, sweet girl," Gram says, her hand circling Emma's back. "Thank you for allowing me to feel young again."

I swallow, looking down at my lap because of the overwhelming sense of gratitude I feel toward Emma at the moment. I sigh, unable to figure out if it's gratitude or something more that courses through me.

"You *are* young," Emma counters to Gram, allowing my grandmother to embrace her for as long as she desires.

Gram finally pulls away, cupping Emma's cheeks in both her hands. "Nothing's made me feel that young—and free—in a long time, and it's all because of you, my dear."

I look up in time to see my mom nodding in agreement. Dad holds his hand out, helping Mom down from the table.

With a sigh, completely at a loss with the feelings that are taking over me, I stand up. I take a step forward, standing at the edge of the table. Holding my hand out, I gesture for Gram to take it.

"Let me help you down," I demand, unable to meet Emma's eyes at the moment.

I don't know what's happening to me, but I know the reason my heart pounds in my chest and my throat feels clogged is because of her. The woman pretending to be my fake girlfriend. The one I'm supposed to never see again after this week. The one smiling at me with flushed cheeks from the dancing. The one who might cause far more trouble for me this week than I was ever expecting.

Gram safely steps to the ground at the same time Jackson helps Peyton get down, leaving Emma standing up there alone.

I extend my hand out for her. I tell myself it's because it's the gentlemanly thing to do and not because I want to feel the press of her skin against mine. I ignore the way my heart lurches inside my chest out of pure excitement when she places her hand in mine.

I don't think I breathe the few seconds it takes to get her off the table.

"Now, you be the romantic one," Gram demands a few feet away from me. She picks up the drink she'd handed to Jackson in the middle of dancing and takes a long drink from it. "Kiss her!"

"Yes!" Peyton excitedly agrees. "C'mon, Preston."

Emma looks up at me with wide eyes. It's the same look she gave me last night when I introduced her as my girlfriend. She tries to laugh it off. "Oh, Preston isn't really one for PDA," she explains, trying to give them all a knowing look.

This makes Gram let out a snort. "Nonsense. Give her a kiss, Preston."

I swallow, not knowing what to do. Gram is persistent. Mix in Peyton also demanding the kiss, and I don't see a way out of this.

Emma and I look at one another. No one knows we've never

kissed. We've never even come close to kissing...we only met last night. I was too busy roping her into being my fake girlfriend to enjoy the night with her and end it with a kiss.

"Who says I don't like PDA?" I ask, slowly placing my hand on the small of her back.

She stiffens underneath my touch but doesn't move.

My lips part.

Her lips part.

"We don't have to," Emma whispers, her hands finding my chest.

I don't respond. It's at the tip of my tongue to tell her I want to, that the thought of kissing her has been at the back of my mind since I first saw her last night.

"Oh, get to it," Gram pushes. Voices ring out in agreement with her.

Emma's trembling fingers tighten around the fabric of my shirt as she pulls me a little closer to her. The front of our bodies become flush with one another. Her body relaxes into mine.

Time seems to stand still as I realize how badly I want to kiss her. The desire only grows when her tongue slips out and licks along her bottom lip to wet it.

I wish the first time my lips met hers wasn't for an audience, but I can't seem to care too much about it right now. I'm too focused on leaning in, on relishing in the feeling of her breath caressing my lips.

If my family says anything, I don't hear them.

I reach for her cheek, my knuckle dusting over it as I look into her eyes. "You good with kissing me in front of them, rebel?" I ask hoarsely.

She presses her cheek into my fingers, prompting me to lay my palm flat against the nape of her neck.

"I'm not the one afraid of a little PDA," she responds, her voice teasing but breathier than normal.

I smile at that all the way until my lips meet hers.

18
Emma

THE KISS STARTS OUT TIMID, OUR LIPS BARELY BRUSHING AGAINST ONE another. While Preston's lips are gentle against mine, his hands aren't. He possessively grabs me by the waist with one hand and pins me against his body. His other hand is on my neck. His hand is so large that his thumb brushes against my cheek and his pinky digs into the skin at the bottom of my neck.

I want more, but I don't want to be the one to deepen it, not knowing how far we're supposed to take this. My hands stay against his chest as I resist the urge to fist the fabric even tighter and bring his mouth against mine harder. I *want* more, but I won't do it, no matter how bad I want it.

Preston moves his lips against mine so softly. It's a tease, something so light but it still manages to make my chest flutter.

He's the one to stop the kiss.

My eyes slowly open, finding his on mine already. My entire body feels warm, and I'm already wishing his lips were on mine again.

I can feel the race of his heart underneath my hand. The feel of it beating wildly against my palm is the only indication that he felt anything from the kiss because his face tells me nothing— except maybe that he might be angry by the way his brows knit together on his forehead.

"C'mon, that was noth—" Gram begins. She doesn't finish

her sentence because before she can get anything else out, Preston is placing both his hands on either side of my face and pulling me to him once again.

I yelp from surprise, not expecting it. This time, he's far more deliberate with the kiss. The moment our lips meet, his tongue is peeking out, licking along the seam of my mouth. I open my mouth, welcoming him in and dying to get a taste.

He tastes like whiskey. Expensive whiskey that's smooth and you can sip slowly, ensuring you never get sick of it.

I pull my hands from his chest and circle my fingers around both of his wrists tightly, attempting to pull his mouth deeper into mine.

It's heated but slow. And ends way too quickly.

Preston pulls away, his hands dropping to his sides and forcing mine to do the same.

Somebody whistles, but I barely hear it over the thundering beat of my own racing pulse. My chest heaves, and I know it's probably flushed from the fervor in which he just kissed me. The intensity is reflected in the way in which he stares back at me.

"Do you two need a room now?" Gram's words catch me off guard.

I rip my eyes from Preston's and look at her. I'm stunned, and I don't know if it's because of her question or if my mind is still reeling from that kiss.

"Gram, you can't say things like that out loud," Peyton scolds, her voice full of humor.

I press my fingers to my lips. My head spins, and I can't decide if I want to pull Preston to me again or to run away from him because the kiss was not supposed to be *that* good.

I decide on the latter. "I just need…" My words drift off, and before anyone can say anything, I'm turning around and rushing away from the table. I'll return to them and make up some sort of excuse about being shy about PDA or something along those lines, but I really just need to get away from Preston.

I knew I was attracted to him. Even before I got a good look at his face, I was drawn to him just by the sound of his voice. But that kiss...that kiss was dangerous because I wanted to get lost in it. I could've gotten lost in *him*, and this summer isn't about being lost—it's about being found.

"Emma, wait!" Preston calls from behind me.

I sigh, folding my arms across my chest and not slowing my steps in the slightest.

"I need a minute, Preston!" Luckily, I'm able to keep my voice composed. I know if I just get a little space from him, I'll be able to return to the dinner and pretend that kiss didn't totally rock my world. I just need a few minutes to gather myself before doing that.

"Where are you going?" Preston asks, his voice closer this time.

A small sound of annoyance comes from deep in my throat. He's the reason I'm in this situation to begin with—the reason I'm having to come to terms with the fact that a kiss that felt so perfect was only just for show.

"I'm going for a walk," I call out, looking around to see where I could even walk to.

"A walk? To where?"

"To anywhere you aren't," I mutter under my breath, thankful that his voice isn't too close to me to hear it.

At least that's what I thought. His fingers wrap around my bicep and spin me, forcing me to face him.

His eyes scan my face with concern. "Did I do something wrong? I wasn't thinking when I pulled you back in for that kiss and—"

I don't let him finish. I'm turning back around and heading in the direction of what looks to be a large garden maze. Luckily for me, Peyton chose a massive property to host her event at, so there are plenty of places for me to escape to. If Preston would just let me.

"Five minutes!" I don't have to look back to know that Preston is still following me. I can feel him there behind me, hot on my heels as I beeline it to the garden maze. "I just need five minutes, and then I'll be back at that dinner, perfectly pretending to be your girlfriend."

"So it was the kiss, then?" Preston pushes, following me into the entrance.

I let out a frustrated sigh, spinning on my heel to face him. He must not expect me to stop because he almost runs into me. His quick reflexes are the only thing that prevent him from doing so.

"Can you just stop with your questions and give me five minutes alone?" My voice comes out more defeated than I want it to, which probably only makes things worse by the way he frowns.

"I'll leave you alone once I know that you're not mad at me for kissing you." He runs his hand through his hair, his eyes anxious as they watch me carefully.

I roll my eyes. "I'm not upset about the kiss." Maybe I *am* upset about the kiss, but not for the reasons he thinks.

Preston takes a step closer to me. I take a step back. We repeat the movement until the leaves of the foliage climbing up the maze wall graze my back.

His eyes rake over my face. "Then what had you running away?"

I wish he didn't smell so good. I wish he didn't have such piercing blue eyes that make it hard to look away. I wish I'd never agreed to be his fake girlfriend without thinking about everything that entails.

I wish he'd kiss me again.

"Emma." My name falls from his lips like a warning.

"I just needed to get away from you for a minute!" My words come out louder than I wanted them to, but he's pushed my buttons by not letting me have a moment to myself.

"From me?" Preston asks. He keeps firm eye contact, making it hard to look away from him, even though I want to fold under his gaze.

"Yes. From you."

"So it *was* the kiss, then?" He sighs in frustration, reaching up to run a hand through his hair. "I should've told my family no. I—"

"It's because I want to kiss you again!" I shout, my resolve finally breaking.

He jolts, my words taking him by surprise.

I take a deep breath in, wondering if I'll regret telling him that. "The first thought I had when you pulled away was how badly I wanted to convince you we needed more practice…that we should do it again."

Preston takes a step closer to me, pressing our bodies together. "You think we need more practice?"

My mouth feels dry. I swallow, trying to fix it. "Maybe," I whisper.

"I don't think we need any practice." His voice is deep and gravelly, causing goose bumps to break out along my arms.

My heart races in my chest. Is this him telling me he doesn't want to kiss me again? Surely not. He seemed just as into that kiss as I was. He can't mask the possessive way he pulled me back to his lips, as if he was starved and couldn't get air from anything or anyone else but me. I know that wasn't in my head.

Preston reaches out, running his knuckle softly along my chin. The touch is featherlight, but it sends shivers down my spine.

"We definitely need more practice," I manage to get out, my voice hoarse. "The kiss felt awkward."

This makes him laugh. God, why is his laugh so sexy? It's deep and rumbles through his chest. I feel it everywhere.

He leans forward, his eyes following the path of his knuckle. He moves it from my jaw to my throat. I wonder if he can feel my racing pulse under his touch. Is his heart beating just as fast as mine? God, I hope so.

"You're telling me that kiss felt awkward, rebel?" His words come out rough and angry.

"Yes," I lie. Nothing about the kiss felt awkward, but maybe if I tell him it did, I'll convince him we have to kiss more to make it seem more natural—so his family won't see through our facade.

He's quiet. So quiet that my heart wants to leap from my chest in anticipation of what he'll say next. Or maybe he won't say anything. Maybe he'll agree with me and kiss me again—giving me exactly what I want from him.

His knuckle makes it to my chest. He traces over the swell of my breast, making my breath hitch. It takes everything in me not to open my mouth and plead for more from him. I'd take anything more than what he's giving me right now.

His lips are so close that I can feel his breath against my skin, but they aren't close enough. They aren't moving against mine.

"Wrong answer," he responds.

"What was the right one?" My voice comes out uneven, and I want him to kiss me again so badly that I don't even care how obvious I'm being. And I'm fairly confident by the look in his eyes he wants the same.

Preston leans in close enough that our lips almost brush against one another's. He's so close that I shut my eyes, waiting for him to close the distance.

He grabs the back of my neck, making me forget that I'd asked him a question. He doesn't have to answer as long as he kisses me. His lips brush against the corner of my mouth. I turn my head to try and line up our lips, but his grip is firm on the back of my neck, keeping my head in the position he wants it.

He continues to tease me, kissing along my cheek and neck instead of pressing his lips where I want them.

A small groan of frustration leaves me, making him laugh. It feels good against my neck, feeling the tickle of his breath against my skin.

His lips make it to my ear. I swear he tries to make me combust when his teeth rake against the sensitive skin underneath it. His tongue pokes out to caress the spot where his teeth just were, and it's the most euphoric form of torture.

I clutch his shirt, trying to pull him closer to me.

"We'll kiss again. That I can promise you."

I smile at his words, waiting for him to do just that. He doesn't move; he keeps his mouth lined up with my ear. "But not right now. I have to teach you a lesson for calling that kiss awkward." As if to nail his point home, he kisses my temple so softly I barely feel it before his body heat is gone from mine.

My eyes pop open, finding him a few steps away from me. He smirks, his hands tucked in his pockets as if his body wasn't just pressed against mine seconds ago.

"What?" I sputter, wondering what just happened.

This only makes him smile wider. I wish he didn't smile so sparingly because it makes my heart race that much faster when he does.

"You called our kiss awkward. It was the furthest thing from that. I know that. You know that. And the next time I kiss you, I'll make damn sure you'll never call it that again."

"I only said that as an excuse to kiss more."

"Do I need an excuse to kiss you?" he counters, his head cocked to the side. "This week, you are my girlfriend, after all."

Before I can respond to him, he's lifting his chin and pointing to the garden exit. "We'll finish this later. Let's get back to dinner before Gram gets any wild ideas about what we're doing."

19
Preston

I'VE NEVER WANTED TO DITCH MY FAMILY MORE THAN I HAVE tonight. Peyton insisted we keep the night going, reminiscing about old family vacations and begging Gram to tell stories about her and Grandpa. The entire time, all I could think about was that kiss with Emma.

I should've just kissed her in that garden. *Fuck*, I know she wanted me to. She kept wetting her lips every time she looked at mine. Even under the moonlight, her entire body was flushed. She wanted me to kiss her just as badly as I wanted to do it—but her comment about our first kiss being awkward didn't sit well with me.

I know she was coming up with excuses like she said, but that was the best damn first kiss I'd ever had. I don't know the last time something rocked me the way that kiss did. I can't help but want to make her pay for calling that kiss anything short of perfection.

Gram is in the midst of recalling the time when Grandpa proposed here in the Hamptons on the same pier they met at and almost dropped the ring in the ocean. I'm too busy regretting not kissing Emma when I had the chance when she leans closer to me.

"Why aren't you finishing your drink?" she asks, pointing to the whiskey the bartender gave me the moment I returned back from the maze with Emma. I hadn't taken a sip of it.

"I'm driving," I answer, not telling her the reason I didn't want to take even a sip was because I didn't want to get rid of the taste of her. She'd tasted of cherry and lime from the fruity cocktail Davis had made her, and I'm still thinking about it an hour later.

My answer must satisfy Emma because she leaves my personal space and goes back to intently listening to the story Gram shares. I thought we might have to come up with an elaborate story to make up for her acting weird when we returned to my family, but she kept it completely cool the moment we returned to the table.

And I think that pisses me off more. She acts cool as can be, even though it wasn't long ago she was almost begging me to kiss her again. I thought I'd teach her a lesson by almost kissing her, but I'm beginning to wonder if she's the one teaching me a lesson.

"Preston?" Grandma shouts, clapping her hands together to get my attention.

I jump, blinking rapidly and looking from my untouched drink to my grandmother. "Yes?"

"Is my story that boring to you?" she teases, her voice soft.

I sit up straight, turning my body toward my grandmother so she has my full attention. "Sorry, Gram. I think I'm just getting a little tired. Emma, you ready?"

"Not really," Emma responds instantly, grinning at me.

Oh, she's definitely getting me back for the moment in the maze.

"Do you have to leave?" Peyton juts out her bottom lip at me, reaching for Emma's hand and locking their fingers together. "Emma and I still have so much to talk about."

Emma nods in agreement. "It's not even ten yet. We should stay longer, *honey muffin*." The way she sarcastically says honey muffin makes me lift an eyebrow. The pet name is terrible and never something two people actually dating should call each other, but none of my family seem to catch on to her dramatic use of a pet name.

"I guess we probably shouldn't stay up too late," Peyton interjects. "Our tennis reservations are pretty early tomorrow morning."

"Tennis?" Emma asks, bringing her bottom lip between her teeth.

Peyton leans forward and now has hold of both of Emma's hands. "Yes, tennis. It'll be the entire wedding party and their plus-ones. It'll be so fun!"

The look in Emma's eyes tells me she may not find tennis to be as fun as Peyton does. She laughs nervously, looking to me for help. I don't give her any, so she looks back to Peyton. "I'm not really a sports kind of girl. But I'd love to wear the tennis skirt I packed and admire from the sidelines."

Peyton shakes her head. "Then Preston won't have a partner. It'll be low-key, I promise. But Preston does have a point. We should all go to bed soon so we're ready and rested for tomorrow."

Mom jumps to her feet, clearly excited at the idea of going to bed. Emma, however, lingers on the ground, staring at Peyton with her mouth slightly open.

I stand up, holding my hand out so Emma will take it. She looks from my hand to me. Her bottom lip is turning red from the way she keeps chewing on it nervously. "Preston, you're going to have to find another partner tomorrow." She keeps her voice low so I'm the only one to hear it in the shuffle of everybody getting up from the table.

I frown as I pull her from the ground. "And why would I partner with anyone other than my lovely, sweet, adoring girlfriend, honey muffin?"

Gram walks up to Emma and me. "That's a lot of adjectives," she notes. "And who says honey muffin?"

I have to avoid making eye contact with Emma because I

know if I do, I won't be able to stifle the laughter threatening to escape.

Emma's the one to respond, although I think she's trying her best to hide her laugh by the way she covers her mouth with her hand. "It's cute and not overused." She reaches up to pinch one of my cheeks. "Plus, look at him. A sweet little honey muffin."

Gram looks between Emma and me with pursed lips. Finally, she lets out a sigh of resignation. "Kids these days. Whatever happened to babe or sweetheart?"

Peyton joins our circle before either of us can respond. "So we'll see you bright and early tomorrow, right?"

Leaning down, I speak close to Emma's ear but still loud enough for everyone to hear my response. "And by bright and early, Peyton means ten."

Peyton narrows her eyes at me. "That's early."

I laugh, rolling my eyes and straightening my spine. "I feel like I've slept in if I get to sleep until seven."

Peyton shakes her head. "And that is why we live very different lives. If the sun isn't high in the sky, it isn't time to get up."

Emma nods her head. "Agreed."

My lips press into a thin line. "Most of the time, I'm up by five in the morning to meet with my trainer."

Emma gives me a pat on the back. "Would you like a medal for that?"

Peyton and Jackson bust out in laughter. I scowl, staring at a smug Emma. She'll pay for that comment later.

I wrap my arm around her, pulling her into my side and keeping her body pressed to mine. "Both Emma and I will be ready to play tennis in the morning. We're ecstatic."

Emma places her hand on my chest, rubbing up and down dramatically. "Can't wait," she lies through a tight smile.

I keep my face neutral as she pinches my abs in retaliation. Emma turns her face to speak against my chest, making sure I'm the only one to hear her.

"Jesus, do you have any body fat there? I can barely even get enough skin to pinch."

"It's the early morning workouts," I respond, giving my sister a coy smile as she watches the two of us.

Emma doesn't respond. She pulls away from me and pulls Gram into a hug.

"Thank you all for inviting me tonight. I had so much fun." She and Gram stay locked in the embrace as Emma continues to talk. "And thank you for sharing all the stories. It was so special to hear about Joseph."

Gram closes her eyes and gives Emma one final squeeze before letting go. "No, thank *you*, sweet girl. I haven't laughed as much as I did tonight in I don't know how long. It might be the most fun I've had since Joseph passed, and that's all because of you."

Gram's words make Emma blush. She swats at the air, trying to take the attention away from herself. "All I did was ask you to dance."

Gram cups both of Emma's cheeks, forcing her to meet her eyes. "No one's asked me to dance in a long time, my dear. And that's why it meant so much."

I can't look away as Emma and Gram share a few more words before Peyton jumps in to also say goodbye to Emma. I watch the interactions, wondering how Emma only met my family yesterday—hell, she only met *me* yesterday—and I can't help but notice how much she fits in. How effortlessly she's connected with them in such a short time.

And I don't know how to feel about that.

I push whatever I'm feeling away, not wanting to address what it is. I'm quick at telling my family goodbye and that I'll see them in the morning. It doesn't take long for Emma and me to be alone once again as I lead her to the front of the estate.

Neither one of us says anything as we walk to the car. The valet left long ago, but they left my car parked in the driveway with the keys hidden in the visor. I expect Emma to say something, but she surprisingly stays quiet.

In fact, she doesn't say anything the entire car ride back to Archer's place. She reaches to open her door, but I stop her before she can do it. "Let me get it," I demand, sliding out of the driver's seat and rounding the front of the car.

I open her door, extending my hand to help her out. She looks at my outstretched hand with raised eyebrows. "Are you done giving me the silent treatment?"

"Here I was thinking *you* were the one giving *me* the silent treatment."

Unlike last night, where I had to almost carry her to the front door, tonight, she's steady on her feet. She won't let me take her hand to walk her to the door. She drops it immediately and beelines for the house.

"Anyway. Good night, Preston," she calls over her shoulder. "I must get to bed since apparently I'm being tortured with tennis in the morning."

Her goodbye doesn't faze me at all. I follow her up the pathway leading to the front door.

She spins to face me before we ever make it there. "What do you think you're doing?"

"Walking you to the door."

"We talked about this last night. I'm fine."

I don't move. I know I don't have to walk her to the front door, but I want to. And she isn't going to stop me from wanting to.

She lets out an annoyed sound and stomps her foot in the most adorable of ways. "Do you ever listen, or do you just not listen to me?"

This makes me smile. "So now I'm not just grumpy, I don't listen either?"

She nods, folding her arms across her chest, and holds her chin high. "Yes. *Exactly*. If you were a gentleman, you would've kissed me in that maze when I was basically begging you to," she mumbles under her breath. The words are quiet and hurried, but there's no mistaking exactly what she said.

I grab her by the elbow, keeping my grip around her firm but gentle as I pull her the rest of the way to the doorstep. "One could argue that the gentlemanly thing to do was to not kiss you."

"I think I preferred it when you were brooding and not talking."

We reach the front doorstep, but I'm still not ready to say good night to her just yet. "Were you giving me the silent treatment because you were mad I didn't kiss you?"

Her eyes go wide as if she wasn't expecting me to be so direct. I've had plenty of time to gather my thoughts and regret not giving in and kissing her when she asked me to. Now, if she asked me again, I'd tell her yes.

Emma is quiet for a moment, and I'm learning that her silence drives me wild. She's not normally quiet. She's vocal about the thoughts running through her head, and right now, I want to know every last one of them.

"You might have been right. Maybe we shouldn't kiss unless it's to make the fake dating thing more believable."

I take a step forward. In return, she takes a step back. It repeats until her back is against the front door, putting us in the same position we were in earlier. "Is that what you want?"

"Is what what I want?"

My fingers twitch at my sides, wanting to reach out and touch her. "Do you not want to kiss me anymore?"

Her eyes flutter shut for a moment before opening again. "I've already told you I want to kiss you. But now that I've thought about it, I can't help but wonder that if we kiss, it might mess things up."

"Mess what up?"

"I don't know. We just met, so I wouldn't call us friends, considering I thought about kissing you since the moment I saw you, but also, we're pretending to be dating. I don't want things to feel...real when they're not."

"Is you wanting to kiss me not real?"

She lets out a sigh of annoyance. "No, that's very real. But I'm only equipped to *play* a girlfriend right now, not *be* one, and I don't want us kissing outside of playing the part to make things complicated."

I laugh. "I do hate complicated."

"So if we kiss—" Her eyes flick to my lips for a moment before she looks back at me to finish her thought. "If we kiss, we have to know that nothing will happen outside of this week. We'll play the part...we'll have fun. But after the wedding, you'll go back to being a celebrity who clearly doesn't want to settle down, and I'll get back to finding myself and not having incredibly hot football players distract me from that."

I swallow, resisting the urge to tell her that it has nothing to do with me wanting to settle down or not. I want my life to slow down, to focus on things outside of football. But I owe it to myself and my teammates to give my all to what will most likely be my last year of football.

Emma anxiously licks her lips, her chest rising and falling in quick breaths. I stare at her lips. They're perfectly full—and the only thing I've thought about for hours.

"Preston, what are you thinking about?"

"Your lips." I know she's wary of kissing in private, but tasting her again is all I can think about. She keeps glancing at mine, something I don't even think she knows she's doing, but something that's driving me wild. I don't agree with holding back, not if we both want it as much as I believe we do.

"What about my lips?"

"They look like they need mine."

20
Emma

For the second time tonight, Preston's lips are against mine.

He kisses me fiercely and possessively. There's no watchful eyes, and he knows it. His tongue sweeps across the seam of my lips as his hands find either side of my face. My mouth opens without any reservations. A small moan falls from my lips at the heated way he kisses me.

I feel the kiss everywhere and all at once. He must've been holding back in front of his family earlier because this kiss is one that'll be burned in my memory forever.

"Fuck, you taste good," he mutters against my lips. "I've been thinking about it all damn night."

I smile as he feathers kisses along my jaw. "That's a good line."

He brings his face close to mine so we're eye to eye. "It wasn't a line."

His thumb brushes against my temple, his eyes roaming my face. My eyes flutter shut at the tenderness of it. "I don't care if it was," I admit. We've set the golden rule for whatever we're doing. It ends after the wedding. So even if he is using his best lines on me, I don't care because I know this won't be anything but a fond memory I'll look back on one day.

And just by the way Preston Rhodes kisses me, I'm confident this week will be full of some of my favorite memories.

He presses his lips to mine once again, and I almost melt into a puddle at how expertly he kisses. It's slow and passionate. Every slip of his tongue against mine is deliberate, as if he thinks he has all the time in the world.

I'd give him all the time he wanted tonight to never have to give up feeling his lips pressed against mine.

The kiss slows and slows until he's pulling away with the faintest smile on his lips. He traces my bottom lip with the pad of his thumb, the smile getting wider, making my pulse skip with how much I love to see him do it. "Yeah. Your lips definitely needed mine."

I shake my head, sliding my hands down his chest. Even with a layer of fabric between my skin and his, the slopes and planes of his muscles are incredibly defined. I did a deep dive of him on Google and saw him shirtless on multiple occasions, but I want to see the ripple of them in person.

With a sigh, I look at the door. "I should probably get to bed if I'm expected to play a sport tomorrow and not injure myself." I don't want to go to bed. I want to invite him inside and see where the night takes us. Would he kiss me more? Would his mouth end up on other places? Those are all things I'd love to find out about, but the wise decision would be to let the night end with the kiss we just shared.

He keeps his fingertips pressed to my skin. "I won't let you get hurt tomorrow."

"You have no way of guaranteeing that. I'm terrible at any sport that involves a ball."

"You're safe with me, Emma," he answers confidently.

"The real question is, are you safe with me? If we're on some sort of team together, you better watch out. Who knows where I'll be swinging that racket."

This gets Preston to let out a small, deep chuckle. "You're something else. You know that?"

I close the distance to the front door and punch in the code to open it. The door swings open, but I wait to step inside, not quite wanting to say goodbye to him yet.

"Do you mean that in a good way or a bad way?" I tease, turning to face him once again. I've always been a lot for people. Loud, energetic, and opinionated are all words to describe me. I don't mind them. I'm not pretending to be anyone but exactly who I am. But when he calls me "something else," I do hope he doesn't mean it negatively.

"If someone has ever said that to you in a bad way, then they do not deserve your time or energy." His words are straight to the point and there's no missing the anger mixed in with them.

I shrug, not wanting to dive deep into all the times I've been called too much throughout my life. I've been too loud, too opinionated, too fun, too much energy…the list could go on and on.

"Good night, Preston." I change the subject. What other people have said about me doesn't matter right now. Not with the way he's looking at me.

I don't know what I expected from him, but when he closes the distance between us again and places his hands on either side of my head, I realize I'd never tire of the feel of his skin against mine. "Night, rebel."

My eyelids flutter shut as he leans in closer. I wait for the press of his lips against mine, but instead, he presses them to my forehead. A small sigh escapes my lips from the intimacy and tenderness of it.

"I'll see you in the morning." His lips move against my forehead. He presses one final kiss to my skin before backing away.

I fake a cough, bringing my balled-up fist to my mouth. "It feels like I have a cold coming on. Might not be able to make it in the morning."

He stops on the front doorstep, shaking his head. "You're not getting out of this. Good night, Emma."

My bottom lip juts out in a pout, but I don't argue with him. His furrowed eyebrows and the hard set of his jaw tell me everything I need to know—I won't be getting out of playing tennis tomorrow.

I stand in the doorway, watching him disappear around the side of the house. Disappointment washes through me at watching him go. I want more from him—much more. I don't know if that should terrify me or thrill me, but right now, it's thrilling. Something about being on the same page about wanting each other but knowing it could never go further makes everything seem even more exciting.

It takes me a few minutes to leave the doorway and shut the door. It's only when I get to my room and pull out my phone to record an update for my followers that I realize the smile still plastered on my lips.

I press record immediately, wanting to capture the moment as best I can.

"So, I'm back from the party," I begin, focusing on my face on the screen. My cheeks are flushed, and there are only slight remnants of the lip liner I applied hours ago. I think through all the different things I could say about the day I had, but some details I want to keep close to my chest for now. "And it turns out garden parties are a blast. I need to find a way to attend them more often."

For the next couple of minutes, I recount the day, leaving out the juiciest details. To keep Preston's name private, I nicknamed him "Sports Guy" and left out the names of his family. Capturing my journey this summer isn't to try and bring any more attention to the Rhodes family. It's a way for me to connect with thousands of people around the world who may be in the same position as I am.

After recounting my afternoon and night, I stare at the version of myself looking back at the phone screen. I'm quiet, even though my phone is still recording. I sigh, realizing that for the first time in a long time, I hadn't spent the day worrying about where I was in life. I didn't look at every person I spoke to and wonder why they'd figured their life out and I hadn't.

I enjoyed myself. And it's a freeing realization.

I blink a few times, pulling the phone closer to me so my face takes up the entire screen. "I think this summer is going to work, you guys. It's only been a day, and I might be dramatic because I'm always dramatic, but I already feel better." I smile, then point to the camera. "And I'm still blown away by the number of you wanting to follow along on this journey of self-discovery. I love you. I'll report back tomorrow on how playing tennis goes. I'll call it a win if no one gets injured!"

I blow the camera a kiss and end the video. As I edit the clips into a more condensed video to post, I wonder what Preston is doing right now. Is he thinking about me? Do I want him to be thinking about me?

Placing my phone on the nightstand, I begin my nightly routine. I don't feel very tired. In fact, I feel wide-awake, my body becoming hot the more I think about the day with Preston.

It was perfect. And the way he kissed me? It's all I can think about as I step into the shower.

So many people wanted his attention today. He was pulled in one direction, then the next, but he continually made sure I was okay. He checked on me, kept his hand on my lower back even as he had conversations with others, and was constantly introducing me to the people he spoke with and made sure I felt included.

All of the articles I read on him before the party dubbed him as a bit of a partier. He'd spent the off-seasons in his twenties going from one party to the next. He was often seen with different pop stars, actresses, and even different socialites. There were rumors he even dated a princess, but there were only ever grainy photos that didn't prove anything.

It seemed as he got further on in his career and turned thirty, he cleaned up his act. Or at least stayed out of the public eye. A company he invested in became a Fortune 500 company, and between his profits from that and the countless brand deals he took and the record-breaking contract he signed four years ago, he was named a billionaire by Forbes before he ever turned thirty-five.

My mind races with all the little details I've learned about him. You can look at him and know that he's athletic, but I'd never think that he played in the NFL. Just like when I first saw him, he still screams "finance guy" and not "sports guy," but the fact he seems to be doing so much with his life is even more intriguing to me.

I want to ask him more questions about his life and his plans, which is new for me because typically no one holds my interest long enough to want to know more.

I wash the soap off my body and turn the water off. Even though I've washed the remnants of his touch from my skin, the memory of his fingertips digging into it remains. If I close my eyes, I'm brought back to feeling his lips on mine.

As I dry myself off and get ready for bed, I can't wipe him from my memory. I feel hot all over, like a rubber band coiled tight. My gaze slips to my suitcase. Maybe there's a way I can get him from my mind. I do need a good night of sleep if I have to play tennis tomorrow. Maybe I could get rid of some of the tension in my body if I gave myself an orgasm.

I chew on my lip for a moment before deciding a helping hand from one of my toys is exactly what I need. Opening up my suitcase, I take out the black velvet bag I'd stuffed my vibrators in. "Fred or Jerry today?"

21
Preston

I TOLD MYSELF I WAS GOING TO LEAVE HER PURSE ON THE DOORSTEP and leave. I already spent all day and evening with her; I don't need to take any more of her time. I really did have pure intentions until I saw the door to the house slightly ajar.

"Emma," I hiss under my breath, ready to lecture her on leaving the house not only unlocked but with the door hanging open. Bringing my knuckles to the door, I knock and wait for her to answer.

My mind swirls with the different lectures I could give her. I know she mentioned thinking it was safe here, but I'd rather her not take her chances. Her carefree attitude about the world is one of my favorite things about her, but not like this. Not when her safety is in question.

A low growl comes from deep in my chest when she doesn't come to the door. I run a hand over my mouth, trying to think through what I should do. I don't know the code to lock the door from the outside, and I probably should make sure everything is okay in there since she didn't answer.

Deciding to check on her, I push the door open and step in. It's eerily quiet. My heartbeat picks up as I begin to walk the house, trying to figure out where she is. There's no sound coming from the kitchen or the living room, so with her purse in hand, I begin to walk down the hallway that leads to the bedrooms.

All the doors down the hallway are open except for one. Since I haven't found her in any other rooms, I'm left guessing the room with the closed door must be hers.

I stand in front of the door, wondering what I should do. If she's sleeping, I don't want to bother her. Although it wasn't too long ago that I'd dropped her off on the doorstep and felt the intoxicating press of her lips against mine. I don't think she'd be asleep yet, but I can't be positive. It's possible she could be in the shower, but I don't hear the sound of running water at all.

Before I can think about my next move, a small moan comes from the other side of the door. Worry courses through my veins as I push the door open to make sure she's okay.

Everything happens in slow motion.

Emma screams. She throws her arms into the air and pulls the covers over her face.

A loud thud rings through the room as I freeze in the doorway. I blink, trying to figure out what I just walked in on.

"What are you doing here?" Emma asks nervously from underneath the blanket.

"Ummm..." I begin, wondering what's making a deep buzzing sound from the other side of the bed.

"Get out!" Emma shrieks, still not showing her face.

"You left your purse in my car," I explain, taking a cautious step into the room.

"Don't come any closer," she demands, her face popping out from the top of the blanket.

I look around the room for a minute, finding her clothes strewn about everywhere.

"What is that noise?" I ask, walking toward the buzzing sound that hasn't let up.

"Stop!" Emma yells, clutching the blankets to her stomach as she sits up. She's wearing an oversized T-shirt with the neck cut out. It slips down her shoulder, showing me a dangerous amount of her skin.

Her plea for me to stop works. I stop at the foot of the bed, unable to see what is making that noise. She stares at me with her eyes wide and her cheeks flushed. Wet hair sticks to her face as she keeps her body pressed into the mattress.

I hold up her purse. "Like I said, you left this in the car. I was going to drop it off on the doorstep and leave, but then I noticed the front door was not only unlocked, but it was hanging open. I wanted to make sure you were okay…"

"You *would* decide right now to be chivalrous," she mutters, her words coming out hurried.

"So you're okay?" I scratch the back of my neck, keeping my eyes on her. "I heard noises and got worried…" My words falter because I don't know what else to say. With her staring at me with an unreadable look on her face, I can't figure out if she's upset that I broke in. Maybe she should be. Maybe this was a mistake.

"I'm fine. Can you go now?"

"Let me just make sure the AC is running okay in here. That buzzing sound doesn't sound right, and I want to make sure you don't get too hot ton—"

"It's Jerry!" Emma yells, her palms hitting the top of the comforter. "You hear Jerry. Nothing is wrong with the AC."

Unwelcome jealousy courses through me. "Jerry?" I get out angrily, taking large steps to where the sound comes from. Is there a man somehow hiding in here?

"Wait, no!" Emma screams, her body scrambling along the top of the bed as my eyes land on the source of the sound.

I'm faster than her. My fingers wrap around the base of a hot pink vibrator.

"Don't touch Jerry!" Emma shouts. She tries to grab it from my hands, but I pull it from her reach.

Her face gets even more flushed, and I know I should leave

her alone. She clearly never expected me to walk in, but my feet stay planted. I can't move. "Are you calling your vibrator Jerry?"

She pushes her wet hair from her face, sitting back on her legs before she answers. I don't hear whatever answer she gives me because I let my gaze slip from her face to discover she's naked from the waist down.

Emma yelps, pulling the T-shirt down over her thighs to block my view. But it doesn't matter. I saw the glisten between her thighs from her arousal. The pretty pink of her pussy. How it seemed to still be begging for a release even after I walked in.

I swallow, blood thrumming through my ears as I come to the realization I can't leave this room, not unless she asks me to.

The vibrator pulses in my hand, stealing my attention. I'm just now noticing the wetness across the tip of it from where it'd been inside her moments ago.

Fucking hell.

"Preston." My name comes out cautious. It catches at the end, and I don't know if the way my name leaves her mouth is a good or bad thing.

"What were you doing in here?" I ask, my voice hoarse with lust. In a few simple moments, she's turned me on more than I've ever been, and I haven't even touched her. The sight of the wetness between her legs, paired with the mental picture of her using the vibrator to get herself off, has me going mad.

"You know the answer to that," she whispers, shifting her weight on the bed. "You weren't supposed to come in." She looks down, her fingers anxiously pulling on the fabric of her shirt.

"Now isn't the time to get shy on me, rebel." My fingers tighten around the vibrator as it takes everything in me to stay where I am instead of taking a step closer to her. If it were up to me, I'd already have her thighs spread open as I show her that her mouth isn't the only thing I can kiss well.

"Sorry, I haven't ever had someone catch me using a vibrator, so this is kind of new territory for me," she remarks, finally getting the nerve to meet my eyes.

I smile. There's the Emma I know.

"Good," I answer. "I don't want to think about anyone but me seeing you with your thighs spread wide so beautifully." I swallow, taking a step toward her. Will she let me touch her? Should I allow myself to touch her? "Fuck, picturing that might be the most exquisite sight I've ever imagined."

Emma's eyelids flutter shut with a moan. The sound of her arousal has me closing the distance between us until my shins are pressed against the mattress.

I lift the vibrator to my lips, peeking my tongue out to lick the tip of it. I groan at the taste of her as my eyes stay locked on hers. I need more. Flattening my tongue, I run it along the vibrator in a slow, long lick, reveling in the way it tastes of *her*.

"What are you doing?" she whispers, her eyes hooded as she watches me closely. I lift my arm, holding the still-pulsating vibrator in front of my face.

"Did you come yet?"

"No." The word is said under her breath, so low that I almost miss it.

"Do you still want to?" I press, imagining what it sounds like when she comes. Is she loud when the orgasm takes over? Do her moans echo off the walls? Or will the orgasm be so intense that her moans get stuck in her chest? Fuck, I'm desperate to know.

"Preston." She rocks back and forth on her knees, rubbing her thighs against one another.

"Answer the question. Do you want to come, rebel?"

She pulls her bottom lip between her teeth. Her fingers have gone white with how tightly she grips the hem of her T-shirt. She nods, keeping her wide blue eyes trained on me.

My eyes flick to the vibrator in my hand and back to her. "Can *I* make you come?" Slowly, I place one knee on the mattress, then the other, until my weight is fully supported. I still don't touch her, waiting for her to answer me.

"How?" Her voice breaks at the end. The unmistakable sound of pure want in her voice has my cock throbbing. I fight the urge to stroke myself to relieve even the smallest amount of pressure. No matter how badly I want to, I don't. Right now, this is all about her.

"Lie back," I instruct, ignoring her question.

She watches me carefully, not budging an inch.

"Was my direction unclear?" I growl.

"Should we be doing this?"

"I won't even touch you. I'll just use the toy. It'll just be like I'm not even here."

She still doesn't lie back, but her body does seem to relax slightly. "Oh, I know you're here. It'd be impossible to forget that."

I smile, relishing in her words. "Lie back," I repeat, aching to see all of her. I want to make her feel good like I want my next breath. I'm desperate for it, but I need her to take the lead—at least at first—to make sure she's okay with what's happening.

She moans—or maybe it's more like a groan—but she does pull one knee out from underneath her. "I'm going to be so embarrassed about this the moment you leave."

"Don't you dare get embarrassed. I'm so fucking turned on by the thought of you touching yourself minutes after I dropped you off. Tell me, was our kiss so good you had to touch yourself to thoughts of me just to relieve some of the tension?"

Her head falls backward. "Preston." My name comes out more like a moan, forcing me to fight the urge to toss the vibrator to the side and use my tongue instead.

"Are you going to be a good girlfriend and follow directions?"

She bites her lip and nods. Time seems to slow down as she pulls her other leg out from underneath her and leans back. She props herself up by the elbows, letting her shoulders rest against the plush pillows behind her.

My tongue peeks out to lick my lips as I take a moment to look at her. She's so fucking sexy, and I love that she knows it. She uses it to her advantage, and it's making me fucking weak for her.

"Spread your thighs," I demand.

"You do it."

She yelps when I place the tip of the vibrator against her thigh. "Preston!" she yells, her thighs inching open slightly.

"What?" I ask innocently, crawling up the bed until my free hand rests on the pillow next to her head.

"I shouldn't be so turned on right now," she mutters, lifting her hips slightly.

"It's about to get even better." I guide the vibrator to her inner thigh, relishing in the small noises she makes. "Now, open your thighs."

Emma surprisingly does as she's told—kind of. She parts her thighs just enough for me to see her but not enough for me to slip the vibrator between them.

"More," I demand, inching my face closer to hers.

She smiles and reaches up to place her hand on the back of my neck. She applies pressure, pulling me closer to her until our lips almost brush against each other. "Do it yourself."

22
Emma

I CAN'T BELIEVE I'M LETTING PRESTON DO THIS. I CAN'T BELIEVE I want him to. The vibrator pulses against my inner thigh, both teasing and torturing me. All I want is for Preston to spread my thighs and place the vibrator against my clit to give me relief, but he doesn't listen.

He's teasing and having fun with it, and I'm doing every-thing I can to hold on to some of the control.

"Do you think you make the rules between us, rebel?" Preston finally asks after being quiet for a few moments.

My hips buck when he guides the vibrator a little higher up my thigh, getting close to exactly where I want him. I moan, my fingernails scraping at the back of his neck. At least if he'd kiss me, it would help with the pressure that's built between my thighs.

Later, I might be embarrassed that he caught me pleasuring myself, but all I can think about right now is how badly I want him to finish the job.

"Answer me," he demands, peppering kisses along my jaw.

"At least for right now, it seems like I'm the one making the rules." I lift my chin, allowing him more access to my neck. Stubble scratches my tender skin as his lips travel the hollow of my throat.

Preston laughs, his teeth raking against the base of my neck.

"Maybe you are. Now, you can either open your legs for me or get this T-shirt off so I can see all of you."

The vibrator in his hand travels even closer to where I'm begging for him to go. It's so close but also so far. I don't know if I hate him for teasing me this much or if it turns me on even more to draw it out like this.

"Guess I'll pick for you, then," Preston announces. Catching me by surprise, he circles my clit once with the vibrator. A whimper falls from my lips at how good it feels.

"Shirt off. Now." He grabs the bottom of my T-shirt and begins to lift it.

"So I'm going to be completely naked while you're clothed? That doesn't seem fair," I argue. My words contradict my actions as I lift my shoulders from the pillows to help him get the shirt off more easily. Only using one hand doesn't slow him at all, and it doesn't take long for the sleep shirt to be discarded on the side of the bed and for cold air to be caressing my nipples.

The only sound in the room is the sound of the buzzing vibrator against the comforter. He stays quiet for so long I wonder if he even heard my question at all. I watch him carefully, trying to read his reaction.

His eyes travel along my body. He looks at me so hungrily with darkened eyes, not ever giving me the time to feel bashful of him seeing every inch of me. I can't feel shy with him looking at me with so much possession and desperation.

No. Now, all I want is for him to touch me. For him to do something whether it be with the vibrator, his mouth, his hands, anything.

"You're fucking magnificent," he rasps.

"Can't say the same about you since you won't take anything off," I quip, trying to cut through the tension in the room. It doesn't help. The heat in his eyes, the hard set of his jaw, and the way he looks up and down my body like he can't get enough lead me all to one conclusion—I have to fuck Preston Rhodes. Because no one has ever looked at me the way he's looking at me right now, and I don't think I can ever get enough of it.

"I love it when you talk back to me." He runs his hand over his mouth, his focus on my lips. Reaching down, he traces my bottom lip with his thumb. "Maybe one day, I'll get to fuck that sass right out of your mouth."

My eyelids flutter shut. His words are filthy, and I'm savoring every one of them. They turn me on, only intensifying the pure lust running through my bloodstream.

"Good luck," I respond, arching my hips slightly. I don't spread my thighs all the way open like he wants me to, but I do want to tease him like he's done to me. He licks his lips, and it's such a simple move but it's so incredibly sexy I want to watch him do it again. "Looking forward to you trying, though," I add.

My entire body is on fire, every inch of me begging for some sort of attention to get some relief. I run a hand along my rib cage until I'm able to palm my own breast. My fingers dance along the tender and aching skin until I pinch my nipple, giving my body just the smallest amount of reprieve.

Preston clicks his tongue. "If I wasn't so fucking eager to watch you come, I might punish you by depriving you of an orgasm."

"Good thing you're eager, then."

A low rumble of a laugh comes from deep in his chest as he picks up the vibrator. It looks small compared to his large hand.

"Tell me what you were thinking about as you fucked yourself with this." His voice is gruff and intense. I wait for him to press the tip of the vibrator to my clit, but instead, he catches me off guard and runs it over my hip.

"No," I answer, pushing my thighs open a few more inches.

He notices the movement immediately by the way he sucks in a breath as a reaction. "Goddamn," he mutters under his breath.

"I need more," I plead, my entire body lighting up because of the way he moves up to circle my nipples with the head of the vibrator.

"I'll give you more, rebel. I promise. But first, answer my question. Were you thinking about me while you touched yourself?"

I shake my head, fighting the urge to reach between my legs and touch myself if he won't.

"Not only a rebel but a liar, too." Preston shifts on the bed, placing his thigh between mine. His warm hand hits my inner thigh as he pushes my legs wide open. There's no hiding from him now—not that I want to.

"You said you weren't going to touch me," I tease, stifling a moan as he trails the vibrator down my abdomen.

"If you can lie, then I can, too." He proves his point by digging his fingertips into my skin, letting his pointer finger drag dangerously close to where I need the relief.

He keeps his hand against my thigh while his other finally guides the vibrator to my clit. This time, he doesn't tease me by only circling it once. He circles it again and again, finally giving me exactly what I want—except it still doesn't feel like enough.

"More," I plead. My fingers grip the comforter as he inches just the tip of the toy into me.

"So greedy. Am I not doing enough for you, rebel? Does it not feel good?"

The moan that falls from my lips is loud and unapologetic. I'm so thankful no one is in this house but the two of us because I've never felt so many delicious sensations at once—and it feels like he's barely even begun.

"It feels good, so good that I need more."

He inches the vibrator in a little further. His knuckle brushes against me in the process, making me moan all over again. "Like this?" he asks, sliding it in and out.

All I can do is nod. I want to keep my eyes open so I can watch the intense way he focuses on every single one of my reactions, but everything is too much, and my eyelids flutter shut.

"This is so fucking sexy." I love the deep raspiness to his voice. I never would've guessed he'd be so vocal when being intimate. He's been so quiet in our time together, letting me do most of the talking. But right now, as he has me completely naked with my thighs spread wide for him, he's driving me wild with every dirty thing he says.

"You going to come for me, rebel?" he continues, his fingertips digging into my skin so deep it's almost painful. I wonder if him keeping them pressed there is the only thing keeping him restrained.

"I'm close," I whisper, unable to form many words beyond those.

"Last night, I went back to the room I was staying in and had to take a cold shower so I could rid my brain of dirty, filthy visions of you."

My eyes pop open with his admission. "You did?" My words come out short because of the building orgasm.

"Of course, I did." He licks his lips again. "How could I not? Look at you."

Goose bumps pop up all over my skin. I'm so close to being sent over the edge.

As if he can read me like an open book, his hand finds the back of my neck as he pulls our lips together. I hadn't realized how desperate I was to feel his lips against mine until he kisses me again. His tongue works against mine as he continues to push the vibrator in and out of me.

"Preston." He swallows my moans, not letting up in the way he kisses me or the way he fucks me with the toy.

My back arches off the bed as his fingers tangle in my hair. The orgasm ricochets through my entire body. It's so intense that my head falls backward as the waves crash over me. Preston uses my inability to do anything but focus on the orgasm to kiss along my throat. He nips and sucks at the tender skin of my neck. It's like he wants to make sure I feel him everywhere as I ride out the waves of pleasure.

He moves the vibrator in and out of me, making sure I enjoy every last second of my orgasm. When my body goes lax, he slowly pulls it out, clicking the top to turn it off.

"I'm going to have to watch you come again, but with my cock buried deep inside you."

I moan, seconds after finding release and already turned on by the mental picture. "Don't make promises you don't intend to keep," I manage to get out despite my voice being breathless.

He laughs, throwing the vibrator to the side. Taking me by surprise, he shifts until his body is pressed on top of mine. His hands are on either side of my face, supporting his weight so it isn't all on top of me. "Oh, Emma, I intend on fucking you, fast and hard and then passionate and slow just so I can discover how you like to be fucked best."

I smile, my teeth digging into my bottom lip. My fingers play with the button of his shirt as I try to come up with a response that isn't me begging him to do that right here and right now. "Maybe we'll get each other out of our systems."

He shakes his head while clicking his tongue. "Not a chance, but we can try over and over again. I'll only end up proving you wrong in the end, though. You'll never get me out of your system, and I'll never get you out of mine."

I lower my head. "Am I dreaming? You can't actually be saying these things in real life."

He places his palms on my cheeks. "You're awake, rebel. This is real."

"Well, if that's true, then I feel like it's time either I put on clothes or you take off some. I'm feeling underdressed."

He smirks, and I remind myself how it's my mission to get this man to smile more. He's incredibly handsome—and sexy—when he does it.

His hands move from my face down my back and cup my ass. "No such thing as you being underdressed. I should let you sleep, though."

I groan, rolling out from underneath him and pulling up my

comforter to cover myself. "I think you barging in on me using a vibrator should get me a free pass out of playing tennis tomorrow."

Preston sits up. "You're not getting out of tennis. Plus, I bet you'll sleep great after that orgasm."

I push my bottom lip out in a pout. "So I'm being forced to still play tennis tomorrow, and you're being a gentleman and not fucking me tonight?"

He leans in and kisses my cheek. "Exactly. But don't worry. You'll be a tennis star by the time I'm done with you tomorrow."

"And what about the other thing?"

"Be a good girlfriend tomorrow, and I'll reward you with my cock tomorrow night."

"Preston Rhodes, you have a filthy mouth. It's always the quiet ones."

He tips my chin up, placing a kiss to my lips. "I've barely even started. Good night, rebel. I'll see you in the morning—with coffee and food."

He slides off the bed, and I miss his heat. I remind myself we only just met. It'd be weird to tell him he could just sleep here instead, but I don't miss the fact that's exactly what I want him to do. Since I only have a few limited number of nights with him, I want to make them count. Instead of asking him to stay, I smile and push the thoughts from my mind. "How'd I get to be such a lucky girlfriend?"

He rolls his eyes while standing in front of my door. "Get some rest. I mean it." He turns around and pushes the door open.

I mock salute. "Yes, sir."

Turning back around, he focuses on me, another smirk on his face. "There will be more of that."

Before I can ask him what he means by that—my cheeks heating with what I think he means with the comment—he's out the door and out of sight.

I'm still sitting in bed with a flush to my entire body and a smile on my face when my phone vibrates a few minutes later. I check, expecting it to be Margo or Winnie texting me. It isn't.

PRESTON

Lock the door.

Sweet dreams of me, rebel.

EMMA

Sweet dreams of me, Rhodes. <3

PRESTON

Not sure I'd call my dreams of you sweet. ;)

Now lock the damn door.

23
Preston

EMMA HASN'T DRIFTED FROM MY MIND SINCE THE MOMENT I LEFT her in her room last night. I'd wanted to stay, but I figured it'd be weird if I told her that. Plus, I'd already barged in on her. I didn't really see any option but to let her have her space, and for me to return back to the guesthouse.

But even though I wasn't with her, she never left my mind.

Not when I had to take yet another cold shower to the memories of the way she moaned my name. Not when I crawled into bed and realized how empty it felt and how quiet the house seemed. Not even when I fell asleep.

I dreamed of her, something that is completely unlike me. Typically, when I dream, it's football related. It's hard for me to get my thoughts to turn off, so instead of resting, I'll come up with new plays, pick apart our opponent's defense, or even think of ways to keep the guys hyped during the season.

Not last night. Even in my dreams, Emma took up all the space.

"Hey, Preston. You still listening?" Ethan's voice pulls me from my thoughts. I'm sitting in the parking lot of Waterfront Cafe, waiting for breakfast and coffee, but it'll still be another ten minutes until my order is done, so I finally answered one of the many calls I'd received from him.

I look at my phone, shaking my head to try and wipe my

mind of thoughts of Emma. "Yes. I'm here," I tell my best friend from college who started out as the roommate who annoyed me.

I wanted to focus on football, and he always wanted to talk about all the business ideas he had floating around in his head. Eventually, he wore me down. I liked the guy, and he had amazing ideas.

When he developed an app that I actually thought was a solid idea, I invested in it so he could bring his ideas to fruition. Then, I became a shareholder and sat on the board. Eventually, we were acquired by one of the leading tech companies, but we were still granted seats on the board and shares that lined my pockets well enough.

"What do you think of the idea?" Ethan pushes.

I've lost track of the number of ideas he's pitched to me over the years. Some of them have been great, while others haven't, but I still listen anyway because he's a genius, and despite me being in a hurry to see Emma this morning, I want to hear whatever idea he's come up with next.

"Tell me again."

"So, you weren't listening?" Ethan laughs. He's always one of the first people to give me shit.

"My head's all over the place with P's wedding and with Ryan breathing down my neck about signing another contract."

He's quiet on the other line for a moment before he sighs. "Have you made a decision yet on what you want to do?"

I shake my head, forgetting he can't see me. "I don't think I want to do it, man," I tell him. The great thing about Ethan is that I can be real with him. Even in college, he didn't give a damn that I was the star quarterback with rich parents and a million connections. If anything, I think the fact I was a student athlete and that I had a trust fund turned him away from me. He was there on a scholarship and gave me long lectures about getting distracted and not devoting myself to my studies. Who I was didn't faze him in the slightest.

Maybe that's why I like Emma so much. She has the same

attitude toward who I am—she doesn't give a shit, and it's refreshing.

"Then don't sign for another year," Ethan offers. "Football doesn't have to be your entire world. You've worked your ass off for years, devoted yourself to the game, but it's okay if that isn't what you want to do anymore, Preston. It's okay to move on."

I scratch my neck, trying to soak in his words. Deep down, I know my answer. I've fallen out of love with football. I'm getting old, and I want to do something else with my life. I want to do more, but it's hard to ignore all the people I'll let down when I retire. And that's the biggest problem with all of this. I know I'll let people down. I know I'll disappoint teammates, coaches, fans, people I respect who want to see me play until I physically can't do it anymore.

But that isn't what *I* want. I want to go out on top. When my body isn't completely falling apart and when I still have enough years left to live my life outside of football.

"Yeah." I clear my throat, hating the way it feels clogged when thinking about what happens when I don't sign another deal. "Anyway, tell me your next great idea."

"Do I *really* have to play tennis?" Emma asks, standing in the front door with her arms folded across her chest.

I ignore her question, holding on to the paper bag filled with breakfast tacos with a death grip when I look at the outfit she has on.

"You're not playing tennis if you're wearing that." My words come out a little more harsh than I want them to, but holy fuck. I'll have to spend the entire day keeping all of Jackson's annoying friends away from her when she looks so incredible.

Emma narrows her eyes at me. She pops her hip and puts her hand on it. "How about a *good morning, Emma. How did you sleep, Emma?*"

"Good morning, Emma," I say, my voice tight. "You can't wear that to play tennis, Emma. Can you go and change, Emma?" Every time I say her name, it comes out a little more struggled because I can't focus on anything other than her in her tiny tennis skirt.

Emma shrugs, opening the door wide to let me in. I really hadn't expected her to be ready. It's barely after nine, but I wanted to make sure I swung by early and brought her food in case I had to pry her from her bed. "Are you telling me you don't like what I'm wearing? Cute outfits are the only reason to play tennis."

I follow her through the door and into the kitchen. Her hips sway in a taunting rhythm as she walks to the kitchen counter. Her blonde hair is pulled into a ponytail, the curled strands brushing the back of her neck with every step she takes.

"The outfit is great, but how am I supposed to focus on teaching you tennis when I know what you're hiding underneath that skirt?" I set the food on the counter and lean a hip against it. She stares at me from a few feet away, her lips pursed as if she doesn't like my response.

"It's not my responsibility to make sure you—or anyone else —can focus because of what I'm wearing. You have to wear a tennis skirt to play tennis—it's like a golden rule. Plus, I already got the green light from my best friends that the outfit looks good. Your opinion doesn't matter." She winks at me, and it's the cutest thing ever.

"You have a point there. But I don't want to hear any grumpy comments from you when I undoubtedly want to snarl like a goddamn caveman at any man that looks at you for too long."

She laughs, reaching for the bag of food on the counter. "Oh, I'm definitely going to comment on you being grumpy. What'd you bring me?"

I was worried things would be weird between us this morning. After all, I caught her getting herself off last night and refused to leave until I could watch her come. But I should've known it wouldn't be like that with Emma. She's acting like last night never happened. "I brought you breakfast and coffee."

She smiles before greedily opening the bag like she's been starved. "Preston Rhodes, are you bribing me to play tennis?"

I slide into one of the barstools at the counter, resting my chin against my knuckles. "No, the orgasm last night was the bribe."

A choking sound comes from her throat. She tries to play it off, but it doesn't work. She's sent into a fit of coughing. I watch with an eyebrow raised as she fills an empty glass from the counter with water and gulps it down.

"You good?" I ask, a taunting tone to my voice.

"Yeah," she sputters. "I just wasn't expecting you to bring up last night. I didn't know if you were the type who wanted to play it off like it didn't happen."

My head cocks to the side as I watch her closely. "Why would I ever want to forget the way you moaned my name? Or the way you greedily begged for more even as I had the vibrator buried inside your perfect pussy?"

Emma looks to the counter, busying herself with unwrapping one of the breakfast tacos. "Preston, you can't say the word 'pussy' this early in the morning."

"I can talk about *your* pussy as much as I want."

Emma shakes her head, her eyes meeting mine. It's the first time I've ever seen her bashful. Her cheeks flush as her lips pull up at the corners with a faint smile. "You keep surprising me."

"You seem like the type of woman who loves surprises."

Her smile goes wide. "I guess I am."

The two of us don't look away from one another. We're locked in a moment. One that seems to hold a lot of weight, but I have no idea why. I just know that my heart rate has sped up just because of the way she looks at me.

I'm the first one to break, having to look away because I'm feeling things I've never felt when I shouldn't be. We barely know each other, yet what I'm feeling for her is stronger than it should be. This thing between us is only for the rest of the week.

She's made it clear she wants nothing to come from our week together, and even if I wanted to—which I'm not sure I do—I'm not in the right season of life to begin a relationship.

But fuck, if I ever was, I think it'd be with someone like Emma. Someone who looks at me like I'm not Preston Rhodes, but *just* Preston. Someone who will call me on my shit and bring me out of my shell. She's perfect, and I want to enjoy every moment I can with her while I have the time.

I clear my throat and straighten my spine. "Eat. You need to fuel your body."

"Ugh. Tennis." Despite her clear displeasure with the agenda for the morning, she does follow directions and takes a bite of the best breakfast taco in town.

Her eyelids flutter closed as she lets out a low moan. She doesn't even finish chewing before she talks. "Oh my god. This is the best thing I've ever put in my mouth."

I smirk. "That'll change tonight."

Emma's eyes pop open, her blue eyes focusing on me instantly. Her cheek juts out like a chipmunk as I've apparently stunned her so much with my comment that she can't even chew her food.

All I do is stare back at her with the cocky grin on my lips. I thought I'd be a gentleman this morning and not bring up last night, but the moment I saw her in that damn tennis skirt, I realized I didn't want to play fair anymore. I was a gentleman by leaving her alone last night, but today is a whole new day.

And I'm not feeling like a good guy. I'm feeling like the kind of man who is starved and depraved and can only get satiated by the woman staring back at me with cheeks flushed and wide eyes.

She finally begins to chew again before she swallows her food with an audible gulp. Frantically, she reaches across the counter and snatches the iced coffee from in front of me. She brings the straw to her lips and sucks almost half of the drink down easily.

"Easy there, rebel," I tease, tapping my fingers against the counter.

She sighs, placing the coffee back down loudly. "I'm going to need caffeine if this is how you're going to be this morning."

"How am I being?"

Emma rolls her eyes. "I don't know...incredibly forward."

"Do you want me to stop?"

She takes another bite of the taco, probably trying to buy herself more time to answer my question. That's fine—I'll sit here and wait until she finally does. I have all the time in the world. Not really, but I do have time to wait, at least for a little bit.

Reaching across the counter, I grab the paper bag and pull it toward me. Immediately, she throws her hand out, her palm hitting the top of the bag with a loud smacking sound.

"What do you think you're doing?" she asks suspiciously.

"Getting a taco? I'm hungry."

She shakes her head, trying to pull the bag out of my grip. "Get your own tacos."

I laugh. "I did. Right here in this bag."

"No. These are mine."

"I got six tacos."

She doesn't miss a beat with her response. "What if I want all six of them?"

I place my hands in the air in surrender. "Then by all means, they're all yours."

She gives me a satisfied smile before shoving the rest of her first taco into her mouth. I don't know why, but I find myself completely endeared by the way she just acted like she was going to bite my head off for even thinking about eating one of the tacos.

"You can have *one* taco—but that's it," Emma says as she begins to unwrap another one.

"One? How generous of you."

She shrugs, tossing her ponytail over her shoulder. "I know."

Instead of taking a taco out of the bag and eating it because I am hungry, I can't do anything but stare at her. Regret washes over me even when I realize I shouldn't be thinking about what will happen after this weekend, but I can't help it.

I know I'll never forget the woman standing in front of me eating a breakfast taco in three enormous bites. She's unlike anyone I've ever met before, and I already regret not having the chance to make her mine past the week I've been given with her.

24
Emma

MARGO

Remember to keep us updated about tennis!

WINNIE

Don't forget sunscreen :)

EMMA

If I embarrass myself in front of an athlete, make sure to bury me in a cute Chanel two-piece set. I won't be able to live after this.

MARGO

I still can't believe you're spending the week with Preston Rhodes. Are you sure I can't tell Beck?

EMMA

I'm pulling the best friend card. No telling husbands until next week when he's no longer here for his sister's wedding.

MARGO

Making an extremely pregnant woman keep a secret from her baby daddy when said baby daddy is barely letting her out of the house is cruel. I need to gossip and both of you are busy.

WINNIE

I love that Beck listens to your gossip.

EMMA

We've all met Archer, Win. We know that man loves when you bring home the tea to spill.

MARGO

Kick some ass at tennis today, Em! Even if you suck, you'll look hot as fuck doing it.

I SMILE, MY FINGERS HOVERING OVER THE KEYBOARD AS I THINK about a witty response. I want to tell her I'm terrified of making a fool out of myself in front of everyone today, but I want to opt out of coming clean on that and pretend to be confident instead.

Preston tries to look over my shoulder at my phone as I step out of the car in front of the tennis courts at Pembroke Hills Country Club. "Who are you talking to?" he asks, trying to peer down at my phone.

I gasp, pulling it to my chest. "That's none of your business."

His body cages me in, pinning me between his sports car and his body. His cologne surrounds me, and I try not to think about the way my sheets smelled like him last night as I drifted asleep to thoughts of him. "I beg to differ," Preston responds, running a finger along my chest. He traces the bare skin right next to where I hold my phone, sending shivers through my entire body.

"No, it isn't."

"You're right. But I still want to know."

I sigh, hating that his answer is perfect. Everything he says is perfect and surprisingly charming—despite him having a sour attitude more often than not. "I'm texting Winnie and Margo."

This might be my head playing tricks on me, but I swear his shoulders loosen a little with my answer. "About what?"

"Admittedly, I did tell them about you. But don't worry, I just said you invited me to be your date for the weekend and that things are very casual. I've sworn them to secrecy from sharing anything with their husbands."

"Fine by me." His answer takes me by surprise. I was ready for him to be upset that I told my friends about us without running through a story with him first. I know he probably works hard at keeping his private life private and that our little charade for the week is probably messing that up, but I can't help but focus on his surprising reaction.

"Really?" I ask, not hiding the shock in my tone.

"It was possible they could be at the wedding this weekend anyway, right?"

I nod. I'm sure they were invited because my friends get invited to everything. But even before getting confirmation that neither of them will be here this weekend, I didn't expect them to be in the Hamptons this weekend for Peyton's wedding.

"Then, of course, I don't care that you told them. I'm the one who called you my girlfriend without ever getting your permission, remember?"

I place my hands against his chest. His muscles are hard underneath my palms, even with the thin fabric between us. I wish he'd play tennis shirtless so I could get a good look at everything he hides underneath his fancy clothes. He saw all of me last night, so it's only fair I see more of him.

"I thought I was going to be put away for murdering you after that."

He leans in close and brushes his thumb along my cheek. "I'm glad you didn't. It hasn't worked out terribly for you, right?"

I lean into his touch, loving the way the calluses on his fingertips feel against my sensitive skin. "That depends on if I make a fool of myself playing tennis this morning."

He presses his lips against mine without any warning, as if he's trying to ease my nerves by kissing them away.

It might work. The man is an excellent kisser. His tongue meets mine eagerly, tracing the seam of my mouth and moving at a speed that has my toes curling in my tennis shoes. I fist the fabric of his shirt and bring him closer to me, needing more from him. I want all of him, but that might be a little R-rated for the country club parking lot.

I know it's possible that anyone could be watching us right now, but I don't care. I place my hands on his shoulders and stand on my tiptoes. Preston understands what I want immediately. His hands run up the backs of my thighs and against my ass until he's lifting me off my feet. My thighs wrap around his middle instantly.

We make out like a bunch of horny teenagers, and it's the best kiss of my life. I swear each time we kiss, it gets better, and I'm slowly beginning to get addicted to the way Preston kisses me. It's possessive and confident. I moan when he squeezes my ass and lets out his own groan of arousal.

"Maybe we skip the tennis," I offer, only pulling my lips away from his long enough to get the words out before I'm going in for more.

He chuckles, the sound vibrating against my core because of the position we're in. "Nice try, rebel. You're not getting out of it. But this does make me even more excited about later."

Much to my dismay, he stops kissing me, but he doesn't put me down. He keeps me in his arms, holding me tight against his middle as his eyes roam my face.

"What's happening later?"

"I'm going to fuck you and show you that my tongue and cock are much better than the fantasy you were having of me last night."

"How do you know I was thinking of you?"

"Because I'll kill someone if you were thinking of anyone but me."

My mouth falls open at his words.

"Murder is taking it a little too far," I tease, keeping my arms wrapped around his neck even when he places me on my feet again.

"Then you better admit it was me you were thinking about, rebel."

I roll my eyes and playfully swat at his stomach. "Of course, I was thinking about you. After the way you kissed me, I wouldn't have been able to think of someone else, even if I wanted to."

This makes him smile. He playfully nips at my neck. "Good," he says, his lips pressed to the hollow of my throat.

"Get a room, lovebirds!" I'd recognize Peyton's cheerful voice anywhere. I duck underneath Preston's arm, finding Peyton and Jackson standing at the hood of Preston's rental with smiles on both of their faces.

"Why get a room when we have a perfectly good parking lot?" I respond, leaving Preston to grab my bag from the car so I can walk in with Peyton.

She makes a dramatic gagging sound as she grabs my hand. "That's my brother. Spare me the details."

Blood fills my cheeks as I think about the details I am keeping from her. Like what her brother did to me last night, and what I hope he does to me tonight. "You're the one who told us to get a room."

"Because I walked up to Pres sucking your neck like he was a damn vampire."

I look at her and wink. "Maybe he is."

Peyton rolls her eyes at me and pulls me closer to her. "I love you. We're going to be best friends...basically sisters."

A pit forms in my stomach at her words. I feel terrible for lying to her. I feel even worse because I like the idea of her staying in my life. If this wasn't fake between me and Preston, if there was a future between us, I know Peyton and I would be the best of friends.

But we won't have the chance.

"Did I make things weird?" Peyton asks, her forehead creasing with worry. She leads me toward the tennis courts, where a large group of people from the wedding party have already gathered. "Jackson keeps telling me that I need to not be such a clinger when it comes to you. I just can't help myself. Preston hasn't ever introduced me to a girlfriend, and the moment we met, it felt like things just clicked. But I don't want to come off weird."

"Not weird at all. Now, can we talk about how incredibly hot you look in this? Hot damn, Peyton. You're the sexiest bride I've ever seen." I yell the last part before putting my fingers in my mouth and whistling the way Aunt V taught me to.

Jackson cheers in agreement from a few feet behind us as he and Preston follow us in. "Hell yes, she is!" He attempts the same whistle, but nothing comes out, which makes Peyton and I double over in laughter.

"I can't believe I'm about to get married."

"I can't believe you convinced me to play tennis." We're getting closer to the group of people, and my nerves are starting to get the best of me. What if I accidentally serve the ball and hit someone in the face? What if I try to get the ball and fall in front of everyone? Jesus. This really isn't a good idea.

Peyton ignores the people greeting her for the morning and instead turns and places her body directly in front of me. "We're just going to have fun today. Don't worry about how you do. I just wanted to get all of the wedding party together for a light-hearted game of tennis. Sound good?"

"Totally," I lie.

She smiles and pulls me in for a hug. "Let's get this started!"

Peyton runs to greet some of her guests, and I'm left standing there wondering if this is a terrible idea. I close my eyes for a moment, praying to the tennis gods that I don't make an absolute fool of myself.

25
Preston

Emma didn't have anything to worry about with tennis. She's held her own with every doubles match we've won. We're in the very last game of the tournament, playing against Jackson and Peyton.

I hand Emma the ball, trying not to notice the way her skin gleams underneath the sun. "It's your serve."

She bites her lip, her eyes looking at a huddled Peyton and Jackson before looking back at me. "I'm nervous."

I scoff. "Don't be. If we lose, at least it's to the bride and groom."

I'm shocked we made it to the final round of the tournament. Not because of Emma swearing she was terrible at tennis, but because I found it hard to concentrate on anything but her. I'm competitive by nature. It's my job to be. But today, my focus has been mostly on Emma.

I couldn't look away during our first match when she realized she wasn't half-bad. The first time she clapped her hands in excitement while she bounced on her feet made my chest feel tight. When we won the first match and she did the most adorable happy dance that was completely out of rhythm, she stole my breath.

And when we won the semifinal match and she threw her

body against mine in celebration, I realized I'll think about this woman for the rest of my life.

"You ready?" Emma asks, grabbing my bicep.

I nod, realizing I'd spaced out in the middle of the court. "Let's get this win."

She gives me a warm smile before taking position. I rock from left to right on the balls of my feet, ready for her to serve. Jackson and Peyton won a set, and so have Emma and I. Whoever wins this next one wins the match, and I know it's a lot of pressure on Emma for it to be her turn to serve.

"You've got this, Emma!" Gram cheers from the sidelines. She's been emphatically cheering for both sides during this match. When Peyton once gave her a look of betrayal, she just shrugged and made a comment about how both of us were her grandchildren and that she wouldn't pick favorites.

Emma bounces the ball a couple of times before lifting it above her head and serving it. I follow it, shocked when it goes straight into the net.

"We won!" Peyton cheers, jumping up and down in excitement.

"Well, shit," Emma says from behind me, her voice not sounding nearly as disappointed as I thought it'd be. If I've learned anything about her during this tennis tournament, it's that she doesn't like to lose. She's extremely competitive, and her reaction to losing this match doesn't match up with how she's acted every other one. Especially since the reason we lost is because of her serve.

My head cocks to the side as I narrow my eyes on her. Peyton's cheers can still be heard behind me, but I don't pay attention to anything but Emma. She comes to a stop right in front of me.

Her hands fall to her sides as she shrugs. "Sorry for losing the game for us, Rhodes."

"You lost on purpose."

Her eyes go wide as she takes a step closer to me. She looks around, her eyes darting back and forth as if she's afraid someone heard me. No one can—they're all busy congratulating Peyton and Jackson on the win.

"I have no idea what you mean." She straightens her spine before throwing her ponytail over her shoulder. I see right through her trying to play it cool.

"You've consistently served the last three matches. You're telling me you just so happened to mess that last one up?"

"Yep."

I shake my head. "Liar."

I keep the rest of my thoughts to myself. If she doesn't want to admit she lost on purpose, she doesn't have to. But I still know. And admire her for it. I would've felt bad as well if we had won and taken the attention away from Peyton today. It made sense to give them the game. I'm just a little shocked Emma cared enough to have that same thought too.

One of Jackson's groomsmen comes running up to us. I'm about to tell him I'm busy when he runs right past me and goes straight for Emma.

"I know the loss is tough, but you played great. I'm impressed." I think his name is Derrick—or was it Patrick—either way, he can fuck right off from talking to my girlfriend.

Much to my dismay, Emma gives him a wide smile. One that I'd tricked myself into thinking she only gives me. "Thank you, Eric. That means a lot coming from a former tennis star."

My teeth grind against each other as I clench my hands at my sides.

He takes a step closer to her as he waves at the air dismissively. "It was just in college."

I fight the urge to make a nasty comment. Instead, all I do is stare daggers in Emma's direction, wondering why she's even giving this guy the time of day.

"That's still very impressive," Emma comments. She places her hand over her eyes to shield them from the sun. The smile on her face never slips, only fueling my jealousy. At least Davis, the bartender from yesterday, isn't here to comment on how I'm acting.

I'm contemplating how mad she'd be with me if I pulled her away and cut her conversation with Eric short. But I find myself not caring, so I clear my throat. "Emma." Her name comes out forced as I take a step closer to her.

She turns to look at me, the smile slipping slightly. "Yes?"

"Maybe we should go congratulate the winners?" I offer, holding my hand out for her to take.

"We probably should. Good talking to you, Eric."

I let out a breath of relief when she takes my hand and lets me lead her away from him.

Peyton and Jackson have a circle of people surrounding them, forcing us to wait on the outskirts of the group until someone moves. I use the opportunity to turn and place my body in front of Emma's, blocking her view of anyone else.

"Do I need to kiss you right now?"

Her pink lips part as her eyes dart to look around us. "No. Why?"

"So Derrick knows he can't have you."

She stares at me incredulously. "You're joking."

"I'm not known to be funny."

Emma shakes her head at me. "You're ridiculous. His name is Eric, not Derrick, and I was just trying to be friendly."

A flash of anger runs through me at the way she says his name. Why do I hate it coming from her mouth so much? "Friendly, huh?"

She nods. "Yes. Just being friendly with him. You have nothing to worry about, sugar muffin." The pet name is said sarcastically. She knows exactly how to ruffle my feathers. I have no doubt she knows how jealous that encounter made me and she's loving it.

Emma starts to walk to Peyton, but I grab her by the waist and pull her to me. Her back is flush to my chest as I lean down and talk right next to her ear. "Are you teasing me, rebel?"

The muscles of her stomach tighten when my hands find the curve of her hips. "Maybe a little," she admits, her voice breathless.

I'm well aware that there are tons of eyes on us at the moment, but I don't care. All I want to do is make sure Emma knows the only man here who can take care of her is me. "I don't like being jealous. I've always gotten everything I've ever wanted; the feeling isn't something I'm used to. I don't want to feel it again."

My fingertips slip slightly into the waistband of her tennis skirt. I want to keep moving them down until I'm met with her pussy, which I'm dying to get a taste of again, but we unfortunately have an audience. Luckily, everyone is focused on Peyton and Jackson to notice us off to the side.

"Then don't be jealous," Emma offers.

"Wish it was that easy, rebel. You look at another man, and I become jealous. It's a problem."

Emma turns to face me. The movement forces my hands from her waistband, making me frown. I already miss the feel of her skin against mine. "Well, that sounds like a *you* problem." She glides her finger across my chest before stepping back and winking. "Now, let's go congratulate the winners."

She shoulders through two of P's bridesmaids—including Marsha—and pulls Peyton in for a hug. "Congratulations," she says excitedly. "Not only are you the hottest bride but a hot tennis star too."

Peyton scoffs, squeezing Emma closer to her body. "I swore we were going to lose. You and Preston were good."

"Not as good as you."

Peyton rolls her eyes. "Enough working out for the day. Now that we won, I'm ready for the spa."

Emma's eyes light up as she looks from Peyton to me. "Spa?"

Peyton narrows her eyes on me. "Pres, did you not tell Emma we had the spa rented out for the day?"

"He seemed to have forgotten to mention that to me," Emma answers with a tight smile.

I shrugged. "Surprise. We're having a spa day."

Peyton sighs, giving me a suspicious look before focusing back on Emma. "Now I really know you were committed to celebrating my wedding. You agreed to tennis, not knowing there was a day of pampering after?"

Emma laughs. Her ponytail swings in the air with the movement, and all I can think about is how badly I want to run my fingers through her hair while I kiss her. "I really was going to take one for the team."

"Well, in that case, you've earned a reward. Right, Preston?"

I smirk, thinking of the exact way I want to reward her. "Yes, she has."

26
Emma

EMMA

They rented the spa for the entire day. It's completely empty.

MARGO

That's rich people behavior.

EMMA

Should I ask Preston if I can just marry into the family? He'd never have to pay me any attention if I got spa days like this frequently.

MARGO

You never know what could happen. Maybe your summer of self-discovery will end up with you madly in love with one of the world's most eligible bachelors!

I ROLL MY EYES, TIGHTENING THE BELT OF MY ROBE SO I DON'T accidentally flash someone from Peyton's wedding party.

WINNIE

I love that idea! Emma Rhodes has a nice ring to it.

EMMA

Stop you two. It's a fun fling that will end as quick as it began and that's fine by me. I'll enjoy the perks.

I exit out of the group chat and pull up the camera. I stretch my arm out and snap a selfie of me in my fancy robe. The locker room is surprisingly vacant. It's so empty I wonder if they have multiple of everything at this spa. Pembroke Hills is a country club for the elite of the elite. I'd been here once before with the girls, but that time, it was far busier than it is today. I've had my nails done and a facial, and I haven't seen anyone from the wedding party after either of those.

My phone vibrates in the locker. I pick it back up, wanting to check it one more time before going off to the sauna to kill time before my massage.

MARGO

No matter what, have the best day today and enjoy yourself! Win and I will be waiting for updates.

WINNIE

Also can't wait to watch another video update on your IG. It's been so fun to hear you talk about sports guy when we know exactly who you're with.

EMMA

It really isn't that juicy. He's a normal guy. Very grumpy honestly.

MARGO

Go have fun with your future in-laws. Love
you, Em!

I'm tempted to tell her there's no way Preston's family would
ever be my in-laws, but I don't. I put my phone in the locker and
shut it for good. I don't have to state the obvious to her that
nothing will transpire between Preston and me after this week.

But I will enjoy the perks of his family's insane amount of
money and enjoy this spa day. Like Peyton mentioned earlier, I
earned this spa day. I'll be on my way to the US Open in no time
with the way I played today—aside from the purposefully
missed serve that Preston noticed. I'm pleasantly surprised with
how well I played. Sitting in a sauna and relishing in my almost
victory is *exactly* what I need.

A massage will be ideal too. Hopefully, I get someone with
strong hands ready to really work at the knots. It's been a long
time since I had a professional massage, and I'm ready for it.

My slippers slap against the marble floors as I search for one
of the sauna rooms. According to the spa attendant, there are
multiple saunas, so it creates a more intimate experience for the
guests. When she walked me back to the locker room after my
facial, she said the ones to the right were all in use, but if I went
to the left and continued down for a minute, I'd find a row of
sauna rooms that were all empty.

I accidentally walk into a break room, interrupting what
looks like an intense lunch group gossip session for some of the
people who work at the spa before finally entering one of the
saunas. When she told me they were private, I expected small
rooms the size of closets. This sauna doesn't seem to be on, so
instead of trying to mess with the controls, I head to the one next
door. It's fogged over, clearly on and ready for me to sit back and
relax.

I pull the door open, barely able to see anything in front of me because of the steam. Stepping in, I relish in the way the steam clings to my skin even through the fabric of my plush robe.

Maybe wearing the robe wasn't the best idea. I slide my feet out of the slippers and leave them in front of the door. I'm placing them neatly to the side when I notice a very large set of slippers already in here.

"Oh shit," I mutter, my back going straight with panic.

"Breaking into my sauna, rebel?" a smooth voice I'd recognize anywhere asks from behind the steam. I squint, trying to see through all of the moisture in the air to find Preston. I think I make out his tall frame in the corner, but I can't be entirely sure.

"How'd you know it's me?" I ask, inching toward the door.

"I'd recognize your voice anywhere," he answers honestly. "You going to join me?"

A small squeak comes from my throat because there's something about the setting in here that makes it far more...intimate. His voice is deep and throaty and sends tingles down my spine.

"Oh, I don't have to stay. I'll find my own sauna. I didn't expect to—"

My words get cut off when he walks through the steam. He turns down the temperature of the sauna a few notches before grabbing my hand. "You're not going anywhere," he declares, tugging on my hand and pulling me deeper into the space.

My heart races, and I don't know why I'm suddenly nervous to be alone with him. The man was fucking me with a vibrator last night and has seen every inch there is to see of me.

Maybe it's the looming threats he's made. I'm ready to see if he follows through with them. The anticipation makes the sauna feel way hotter than it actually is.

Preston leads me to a stone bench that's part of the wall. Over here, the steam is a little thinner, but not by much.

"Enjoying your spa day?" he asks, gesturing for me to sit. I do, even though it feels weird because he's still standing with his eyes pinned on me.

All I can do is nod as I try to keep my eyes on his, but it's hard when he's shirtless. Not only shirtless, but the man is wearing nothing but a plush white towel wrapped around his hips.

And oh my god, he has the body of a Greek god. Actually, scratch that—I think the gods would've been jealous of the perfect slopes and planes of his body.

He chuckles, the sound barely audible over the spa music that plays through speakers I can't see. "You like what you see, rebel?"

I jump, my eyes finding his. The corners of his lips twitch with the hint of a smile.

"I wasn't staring," I lie, sitting back and trying to play it cool.

"You were. And that's okay. I like it when you stare."

My mouth falls open. *Is it hot in here?* I guess it *is* a sauna. That must explain why my whole entire body feels flushed, and not because I'm fairly confident Preston's muscles have muscles, and I have the strongest urge to run my tongue along them.

He takes a step closer to me. I've seen him in a suit and clothes that no doubt probably cost an ungodly amount of money, but I think the hottest thing I've ever seen him wear is this towel. It's knotted low on his hip. The deep v that disappears underneath his towel is so pronounced I want to lick it and feel it against my tongue.

"You're normally *so* chatty. Why so quiet now?"

I swallow, the pronounced outline of his abs now so close to me I could reach out and touch them if I wanted to. "I'm just very relaxed."

He laughs again, and it's quickly becoming one of my favorite sounds. It's because I know he doesn't do it too often that it makes it that much more special when he does. "Are you enjoying the spa?"

I nod. "Yes. Are you?" My voice breaks a little at the end

because he's taken another step closer to me. My knees now brush against the towel around his waist.

Leaning in, he places his palms against the wall on either side of my head. He's caging me in, his presence now the only thing I can concentrate on. Not that I'm complaining. He's the hottest man I've ever seen, and I'll bask in the heated way he's watching me right now. "I'm enjoying my day a *lot* better now."

He sticks his knee between my thighs, forcing them open. It's such a simple move, but it sets my entire body on fire. My clit throbs because of it.

"So, you're really into saunas?" I twist my hands together in my lap. He leans over me, so close I'm wondering if I'm supposed to place my hands on his chest? Slide my fingers underneath his towel? The way he stares at my lips angrily, I'm thinking I'm about to have my first public sexual experience, and I can't even be embarrassed by it because my body is on fire with desire for him.

"Yes. If you're in them. I didn't think I'd see you until our scheduled couples massage, so this was a very welcomed surprise."

He keeps one hand braced against the wall while the other begins to trace the side of my face. His fingers keep drifting down until they're wrapped around the tie of my robe.

"I didn't know it was a couples massage."

His fingers are quick at getting the tie undone. He pulls it from the loops and places it on the bench next to me. I'm transfixed by the way his muscles ripple with every movement.

He slips his hand underneath the collar of the robe, his fingertips splaying against my collarbone. "You don't have to just look. Touch me, rebel."

My eyes flutter closed for a moment. "Preston." His name is said like a warning—or maybe a plea. I've never wanted someone as badly as I want him, and now that he's right in front of me, clearly mine for the taking, I don't know what to do.

Preston decides for me. He pulls his hand free from my robe

and grabs on to my wrist. His fingers are strong as he guides my hand to his abs.

I gasp the moment my fingertips press to his skin. Now that I'm touching him, I want *more*. I flatten my palm against him, wanting to memorize every dip of his muscles.

"All I've thought about since last night was how badly I needed to touch you…" His fingers return to my skin again, but this time, his movements are faster with more intention. He pushes the fabric of my robe off my shoulders, baring more of my skin to him.

His fingertip traces the swell of my breast. There's no way he doesn't feel my racing heart under his touch. He tugs on the robe one more time until it's completely open, freeing my breasts as the fabric falls to my hips. He lets his knuckle brush over my peaked nipple, teasing me in the most excruciating way. "I've thought about how badly I wanted to taste you…"

"You have tasted me." My voice comes out strained as he circles my nipple with his fingertip. His touch is so light that all it manages to do is tease me and have me yearning for so much more from him.

He clicks his tongue, and his hand drops to my lap. His fingertips slip between my thighs. "No. Taste you *here*." He slides his fingers through my wetness, letting out a grunt of approval to find just how wet I already am.

"Oh god," I moan, my head falling backward as he presses his thumb against my clit.

"I'll make you see god by the time I'm done with you."

27
Preston

EMMA MOANS AGAIN—THIS TIME MUCH LOUDER THAN THE LAST time. I don't know if it's from my comment or the fact that I've slipped one finger inside her. Either way, I'm determined to get many more from her. She's so reactive to every touch of mine, and I'm desperate to know what else she'll do by the time I'm done with her today.

I was pissed the moment we were split up at the spa. I thought I'd have all afternoon with her, and instead, it's been hours since tennis, and all I've been left to do in that time is think about all the different ways I wanted to fuck her. First with my fingers, just like I'm doing right now. Then with my tongue. I want to feel her come, to taste her arousal and feel her orgasm against my tongue before I finally fuck her.

"Preston, anyone could walk in on us. I didn't lock the door." Emma's words don't come out weak. It's like she knows this is wrong, but she doesn't care. Good. I don't care either.

"I guess they'd get a show, then," I respond, pulling the robe from around her hips and throwing it behind me. It's the second time I've seen her completely naked, and it's still the most beautiful sight in the world.

She's slightly flushed, and moisture clings to her skin, making it have a sheen to it underneath the dim light of the sauna.

"Maybe we should wait until we get back to the house," she continues, rocking her hips against the heel of my hand.

I smile, knowing there's no way in hell I'm stopping now. By the way she's riding my hand, trying to get more from me, she doesn't want me to stop either. "Oh, I have no intention of stopping, rebel. Not until you've come at least twice."

"*Twice*?" she asks breathlessly. "That's a little cocky of you to assume you'll get multiple." Her back arches, placing her perfect tits and peaked nipples right in front of my face.

"I'm not being cocky. I'm just confident it'll happen." I inch my finger deeper, feeling her clench around me. It's tight around only one of my fingers. It's going to take some time to get her ready to take my cock, but she'll get there. I'll make sure of it.

I can't resist leaning in and taking her nipple into my mouth. She moans, her fingers sliding underneath the towel at my hips. She tries to tug at the fabric, but I pull my hips away from her and out of reach. I continue to work my finger in and out of her while my tongue circles her nipple.

"Preston, let me—" Her words die off as I slide another finger inside her. She's tight around them, but I'm slow, allowing her body to adjust to me.

I kiss a path all the way up her chest and neck until my lips are lined up with hers once again. "Let you what?" I ask, taking her bottom lip between my teeth.

Just like I want to memorize every one of her smiles, I also want to memorize each one of her moans. Some are loud and untamed; others are soft but shake her entire body with pleasure. All I want is to make her do it more and more until her body is spent from orgasms.

"Let me touch you," she responds as I pick up the pace of my fingers. I open them inside her, wanting to stretch her as much as possible.

"You don't get to touch me until you come."

"Preston," she whines, her head rocking back and forth. "I don't want to until you—"

"Until I what?"

"You're inside me." She tries to reach for me again, but I knock her hand away.

I spread my fingers further apart, spreading her even wider as I hook them. "Am I not inside you right now?" Her head falls backward with pleasure. I'm soaking in every single one of her reactions to what I'm doing to her, committing them to memory so I'll never forget having her just like this.

"You are, but I mean your..." She reaches forward and tries to grab my cock, but I don't let her. If she touches me, I'll be done for. One brush of her fingertips against me, and I'll be buried inside her in a heartbeat. I don't want to rush this. I want to take my time and savor every second of having her.

"Are you eager for my cock, rebel?" I sigh, reveling in her body's reactions to my words. "You are, aren't you? Know how I can tell?"

"How?" she pants.

"Your pussy hugged my fingers nice and tight when I said cock."

"Fuck me," she pleads as she lifts her hips from the bench.

"I will, baby. That's a promise."

She moans in disapproval when I pull my fingers from her pussy. Her eyes pop open. "Don't stop." I love that she begs, not afraid at all about asking for what she wants.

I keep my eyes locked on hers as I bring my fingers to my mouth. I stick them inside, pressing my fingertips to my tongue so I can taste her. My eyes close as pure want for the woman in front of me courses through my body.

"Fuck, you taste good."

"Preston." I fucking love the way she says my name. It's needy and filled with so much lust that I almost want to give in and give her my cock to reward her for moaning my name like that.

My cock aches, and I can't fight it any longer. In one tug, I rip my towel from my hips and let it fall to the ground.

Emma sucks in air, her wide eyes focused on my length. She swallows, her eyes anxiously finding mine. "I don't think it'll fit."

I smile, gently grabbing both of her wrists and placing her hands above her head. "It'll fit." She watches me carefully as I pick up the discarded rope from her robe. I begin to loop it around her wrists, binding them tightly together but not enough to hurt her. "But we've got to work you up to my cock, baby. Get you nice and ready." I tie the other end of the rope to a shelf above her head.

She pulls on the restraint, unable to get her hands free. "What is this?" she asks, her voice breathless. She rubs her thighs together, trying to get some sort of relief. It makes me smile, seeing her so needy and ready to come.

"Keep your hands up there like a good girl and I'll reward you. It isn't time for you to touch me yet."

"Why?"

I lower myself to my knees, placing my hands on her tan thighs. My fingertips press into her inner thighs as I push her knees open. "So I can eat this pussy without any distractions."

Her moan is loud, and I fucking love it. I don't care if someone is in the sauna next to us or not; nothing will stop me from getting to taste her pussy—to feel her come against my tongue. She tries to close her thighs—to get friction, I'm sure—but I don't let her. I keep my hands pressed to her inner thighs, keeping her spread wide for me as I admire the view.

"You're so sexy. You know that?" I lick my lips, practically salivating to taste her. As light as I can, I circle her inner thigh with my callused finger. "I love having you like this. Tied up and at my mercy, your pussy dripping wet and desperate for my attention."

Her eyelids flutter shut as she runs her teeth over her bottom lip. "Preston, you're teasing me," she whines, bucking her hips in protest.

I smirk, letting my fingertips drift even higher. She jumps when I run a finger over her clit. "Can't help it, rebel. You're so fucking sexy when you're being teased."

Lucky for her, I can't resist tasting her any longer. I lean in and lick her pussy the way I've been dreaming about all day.

28
Emma

I'M NEVER LEAVING THIS SPOT. BURY ME IN THIS SAUNA WITH Preston's head between my thighs because nothing—and I mean absolutely nothing—has ever felt as good as what he's doing right now.

He kisses me down there like a man starved. His tongue doesn't stop as he licks me up and down. Every lap of his tongue is only heightened by my hands being tied above me. I can't do anything but give my body to him completely.

I want to run my hands through his hair and grip to have something to hold on to, but I can't. Too many sensations are happening at once, and I don't want to admit to him that making me come twice won't be as hard as I thought it'd be—not with him.

Preston's fingertips dig into my thighs so hard I think he might leave bruises. I love the idea of being able to look at my skin days from now and remember this moment. I want to etch the sight of him on his knees in front of me into my mind forever; his hands holding on to my thighs so hard and desperate it's like he can't breathe unless his tongue is working against my clit. He slides a finger inside me, his tongue not pausing at all.

"Preston," I moan his name out loud and can't even begin to care if someone might hear it. It doesn't matter to me, not in the moment. All that matters is how I convince him to never stop unless it's to actually fuck me the way I'm aching for him to do.

"Yes, Emma?" His breath is hot between my thighs, and I don't know why that turns me on so much more, but it does.

"I'm going to come," I admit, missing the feel of his tongue against me. I lift my hips, trying to find some sort of reprieve after the absence of his mouth sealed to my core.

"What happened to you only being able to come once?" There's a taunting tone to his voice that only turns me on more. It's hot as hell how he doesn't let me get away with anything.

I look at him, finding his eyes already on me. I pull at the rope around my wrists, wanting nothing more than to grab his face and guide it right back to my clit.

He laughs, his eyes briefly looking at where my hands are tied above my head before meeting mine once again. "I'll free your hands once you've come against my tongue like the good girl you are and not a second sooner. You got that?"

I nod, letting my arm muscles relax. That's exactly what I want, and I'm not too proud to admit it. I close my eyes, waiting for him to return to what he was doing instead of dragging out my building orgasm.

He doesn't. When I open my eyes again, I find him staring at me with lust-filled eyes.

One side of his mouth picks up in a cocky smirk. "I'm waiting." He pushes his fingers in and out of me slowly, doing it just fast enough to feel good but not enough to send me over the edge.

My back arches in anticipation of him sealing his mouth to me once again. He takes the opportunity to take one of my nipples into his mouth. I moan, not knowing if it's in pleasure or displeasure that his mouth isn't working me.

"Waiting for what?" I ask, my desperation for him obvious in my tone.

"For you to admit you'll come multiple times." He bites down on my nipple slightly, making me yelp with pleasure. *Holy shit.* That felt so much better than I ever thought it would. My entire body tingles from both the pain and pleasure from it.

"I will," I hurriedly say, ready to stop talking about coming and actually doing it. "I will because it's with you."

A low growl comes from deep in his throat, and fuck, it's hot. "That might be the sexiest thing you've ever said to me."

Before I can respond, his mouth is right where I want him, but this time, it's even better. He slides two fingers inside me while his tongue circles my clit, and it almost feels like he's rewarding me for my comment. It's the best feeling in the world, and it doesn't take long for tingles to run down my spine with a budding orgasm.

As if he can feel me getting close—or maybe he really can—he reaches up and pinches one of my nipples between his thumb and pointer finger. That, mixed with his tongue and his fingers from his other hand pushing in and out of me, has my toes curling as the orgasm takes hold of me. I don't know what comes out of my mouth as I ride the waves of pleasure. It's all a blur, but I know I chant his name over and over again with some other things I doubt are even understandable.

Even as my body writhes with pleasure, Preston doesn't stop. I swear his persistence in licking me up and down even as I ride out the orgasm makes it last even longer. By the time my body goes lax, I have no idea how something can ever be more intense again. He put every time I've ever touched myself—or even used a toy—to shame.

"Oh my god," I mutter, my voice breathless from how intense the orgasm was.

Preston stands up, bringing his face in front of mine. "Yeah? Did you see him while you screamed my name?"

"No. All I saw was you." I smile, my gaze focusing on his lips. They're wet—with me—and it's fucking hot. I like seeing my arousal all over his face. I don't stare at his lips for too long— not when his dick is finally this close to me.

"I think it's you that knows all the right things to say, rebel."

He runs his thumb along my cheek. It seems so intimate after the way he just ate me out, but I soak it in.

I love the contrast. How he can be so filthy in one moment and tender the next.

My heart races at the way he looks at me. It begins to want things it shouldn't want, and I tell myself it's the aftermath of the orgasm messing with my head. I know deep down it isn't, but that's a problem for later. Right now, I'm desperate to finally return the favor for him.

I pull on my bound hands, itching to touch him and feel his skin. I want to study his reactions to find out what drives him wild. But I can't do any of that until he unties my hands.

"My turn," I say, licking my lips as I look at his dick. It's far bigger than I imagined. I don't know if I'll be able to fit it in my mouth—or anywhere else—but I'm determined to try.

"You want to suck my cock, Emma?" His voice is hoarse as his fingers move my wet hair from my face. My entire body is coated in moisture from the sauna, and so is his. It sticks to his muscles, making them gleam and taunt me while I still don't have my hands free to touch them.

I nod, smiling at him. "Yes."

He reaches up and begins to untie the knot around my wrists. "Then who am I to stop you?"

29
Preston

The moment I untie Emma's hands, she's wrapping her arms around my neck and throwing her body against me. Her lips crash against mine, and her fingers tangle in my hair. She kisses me hurriedly as if she's afraid I'll stop the kiss.

I don't. I lift her off the bench and revel in the way she wraps her legs around my middle. My cock brushes against her ass as she rocks against me, but it doesn't seem to deter her. If anything, it makes her more vocal.

She pulls at my hair as our tongues clash against each other. *Fuck.* This woman will destroy me. I already know it, and I don't even care that she'll leave me in ruin. I'll be grateful for it, that at least for a small moment in time, I had her the way I do at this very moment.

Finally, she slows, pulling her head back far enough that our eyes meet. "I just had to kiss you before doing anything else."

I squeeze her ass cheeks, keeping her pinned to my body. "No complaints here."

This makes her smile. She bites her lip, looking at me from under her eyelashes. "I like the way you taste."

"And how do I taste?"

"Like me."

An unrestrained groan comes from my chest at her words.

She smiles wide at my reaction, telling me she knows just

how crazy she's driving me. If it were any other person, I'd be upset for them to know how much power they have over me. But with her? I don't give a damn. In fact, I *want* her to know how fucking wild she drives me. How I'd do anything to see her sultry grin or hear her needy moans for far longer than the week I have with her.

My cock strains. I'm so close to her entrance that if I just shifted her a bit, I could slide right in. I want to, but there's something I want from her first. It's past wanting and now something I absolutely need from her.

I let my hands slide down the backs of her thighs. "On your knees," I demand, needing to feel her mouth around my cock.

Emma hums, her head cocking to the side. "You don't get to boss me around, Rhodes."

Her words contradict her actions because she unwraps her legs from around me and places her feet on the stone floor once again. Her cunt brushes against my cock in the process of her getting down, making me suck in a breath of air.

She takes a step back, and I use the opportunity to look at her body. I don't know how many times I've already admired her today, but just the sight of her has me breathless. She's sexy and beautiful, confident but careful with her movements, and fuck, I'm obsessed with the sight of her. Her tits, which are the perfect handful, her sun-kissed skin, which glows underneath the dim sauna lights. The slight curve from her waist to her hips that fits my hands perfectly. I've already imagined placing my hands right there as she sits on my cock and rides me at whatever speed and rhythm she wants.

Everything about her is perfect, and that thought occurs to me seconds before she drops to her knees.

Now, this—*this* is the best view I'll ever have.

She shifts her weight from one knee to the other to get comfortable. Her hands rest on her thighs as she just stares at me. I swallow, desperate for her to do something other than just look at me.

"Do something," I demand—or maybe it's more like begging. My voice is thick with passion as I wait for her to take me into her mouth.

Emma looks up, a smile playing on her lips. "I'm appreciating the view."

I love the way she argues with me. I'm always on my toes with her, never able to guess what she'll say. It's a thrill I'm addicted to—even though at the moment, it's frustrating because all I want is to feel her lips wrapped around my cock.

Needing relief, I wrap my fingers around my length and pump up and down. She watches the movements carefully, not stopping me from doing so. *What a shame.* Part of me was hoping if she saw me stroke my own length that it'd encourage her to take over.

I should've known she'd tease me just the way I teased her. I deserve it. Hell, if she really wanted to taunt me, she'd restrain my hands and prevent me from chasing the relief I so desperately need just the way I did to her.

She doesn't, but the way she teases me might be even worse. All she does is stare as I pump up and down. I do it slowly, showing her just how I like my cock to be touched. A bead of precum sits at the tip. I wipe my thumb over it, spreading it around as I watch her closely.

Just when I wonder if she's not going to touch me at all, she reaches out and wraps her fingers around my wrist. She pulls, wanting me to move my hand. "Now it's my turn," she demands, letting out a hum of approval when I move it.

Air hisses through my teeth when her fingers wrap around my length. She squeezes slightly, trying to get her fingertips to touch around me but failing at it. For a moment, she keeps her hand there without moving, and it's still enough to make my head spin with lust.

"Fuck." I groan, my head falling backward when she begins to move up and down. It's a good thing I've stopped her from touching me until now. I don't know if I'll be able to last long with how fucking good she strokes my cock.

Her hand picks up pace, and a strangled sound comes from my throat when her mouth joins in on the action without any warning. With one long and achingly slow drag of her tongue, she completely unravels me.

I'm fucking *gone* for her.

She licks from the base all the way to the tip, circling the head as if she has all the time in the world to give me head at the pace she chooses.

I need more. I'm desperate for it. Her tongue licking up and down feels fucking amazing, but it still isn't enough. Even her hand pumping up and down the base isn't enough. It won't be until my cock is buried down her throat, taking her to the limit and then going past that.

My fingers tangle in her hair as I wrap the wet, blonde strands around my palm. It gives me control, allowing me to guide her head right where I want it. I thrust my hips forward, trying to coax my cock between her lips.

Emma has the nerve to laugh, the sound sexy despite her not doing what I want her to. "You trying to rush me, Rhodes?"

"Yes. Take my cock, rebel. I know you want to."

Her thumb slides over the tip of my cock. She spreads precum around, staring at it intently before leaning in and licking my cock free of it.

"What if I want to take my time?"

My jaw clenches. The last thing I want is for her to take her time. I want her to rush this, to shove my cock down her throat and go at it with the same eagerness she showed earlier when she was practically begging for me to untie her so she could touch me.

"You don't want to take your time. You want to gag on my cock just as badly as I want you to. Be a good little whore and do it."

Her lips part, and she slowly coaxes me into her mouth. My

head rolls backward with pleasure. She's only fit the tip into her hot, wet mouth, and it's already making my entire body feel like I could combust at any moment.

I tighten the hold I have on her hair, pushing her head forward to take even more of me. She does so, opening her mouth wide in an attempt to fit all of me. My muscles shake as I fight the urge to ram my hips forward and shove my cock to the back of her throat. I don't want to be rough with her. I want her to take me at the pace she chooses, but she's driving me fucking mad with how slow she's allowing her throat to adjust to me.

"Fuck, Emma." I slowly move my hips, the tip of my cock hitting the back of her throat. Her body jerks in response, but she doesn't stop. Her teeth graze my shaft, and it just adds to how fucking good this feels.

She keeps her fingers wrapped around my base, making sure she gives every inch of my cock attention, even though all of me can't fit in her mouth.

"Faster, baby," I rasp.

She hums, and it feels incredible with her mouth still wrapped around my cock.

At this point, my fingertips dig into her scalp, but I can't loosen my grip. I need more. I need to fuck her mouth, and then I need to finally fuck her.

I push my hips forward, testing her boundaries. Her eyes widen as they find mine. She doesn't look away from my gaze, even as I repeat the motion again, but this time with a little more force to fit even more of me inside her.

She gladly takes it both times, letting me take control. Every time the tip of my cock hits the back of her throat, she gags a little but never relents. If anything, she seems to try to take even more of me every time her body jolts, and that realization has me closer than ever to coming far sooner than I expected.

"God, you look so fucking sexy on your knees, taking every inch of my cock you can manage. Will your pussy be just as greedy?" I ram my hips forward, making her hand fall from the base.

She moans again, her hand brushing the inside of her thigh. I watch with pure fascination as her fingers drift to her clit. She's needier than I thought she was. It's incredibly sexy to know that she's getting off on taking my cock like this and that she has no option but to touch herself while taking me.

I'm opening my mouth to tell her it's time I finally fuck that perfect cunt of hers when a knock sounds against the door.

30
Emma

I yelp, trying to pull my mouth from Preston, but he doesn't let me. He keeps digging his fingertips into my scalp, his grip on my hair so tight I can't move. I look at him, wondering what we should do about the person knocking at the door.

Preston lifts his hand and presses one finger to his lips. His hips rock forward as if there isn't someone on the other side of the door that could walk in and find his cock halfway down my throat.

It shouldn't turn me on to know we're seconds away from being caught, but it does. I try to hide my moan when he moves again, forcing his cock as far into my mouth as I can possibly take him. This man doesn't believe in being gentle, and it's driving me wild. My clit throbs with need for him. Not even my own fingers circling the sensitive spot is providing relief.

Another knock fills the space around us, this time louder than the first. "Mr. Rhodes?" the voice calls on the other side. "It's time for your couples massage."

"I'll be a minute!" Preston responds, his voice tight as I circle the head of his cock with my tongue.

"You're ten minutes past your appointment time, sir."

"Got it," Preston clips.

"Do you have any idea of where Ms. Turner is? We want to make sure she knows about the massage as well."

Preston laughs, his thumb brushing over my cheekbone. "I'll make sure she doesn't miss it."

It's quiet on the other side of the door for a moment before someone speaks up again. "See you soon, Mr. Rhodes. We'll be waiting."

Preston's grip loosens just enough to pull him from my mouth. I sit back on my heels, my heart racing at almost being caught. "Oh my god," I manage to get out. "A poor spa attendant almost walked in on us."

"He would've got quite the show," he responds, not at all appearing worried that we were seconds away from being discovered.

His lips turn into a frown when I stand up. "What do you think you're doing?"

"Going to the massage before they come looking for us again…and *actually* open the door."

He frowns, his hand wrapping around his cock. I feel bad—I know if I kept at it, I could've finished him off if we hadn't been interrupted. "We're not done." His voice echoes off the stone walls of the sauna. It's deep and intoxicating, caressing my skin without him having to touch me at all.

I bite my lip, excited for us to finish things. It's already been so good with him, and he hasn't even fucked me yet. Maybe it's for the best that we were interrupted. We can rush back to the house after the massages and finish what we've started. "We'll enjoy the massage and then make up an excuse to go back to the house for a bit."

"Just a bit?"

I shrug, taking a step toward my discarded robe. My entire body feels like it's on fire with need for him. "Or longer," I suggest. "We just have to make it through the massage and you're all mine."

Finally, he smiles, but it doesn't reach his eyes. It's more predatory—and becomes even more untamed when his eyes darken as I shrug the robe on.

"Just so we're clear, if it were up to me, the massage would be forgotten about, and my cock would already be buried inside you."

"Even if someone could walk in at any minute?"

"I don't give a shit about that. Not when all I can think about is fucking you."

I pick up the tie for my robe off the ground. My mind flashes with how it wasn't too long ago when it was tied around my wrists as Preston gave me the best orgasm of my life. The back of my neck heats with the memory as I tie the rope around my waist as tight as I can manage. "I can't stop thinking about that either. After the couples massage, I'm all yours."

"I've never dreaded having to go to a massage more," he tosses out, picking his towel off the floor. His movements are jerky as he ties it around his waist. I try not to smile at the small tantrum he's throwing at being interrupted. It's kind of hot.

"Really?" I ask, pretending to be completely unbothered by the fact we didn't get to finish what we started. He doesn't have to know that my body throbs in desperation for him...for another release. "I've never had a couples massage before. I'm ready for it."

I slide my slippers back on and carefully open the door, making sure to peek out and make sure no one is in the hallway. I scurry out of there and try to play it cool. If someone were to walk down the hallway now, they wouldn't know I was in the same sauna as Preston. I could've come from any of them. Even though I'm tempted to, I don't even look behind me to see if Preston follows me.

Luckily, I paid attention earlier when the spa attendant told me where the massages were. I scan the doors, finding both Preston's and my name written on one of them. Slowly, I push the door open and find two massage therapists waiting inside.

"You must be Emma," one of them says. I recognize his voice from outside the sauna.

"Yes."

"I'm Lowry." I try not to blush as he holds his hand out for me to shake. I timidly take his hand in mine right as Preston opens the door, his eyes immediately focusing on Lowry's hand around mine.

"Nice to meet you," I squeak, unable to look away from Preston's angry glare.

"And I'm Hannah," the other massage therapist says, holding her hand out for me to take. I'm able to meet her eyes better than I was meeting Lowry's, only because I know Lowry was close to finding me in a very interesting position.

"Glad you made it, Mr. Rhodes," Lowry says, holding his hand out for Preston to take.

Preston doesn't take it. Instead, he keeps his hand over the front of his towel to try and hide his erection. He looks at the two tables placed in the middle of the room right next to one another. "Are we ready to begin?"

Lowry's hand awkwardly drops to his side. "Yes. Hannah and I will step out for a minute to let the two of you get comfortable. Feel free to undress to your comfort level. We'll knock before entering." He flips a light off on the way out, making it dim in the room.

My eyes go wide as I realize I never returned to my locker. I look to Preston, finding him staring at me with an unreadable look on his face.

"I forgot my underwear." I panic. I know there's a huge debate on whether or not you're supposed to keep underwear on during a massage, but I sit firmly on the keep-the-underwear-on side. In the heat of what was happening with Preston, I completely forgot about going back to grab mine.

"Get on the table so we can get this over with. And keep that sheet over you."

My heart races at the roughness to his voice. He isn't happy, and it's terrible of me to admit, but I love it.

"Someone got grumpy *really* fast," I mutter as I strip out of my robe and hang it on the hook in the room. I climb up onto the table and lie down. Preston lets out a sigh of approval when I pull the sheet up my body to cover me.

"Maybe I'm grumpy because my dick is still hard as a rock, thanks to the mind-blowing way you sucked me. Seeing your ass in the air as you climbed onto the table didn't do me any favors."

I smile, even though he can't see it. I love the power I feel knowing I'm doing this to him. "Soon, you'll be able to do whatever you want to me."

"Oh, I plan on it." The table beside mine creaks as I assume he lies down. I keep my face pressed down into the pillow, not needing to look at him. He has the same effect on me that I have on him. If I saw the beautiful ripple of his muscles or the chiseled line of his jaw, I might concede and cancel the massage, even though I was looking forward to it.

Patience. It's not something I've ever had, but I'm all about bettering myself this summer. Doing some self-care before having what will no doubt be the best sex of my life counts as making better life decisions...right?

As if on cue, there's a knock on the door.

"Come in," I call, my voice muffled thanks to being face down against the pillow.

All Preston does is grunt, not bothering to hide his opinion on the current situation.

"All set?" Lowry asks, stepping up to my table.

I swallow. I'd assumed Hannah would be my massage therapist and Lowry would be Preston's, but apparently, I was wrong. Lowry adjusts the sheet on my body, tucking it against my side.

Lowry's fingers wrap around my wrist, and before I can ask him what he's doing, he's placing my hand in Preston's.

"Couples massages are all about connecting at a deeper level," Hannah says in a slow, whimsical tone. "Think about your linked hands, about the connection thrumming through both of you."

My hand feels so small in Preston's. We only touch at our hands, but the small press of our skin has my body ablaze all over again. I try not to jump when his thumb begins to rub the inside of my palm in little circles.

"Tell me if it gets too hard," Lowry whispers.

Preston coughs next to me, his thumb stalling for a moment.

"You okay?" Hannah asks Preston.

"Great," he clips.

Lowry's hands find my shoulders. They're wet with oil as he carefully moves my hair from my neck. He begins to rub my back gently, but every now and then, his thumb applies more pressure that hurts in the best way possible.

I try not to moan, but his fingers work a knot that feels incredible. Preston's thumb continues to trace circles against my skin. I don't know why, but the small circles almost feel as intimate as having his tongue against me. Maybe it's because I'm still turned on from the sauna, but the small scratch of his calloused thumb against my palm might be one of the most erotic things I've ever felt.

Lowry's fingers continue to work at the knots of my back, but that isn't what I'm focusing on at all. It's Preston and the way he continues to trace my skin as if he doesn't want me to forget he's here. His touch is so light it almost tickles, and every minute that goes by, my body feels tighter.

Eventually, a moan falls from my lips as the tender press of Preston's skin against mine becomes too much.

My hand falls to the side of the table in an instant.

"We're done here," Preston clips, the sound of his body shifting on the table.

"Everything okay, Mr. Rhodes?" Hannah asks, her voice uneasy.

I lift my head, wanting to make sure I stay covered as I try to figure out what's wrong with Preston. He doesn't look at Hannah or Lowry. He stares right at me.

"I'm not feeling so well. Can we have the room, please?"

"Maybe if you just lie down for a minu—"

"*Out.* Now." Preston's tone leaves no room for discussion.

My cheeks heat at the sound of his booming voice. I can't even look at Lowry or Hannah as they both scurry out of the room.

The door shuts, and Preston is immediately sliding off the table. In a few easy steps, he's locking the door and turning to face me.

I sit up, crossing my arms across my chest to hide myself, even though he's already seen it all. "That was rude."

"I don't give a fuck." He takes a step in my direction. My adrenaline spikes at the hungry look in his eyes. I don't have to ask why he stopped the massage minutes after it began or wonder what he wants from me.

"Should we go back to the house?"

He steps up to the end of my table. His strong fingers wrap around my ankles as he pulls me across the table. "We're not going anywhere until I've fucked you."

"You didn't even let me finish the massage. Lowry was doing an excellent job at—"

His palm covers my mouth before I can say anything else.

"I don't want to hear his name from your mouth ever again. Hearing you moan while his hands were on you... I've never seen so much red."

Wetness pools between my thighs at the pure jealousy in his words. He keeps his hand pressed to my lips, not even giving me the chance to respond. I don't even know what I'd say. His jealousy was misplaced. My moans had everything to do with the seductive way Preston softly rubbed my skin.

Preston pushes my thighs open and steps between them. The tip of his cock brushes my inner thigh, and I moan at the sensation. He's so close. He could easily slide inside me if he wanted to. The only problem is we're still not in private.

"Now, I tried doing it your way. It didn't work for me. So now, we're going to fuck here, right now, and you're going to stay quiet for me. Can you do that?"

I moan at his words—at the idea of him taking me right here.

I know we shouldn't, but I was more than willing to do it in the sauna where we didn't have a lock on the door. At least in here, we do. But Hannah or Lowry could come back any minute to check on us, and I don't know if I'll be able to stay quiet enough to hide what we're doing.

"Nod your head yes, baby." His free hand skirts across my thigh. He's not teasing me this time. His fingers push inside me instantly.

A satisfied grin spreads over his face. "Fuck. You're still so wet. This pussy is ready to take me, isn't it?"

He lets his hand drop from my mouth, but his eyes stay on me with his eyebrows raised. He doesn't have to say anything else. I know he's gesturing for me to stay quiet.

I look down at his dick. It stands straight up, almost hitting his belly button with his impressive length.

"I don't see how that's going to fit," I whisper.

He begins to slide a second and then a third finger inside me. I gasp at the fullness. I can feel him stretching me, his fingers curling inside to bring even more pleasure. "Of course it'll fit. This pussy is mine. It was made for me. You're going to take my cock—every inch of it."

My head falls backward, and the only thing that stops me from falling against the table is Preston's quick reaction. His hand rests on the small of my back, keeping me upright as his fingers continue to work in and out of me.

The heel of his hand presses against my clit as he continues to push in and out of me at a slow and taunting pace.

"Tell me you're on the pill. My last tests were negative, and I don't want anything between us if that's okay with you."

I nod, forgetting all about where this is happening. "Yes. Mine were negative too." He's broken down my resolve to try and wait until we get back to the house. I need him. Right now.

31
Preston

Emma spreads her legs open for me, her fingers drifting between her thighs once again. I love that she doesn't wait or try to drag this out. It's evident she's as ready for this as I am.

She takes me by surprise by grabbing me and beginning to pump up and down my length. She's so eager for me, and I love it. Her pace is quick and rushed, even though it doesn't need to be. I don't care where we are right now, I'm still going to take my time with her and enjoy every second of this finally happening between us.

"Ready, baby?" I ask, leaning in to kiss her. I'll never tire of the taste of her. The crazed way she kisses me back is something that'll stay burned in my mind far beyond this week.

"Yes." She sighs against my lips as I brush the tip of my cock through her wetness.

"You're nice and ready for me, aren't you?"

She nods, and my tongue dances in her mouth as I give her exactly what she wants. I run my cock again through the wetness between her thighs, and when I feel like it is wet enough to slide into her easily, I line it up with her perfectly. With one small push of my hips, I'm finally inside her.

We taste each other's groans at the feeling of our bodies finally being linked. She's tight around me, but it doesn't stop her from moving her hips to get more.

"Fuck." I groan, my forehead finding hers. We stay in that position for a moment, both of us trying to calm our racing hearts. Our breaths fall in sync, her chest rising and mine falling and vice versa.

I'm not even halfway inside her, and I can't shake how right this feels. It's like she was made for me and I was made for her.

"More," Emma pants. She kisses me hungrily, like she's trying to get as much of me as possible.

I pull away but don't break contact for long. "I'm trying to let you adjust to me, baby." My lips trail along her jaw. I nip and suck at her soft skin, wanting to leave my mark anywhere I can.

"No," she pleads, grinding her hips. "More, Preston. *Please.*"

The way she says please snaps my resolve. "You want more?" I wrap my fingers around the back of her neck to cradle her head. My other hand presses to her chest as I push her body onto the table.

She allows me to lay her flat. I make sure she's comfortable before moving my hands to her hips. I hold on to them, committing the slight curves of her body to memory. Slowly, I coax myself in another inch, feeling her tighten around me.

My hands find her breasts. I cup them in each hand, rolling her nipples between my fingers. She writhes under my touch, her eyes fluttering shut in pleasure. I use the chance to seat myself deep inside her.

"Oh my…" Her words trail off.

"You said you wanted more." My voice is hushed and strained. I'm unable to make any more sound than that. Not when her cunt is hugging me so perfectly. "I won't just give you more. I'll give you every fucking inch of me."

She lets out a loud, unrestrained whimper.

I groan, having to pause for a moment because of how good it feels. I need to get ahold of myself. I don't want to rush things between us, and she feels too fucking perfect that I'm worried if I begin to rock in and out of her, I won't be able to last long.

I take it slow, grinding my hips only the smallest amount. I knew she'd feel like heaven, but this—us together—it's even better.

"Yes," Emma pants when I pick up the pace.

I pull her all the way to the edge of the table, wanting to get as deep as possible. Even this position doesn't feel deep enough. I need more of her. I don't know if I'll ever feel like I have enough.

Without pulling free from her, I reach to the table next to us and grab the pillow at the end of it.

"Lift," I demand, my finger tapping her hip.

"What?"

A low growl comes from deep in my chest. "Lift your hips, baby."

She groans as if she's annoyed I'm talking instead of rocking in and out of her. I laugh, knowing things are about to feel even better for her. Despite her low groans of protest, she lifts her hips slightly. I slide the pillow underneath her, allowing me even deeper inside her.

"Oh my god." Her voice comes out like a high-pitched cry. "You're so deep."

I hook my arms around her thighs and spread them open, giving me the perfect view of my cock moving in and out of her. "You like taking all of my cock?" I growl, my hips beginning to move at a punishing rhythm. "You do, don't you? Because you're a greedy slut who can't get enough."

"Preston." My name falls from her lips loud and unapologetically.

"You like it when I call you names, don't you? You love being called my dirty slut. No one else's but mine." My head falls backward for a moment in pure ecstasy. She fits my cock like a damn glove. I drive in and out of her, knowing nothing will ever come close to this feeling right here.

Her pussy clenches around me, telling me she's relishing every second of this like I am. My hips jam against the backs of her thighs with each punishing thrust.

Emma's moans grow louder and louder until I realize they're probably getting to the point where somebody could hear us. I don't want someone to knock on the door to try and stop us, so I need to think of a way to keep her quiet.

"Baby, you're being loud," I tell her.

Her eyes open and find mine. "I'm sorry. I can—"

Before she can finish her thought, I'm grabbing her hips and turning her. She yelps, not expecting the movement. The new position has her ass in the air, her pussy still wet with desire. I wish I had time to take a step back and look at her, but all I can think about is getting inside her again.

I trail my fingers down her spine, pushing her chest into the massage table as I climb onto it behind her. The table groans underneath both our weight, but it doesn't stop me from doing it.

"Your ass in the air like this is a spectacular sight," I note, lining up my cock with her once again. "Soon, I'll have to eat your pussy in this position. But right now..." I caress her spine, letting my fingers drift higher until they rest at the back of her neck. "Put your face in the pillow, baby. Let it muffle your screams so I can fuck you hard and fast."

"Preston." My name comes out so loud there's no doubt in my mind if someone was in the room next to us that they heard it.

I shush her, applying pressure to the back of her neck to direct her face against the pillow. "Use the pillow to keep quiet, or I'll have to stop."

She turns, pressing her face into the pillow with a muffled moan. I reward her by thrusting forward, shoving all of me inside her. Her body folds underneath the feeling. I use my free hand to grab her by the hip and keep her on her knees.

It allows me to wrap around her front and brush my fingers against her clit. I've watched her closely, noticing how she's always making quick circles around her clit. I repeat the same action, my body going tight at the muffled moans that come from her because of it.

I swear my name comes from her lips again, although it's hard to tell because of her face in the pillow. The table continues to creak underneath our movements. My hips move faster and faster as her moans get louder and louder.

My fingers tangle in her hair, needing to feel even more of her as she clenches around me. Even muffled, her moans get louder, and I know she's coming.

I don't stop my pace at all, wanting to milk every last second of the orgasm from her. My finger continues to work her clit as my cock pushes in and out of her at a punishing rhythm. She's now even tighter around me as she comes down from the high of the orgasm.

My grip in her hair has loosened slightly, allowing her to turn her head. "Preston, I came." Her words come out breathless.

Moving from her neck and wrapping around her middle, I pull her off the table until her back is pressed to my chest. The new position gets me even deeper inside her—deeper than I've been before.

I kiss her shoulder as her calves are right on the sides of my thighs. "I told you you'd be coming multiple times. Now, give me one more, baby. Come on my cock while I fill you with my cum."

Her head falls against my shoulder. I press my lips to her temple, wanting any connection to her I can get. I'm fully inside her—as deep as I can possibly go—and it still isn't enough. I'm not sure anything will ever be enough.

"Like this, you're too big. It's too mu—" Her words stop as my fingers find her nipple. I pinch it before massaging her breast and repeating the motion.

"No, I'm not. I'm perfect for you. And you're perfect for me. We fit. Now, breathe and give me one more." The last words come out as more of a growl than a sentence, but I know she still hears me because her body goes lax against mine. She's giving me full control, and I fucking love it.

My thrusts have slowed and become more deliberate. With every one of them, she takes me to her limit, and it feels so fucking good that I know I'm close to finishing. It's like a spring coiled tightly and threatening to release. I continue to work in and out, enjoying every second of being inside her.

The slow thrusts feel impeccable, but as my vision begins to blur with the looming orgasm, I have to pick up pace again. Emma doesn't seem to mind; with every quick move of my hips, her moans get louder. My hand clasps over her mouth to keep her quiet as I drill into her.

Her breath is hot against my palm as a moan overtakes her. She's coming, and her release has me finding mine. Bursts of fire trail down my spine as the orgasm takes over me. I grunt, unable to form words at how intense the orgasm is. Her moans vibrate against my skin as time seems to pause. I continue to work in and out of her to savor every second of it, and with one final thrust, the massage table comes crashing down.

32
Emma

I'M STILL RIDING THE HIGH OF A THIRD ORGASM I DIDN'T EVEN THINK was possible when Preston and I go crashing to the ground. The table completely gave out underneath us, two of the legs snapping in half from the weight.

Preston keeps a grip on me, even after we hit the ground in a tangle of limbs.

"Are you okay?" The concern in his face is evident as he twists my body in his lap to face him. He pulls himself from me, and despite the unexpected ending to our first time together, I miss the fullness I felt with him inside me.

For a few seconds, I don't speak, too stunned about what just happened. Both our breaths are heavy and quick as we regain our composure.

Preston's hands find my cheeks. "Emma. Are you okay?"

My eyes meet his at the same moment the loudest laugh erupts from deep in my chest. It's probably the most unattractive sound ever, but I snort, unable to get control of myself.

"Oh my god," I wheeze, trying to get air into my lungs but finding it difficult because of the laughter overtaking my entire body. "We just broke a table."

Preston's eyes go wide before he rolls them at me. "Fuck, Emma, I thought you got hurt." His cheeks hollow out as he lets out a breath. He places his hand to his chest, rubbing over it dramatically. "My heart actually fucking hurts with how worried I was there for a moment."

I wipe at the tears that prickle the corner of my eyes. My body still shakes with another laugh that threatens to burst free. "I'm sorry," I manage to get out. "It's just that I just got fucked so good that we ended up breaking a table."

This gets him to relax the hard set of his jaw. His thumbs brush against my cheeks. "It really did end with a bang." His lips twitch before he lets out a deep rumble of a laugh.

I join him, unable to play it cool for another second after his words. The two of us break out in laughter like it's the most normal thing in the world for us to be cracking up after having mind-blowing sex in public and accidentally breaking a table in the process.

I don't know how long the laughing lasts, but as we both get our breaths back—both from the laughter and the sex—I realize I don't know if I've ever felt such a rush of happiness. I'm completely content, and as Preston stares at me with his deep blue eyes, I find myself wishing all of this didn't end after Peyton's wedding.

Preston's eyes travel my face as our breathing evens out. The humor is gone from the room, and now, a heavy tension fills the space around us. His thumb traces over my bottom lip, and all I can do is hope that he's feeling the same overwhelming rush of feelings I am.

"Tell me that was as good for you as it was for me." His voice comes out hoarse and unsure. It's the first time I've heard anything but confidence in his tone.

I place my palms against his cheeks, copying the same position as his hands on my face. I don't even try to hide my smile or the effect he's having on me. If I only have a few more days left with him, I'm okay with wearing my heart on my sleeve.

I agreed to be his fake girlfriend because I didn't want to live with what-ifs. That mindset goes for this too. I don't want to look back and wonder what could've happened if I'd been more open and honest with him. What's the worst thing that can happen? I never see him again? That's already happening once Peyton gets married. I don't have anything to lose.

Preston swallows, his fingertips applying slightly more pressure. "Talk to me, Em."

Em. I like the nickname. I like rebel, too. I like anything he calls me—even if some of them are filthy.

I loop my finger through the chain necklace around his neck and pull his face closer to mine. "I'm the one who came three times. For me, it was probably better." I kiss him before he can even respond. He doesn't seem to care. His tongue meets mine, slowly circling my mouth.

We kiss like that for a few moments before he pulls away enough to talk. "I'm already thinking about making you come again."

I gasp, pulling my finger free from his necklace. "Preston Rhodes, you animal. You just gave me the best sex and orgasms —yes, *plural*—of my life, and you're already talking about when it'll happen again."

He smirks, and it seems so boyish on him. I love it. When we first met, I wondered if he ever really smiled. It turns out he does. He just saves them for the special moments, and I feel a high knowing he'll freely give them to me. "Yes. I am. I don't remember what the itinerary Peyton gave us for the rest of the day is , but I vote we skip it."

I playfully swat at his chest. "It's your sister's wedding week. You can't skip anything."

He narrows his eyes on me, clearly not happy with my answer. "Guess I'll be keeping you up late, then."

My cheeks heat with what I'm sure is a blush. I never thought I was someone who blushed, but apparently, I just hadn't met the right person. I look underneath us at the broken remains of the table. "What are we going to do about this table?"

I don't want to, but I slide from his lap and look down at the mess we made. The pillow has fallen to the ground, and one of the legs of the table is completely bent in half. I don't know how we managed to break it this badly, but somehow, we did.

Preston sighs as we both stand up. He puts his hands on his hips, looking down at our mess. I try not to laugh at the sight of us because we're both completely naked, staring down at what used to be a perfectly working massage table.

I cannot wait to tell my friends about this. I finally have the hottest sex of my life, and instead of it ending with us passionately gazing into each other's lust-filled eyes, it ended with us on the ground, surrounded by broken pieces of a massage table.

"I could try to fix it." His words come out as more of a question than a statement.

I grab my robe off the hook and pull it on, looking down at the leg of the table that's completely broken in half. "I'm not sure that can be fixed."

He chuckles. "I'll tell the staff I'll buy them a new one."

"That's probably a better idea. Do you have your wallet?"

"Why would I need my wallet? They can put it on a tab for me." He raises an eyebrow before grabbing a spare robe from the back of the door. It doesn't fit him at all. His tall frame makes it far too short for him, and it can't close because of his broad shoulders, but he still pulls it off, looking incredibly too good for his—and my—own good.

I squat down, seeing if there's a way we could stage the table to make it look not so broken. There isn't. The moment Hannah and Lowry return, they will know exactly what happened between me and Preston. I need to make sure I run out of this spa and never ever return. "No, not for the table. Although you do owe them a new one. I wanted to know if you had your wallet so you can leave a tip for Lowry and Hannah. I think they, uh…" I laugh, shaking my head. "Well, I think they earned a tip."

Preston nods. "I don't have my wallet because the towel I was wearing didn't have pockets, but I'll make sure they get a good tip. As long as you never say his name again."

I roll my eyes. "You were literally inside me five minutes ago, and you're jealous of the massage therapist because I said his name?"

"And the way you moaned while his hands were on you."

"I moaned because, for some reason, your thumb brushing against my palm was the most erotic thing ever."

"More erotic than my cock buried inside you?"

I shrug, trying to hide the blush blooming on my cheeks. "We hadn't gotten that far yet. Now, let's go before Hannah and Lowry come back and I die of embarrassment."

33
Preston

"Preston, you have to wear the T-shirt."

I stare at my sister, questioning how much I actually love her for what she's asking me to do. "Peyton," I begin, saying her name nice and slow. She stares at me with the same wide eyes that used to get her anything she wanted out of me when she was a kid. "I'm not wearing a cheesy bachelor party shirt that says 'I'm on a yacht before tying the knot.'"

Peyton juts out her bottom lip and takes a step closer to me. She grabs my hands and takes them in hers. She's close enough that I can see that she got sunburnt earlier today during the tennis matches. "It's fun. Jackson and I didn't want to do individual parties, so we combined our bachelor and bachelorette parties, but I didn't want to miss out on the cute, corny T-shirts."

My eyes dart to the people around us. We're waiting on a dock for the rest of the wedding party to arrive before starting the celebrations for tonight. I'm *thrilled*. "P, Mom and Dad chartered us a yacht for the night—where we were told to dress nice —and you want to put these on?" I hold up the T-shirt in question. The cotton is rough against my skin, and just by holding it up, I can already tell it isn't going to fit right.

"Do it for me. Please. It'll be fun. We can take a few pictures in them, and then you can change if you want."

"Look who I found!" Emma calls from down the dock. She

disappeared fifteen minutes ago, saying she wanted to go check out one of the gift shops. I was about to go looking for her, not wanting to spend much time away from her at all after the day we had.

"Gram!" Peyton excitedly cheers, forgetting all about me and running down the dock to Emma and Gram.

"I can't believe you invited me to your bachelorette party," Gram quips, rocking the T-shirt Peyton is so desperately begging me to wear. "Shouldn't you have strippers at yours? Grandmothers don't belong at bachelorette parties."

Emma lets out a loud gasp. "No, you're the life of the party, Gram. Of course, you're here."

It's only now I notice that somehow Peyton's managed to get Emma in one of the cheesy T-shirts. I took a phone call from my agent for a few minutes not too long ago, but I didn't think Emma came back in that time. Apparently, I was wrong.

"Exactly," Peyton chimes in, smiling as she takes in the matching shirts both Gram and Emma are wearing. I frown, knowing any minute now, Peyton's attention will return to me, and she's going to beg me to put on that damn shirt.

I look back, glaring over my shoulder for a minute at Jackson. Not only is he wearing the T-shirt proudly, but he's even wearing a temporary tattoo of Peyton's face on his bicep that he shows off to anyone he talks to.

Gram lets out a grunt as they come to a stop right next to me. She stares at the yacht our parents chartered for Peyton and Jackson in front of us. Her eyes narrow before she reaches into the small purse at her side. She pulls her glasses onto her face, her eyes still focused on the yacht we're about to board.

"Peyton, darling." Gram pulls her eyes from the yacht and wraps an arm around Peyton.

"Yes, Gram?"

"Why is there nothing penis-shaped at this party?"

"Gram, I never want to hear the word 'penis' from your mouth ever again." Peyton shivers.

"They're ready for us!" Mom calls, taking the hand of one of the crew members as he escorts her up the stairs to the boat.

Peyton excitedly claps before she throws the T-shirt at me. "Put it on, Preston. Let's go celebrate one of my final nights as a Rhodes!" She runs away before she can hear any of my protests.

"Put the damn shirt on, and let's go, Pres," Gram chimes in. She gives me a look that leaves little up for discussion.

Emma smiles at me, clearly aware of how little I want to wear this shirt. She's wearing hers proudly. It's tied at the side, covering the pale yellow dress she wore for the party tonight. If Gram wasn't standing within earshot, I'd tell her how I hate the T-shirt and not because it's cheesy but because it hides the perfect swell of her breasts.

When we left the spa, I thought we'd hurry back to Moore's place and spend the rest of the afternoon in bed. Unfortunately, Peyton caught us on the way out and insisted we do a late lunch with them. By the time we were done, it was time for us to get back to the house and get ready for the night.

It's been hours since we had sex, and I need more of her. The kisses I've stolen between then and now aren't enough. Which leads me to question if I'll ever get enough of her? Probably not, but I'll have to try. Especially with the knowledge that Peyton's wedding is in two days, and after that...well, I don't want to think about what happens after.

"Preston," Gram calls, she and Emma are a few steps ahead of me. They're still arm in arm, both of them looking over their shoulders with confused looks.

"Coming," I respond with a groan, already shrugging out of my suit jacket so I can put the damn T-shirt on.

I'm begrudgingly following them to the yacht and changing into the silly T-shirt when Emma leans in to talk next to Gram's ear. She tries to lower her voice, but she fails at it.

"For the record, I agree with you. There aren't enough penis-shaped things at this party for my liking."

I try not to laugh at her comment.

Gram looks at Emma with a wide grin. "Oh, darling. I'm never letting you leave this family."

"You know, I think I look hot in the T-shirt," Emma comments, finishing off the last bite of her bananas Foster.

"I never said you didn't," I respond.

Luckily, Peyton held true to her word and only had me keep the shirt on for pictures. After that, most people changed back into their formal wear as the yacht set off for the dinner cruise. But not Emma—she's worn it proudly the entire time. She's the only one still wearing it besides Peyton and Jackson.

"Yeah, but you keep glaring at the shirt like it offended you. Through every course of dinner, you were staring daggers at it."

My eyes scan the boat, trying to figure out if anyone is looking our way. Some people have left the table altogether and are exploring the boat; some are deep in conversations I haven't been paying attention to. But all that matters is no one is looking our way.

I lean in, kissing right underneath her ear. "Maybe I'm glaring because I don't want to be here. I want to be back at the house with that goddamn shirt—and everything else you're wearing—on the floor."

Emma tilts her head, allowing me more access to her sunburnt skin. "This dress is silk, and I saved up for months to buy it. You will *not* be throwing it on the floor."

My teeth graze her throat. "I'll buy you a new one."

"Or you'll take care of the one I already bought."

"I don't know if I can think about taking care of anything but this right here." I casually place my hand underneath the table and inch my way up her thigh. My fingers slide underneath her dress and brush over her pussy.

A strangled breath falls from her lips when my fingers don't meet any fabric. I grunt, not expecting to find her bare under her dress. "Emma Turner, where are your panties?" I growl, running my fingers along her pussy.

"Did you just scold me using my full name?" Her blue eyes light with mischief underneath the moon. Fuck, I wish my grandmother wasn't sitting three chairs down from me. I wish we were alone so I could push the dress up to her hips and devour her pussy again.

"I did. How am I supposed to go the rest of the night knowing you're not wearing any panties underneath this dress?"

She tries to squeeze her thighs together to stop my finger from circling her clit, but it doesn't work. If anything, it keeps my hand pinned between her legs. "I guess you're going to have to figure it out. I couldn't wear a dress like this and have panty lines. That's a cardinal sin, Rhodes."

Before I can respond, she slides her chair from the table, forcing my hand to drop away from her. I growl, already missing the feel of her, but all she does is smile at me. She knows exactly what she's doing to me, and the wide grin on her face tells me she's loving it.

"No, what's a sin is what I plan to do to you later, rebel."

She bites her lip eagerly. "Is that a promise?"

I cough, completely taken aback by her response. This woman. I'm so fucking gone for her that there's no point in me even fighting against it... Fuck, I think I'm developing real, actual feelings for her.

"Now, I've never been on a yacht before, and I just have to explore. Walk with me?"

My chair scratches against the floor as I stand up abruptly. A few curious stares look our way, but for the most part, it doesn't capture the attention of others. I close the distance to her, proudly taking her hand in mine.

"I'd love to show you somewhere more private."

"Oh, don't get any ideas," she whispers, letting me lead her away from the crowd. "I've had enough public sex for the day. You're going to have to wait until we're back at the house."

34
Emma

"I THINK I COULD GET USED TO BEING ON A YACHT," I TELL PRESTON as he leads me to the second level of the boat. The stairway is narrow and dim, but I trust him to guide me. We've already toured the first floor, even though I don't know if calling it a boat is the right word because it's massive and elaborate.

"Yeah?" Preston asks, leading me down a walkway. If I remember correctly, the blacked-out windows next to us are where the captain steers the boat from, and there's enough space for living quarters for him if at sea.

We stop at the back of the boat, both of us standing against the railing that overlooks the deck below us. "Yep. It's official, I'm a yacht person. Next, I need to find a way to actually go out to sea on one of these."

"We'll have to do that sometime," he responds.

I watch him carefully, wondering if I heard him correctly. He stares right back at me, his features set in stone. Either he doesn't realize he's said it, or he sees nothing wrong with it.

"Will we?" I ask cautiously.

My heart races in my chest as I wait for his answer. I don't know what I want it to be. I'm a mess—the biggest mess—and I'm under no impression I should be diving into some sort of relationship with anyone, not that I assume he'd even want that.

But it does make me sad to think about never seeing him again after Saturday. Maybe we should've talked more about this.

"Maybe." He makes the word sound so confident.

I search his eyes for answers. "I thought we were never going to see each other again after Saturday," I confess. I know it's probably not the right thing to say, but I don't care. I don't want to dwell on what-ifs anymore. I want to know how he feels and not have regrets or wonder what would've happened if I'd been honest.

Preston reaches out and tucks a piece of hair behind my ear. His hand lingers as he cups my cheek.

"What are you thinking?" I whisper, wishing he wore his emotions on his sleeve. Occasionally, I've seen breaks in his resolve and could read his features, but he's so good at keeping what he feels hidden that right now, I have no idea what's running through his mind.

"I'm thinking that I have no idea what's happening between us. And that when I conned you into being my fake girlfriend for the week, I thought that I'd be okay with letting you go at the end of it."

"But now?"

"Now I hate the thought of saying goodbye to you."

"I know." I should probably say more, but I don't know what else to say to him. I could tell him that I feel the same and I hate the idea of never seeing him again after this. But I'm trying to think more long-term—something I clearly haven't done before.

I don't know what anything past this week would look like for us. I don't even know what *my* life will look like weeks from now. I'm a mess and have so many things to figure out, but for right now, I just want him to know that I don't want to say goodbye either.

He moves his hand to the back of my neck as his thumb tilts my chin up. "I don't let anyone in my head." His free hand taps my temple before both of his hands are cupping my cheeks. "But you managed to do it, Emma. You're in my head. And the craziest part is that I don't even want you out of it."

"You really say all the right things." I lift on my tiptoes, my hands finding his forearms as my lips find his. I don't have the right words to say to him, so I don't use words at all. I kiss him, not caring if someone were to see us. Nothing matters but reveling in every second I have with this man.

The kiss is slow, but it still makes my heart beat furiously. I don't know how long we stay locked in it, but somehow, it feels like time both stands still and flies by all at once.

Eventually, he pulls away, a whisper of a smile on his lips. "Tell me where you'd like to go on this yacht."

My eyes widen with excitement. I sigh, turning to look out over the deck and at the ocean around us. "*Anywhere.* I don't think you could pick a wrong place to visit when aboard something like this."

He steps behind me, pressing his front to my back. His arms come around my waist as he rests his chin on my shoulder. I let out a sigh, my body feeling completely content as I let myself melt into him.

"Well, where have you gone?" he asks. His chest rumbles against my back with his deep, throaty rasp.

"On a yacht? Wherever we're going tonight."

"No, I meant where have you traveled to before? I don't want to take you somewhere you've already been when I could take you somewhere completely new."

"I've never been out of the country, so your options are pretty limitless."

His fingers tighten slightly at my hips. "Never?"

I shake my head. "Never. I'm not very well traveled, Preston Rhodes."

"Now you're making me want to take you to every country in the world."

I smile at the thought, imagining what it'd be like to travel the world with him. I bet he's the kind of guy who has a perfect itinerary planned out to the hour. "Is that a promise?"

He hugs me tight to his chest, completely enveloping me in him. "I hope it is."

35
Preston

"Never did I think I'd hear the word *penis* that many times from your grandmother's mouth in one night." Emma laughs from the passenger seat of my car as she stares out the window.

I pull into the driveway of Moore's house, trying not to cringe at Emma's comment. Hearing the word *penis* come from my Gram's mouth once was enough for me to last a lifetime. Tonight, she felt the need to ask why there was nothing penis-shaped or why there weren't strippers far too many times for my liking.

"She really is something," I say, trying to wipe the memories from my mind with a grimace.

"I love her. She's a national treasure that must be protected at all costs."

I laugh, wondering if Gram would love Emma calling her that or if she'd make a snide comment asking if Emma was calling her old. "Let's change the subject from Gram's disappointment on Peyton's lack of a penis-themed bachelorette party."

"I'm sorry." She laughs again, shaking her head as I put the car in park. "It's just so funny. She's hilarious, and I'm obsessed with her."

I wish you were obsessed with me. My eyes go wide with the thought as I try to push it aside. I need to rein myself in and remind myself I only just met her. I shouldn't be thinking any of those things about her, but I can't help it.

"Can I walk you in?" I ask Emma, turning to face her.

She nods, the whisper of a smile on her lips. We stare at one another, searching each other's eyes for I'm not sure what.

The summer breeze picks up around us. It was the perfect night to keep the top down on the car. I loved taking the back roads on the way home from the marina. Normally, I like to get from point A to point B as quickly as possible, always in a rush to get to the next thing. But tonight, after the party, I wanted to take things as slow as possible. I wanted to savor the moment with her.

I wanted the chance to commit to memory the way her hair blew in the wind, the way she'd let out the cutest giddy noises when I took a turn a little faster than I should, or when she'd closed her eyes and leaned back in her seat to feel every curve we took in the road.

I love how she seems to live in the present and wants to enjoy every second of it. I need more of that in my life.

"Let's go in, then," I finally get out. My voice is hoarse, clogged with the overwhelming feeling that she's someone I'll think about for years to come.

"Can we just sit out here for one more minute? It's beautiful out."

I nod, reaching across the center console and grabbing her hand. I let our intertwined fingers rest in her lap as we sit in silence in the middle of the driveway. It's peaceful and just another time she's forced me to slow down and appreciate the small things, like a beautiful summer night sitting next to the perfect girl.

"I really love your family." Emma finally speaks up.

I look over at her, expecting her to be looking at me, but she isn't. She has her eyes closed and her head against the headrest. I don't know how I managed it, but somehow, I got the most beautiful woman on the planet to pretend to be my girlfriend, and I'm well aware of how lucky I am that she said yes.

"They love you," I respond, just now remembering she'd said something. I was too lost in admiring her high cheekbones and slightly upturned nose to respond right away.

She smiles but still doesn't open her eyes. "That makes me happy. I feel bad. I was wrong about you guys when we first met at the club."

I let out a small breath of air. "Don't feel bad. You weren't wrong. There was just more to us."

Her eyes finally open, and my chest hitches at the sight of her big blue eyes aimed right at me.

"Thank you for sitting out here for a little longer."

I squeeze her hand, loving how perfectly it fits in mine. "I'd sit out here as long as you wanted, if it meant spending more time with you."

Her eyelids flutter shut for a moment as she shakes her head. "You've got to stop being so honest. Especially when everything you say is so perfect."

"Only with you," I confess. I lift her hand and bring it to my lips. I press a kiss to the back of her hand before I turn it over, exposing her wrist to me. I begin to pepper kisses down the inside of her wrist. She lets out a contented sigh, her lips turning up in a slight smile. "I'm not always the most open person with others."

"Trust me, I know," she responds sarcastically. I continue to trail kisses along the inside of her wrist, letting my tongue peek out occasionally to tease her. "Your grumpy demeanor doesn't go unnoticed."

I shake my head, dropping her hand and leaning across the center console to place my face close to hers. "Will you ever drop the grumpy nickname? You make me sound like one of Snow White's dwarves."

Emma laughs, the sound like a melody. "Oh my god. Now I

can't get the mental picture of you whistling and marching through the meadow out of my head."

"What am I going to do with you, Emma Turner?"

"Take me inside."

I smile before leaning in and stealing a kiss. "You don't have to tell me twice," I respond as I pull away.

I'm quick at opening my door and rounding the car so I can open hers. She waits for me to open it, eagerly taking my outstretched hand as I help her out of her seat.

We're quiet as we walk to the front door. She doesn't stop and turn to face me at the door like she has in the past. She goes straight to pressing the code into the lock. The door swings open, and she takes a step inside. I wait at the doorstep, not sure if I'm supposed to go back to the guest house or if I can go inside and spend all night taking my time with her.

She turns to shut the door and frowns when she finds me still standing on the welcome mat. "Why aren't you coming in?"

"You didn't invite me in."

"Are you a vampire? Come in, Preston." She dramatically waves me forward with a roll of her eyes.

I stare at her, confused as I step inside. "What? No, I'm not a vampire. I was just trying to be a gentleman."

She closes the door before leaning against it. Her purse drops to the ground with a soft thud as she keeps eye contact with me. "I don't want you to be a gentleman. You've been making promises all day about what you want to do to me, Rhodes. It's time you make good on your promises."

I swallow as the playfulness between us seems to disappear, replaced with a thick sexual tension as my mind races with all the things I said I wanted to do to her once I got her alone again.

Emma lifts a foot and begins to undo one of her heels.

"No," I speak up, my voice echoing off the high ceilings of the entryway. "The heels stay on."

She smiles before putting her foot back down. Her fingers

drift up her thighs as she bunches the smooth fabric of the yellow dress. "And what about this?"

My pulse thumps erratically in anticipation of what's to come. I've been dreaming about getting that damn dress off her all night, and now's the time.

"The dress needs to come off. *Now*."

I close the distance between us, taking her face in my hands and yanking her to me. She yelps, but her mouth is still ready for me the moment our lips connect. Her hands drop from her dress and instead grab at the lapels of my suit jacket. She tugs me lower as her mouth opens up even wider for me.

She's been thinking about doing this again as much as I have, and I fucking love it.

I grab the fabric of her dress and begin to lift it up, needing to see every naked inch of her again. She grabs me by the hands. "Wait," she pants, her breaths becoming more labored by the second.

"What is it?"

"Make one more promise to me before we do this again."

I kiss along her collarbone, loving the taste of her skin against my tongue. "I'll promise you anything you want, rebel."

"Don't leave tonight. After this happens—" She lets out a shaky breath. "After we do this again, just tell me you'll stay after."

My lips pause against her shoulder at the vulnerability in her tone. I straighten my spine and bring my eyes to hers. "I'll be here in the morning, Em. There's nowhere else I'd rather be. I promise you that."

36

Emma

I wake up from the most peaceful sleep I've ever gotten to a strong arm wrapped around my middle. Warmth surrounds me from Preston's solid body behind me. He's got me tucked against him so we touch almost all the way from head to toe. Even my foot is trapped between us underneath the sheets as if he was trying to get every point of contact possible.

Aunt V once went through a phase where she wanted to talk about people's different love languages. We'd go out to eat and watch people around us, trying to guess what we thought theirs was. It's something I still do, and with how much Preston always seems to make sure our bodies are making contact, I'd bet his love language is physical touch. And I love that. Anytime our skin no longer touches, I miss the heat of his body.

A content sigh falls from my lips as my eyes flutter open. Sunlight fills the room, illuminating the piles of our clothing from the night before. My stomach flutters at the thought of last night—*and* this morning.

Preston definitely made good on his promises. I thought nothing could top what happened between us at the spa, but I was very wrong. Last night was...everything. My body is sore, and I don't know if it's from tennis yesterday or from him. He had me bent into positions I didn't know were possible. I knew he gave off vibes that he liked to be in control...but last night only proved that he thrives on control. And I surprisingly love giving it to him.

Don't even get me started on the number of orgasms he gave me.

I'm grateful that the only thing we have to attend today is the rehearsal dinner tonight. The rest of the day is free for us to do whatever we want. Which apparently started with us sleeping in pretty late, judging by how bright the room is.

I gently grab Preston's hand, wanting to sneak out of bed and make us coffee. I've lifted three of his fingers when his grip on me tightens.

"Where do you think you're going?" His voice is raspier than normal. Shivers run down my spine at how sexy it is.

"I was going to make us coffee." I turn to face him, propping my head up by my elbow against the pillow.

"Screw coffee. Stay in bed with me for a few more minutes." His fingers trace circles along my back, a gesture that means more than I could ever express.

His dark hair sticks up in different directions while some of it lies flat against his forehead. It makes him look younger and more carefree. I reach over to brush his hair back, my eyes momentarily closing at the memories of running my fingers through it last night while he rocked into me nice and slow, prolonging an orgasm he let build for what seemed like an eternity.

"Something wrong with my hair, rebel?" He pulls me closer to him by the hips until our middles are pressed against one another.

I shake my head. "No. I like your hair. You should wear it messy more often."

He reaches up and pushes my own hair from my forehead. I don't want to know what it looks like. I know it's got to be a tangled mess from last night, but it doesn't matter how it looks. Not when Preston's staring at me like I'm the most beautiful woman in the world.

"Sleep good?"

God. The deep, throaty tenor of his voice this morning is about to have me climbing on top of him to have a repeat from last night. It's like a caress to my libido every time I hear the scratch in his throat from the early hour.

I nod. "Slept great. I think it was the workout yesterday."

He smiles, running his thumb along my cheekbone. "We did get a good workout...worked lots of different muscles last night."

"Oh, I was talking about the tennis."

His morning voice is hot, but his morning laugh? I might be obsessed with it.

"I know I gave you a far better workout than tennis did."

I shrug, trying to play it cool. "Maybe."

His fingers trail to the back of my head before he pulls me to him. He kisses me, and I want to protest that I haven't brushed my teeth yet this morning, but he doesn't give me time.

This kiss is more chaste than the ones we shared last night, but somehow, it might do more to me than any other kiss we've shared. This one goes right to my heart, the thing I've been trying to protect this entire time.

I told Preston after he kissed me in front of his family that I wasn't girlfriend material, and I meant it. I'm not sure he's even in the right spot in his life to be in a relationship, but when he kisses me tenderly like this, I find myself hoping we could make it work.

He pulls away but doesn't make any kind of move to get up. The only thing he does is copy the same position I'm in. He rests his chin against his palm and pushes his elbow into the pillow to support the weight.

For a few moments, all we do is stare at each other. He looks good in the morning light. Never did I think I'd ask him to stay the night with me. I never ask *anyone* to stay with me. I prefer my own space and to wake up alone, but I'm loving waking up to him a little too much.

I'm the first one to break eye contact, needing a moment away from the intense way he looks back at me. I choose to trace the defined shape of his bicep with my gaze. I swallow before I get the nerve to reach out and trail over the lines of his snake tattoo with my fingertip.

"I feel like I should tell you something," I confess, my heartbeat picking up with nerves. I've never once said his name online, but since I posted that first video when I arrived in the Hamptons, my following has grown exponentially. I've tried to keep as many details about Preston and his family secret while only speaking on my experience this week, but I don't want to hide it from him anymore. Not that I wanted to hide it from him to begin with; it just never felt like the right time to let him know.

"Yes to whatever you want," he responds.

I roll my eyes, my finger pausing its lazy trail along the ink on his skin. "I said I have to *tell* you something, not *ask* you something."

"Then tell me."

I rub my lips together, wondering what's the best way to start the conversation. My cheeks puff out as I let out a deep breath. "The first night we met...my first night here..."

He lifts an eyebrow, the hint of a smile on his lips. "I remember it very well."

His response makes me smile and calms my nerves slightly. "Well, that night, I decided to make a video—while very tipsy— and tell my small number of followers at the time about coming to the Hamptons to figure my life out. I was honest, almost *too* honest, telling them how I wanted to make mistakes and learn this summer and find myself by the end of it. I guess it resonated with a lot of people in the same position as me because I woke up the next morning to a ton more followers and that video at millions of views. Instead of panicking about being in the limelight, I decided to try and embrace it. I've been filling them in on the week we've had together...leaving out the exact details, of course, to keep your family's privacy."

My stomach is in knots awaiting his response. I should've told him sooner—I know that—but I also just didn't know how to admit to this man that I've gone viral for being a complete mess.

My heart is about to beat right out of my chest when he finally responds. The corner of his mouth turns up in what I swear is the start of a smile. Maybe he's not upset like I feared he'd be.

"I know."

I've already opened my mouth to begin apologizing when it snaps shut as his words register. "You know?" Out of all the responses he could've given me, the one he gave was one that never crossed my mind.

Preston nods. "One of Peyton's bridesmaids saw the video and showed Peyton, so then Peyton showed me. I liked the video. It takes a lot of courage to be that vulnerable with strangers."

My face feels hot with his answer. I never thought about how viral the video went and how people I'm spending the week with could be watching my updates without me even knowing.

He reaches out and lifts my chin so I look at him. "Why are you turning red? It isn't a big deal. Peyton changed my name in her phone to Sports Guy as a joke. You couldn't think of a better nickname?"

I groan as I fall facedown into my pillow. "I can't believe you knew and didn't tell me."

"I figured you'd tell me about it when you wanted to...*if* you wanted to." He places his hand on my back. The weight of it feels good despite the utter embarrassment rushing through me.

I keep my face buried in the pillow. Realistically, I should've thought about the fact someone attending the wedding would see the video. Not to mention, the videos I've posted after are getting way more views than I can even comprehend. I should've known better.

"I can't believe your entire family knows I'm such a mess."

"I don't know if Peyton told anyone but me. If anyone in the family knows, they haven't mentioned it. You're not a mess. You're just figuring life out."

With a dramatic sigh, I push my body off the pillow and muster up the confidence to meet his eyes. The skin around them crinkles at the sides from his grin. "You're kind of cute when you're embarrassed."

"So, you're not mad at all?"

His fingers still rest on the small of my back, except now they trace little circles that make my skin break out in goosebumps. "No, I'm not mad. You haven't done anything wrong. I hate anything on the internet only because of the narrative they paint of me. I like how you're choosing what you're putting out there and telling your own story the way you want it to be told."

"You're acting like anyone cares about my story."

His head cocks to the side. "Clearly, tons of people care not only about your story but about *you*, rebel." He's quiet for a moment, his eyes tracking my face before his next words are said in an almost whisper. "I feel the same as them."

My chest hitches with his admission. Something in the air feels different between us this morning, and I don't know why. It might be the fact it's the morning, and I've never spent the morning in bed with someone before. Or maybe it's the fact that the sunlight filtering through the curtains paints everything in a more vulnerable light. The way his hair is messy or that there's a tiny line across his cheek from where he slept on his pillow. It makes everything feel less guarded.

"I promise I won't tell people about us. Even after this week...I won't put your name out there when it's so obvious you try to stay away from social media."

I've never once mentioned what sport he plays or what club all of the events are taking place at. There are tons of country clubs here in the Hamptons, just none of them as exclusive as Pembroke Hills. I've read comments where people swore they saw me and a former baseball player at Hilltop Country Club, and more where they argued I've actually been spotted with a former Olympic swimmer at Fairway Club.

I can't keep track of all my comments, but I have been reading some, and from what I can tell, no one has caught on to the fact I've been at Pembroke with Preston, but then again, no one has been posting about Peyton's wedding at all.

She mentioned to me at the garden party that she didn't want any pictures from the events posted online until after the nuptials took place just so she could post the professional ones first. Still, I should probably check with her that my videos haven't given too many details about her wedding celebrations to the world before she was ready.

"You don't have to make that promise to me. I trust you. All you're doing is sharing your story, and I'm the lucky sports guy that gets to be a part of your journey."

This conversation has gone way better than I thought it would, making me feel almost worse because I should've just told him the moment he picked me up for the garden party. At that point, I was still coming to terms with the fact my face—and my hot mess of a story—was in front of millions of viewers. Now I'm just...

"Oh my god," I rush out in a panic as a thought pops into my head. "Did I blow our cover for Peyton, then? I've said in my videos how we just met and—"

He places his fingers to my lips. "I told her we came up with that part of the story ahead of time for privacy reasons."

I frown. "And she believed it?"

He lifts a shoulder. "I think so. We really didn't talk long about it, I promise. It isn't a big deal."

37
Preston

Emma stares at me apprehensively, her eyelids slightly narrowed as if she doesn't quite believe me that her making videos isn't a big deal. I don't know why it'd shock her. What she posts on the internet—especially when she never once mentions my name—has nothing to do with me. If part of finding herself this summer is doing it with millions of people witnessing it, then that's her journey and not really my business.

"Will you stop worrying about this? I don't care. Peyton doesn't care. Continue on with what makes you feel good the way you have been." I reach out and pull Emma's bottom lip from between her teeth. Even after I do it, she goes right back to chewing it anxiously.

I roll my eyes, deciding to pull her body against mine. I've never been one that gets the best sleep. I've had many trainers over the years lecture me on how essential sleep is to recovery and that I need to do more to rest better at night, but nothing ever really worked. I just got used to functioning on little rest. But I'm scared to admit how great I slept last night with her in my arms. I don't know if I've ever felt so at peace, and I definitely can't think of the last time I woke up feeling so well rested. And it's all because of the woman I've pulled to my chest, who watches me with a careful expression.

"Peyton's probably wondering why you're with someone who is such a mess."

I sigh. "Stop calling yourself a mess."

"But I am a mess."

"You're young. You aren't supposed to have your life together yet. At least you aren't pushing forty, about to go into your last year of the only job you've ever known and have no idea if it'll be the worst or best decision you've ever made."

She folds her hands over my chest and places her chin on top of them. My arm snakes around her waist, my hand pressing to her back as I wait for her response. If she can feel my heart rate increase with my honesty, she doesn't say anything about it.

"Which one do you think it'll be?"

"Like I said. Although I haven't formally let the team or my agent know that I won't be signing another contract, this next season will be my last one."

Emma nods. "I know that. I meant, do you think leaving football will be the worst decision or the best one?"

Her question surprises me a bit. I figured she'd ask me why I wanted to be done with football or if I was actually sure in my decision. What I didn't expect was for her to ask me something that seems to have an obvious answer. "If I thought it'd be bad for me, do you really think I'd be choosing to quit?"

Emma shifts her body until she lies fully on top of me. Her feet kick in the air as she gets comfortable lying across my torso. "First, don't use the word *quit*. It takes away from the years— well, actually, I guess at your age, decades—you spent dedicated to the sport." She winks at me, probably trying to soften the blow of the age comment.

"Did you just call me old, rebel?"

She raises her eyebrows and purses her lips. "Never once did I use the word *old*. And don't try changing the subject. There's a difference between quitting and knowing when it's time to move on. And if you feel like it's time to move on, then you already know the decision could never be the worst thing for you."

I stare at her for a moment as I wonder how the universe works. What had to happen for her to scale that fence at the exact time I'd stepped out to take a break? Were we meant to meet no matter what? If I'd been five minutes later going outside, would our paths still have crossed somehow?

I'd like to think so. I can't imagine a universe where Emma Turner wasn't meant to crash into my life. I refuse to accept that even if she hadn't decided to sneak into Peyton's party or I hadn't needed some air, that we wouldn't have met some other way.

What I'm confident in is that she's doing things to me no one else has done before. She's making me feel things I've never felt. And it's terrifying because she made it very clear she wasn't looking for anything outside of this week. I didn't think I'd want anything after either, but now I feel empty at the thought of never seeing her again after this weekend.

Emma scrunches her nose, lifting her head slightly so she can better look at me. "Was that last part too much? Did it sound a little too much like a life coach?"

I laugh, the deep rumble of my chest bouncing her up and down from where she lies on me. "No. What you said was perfect. I haven't told many people about wanting to retire, so your response to it just wasn't what I was expecting."

"And what were you expecting?"

"For you to tell me I should give it a couple more years. That I'm just disappointed after losing the Super Bowl last year and I just need to get some more wins under my belt again."

"Is this the right time to tell you I know nothing about football? I had no idea you made it to the Super Bowl or that you lost. Super Bowls for me have always been about the halftime show and amazing food."

I shake my head. I don't know how I've ended up developing feelings for a woman who not only doesn't give a shit that I play football but also has no idea about anything to do with the sport. "I'm shocked you didn't bring up the commercials."

Her eyes go wide. "Oh my god, I forgot about the commercials. Those are for sure a main reason to watch."

"And not the actual game going on?"

She playfully bites her lip. "I've already confessed to you I don't care about the game."

"You will next year when I'm playing in it." The moment the words leave my mouth, I wonder if I should've said them or not. It isn't the first time I've alluded to the fact I want her past this week. I'm waiting for her to call me out on it, for us to broach the subject of our arrangement again so I can tell her I don't think what we previously decided on will work for me anymore.

I can't help but feel a tinge of disappointment when she seems to gloss right over my comment. "I think you need to make the official call that this will be your last year. Stop waffling on your decision and make it. Let anyone who tries to change your mind know that it's useless. Be confident in your choice and stick to it."

"You make that sound so simple."

Her hands find either side of my face. I love the feeling of her fingers brushing through the overgrown locks of my hair. She looks at me with her bright blue eyes and her beaming smile, and it's almost painful how happy I feel in this very moment. "It is simple. You're just making it complicated because you don't want to disappoint people."

I raise my eyebrows because damn...she's spot-on. For someone who loves to mention how much of a mess she is, she really does have a grasp on others. "I think I'm done with the analyzing for the morning. Maybe we should talk more about what you want to do with your life after this summer and what makes you happy?"

I grab the back of her neck and pull her face to me, trailing my lips down her neck. She laughs against my chest, and I love the feel of it. I love the feel of her. I continue to dust kisses along her neck until I pull away to meet her eyes.

She looks between my lips and eyes. Her lips rub together

before she gives me a shy smile. "Right now, what makes me happy is *you*. And that's all I want to think about at the moment."

When she leans in to kiss me, I let her, even though it's at the tip of my tongue to ask her to make me part of her plans for the summer and even after that.

38
Emma

I STARE AT MYSELF IN THE MIRROR, SMOOTHING THE FABRIC OF THE dress I'm wearing for what seems like the hundredth time.

Preston steps behind me, placing his hands on my hips as he stares at our reflections in the mirror. "Stop running your hands over the fabric," he instructs, kissing right below my ear. "I spent almost an hour steaming all the wrinkles out."

I smile, remembering the sight of him steaming my dress in nothing but a pair of his boxer briefs. It was hot as hell, and I almost want to wrinkle the dress all over again just to see him like that. "Oh, but you looked *so* good doing it," I respond.

He trails his lips down my neck, making my eyelids flutter shut. We spent almost all of yesterday in bed together until we had to get ready for the rehearsal dinner. It felt almost normal. Like he wasn't one of the most famous athletes in the world, and as if I wasn't only pretending to be his girlfriend for the week.

"Have I told you how beautiful you look today?" His hands tighten around my hips as his lips continue to blaze a path across my skin, sending shivers down my spine.

"You might've mentioned it a few times." The moment I opened my eyes this morning and found him already awake and watching me, he told me I was beautiful. He mentioned it again as I helped him make breakfast wearing nothing but a Manhattan Mambas shirt of his. I know he told me other times today as we got ready for his sister's wedding day, and every time he said it, my heart leapt inside my chest.

"Well, I'm saying it again. I have the most beautiful date for the wedding, and I cannot wait to show you off."

"Speaking of the wedding, we probably should get going." I give him a smile through the mirror, even though inside, I'm twisted up with nerves. It isn't because of the wedding. It's because of what comes after.

Preston hasn't given me any details about when he's leaving or what his plans are, but our little agreement was only for me to be his date to the wedding. I've done my job. His sister's friends have left him alone, and I haven't overheard anyone trying to meddle with his love life since he introduced me as his.

Every time he mentions something about having me come to his games next year or that he's getting used to waking up to me, I wait for him to say he wants more than this week. He hasn't, and since I know I shouldn't want something more from him when I have no idea where I'll end up, I keep my mouth shut.

But faking it with him doesn't feel fake at all anymore. And I don't know what happens next.

All Preston does is continue to kiss along my neck and bare shoulder. I wish he wasn't due for pictures at Pembroke soon. I want to get back in bed with him and forget that it's already the end of our week together.

"Preston," I say, his name coming out breathy as my entire body lights up with desire. "We have to get to your sister's wedding. You can't be late for pictures."

"But I'm having so much fun watching my girlfriend blush for me."

My girlfriend. God, the way he says it makes me believe everything between us is real.

"I think this is the first time in my life that I'm the responsible one," I joke, pushing his hands from my hips, even though I miss the warmth the moment they're gone. "As much as I'd love to stay here with you, we have to go, Rhodes. Now."

He lets out a low groan of disapproval but doesn't protest anymore. "I don't like responsible Em as much." He takes a step closer to the mirror and fixes his tie in it, something he's done multiple times already.

If it isn't perfectly straight, he'll obsess and fidget with it until it's to his liking. I find it incredibly cute, though I wonder if that's something he's going to still fuss over even at the wedding when he's supposed to be having fun.

I use the opportunity to check him out again. Peyton's wedding is black-tie. All of the guests were asked to wear black, and Preston looks incredible all dressed up. I thought I'd seen him dressed up this week in his button-ups and linen shirts, but none of them hold a candle to how he's dressed right now.

The black suit is perfectly tailored to his body, and I might get in trouble tonight staring at the way the fabric hugs his perfect arms. I wet my lips just thinking about the tattoos he hides under the jacket. They're my kryptonite.

"Ready?" he asks, stepping away from the mirror.

I nod, forcing a smile even though I just want to stop time for the night. Soon, I won't be able to trace the ink on his body with my fingertip while he falls asleep or see his tousled hair in the morning, and that knowledge makes me sad.

I wanted to find myself this summer, but within the first week of being here, I've found something else. Something so deep and powerful I want to hold on to it forever, but I don't know how.

Preston stops in front of me, grabbing each side of my face and cradling my cheeks in his palms. His thumbs brush over my cheekbones. I should tell him to be careful of the makeup I'd spent an hour applying, but I don't. I want this moment with him. I want any moments I can get with him.

His eyes flick to my lips. I lined them with lipstick which now, looking back, was a dumb idea because I don't know if he'll want to kiss me and risk getting it all over him. Especially before the wedding.

As if he can read my mind, he leans in and softly brushes his lips against mine. He's asking to kiss me without using any words, and in an instant, I'm standing on my tiptoes, even in my heels, to get better access to his mouth.

I press our lips together harder, needing more of him. He doesn't protest. His grip on my face tightens as we fuse our mouths together. We stay like that for a few moments, savoring the nearness of one another.

I'm the first one to break contact, worried that if I allow myself to feel the press of our lips any longer, then we really will be late to Peyton's wedding.

"Alright, Rhodes, we really do have to go. Peyton's been talking about how over-the-top today's going to be. I'm ready to witness it."

This makes him laugh. He holds out his hand, and I gladly take it, letting him lead me out of the room. I grab my small purse from the kitchen counter, opening it to make sure I have everything I need.

Preston's about to open the front door to leave when he turns around and looks at me. "Didn't you want to make a video before leaving? Tell your followers how this elusive wedding is finally happening?"

I smile, unable to rein in the way my heart races at the fact he remembered me mentioning how I wanted to film something today. Time kind of got away from us—mostly because when he started running his hand up my thigh during breakfast, I couldn't help but have him right there in the kitchen—so I didn't have time to get ready and film something. "I wanted to, but it's okay. I can give them an update later."

He gives one shake of his head. "No. Update your followers, and then we'll leave."

"I'll do it in the car."

He stares at me, and I stare back. I've learned we're both incredibly stubborn. I refuse to make him late for this wedding, so if he thinks I'm going to sit here and make a video when we should be on our way, he's very mistaken.

Today, I win this round because with a long sigh, he turns around and opens the door, waiting for me to walk through before he closes it. As I make sure the house is locked, he's opened the door to his rental already and is waiting for me.

"Hottest chauffeur I've ever had," I joke, sliding into the seat. He put the top on for the day, something that I'm a little sad about, but I understand why he did it. I carefully curled my blonde hair for the occasion, and as much as I love feeling the breeze against my cheeks, I want to keep it nice, at least until the reception. Then all bets are off because I love dancing at weddings. Pair dancing with an open bar and my hair's bound to be a mess by the end of tonight.

"I better be the hottest *anything* you've ever had," Preston responds as he slides into the driver's seat. I always find it funny how massive he looks in the sports car. He has to push the seat all the way back, and it still seems like he doesn't quite have enough room for his long, toned legs.

"Mmmm, you'd like that, wouldn't you?" I fire back, getting out my phone to at least take a picture of myself before going to the event. I don't know if I could record a video with Preston here even if I had the time. It's a lot easier to talk to the camera when no one is watching you do it.

Before Preston can counter with some sort of jealous remark that'll send my pulse spiking, I open the camera and hold my phone out in front of me. I focus my face on the screen and then snap the picture to share on my story. It's only when I bring the phone closer to me that I realize that Preston's arm is in it.

He puts the car in drive as I look over at him. "Your arm ruined my selfie."

"Let me see."

I angle the phone towards him. You can't see his face or anything that proves who I'm with, but his arm and shoulder are in the corner of the photo, and I'm sure many people would notice him being there if I were to keep it.

"Post it. They can get a little tease of your sports guy."

I stare at him, trying to figure out if he's being serious. "You sure?"

"Positive."

I can't hide my smile, and I don't want to. I know it isn't a big deal. You can't even tell who he is. But I like that he wants me to post him, even if it's just his arm. It still means *something*. It feels special. So I post it with no caption at all and put my phone away.

Tonight, I want to live in the moment with him and not worry about what happens tomorrow. For tonight, he's mine— my sports guy—and that's got to be good enough for me.

39

Preston

My baby sister is married.

I didn't think I'd feel emotional at the fact. From the moment Peyton met Jackson, she'd said the two of them would get married, but watching them exchange vows made it real. She's all grown up, and it happened so fast. It feels like just yesterday she was forcing me to sit at tea parties with her stuffed animals, and now she's had the most beautiful wedding, which hopefully all came together to be her dream event.

The entire club was rented out for the day, and their ceremony took place on the golf course overlooking the ocean. The weather was perfect, and the event was so beautiful. I'm just waiting for Emma to comment on how she caught me wiping my eyes during their vows. Jackson is one of the most unique guys I've ever met, but it was clear today how happy he makes my sister. His vows were so good it made up for all the things I've questioned about him in the past.

Emma slides into her chair next to mine with two glasses of champagne in her hand. "Not to alarm you, but I almost just accidentally knocked over the entire champagne tower grabbing these."

I pull my eyes from where Peyton and Jackson embrace on the dance floor, raising an eyebrow in Emma's direction. "How'd that happen?"

"I was trying to get one of the ones at the top with the cotton candy in them because duh, cotton candy. While I was reaching for one of them, my hip bumped the table, and, well...I almost ruined your sister's wedding."

She hands one of the champagnes to me. I take it, mesmerized by her animatedly telling the story. I hand the piece of cotton candy from mine over to her since she clearly wanted the cotton candy badly. "You didn't almost ruin Peyton's wedding." I point to where Jackson and Peyton are lost in their own world on the dance floor, even as other people join them. "I don't think Peyton would've even known if the glasses came crashing to the ground."

"Well, I'm still glad it didn't happen. Someone could've gotten that on video, and I'd be viral all over again." She sticks her tongue out and places the cotton candy on it. I watch it melt and fight the urge to lean in and taste the cotton candy straight from her mouth.

I smile at her, staring at a small piece that's stuck to the corner of her mouth. She continues to rattle on about how she's ready to go out there and start dancing, but I don't catch all of her words. I'm too transfixed in staring at her to say anything.

Emma pauses, her hands flying to her face. "Do I have something on me?" She wipes across her face, still not getting the small piece of cotton candy.

"Let me help," I respond, my voice hoarse. Emotions are bubbling up inside me, and I don't know how to process them. All I know is she means far more to me than I care to admit, and I refuse to believe our story ends after tonight.

I lean in, licking the cotton candy from the corner of her mouth.

Emma watches carefully, her eyes zoned in on me. The cotton candy melts on my tongue, making me want more. But not from the drink—from her mouth.

"Eating cotton candy shouldn't be so hot," Emma comments, shoving another piece in her mouth.

I laugh, not quite expecting the remark. "Trust me. I know." Her tongue peeks out to lick the extra pieces from her lips. The sight reminds me of this morning when she flattened her tongue along the length of my cock before licking me from base to tip. I shake my head, trying to rid my mind of the memory before I pull her from her chair and lead us somewhere private so I can have her again.

"Your sister's one of the most beautiful brides I've ever seen," Emma notes, her eyes finding Peyton and Jackson on the dance floor.

"She's really something."

Emma reaches over and grabs my hand, lacing our fingers together. I slide my foot underneath her chair and pull her closer to me. I feather kisses along the top of her hand, and she gives me a radiant smile. "Are you going to ask me to dance?"

My lips pause against her skin. Despite the constant events I've attended over the years where knowing my way around the dance floor is needed, I still hate dancing. But for her, I'd do anything.

I stand up and nod my head toward the dance floor. "Will you dance with me, rebel?"

"I've just been waiting for you to ask."

"Preston, I don't think you've looked away from her once today," Gram pipes up from my side at the table.

I pull my eyes from Emma dancing with Peyton on the dance floor and look at my grandmother. I cough, mildly taken aback by her calling me out like that. "I don't know what you're talking about."

Gram purses her lips. "Don't try to lie to me, dear. I can read you like an open book, and that sweet girl has you twisted up in knots."

I sit up in my chair, staring at her with a blank expression.

I'm not sure how to respond to her. "Us dating. It's very new. I'm still getting to know her." It isn't a lie. I am still getting to know her. We're just technically not dating, even though the thought of her with any other man makes me sick to my stomach.

Gram hums, her eyes staring at me like she can read every single one of my thoughts. As a kid, I used to think that she could because she'd know things I swore I never told anyone. She's insightful that way, and I should've known better than to sit alone with her. She loves to meddle, and she loves to be right; I'm not going to hear the end of what she thinks about how I feel about Emma.

She clicks her tongue, folding her arms across her chest after she realizes I'm not elaborating on my comment. "I know you're not trying to lie to me, Preston Nathanial Rhodes."

"I'm not lying. I just do—"

"You don't understand your feelings enough to admit them to me."

My thumb rubs along my bottom lip as I look at her and think through her words. "Yeah. That."

"Just because you don't admit your feelings doesn't mean they're not there."

"Are you my grandmother or my therapist?" My tone has a bit of a bite to it, but it doesn't deter her at all. She's used to my mood changes, so all she does is aim a knowing smile in my direction.

"Right now, apparently both because you can't get your head on straight to realize you're crazy about this girl."

I let out a defeated sigh as I fall backward in my chair. Gram's right. I *am* crazy about Emma. I just don't know what to do about it. The timing of us meeting seems all wrong. She's set on finding herself and has made it clear a relationship isn't in the cards for her right now, and I'm about to go into the last year of my football career. Logistically, it seems all wrong for me to feel this way about her. But logistics don't matter when it comes to the heart.

I just want her, no matter the cards stacked against us.

Gram leaves me alone to gather my thoughts. She surprisingly doesn't poke or prod to figure out what's going through my mind. She sits there quietly, letting me come to terms with my feelings.

Finally, I look up from staring at my hands in my lap and meet my grandmother's eyes once again. "I've never met anyone like her. How could I not be crazy about her?"

Gram nods, her lips pulling into a wide smile as she looks to Emma. My gaze follows her lead, finding Emma shimmying on the dance floor as Peyton laughs next to her.

"It's okay to feel that way about her and to be scared about the future. Being scared is just a sign that you care."

"That might be my problem. That I care."

"Only if you look at it that way. Or you could look at it as a good thing and think with your heart for once." She reaches across the table and taps my forehead. "You've always been wise beyond your years, Preston. But what if thinking with your head makes you miss out on what might be the best thing to ever happen to you?"

I swallow past the lump in my throat. I've been dreading tonight, knowing I'm supposed to go back to the city tomorrow. Now, I'm having to sit through my grandmother playing philosophical matchmaker, knowing she's making very valid points.

Emma and I cannot end tonight. We started as what was only supposed to be a week together for Peyton's wedding, but it's turned into something that feels like so much more. I don't know what more that will be long-term, but all I know is it can't end tonight.

"So, are you going to tell her how you feel?" Gram asks from my side. I'd been so deep in thought I hadn't realized how her cold hand had moved down to massage the back of my neck. She continues to circle the tender spot as I think about her question.

"Do I have much of a choice?" I tease, appreciating my

grandmother for giving me a push to admit my feelings. "If I don't tell her, it seems like you might."

She winks at me. "You know me well, dear."

The conversation falls off because there's nothing else to say.

For once in my life, I'm scared of losing something. I'm more than scared—I'm terrified. No matter my feelings, Emma could tell me that she isn't feeling the same things as I am. I feel dizzy about the thought, but it's something I have to prepare myself for. At this point, even if she tells me this isn't something special to her like it is to me, I have to try.

Tonight, I'm going to ask her for more, whatever more she'll give me. And all I can do is hope she wants the same.

40
Emma

"What a night," I mutter as Preston and I walk through the front door of the house. I don't even know what time it is, but I know we celebrated Jackson and Peyton into the early hours of the morning. I'm exhausted but also incredibly exhilarated by how perfect the night was.

"You hungry at all?" Preston asks, setting my heels he was carrying for me by the door.

I smile and nod. "I'm starved. It seems like the late-night snack the club served was hours ago."

"It *was* hours ago," Preston points out, walking over to the refrigerator. "And you barely left the dance floor. You need fuel for your body. I'll make us something." He's been quiet tonight. Even more quiet than normal. Even as he spun me around the dance floor, he wouldn't voice whatever was running through his head. Which is unfortunate because all I want to know is what he's thinking about.

"You being a good cook is really sexy." I still don't have the nerve to ask him why he's been so quiet, but I do want to break the tension now that it's just us.

I slide onto one of the barstools at the large island. I'd had a few drinks over the course of the night, but by this point, I barely even feel them anymore. I'm riding a high from the incredible time I had with Preston at the wedding.

But with that high comes the knowledge of what tomorrow will bring. Peyton and Jackson leave for their honeymoon, and Gram's already told me that a private plane is taking the rest of them back to Manhattan tomorrow afternoon.

My time with Preston is coming to an end, and I hate it. I want more of it. I want more of *him*. I don't even want to sleep until he steps onto a plane so I can soak in every moment I have with him.

"What sounds good to eat?" he asks as he rifles through the contents of the fridge. He'd put in a massive grocery order yesterday that completely stocked the fridge, which I found odd since he's leaving tomorrow, but I didn't question him on it.

"You know what I want?" I lean forward, placing my chin in my hands as I stare at him.

"What do you want?"

You. All I really want is you. "I want a grilled cheese."

Preston cocks his head to the side. "We have a fridge full of different ingredients, and you want something with only two?"

I nod. "I love a grilled cheese. But technically, it has to have a pickle on the side, so there's three right there."

"A pickle?"

"Yes. A pickle."

He watches me over his shoulder for a moment before turning back to the fridge. "Got it. One grilled cheese with a pickle coming right up."

"Hopefully you make two or you aren't hungry because I'm not sharing my food."

This makes Preston laugh. "Okay. No sharing. *Two* grilled cheeses, then."

We fall into a natural conversation as he makes the sandwiches. I love watching him cook and having normal conversations with him. I learn about his favorite movies, that he actually hates snakes but the tattoo was something he got done with the other rookies his first year, and he didn't want to admit to them he actually hated snakes. He tells me about his best friend from college, Ethan, and all the wild ideas Ethan's come up with over the years.

Time moves too quickly, and all too soon, both of our plates are completely wiped clean, and we're sitting in silence, the tension between us thick.

Preston swallows, his eyes focusing on my mouth. "How was the food?"

"Awful. The worst grilled cheese I've ever had."

His head cocks to the side. "So bad you ate every last bite?"

"Only because I was starving." I try to fight my smile, but it's no use. My lips turn up in a wide one. It was actually the best grilled cheese I've ever had, but I don't want to admit that to him and have it go to his head.

Preston shakes his head. Reaching out, he grabs the barstool I'm sitting on and pulls it toward him. The legs of the stool make a scratching sound against the floor as he pulls me between his thighs. He cages me in on either side as he stares me down with raised eyebrows. "Take it back."

I rub my lips together, slowly shaking my head at him. "No."

"Rebel." The nickname comes out as a warning as he stares at me. His gaze is intense, making me feel hot even though he isn't even touching me.

"Rhodes," I fire back, trying to mimic the warning tone to his voice but failing miserably. I'm having too much fun messing with him that I can't mask the teasing tone to my words.

"One more chance to tell me that was the best damn grilled cheese of your life."

I playfully shrug. "I've had better."

The words have barely left my mouth when his fingertips are pressing into my sides. I scream, not expecting the pressure he applies to my ribs.

"Preston!" I yell, squirming in the stool to try and get him to stop tickling me. He doesn't, making me laugh so hard that it gets hard to breathe.

"I warned you," he says next to my ear, playfully nipping at my ear as his fingers continue to dig into my sides.

"It was the best grilled cheese ever," I yell, ready to do anything to get him to stop tickling me. I can barely get words out through the laughter. I wouldn't be shocked if he wasn't even able to understand what I said through the fit of giggles.

Finally, Preston's fingers still. He keeps them pressed to my ribs but doesn't move them. My chest heaves up and down as I try to catch my breath. Suddenly, all the humor is gone. The air has thickened in just a few short seconds, and it's all because of the heated way he looks at me.

Everything pauses for a minute as we stare at one another. One second, I'm still in my own seat, only feeling the press of his fingertips through the fabric of my dress; the next, I'm being pulled onto his lap as I straddle him.

Our lips crash together like a powerful wave. We're teeth and tongue and the press of heated bodies against one another. My fingers fumble with the buttons of his shirt as he pushes the skirt of my dress up my hips. We're frantic at getting one piece of clothing off the other until I'm in nothing but a pair of panties and he's stripped down to his boxer briefs.

Preston sets me on the island. The stone is cold against the backs of my thighs, but I don't care. All I care about is his lips as they trail across my collarbone. His thumb brushes over my sensitive nipple, making my hips buck with eagerness. I want him to touch me. I'd take feeling the press of his skin anywhere, and he knows how touch-starved I am for it as he continues to let his fingers brush along my body as his lips travel down.

Finally, his mouth hovers above my peaked nipple. His breath is hot against my skin, teasing me as I wait for him to finally take my nipple into his mouth. He makes me wait, instead running his tongue along the skin around it. I moan, needing some sort of relief. It feels like I could combust with how much I need him.

His tongue circles my nipple one more time before he takes it in his mouth. His other hand cups my other breast, sending tingles down my spine. My toes curl as he switches from one nipple to the next, giving them both attention.

"Preston." His name comes out as a plea. As good as his mouth on me feels, I need more. I want him inside me, to feel him stretching me and molding my body to perfectly fit him.

"I know, baby," he mutters against my skin. "You need me, don't you?"

I nod, meeting his gaze when he lines his face up with mine. The movement makes him smile, his teeth raking against his lip in anticipation.

He leans in to kiss me, and I meet him halfway, letting him pull my body from the counter. I wrap my legs around his waist as he carries me to the bedroom. He kisses me the entire way to the bed, our lips only disconnecting for us to catch our breath before it continues.

Softly, he lays me down on the mattress. Our kiss breaks as he stands above me, his gaze intense as it traces my body.

"You're beautiful," he whispers.

I swallow. The air between us is still thick, but this is different. It feels heavier, like something more than lust.

His eyes don't leave my body as he pushes his boxer briefs down his thighs. I watch in awe as he wraps his fingers around his length and begins to move up and down.

"Come here." My voice is shaky from how badly I want—need—him. If tonight's the last night I have him, I want to spend every single second of it in his arms with our bodies joined.

Preston takes a step forward, his fingers hooking through the fabric of my thong at my hips and pulling down. I help him get the panties off me, needing them gone and nothing between us. It's one step closer to him being inside me.

The mattress dips with his weight as he places his body between my legs. His hands run up the sides of my thighs as if he's memorizing the feel of my skin against his fingertips. My heart races with the thought. Is he trying to commit every single moment of this night to memory? Does it pain him as much as it does me to think we might not get another night together after tonight?

"I know I should take my time with you," he begins, leaning over me and pressing his hand into the mattress next to my head. "If I was a gentleman, I'd let you come against my tongue before pushing inside you, but I don't want to be a gentleman tonight, Em. I need you—all of you—right now."

As if to prove his point, he runs the tip of himself along my clit. I moan, agreeing with him that it's exactly what I need.

I nod. "I need that too. Please, Preston."

He laughs as his lips travel along my jawline. "I love that my girl has manners, even when I'm being the furthest thing from a gentleman."

My clit throbs as he continues to circle it with his tip. I moan, ready for him to stop teasing me and push inside.

I'm getting ready to open my mouth and start begging for him to fuck me when he finally lines himself up perfectly and begins to push inside me inch by inch. He doesn't wait to give me time to adjust to him; his hips begin to move in and out of me in a slow, tantalizing rhythm.

I moan, letting out a shaky breath as I get adjusted to the size of him. He's been inside me plenty of times now, and still, I have to give my body a moment to take all of him. He stretches me perfectly, making my toes curl against the comforter with how good it feels.

My eyes flutter open as his fingers tenderly push the hair out of my face as he continues to rock in and out of me. He watches me with hooded eyes, intensity reflecting in his cobalt-blue eyes.

Leaning forward, he takes my lips in his and kisses me slowly in the same unhurried rhythm as his hips. I thought this time would be rushed after the frenzy of our bodies in the kitchen, but he's slowed it down. I don't mind—something I can't explain is happening between us.

He pulls away, the both of us staring into each other's eyes as our moans mix together with every thrust of his hips.

"Emma..." My name comes out like a question, broken and raspy. He looks at me so intensely I'm scared of what's running through his head.

"Yes?"

41
Preston

MY HIPS DON'T STILL AS I CONTINUE TO PUSH IN AND OUT OF HER. Emma watches me cautiously, her eyelids fluttering open and shut with pleasure with every thrust.

"What if I don't leave tomorrow?" My heart beats erratically in my chest. I've had enough of being sad all day, dreading tomorrow. There's no reason I have to leave with my family, and even if I had something I needed to get to, I'd cancel it for her.

This can't be the end of us. I can't say goodbye to her. Not when it feels like we're just getting started.

"What?" Emma asks, her hips rocking against mine. I hadn't even realized my thrusts had stilled until she moves against me.

"I don't want to leave tomorrow. I can't say goodbye to you, Emma. Not yet." *Not ever.* I keep the last part to myself. I don't know if she'll run if I'm completely honest with her, but I do need her to know that no part of me can stand the thought of never seeing her again after tonight.

"Do you mean that?" she whispers. Her eyes flutter shut as I thrust inside her, deep, wanting her to know that this thing between us is far from over. Things can't feel this perfect to not continue. I refuse to let that happen, and by the tentative way she asked if I meant it, I'm hoping she feels the same.

I run my thumb along her temple, feeling the weight of what's happening between us as I stare into her eyes. "Of course,

I mean it. Tell me to stay. Fuck, tell me to do anything, and I'll do it for you."

Her body trembles as she leans into my touch. I can feel her tighten around me, as if my words and me being inside her are too much. Maybe they are—I could come any minute with the way she perfectly fits around me paired with the loving look in her eyes.

Instead of answering, a low moan falls from her lips. She squeezes me so tight I know she's close to coming. I pick up my pace, wanting to get her that release.

"Tell me to stay," I repeat, my voice hoarse with emotion. "*Please.*" My voice breaks at the end of the word, but I don't care. I can't care when the look of adoration on her face tells me everything I need to know.

"Stay." Her breath hitches, as if it took her breath away to say the word out loud.

I don't let her say anything else. My mouth crashes against hers as soon as she gets the word out. It feels like my heart might beat right out of my chest with happiness. I still don't understand the depths of my feelings for her since we've only just met, but I know she's someone I can't let go.

With the tangle of our tongues and the punishing rhythm of my hips, it doesn't take long for her back to arch off the mattress.

"Preston." She practically screams my name, her nails digging into my back as she's sent over the edge. Her reaction to the orgasm has me chasing my release as well. My hips don't still as I continue to thrust in and out of her, making sure to draw out the orgasm for the both of us for as long as possible.

My lips find hers again, needing to feel that connection to her as we ride out the end of our releases. She kisses me back with so much passion it probably wouldn't take long for me to get worked up all over again. I slow down, because as much as I want her again, I need to talk to her more. I want to know if she meant it when she asked me to stay. I don't want to get my hopes up only for her to not feel the same as I do.

Finally, my hips stop altogether while we continue to kiss at a slow and lazy pace. Emma's the one to pull away, but it's only to aim the most beautiful smile in my direction. Her chest heaves up and down as she catches her breath.

"Did you mean it?" she finally gets out. Her voice is timid, as if she's nervous to ask the question.

I nod, slowly sliding out of her but not going far. I keep my hands pressed to either side of her head, holding my weight by my elbows to keep from crushing her. I have to swallow, my throat feeling clogged with how badly I wanted her to ask me to stay and how happy I am she did. "Of course, I mean it."

She pushes off the mattress and grabs my cheeks and pulls me closer to her, kissing me all over. The kiss slows before she stops it again and presses her forehead to mine. "I need two seconds to get cleaned up, and then we're talking about this more."

Before I can respond, she's slipping under my arm and dashing to the bathroom. I lie there for a few moments, basking in the happiness I feel at tonight not being our last, before I follow her in there.

"Maybe we just shower?" Emma offers with a smile.

I nod, loving the idea. She reaches inside and turns both showerheads on. We wait a minute for the water to heat up before getting in. The hot water feels good against my muscles as I close the door to the shower. Emma stands underneath the cascading water, letting it run over the blonde tendrils of her hair.

I take a step closer and stand underneath the water with her, wrapping my arms around her and pulling her body close to mine. She relaxes into me immediately, and for a moment, we just stand there with the water falling around us, enjoying the moment together.

Emma looks up, resting her chin against my chest. I turn our bodies slightly, wanting to make sure the water doesn't get in her eyes.

"Hi," she gets out. Pieces of hair stick to her face, and I move them out of her eyes, wanting to see them perfectly.

"Hi," I answer, my thumb brushing over her cheekbone.

"So about tomorrow…" Her words trail off as a bit of hesitancy makes its way into her tone.

"Yeah, about tomorrow. What should we do? Go to the club? Grab food somewhere? Or maybe we should visit the beach."

She smiles, her arms tightening around my middle. "Are you making plans with me, Rhodes?"

"I'm trying to."

Emma shakes her head and lifts to her tiptoes, bringing her face closer to mine. "I like the sound of plans with you. I'd love to hit the beach."

"So we'll go to the beach."

She looks down at her feet. "I'm nervous," she admits quietly. I barely hear it over the sound of both streams of water.

"Nervous about what?" I cup her cheek, trying to tilt her chin up so she'll look at me. She doesn't let me; instead, she keeps her face down as she stares at the shower floor.

When she finally meets my eyes, my stomach drops. There's so much vulnerability in the way she looks at me it makes my breath hitch for a moment. Vulnerable is not something I'm used to her being. She's always so confident and carefree, but right now, it seems she's scared—I'm just not sure of what.

"What if I'm too much for you?" Her words come out hurried and timid. She winces at the end of the question as if she regrets even asking it in the first place.

I tip her chin up, letting out a breath of relief when she lets me do it this time. I watch her for a minute, wondering how a woman so perfect can believe she's too much of anything. "What if you're perfect for me?" I respond, meaning every word.

Her eyes flutter shut for a moment. She leans into my caress. I love that she takes comfort in my touch. Now, if I can't feel her skin against mine, things feel off, so it's reassuring to know she might be feeling the same way.

"It's just that I'm only here for the summer. And I'm still a mess. What if you—"

I cut her off by kissing her. I don't want her to even waste her breath worrying about what could happen. My entire life has revolved around the future, so for once, I want to live in the right now and enjoy the time I have with her. I know eventually, we'll have to worry about what happens when I inevitably do have to return to Manhattan, and she has to decide what she wants for herself, but those decisions don't have to be made tonight.

Tonight, I'm going to enjoy knowing that tomorrow doesn't hold a goodbye for us. For right now, that's more than enough.

42
Emma
two months later

MARGO

EMMA!!!

EMMA

Yes?

MARGO

I know you're an influencer now and post the
links to everything you're wearing on your
grand adventure parading around the
Hamptons this summer, but I need the best
friend hookup and for you to tell me where your
dress is from in these photos.

PRESTON IS ON THE PHONE WITH HIS AGENT WHILE I WAIT FOR THE
photos from Margo to come through. There have been a few
different instances where photos of Preston and me have reached
the press in the almost two months we've spent together here in
the Hamptons.

For the most part, we've laid low and stuck to doing things at
the club or tried to go places that weren't busy, but it's been hard
to avoid the media completely. While there's plenty of specula-

tion that I'm the one seen in photos with Preston, I've taken up wearing hats and large sunglasses while I'm out with him.

No one has been able to confirm anything, but the grainy photos the paparazzi have taken, and me still teasing being with a sports guy on my still-growing social media platform, have the world catching on to what Preston and I have going on.

He smiles at me, his phone pressed to his ear. Butterflies still take flight in my stomach every time he graces me with the curve of his lips. We've been in our own bubble of happiness and getting to know one another for almost two months now, and every time he aims a smile at me, my heart feels like it skips a beat.

His smiles are easier to earn than they used to be, but his default setting is still his typical grumpy scowl, so I love softening him up every now and then.

My phone vibrates, pulling me away from my thoughts of him. I open up my texts, finding the photo from Margo.

MARGO

This one!!!

In the photo, I'm wearing a lilac-colored halter dress. It's taken from far away as Preston and I leave a small local seafood place we're obsessed with. There are only ten tables inside, and the owners have been generous enough to let Preston rent the place out for a couple of hours a few times so that we could dine in private. Preston pays them well for it, and it's allowed us to continue to avoid the media as much as possible. The moment we'd stepped out of the back exit of the restaurant, you could hear the familiar click of a camera—something I never thought I'd get used to.

EMMA

I got it at one of the local boutiques here. Come visit and we can go shopping!!

MARGO

I'd love to visit but this baby is due any day now and Beck won't let me out of his sight.

He's watching me closely right now with his hands braced on the chair like he expects me to make a run for it.

EMMA

I'm dying at the mental picture of you so pregnant you're about to pop running from him.

MARGO

I need this baby out of me immediately. Maybe then he'll let me get fresh air.

EMMA

My final guess is you're having a girl!! Can't wait to prove both you and Winnie wrong.

MARGO

It's a boy. I'm convinced of it.

EMMA

Can't wait to snuggle your precious little girl!

I laugh, finding myself hilarious. Throughout Margo's entire pregnancy, both she and Winnie have sworn she's having a boy, and I've been adamant about the fact that she's having a girl. Her due date is next week, and I'm ready to prove both of them wrong.

I look down at her response when my phone vibrates again in my lap.

MARGO

> MARGO
>
> Can't wait for you to come home so you can get all the baby boy snuggles. When are you and Preston coming back to Manhattan?

My stomach drops at her question. Preston has to be in Manhattan in two days for the start of practices. He's made it clear that he wants me to come back with him so we can continue to spend time together, but even though I've told him I will, something still makes me uneasy about it all.

I think I'm just nervous that once we leave the Hamptons and the real world catches up to us, our perfect summer bubble will burst. I look over at him, finding him still on the phone with Ryan. They're deep in conversation—probably because Preston officially notified the team this will be his last year. The word hasn't gotten out to the public, but I know it's been making him anxious to finally make the announcement.

I take a deep breath, not wanting to think about how much things are about to start changing with the upcoming football season. Whatever happens when we trade our summer nights for both the bright lights of the stadiums and the public interest in our relationship is something we're going to have to figure out.

All of this might feel better if I had an idea of what my next steps are. Sharing my life on the internet—as well as my outfits and favorite products—kind of fell into my lap. I just hired a manager who helps me secure brand deals, but I still don't know how long this will last. My life is nowhere near figured out, and I hate that part of me wonders if that will get in the way of the relationship me and Preston have built.

Sadness washes over me as I look down at my phone and type a response back to Margo.

It's our last night here so we come back tomorrow. Think Winnie's excited for me to finally stop crashing at her place?

I throw the joke in there to try and lighten the mood, but I still feel a little sad that my time here is coming to an end. If anything, I feel even more lost than when the summer started. I have a relationship that I desperately want to hold on to but also know will be hard to navigate once the season starts and we rarely see each other. We've both avoided the topic of what's next, wanting to just enjoy the time we do have together.

I keep reminding myself of the comment Winnie made before I left for my trip. Maybe it does take getting lost to be found. At least I hope it does because right now, I'm lost in how I feel for Preston. Every day we spend together, the feelings I have for him grow stronger and stronger.

It's equally as terrifying as it is exciting.

"Sorry that call took so long." Preston's hand snakes around my waist as he turns my body to face his.

I smile, trying to push the fear of the future to the back of my mind. "Don't worry about it."

"You ready to go?" He presses a kiss to my cheek.

I nod.

For our last night here in the Hamptons, we're going into town for some shopping and dinner. The smart thing to do would probably be to hang out at the house or book somewhere private so no one sees us, but I want one last night to feel normal with him. I know things will change when we get back to Manhattan.

It'll be harder to hide, and soon, our relationship will be confirmed. We've had numerous conversations about being ready for the spotlight, and I think I can handle it, but for one more night, I want to pretend he's just a guy and I'm just a girl and we can do normal things together.

Besides, I need a shopping session. Even though Winnie and Margo have been to the Hamptons before and even own properties here, I want to get them something. I also want to get a gift for Baby Sinclair and for Aunt V as well. I've promised her that I'm going to come home soon to visit. I want to bring her back a memento from my summer away.

Preston grabs my chin and gently tilts it up to look at him. "Everything okay?"

I force a smile and nod. "Yes. I think I'm just a little sad to leave tomorrow. We've had such a great time here together."

His eyes track my face. Two little lines of concern appear between his eyebrows as he watches me carefully. "We'll have a great time together in Manhattan too."

"I know." *But it won't be the same,* I don't say out loud.

What we have won't just be ours anymore, and that's terrifying.

43
Preston

THE MOMENT I STEP UP ONTO THE PODIUM, I HEAR THE DISTINCT sound of clicking cameras. Someone clears their throat in the background as they all wait for me to make the announcement that's weighed on my chest all summer.

I've been back in Manhattan for a week now. The first day back at practice, I was able to tell the entire team that this is my last year. It was important for me that they heard it from me and not anyone else.

Somehow, in the week since I've told them, we've been able to keep the news under wraps. I thought I was excited that it hadn't leaked to the media. My publicist and PR firm have been working overtime navigating all the media attention of not only my relationship with Emma but the record-breaking deal I'd supposedly signed.

As I stand at the podium, countless pairs of eyes watching me closely, I wonder if I would have preferred a leak about my retirement to have happened. I know what I'm about to say will shock a lot of people, and now that I'm faced with doing it, I'm actually terrified.

I swallow as my knuckles turn white with how hard I grab the corners of the podium. "Good afternoon, everyone," I begin. I clear my throat, my words coming out a little raspier than I'd intended.

More cameras click. It's the only sound in the room besides my own voice. I wish someone would go against the typical code of these interviews and just begin asking me questions instead of waiting for me to talk.

I look to the side of the media room, finding my team of people all watching me closely. Emma even stands with them, but I can't see her well behind Ryan. I don't know if she'd admit this, but I think she's trying to stay out of view from any cameras.

Even though we haven't confirmed our relationship, she's been under intense scrutiny now that we've been seen together more. I don't blame her for wanting to stay away. I'd hide from it if I was able to.

"I've never been a man of many words. In fact, many of my teammates—both current and former—could attest to the fact that I'm a firm believer in less words being more."

I pause, letting the room full of reporters and media personnel laugh at my joke before continuing. "Because of that, I won't waste your time up here and get straight to the point."

I take a deep breath before continuing. I don't have any regrets about my decision. I know it's for the best, but I'm still nervous about finally telling the world. Other people's opinions of me have never mattered, but for some reason, I know I'm going to be sensitive to what others think of this announcement. "This next season will be my last with the Mambas. It'll be my last season altogether."

There's a collective gasp. People look at one another as if they're trying to figure out if they heard me correctly. The clicks get faster, and the cameramen straighten their spines as if they're trying to get the best angle of me possible with this announcement.

The words are already out in the universe, and before they can start throwing questions my way, I continue to speak. "For over two decades, I've devoted myself to football. When I make a commitment to something, I stick to it. I like to think through my many seasons on the team that my teammates, coaches, and even the fans feel like I've fully committed myself to both the team and sport we all love."

I pause for a moment, my emotions beginning to run high. Suddenly, I feel hot and am all too aware of the attention focused on me and only me. I sigh, looking down at the podium for a moment, my eyes finding my carefully thought-out, publicist-approved speech that sits on top of it.

When I look back up and meet the eyes of the reporters who have interviewed me numerous times, I decide to veer off course just a little. "To be honest, I'm getting tired. I'm getting old." I pause again to allow for all of them to laugh. I shrug as I plaster on a smile for them. "We all know you're thinking it. Could I play past this season? Sure. But I think it'd be a disservice to not only myself but everyone who believes in me on and off the field. I'm ready to make other commitments in my life." My eyes flick to the side where Emma is. "I just can't devote myself to the sport like I used to. I've got this one final season where I'll give it my all, and then it's time for me to let someone else find the beauty in committing themself to a team and league that's given me so much. I'm at peace with my decision, and I hope in time everyone else will understand it as well. I'll take a couple of questions and then I'll leave the podium for my teammates."

I'm worried the sound of my pounding heart can be heard through the microphone in front of me. It beats so fast from nerves that I feel like I just got done with a workout. Everyone starts yelling questions at me at once, all of their voices blending together.

I swallow, trying to make out any question through the chaos so I can actually answer it.

Finally, one of them raises their hand, waiting for me to pick them. I nod. "Yes?" I speak into the microphone as the other voices die down, realizing they'll have to wait.

"Preston, I know you guys are the favorites for the Super Bowl coming into the season. Your team is very young and still has so much star power. Are you afraid to leave that all behind at the end of the season?"

"I believe in the guys around me this year. I believe if we have the right mindset, the Super Bowl is ours. As for your question, I can't play football forever. I want to go out feeling good about my performance. This team is great, and it will continue to be great even after I leave."

Cameras click, and more hands go up to aim questions in my direction. I point to a woman in the back of the room. I don't recognize her, but she seems respectful and waits instead of yelling things out to me.

"Preston, how did your teammates feel about the news? Did they take it well?"

I run my hand over my mouth, thinking of how intense it was in the room when I told everyone I was retiring. It was solemn. A part of me felt like I was letting them down, even though I know none of them would ever actually say that. It's part of the job, having guys leave, get traded, or even retire. But I still know it hit some of them harder than others.

"There were a lot of emotions, but the guys have been nothing but supportive of my decision."

She smiles as a thank-you before sitting back in her seat.

My eyes scan over the room, but before I can pick someone next, a man stands up in the front row, his handheld recorder aimed in my direction. "Preston, you've been seen a lot lately with an influencer named Emma Turner. Is your decision to retire because of her?"

I stare at him for a minute, my blood pumping. The room seems to go quiet with the question, and I hate that he even asked it. I swallow, my grip tightening on the podium in anger. Leaning closer, I make sure to line my mouth up perfectly with the microphone so no one can misconstrue my words. "My mind's been made up for a long time. My life outside of football is not up for discussion." I grab the piece of paper from the podium and tuck it back into the pocket of my suit. "I'm done with questions for the day. Have a good rest of your day, everyone."

The room breaks out into a chaos of questions, but I ignore all of it. I don't pay attention to anyone. All I want to do is find Emma. Ryan tries to stop me, but I walk right by him, finding Emma hidden behind a stack of boxes.

"Well, that was something," she notes.

I pull her body into mine, needing to feel the connection. That last question rubbed me the wrong way, and I just need to know it didn't go to her head. *I'm* trying not to let it get to mine. We both know my mind was made up way before I ever met her, but I hate that the question is now out there. Countless people got it on video, and now I'm fairly confident the media will get a hold of it and spin Emma as the reason I'm retiring.

"It's over with," I say against her ear, keeping her close. They've closed the door to the media room, allowing us some privacy from the press.

"How do you feel?" she asks me.

I pull away, cupping her cheeks in my hands. "I'm more worried about how *you* feel."

She frowns a little. "I'm not the one who just announced my retirement. I don't even have a job to retire from."

The sarcastic tone of the second part of her sentence sends a twinge to my heart. I don't like how negatively she talks about not having a job because she does have one now. Social media has become her job, with a manager and everything, but she still won't admit to herself that maybe she has found her passion.

"I'm sorry about that last reporter," I begin, wanting to address the elephant in the room before it can get worse. "He has no idea what he's talking about, and anyone with even the smallest amount of logic will know my decision wasn't made because of you."

"It's fine, Rhodes. Promise."

I've memorized her smiles for some time now. I know the one she's giving me right now is fake, and it isn't fine, but I don't know what else to say. I can't change the opinions of others or how they perceive my retirement.

I make the mental note to have my publicist do some damage control after that last question, but there's not much I can actually do to change people's minds. All I can do is make sure the public opinion on Emma's and my relationship doesn't get between us.

As I lead a quiet Emma through the stadium on the way to my car, I can't help but feel a pit of dread in my stomach over what's to come.

44
Emma

"SHE'S THE MOST BEAUTIFUL BABY EVER," I MUTTER, CRADLING Margo's newborn baby to my chest. A giant pink bow sits on top of her head as she sleeps peacefully in my arms.

Winnie leans close to me, her finger wrapped in baby Celeste's tiny hand as we both marvel over our newest best friend. "I just love her so much already," Winnie coos, a wide smile on her face.

Margo sits on the other side of us, a to-go box of sushi resting in her lap as she shoves one raw roll after another into her mouth. "She's pretty cute, even if she took thirty hours to exit my vagina," she mutters through a mouth full of food.

I laugh, looking down at Celeste. She's got a head full of blonde hair and the cutest button nose. I haven't been around a lot of babies in my life, but she's got to be the most precious newborn to ever exist. "She's a perfect angel. Perfection takes time, Mar."

Margo rolls her eyes at me, too focused on devouring the sushi to even respond.

"Em, you're hogging all the baby snuggles. I want some," Winnie whines from my side.

I pull Celeste a little closer to my chest, not wanting to give her up. It feels like Margo just handed her to me, and I want to continue to bask in her sweet newborn scent for the rest of the day.

Winnie lets out a low groan, clearly not amused by me not handing Celeste over.

I let out a dramatic sigh, being careful to sit up as I hand the baby to Winnie. "You get five minutes, then it's my turn again."

Winnie rolls her eyes at me, something she doesn't do often. She sits back on the couch and snuggles Celeste into the crook of her elbow. "I'm getting at least ten with her. You had so long."

"Did not," I respond, pulling my phone from my pocket.

Preston's at practice for the day, so I know I won't have any messages from him, but I'm waiting to hear back from Aunt V. I'm visiting her for a week this weekend before Preston's final season starts and I travel to all of his games. I don't have any texts from her, but it's probably because she's still working.

Winnie and Margo begin to talk about who they think Celeste looks like while I thumb through some of the notifications on my phone.

This morning, I posted something different than what I've usually been posting since we returned from the Hamptons. It's felt weird to tell everyone that I still feel like a mess because it seems like all people care about in my comments is Preston.

To try and move the topic back to me and not just my relationship with him, I'd posted a video this morning asking for my followers to ask me questions in the comments and I'd make a Q&A out of it to post on my page.

Some questions are inevitably about Preston, which I gloss over, but some of them catch my attention, and I know I'll want to answer them. There's some asking where I grew up, for tips on how to grow on social media but still stay authentic, and a surprising amount asking what my plans are now that I'm back in Manhattan.

I'm about to close the app and join in the conversation with Margo and Winnie when a comment thread catches my eye.

> **user9509345821:** *Didn't this girl get famous about wanting to find herself? Did she just forget all about that and found herself underneath a man instead?*

My heart sinks. I know I should close out of the app and not read any of the comments below this one, but I can't help it. Winnie and Margo's voices fade out as I decide to torture myself by reading more comments.

> **MrsRhodes509:** *She was his fun before the season started. He'll realize he needs to be with someone who has their life figured out in no time.*

> **hannahmarty2:** *is anyone else really disappointed she followed preston back to manhattan? i followed her because she was relatable about not knowing her next steps. i wanted to watch her find her footing. instead she decided to give up everything she wanted to do for a man. i guess maybe that is relatable, just not in the way i was hoping.*

> **kirstensings:** *What happens when he leaves her for someone better? Does she come on here drunk again and give the same speech as last time hoping we'll all forget she dropped everything for the first guy she met?*

"Em?" Margo's hand on my thigh pulls me from the comments. My phone drops to my lap like it's on fire as I meet my best friend's worried eyes.

"What's wrong?" Margo prods.

I shake my head, not wanting to ruin the afternoon with my best friends. "Nothing's wrong." I'm mad at myself for thinking it was a good idea to read my comments to begin with, let alone doing it while I'm supposed to be focused on nothing but my friends. I barely saw them over the summer, and Margo has a precious baby who deserves all the love.

People on the internet who have no idea who I am don't deserve a single second of my time, even if I'm learning how hard it is to not let them in my head.

"You're lying to me, and I don't appreciate it," Margo tells me, narrowing her eyes.

I smile at her, not wanting to waste my breath talking about the trolls in my comment section. "I'm not lying at all. Is it my turn to hold Celeste again?"

"It hasn't even been five minutes," Winnie argues.

I laugh, leaning in to fix the bow on Celeste's head. "You've got five more, and then that baby is all mine."

For right now, I try to push all the negative thoughts from my mind. I try to be present, but in the back of my mind, one comment sticks out amongst the others. Is following Preston through this upcoming season the opposite of what I've been trying to do all summer? Instead of finding myself, am I losing who I am instead?

45
Preston

"Emma," I call as I open the door to the condo where I stay during the season.

It's quiet, something I'm not used to with Emma around. I'm used to opening the door after getting back from practice and hearing the TV blaring with some cheesy chick flick, or she'll have music playing throughout the condo's speakers.

But today, it's just silence.

I set my practice bag down by the door, an uneasy feeling coursing through my veins. There's probably no reason for me to feel this way. Just because it's quiet doesn't mean something's wrong. She'd told me she was going to Beck and Margo's house to meet their new daughter. Maybe that went later than I thought.

I try not to feel disappointed at the idea that she may not be here. She leaves tomorrow for a week to visit her aunt, and while I know it's important for her to see the one family member she still has in her life, I'll miss her.

From the day we met, we've spent every day together. So, this will be the first time we're apart, and I miss her already.

I walk through the hallway that leads to the kitchen and main living space in search of her. It's possible she fell asleep or is in the shower and can't hear me.

My stomach drops when I find Emma sitting on the edge of

the couch with two suitcases and a duffel bag sitting next to her. I swallow, trying to tell myself the bags are just for her week away, but the way she won't meet my eyes makes me fear something else is happening.

"Hi," I manage to get out. The condo seems so eerily quiet, and I hate it. It's so quiet I wonder if she can hear the anxious beat of my heart through the silence.

When her eyes finally meet mine, I know something's wrong. It seems like the light I've grown accustomed to seeing in her eyes is gone. "Preston, we need to talk." Her words are quiet, but they still wreak havoc on my heart.

I'm losing her. She's barely said a word, and I still know I'm about to lose her.

I reach out, needing to touch her. My fingertips brush over her jaw. "Whatever's wrong, I'll fix it."

The color drains from her face. She closes her eyes, as if it's too painful for her to even look at me with what she has to say. "You can't fix this," she whispers, her eyes still shut.

I cradle the back of her neck, clinging to anything to get her to tell me what's wrong. My feelings for her have gotten so strong there's nothing I won't do to fix whatever's the matter. "Yes, I can. What is it, baby?"

She shakes her head slowly, her eyes finally finding mine. They're glossy with unshed tears. The only time I've seen Emma cry was during Jackson's speech at Peyton's wedding. Those were happy tears. These are the complete opposite, completely wrecking my heart with the sight of them. "I'm sorry," she begins, her voice breaking at the end.

"Sorry for what?" I press my forehead to hers, needing to feel her skin against mine so that I know we'll be okay. The suitcases sit in the corner of my vision, taunting me with the idea that she's leaving me.

"I'm going home, but I've decided to stay there…"

"For how long? Stay there as long as you need—you don't have to come to the preseason games. Or even the season op—"

She pulls away, the tears freely falling down her cheeks at this point. "No, Preston. I'm going home for good."

"What does that mean? How long is for good?"

"However long it takes me to figure myself out. I had the best summer with you, but now that we're back, it's hit me that I never really focused on myself like I'd wanted to."

My throat feels painfully tight. I swallow, trying to fix it, but it doesn't help. "So, you're going home for an unknown amount of time. That's okay. We'll still talk and figure it out. Whatever games you want to travel to, I'll get you tickets from the closest airport to Vanessa. I can even try to come see you when—"

Emma sighs, her head shaking. I try to wipe the tears from her cheeks, but she nudges my hand away, wiping her tear stained cheeks herself. "No, Preston. That's the thing. I can't just follow you around this season." Her bottom lip trembles, but she manages to keep her words clear as she continues to break my heart. "The whole reason I met you in the first place was because I was finally doing something for myself. Before, I used to follow my best friends from one place to the next, never really thinking about what *I* wanted for my future. I didn't have to think through my next steps because Winnie and Margo were doing it for me. But going alone to the Hamptons was the first time I did something for myself, and instead, I let myself get lost in you."

It feels like she's taken a knife to my chest. For a moment, the world goes blurry as I try to process if she regrets what started between us over the summer. "I don't understand," I get out, my voice thick. "Are you saying you regret us?"

"I could never regret you. But I do feel like I've let myself down in a way. I've fallen into the same pattern, following someone else and their dreams instead of figuring out *my* dreams."

My lips pinch together as I try to keep them from shaking. I don't want her to know how every single thing that comes out of her mouth is slicing me open. She's hurting me, but I don't want her to know it. I don't want to make her feel guilty when it's clearly painful for her to tell me this.

"It feels a hell of a lot like you regret me." My voice cracks, and I wish I could hide it, but it's already out there. "Why can't you figure out what you want to do next while still making our relationship work? Why are you making it a choice between yourself or me? I'm not asking you to choose, Em. I'll wait for you to feel good about whatever you want to do with the rest of your life. Just let me be a part of it."

"Because right now, I owe it to myself to give *myself* a chance. I think if I let myself follow you for the season, I'll end up falling in love with you."

"Is that so bad?"

I've never been in love because I was always focused on other things. I have no idea what it feels like, but it must be something close to how I already feel about her because it couldn't hurt this bad at the thought of her leaving me behind if I wasn't close to being in love with her.

Her shoulders shake as she takes a deep breath. I try to console her by caressing her cheek, but it doesn't stop her body from trembling. I don't think it helps that I think my fingers also tremble with the fear of losing her and everything we've shared in the time we've known each other.

"Not if it means losing myself in the process. I want to love you right, Preston. And I don't think anyone deserves to fall in love with me until I love myself and who I become."

I rub my chest, feeling nothing but pain at her words. How do I convince her that no one deserves love more than her? She deserves every happy thing life has to offer—including love. She's funny and kind and is always putting others over herself, even though she doesn't even realize it.

But perhaps that's why, this time, she's choosing herself.

That might be my hardest realization no matter how much it pains me. I could tell her that I'm ready to fall in love with her, to give it my all and do anything necessary to keep her for the rest of my life.

Every time I wake up next to her in the morning, I imagine doing it for the rest of my life. I think about the vacations we'll take our future kids on and how we'll have to take them to the place where we first met. I never told her this, but I've imagined a whole life with her.

I can't convince her she's worthy of love no matter where she's at in her life until she's convinced of it herself. There's nothing I can do but support her in whatever decision she makes. No matter how much it hurts, what she needs right now isn't me. I just hope that she'll still want me after she discovers who she wants to be.

46
Emma

I HOPE ONE DAY I'LL BE ABLE TO FORGIVE MYSELF FOR HURTING HIM. I hope I look back and realize this was the best decision for both me and Preston because right now, I want to pull him into my arms and tell him I didn't mean anything I've said.

From the moment I left Margo's house, the comments on my video have been at the forefront of my mind. I think some of their points have been in the back of my mind from the moment I decided to come back to Manhattan with Preston and follow along with him this season.

Deep down, I knew I was falling back into a cycle I wanted to break. I kept telling myself that I had this career and that perhaps I could find myself while still being with him. But Preston deserves to have all of me, and *I* deserve to find myself before I end up losing myself in someone else.

I hate that I let the trolls get to me, but some of them had a point. The timing for Preston and me isn't right at the moment, no matter how much it hurts to admit that to myself.

"I'm sorry," I tell him, wrapping my fingers in the fabric of his T-shirt.

"Can you at least tell me what changed your mind?" I hate the way his voice breaks. I know he doesn't like to be vulnerable. He takes a deep breath, his cobalt eyes searching my face for answers. "This morning, everything seemed so perfect. What changed that?"

I swallow, not knowing how to answer him. So instead, I go with the truth, wondering if it'll sound silly when I say it out loud. "I was looking at comments on my most recent post, and there was comment after comment of people saying you could do better than m—"

"I don't give a fuck what any of them think. Please don't tell me you're ending this between us because of that. Because of them." He practically spits the last word, making me second-guess even bringing up what got me thinking deeper into our relationship.

"No, it's not that. I want to find myself in this world and on my own terms. But I'm not ready to have people dissect my life the way they are. If I keep going the way that I am, I feel like I'll lose more of myself every day, and you don't deserve that. *I* don't deserve that."

He winces, his eyes closing for a minute as he lets out a long breath. I hate how stiff his muscles are under my hands, that not even the press of my skin against his is comforting him.

I never wanted to hurt him, but it's better to walk away now than down the road when we're even deeper in this. It isn't a secret that I started my journey by openly sharing it with the world. I was opening myself up to scrutiny, but the opinions that came from me posting on social media are nothing in comparison to the attention I've received since the public caught wind of me dating Preston.

People follow us everywhere, always screaming their opinions at us anytime we go out in public, and I thought I was tough enough to swim in this fishbowl with him with the constant attention he gets, but the reality is, I'm not.

I hope to one day be, but that time isn't now.

"I wish I could change your mind," he mutters, his voice emotionless. "I wish you weren't just letting this end between us.

Not when I feel like things are just beginning. Not when I really thought things were perfect."

His words feel like a punch to the gut. Everything would be perfect if I felt like I was in a place where I was ready. I want that with him, but not until I feel better about where I'm at in my life.

I let out a shaky breath, trying to regain my composure. "I'd never ask you to wait for me. I want you to live your life, but maybe the universe will work out for us and the timing will be right. Maybe we'll find each other again when I'm happier with the path my life has taken, and you've won that Super Bowl you so deserve."

He doesn't say anything. All he does is stare at me. His jaw flexes as his eyes scan my face. I want to know what's going through his head—or maybe I don't. I'm already trying to stay strong by doing what I think is the right thing and putting a pause on things between us.

Although the past couple of months have been nothing short of amazing, I don't want to do long distance, only for us to end up getting torn apart. I don't want to grow to resent him because I didn't get to follow my own dreams.

At least now, maybe if things are right, we'll find each other again.

We've both never been in a relationship, and I don't want us to start on an unsteady foundation. He deserves to be all in for his season. When people interview him, I want them to ask about his success in the season and not about his relationship status. Especially when it's clear that more and more people are wanting to know about us.

If he loses a game or throws a bad pass, I don't want my name to be the reason it happened. He's gone his whole career focusing on the sport; I want to give him that last year of doing it without me there as a potential distraction.

"If I focus on football and give you the time you need, will you promise me that we'll revisit this? That this isn't over between us?"

The right thing to do would be to tell him he doesn't have to give me the time I need. I don't want him to think I'm asking him to wait for me, but I've already said it once. If he's sure that we're meant to be and that we'll find our way back together after this, I don't have it in me to change his mind.

I nod, reaching up to cup his cheek in my hand. He was running late to practice this morning because I wouldn't let him leave our bed. Because of that, he didn't shave, so now that it's almost dinner, stubble dusts both his cheeks. It scrapes the palm of my hand, and I try to memorize the feel of it.

"If we're meant to be, we'll find our way back to each other," I get out, tears falling down my face.

I'm trying my best not to cry and make this worse than it already is, but I can't help it. He's everything I want in a boyfriend and partner. I'm just not who *I* want to be yet, and I don't want to lose the perfect guy later down the road because I never took the time to love and find myself first.

Preston leans forward and presses a kiss to my forehead. He keeps his lips there, his arms clinging to my sides with his next words. "I already know we're meant to be, Emma. I want to give you the time to not only find yourself, but fall in love with who you are too. I'll wait until you're ready."

A loud sob erupts from my chest. I wrap my arms around his middle, clinging to his body and wishing I never had to let go. I'd spent all afternoon thinking this through. I know I'm making the right decision. I know I need to spend time with Aunt V and take the time to figure out my next steps. I also know that he deserves to focus on his career one last time without any distractions. I know all of this, but it doesn't make it any easier.

"I'm so sorry, Preston. Everything with you was perfect—*is* so perfect. I just need some time. I'm still happy I snuck into the club that night."

"I'm *so* happy you did too, Em." His voice is sad, shattering my already broken heart into a million pieces.

I don't know a lot about love. I've never been in love, but as I cling to his warm body, I'm wondering if I was wrong for worrying about eventually falling in love with him. I think I've already fallen. I didn't mean to. I tried to guard my heart and be realistic that the odds were stacked against Preston and me, but my cautiousness was useless.

"I refuse to believe this is the end for us," Preston says against my hair. "For the next several months, I will devote myself to nothing but football. I hope you'll do the same and realize that you don't have to have your whole life figured out to be loved. And then, it'll be us together in the end. The rest of the world and their opinions be damned."

I don't respond. All I do is savor the last few moments of feeling what it's like to be wrapped in his arms. I've become so used to the feel of his body against mine, to his scent, even to the familiar beat of his heart. We may not have known each other the longest, but we've spent every day together for months. I know him better than I ever thought, and it's killing me having to let him go.

"Goodbye, Preston." My words come out muffled because of my face being pressed to his chest. His arms tighten around me with the farewell, as if he's trying to prolong the inevitable just a little bit longer.

I brace my palms against his chest and push off him. I'm scared if I stay in his arms any longer that I'll change my mind. Changing my mind won't help either of us, not in the long run. Not if we actually want this to work between us.

"You better win that Super Bowl, Rhodes." I force a smile, wanting him to get that dream more than anything.

His eyes are red, making the cobalt blue color pop. "Only if you'll celebrate with me after."

"Deal." There's a lot of time between now and the Super Bowl in February. Maybe it isn't too far-fetched to think I'll be in a better place by that time. I'd love to celebrate his success after he wins it all like I know he will.

Preston tucks a piece of my hair behind my ear, letting his

fingers linger against my neck. "I'll miss you, Em. You let me know when you're ready and I'm yours."

One last tear falls down my cheek. He watches it fall and land against my T-shirt. He stares at the small wet spot for a moment before he rips his eyes away and looks at my packed bags. "Let me help you get these to the elevator."

"I've got it," I argue, trying to take the bag from him.

"Emma, if you're going to break my heart, let me at least help you to the door."

All I can do is nod, not knowing what to even say back to that. I let him lead me to the elevator, holding nothing but my purse as he grabs everything else. He presses the intercom next to the elevator, calling for one of the doormen to help me the rest of the way.

Standing in front of the metal doors, waiting for the elevator to reach our floor, makes everything seem so final. He stands a few feet away from me, his eyes on the ground. He doesn't say anything, and I don't either. I don't know if there's really anything else to say.

When the doors open, he hands my bags over to Benson, one of the doormen I've grown fond of since we came back to Manhattan. It happens too quickly. I want more time with him even when I know I shouldn't, when I'm the one that made this decision for us.

Preston's eyes find mine, and I feel like the defeated way he looks at me will forever be burned in my mind. "Remember what I said, Em. I meant every word."

And without any further goodbye, he turns and walks down the hallway to his condo.

I watch him the entire way.

When I turn to face Benson, I know the tears streaming down my face are obvious. I step in the elevator, trying to wipe them away. All my life, I've said I just wanted a man to want me and spoil me, and here I am finally getting one, and I'm walking away from him. But it's necessary. No matter how much it hurts.

Sadness washes over me as the elevator descends. All I can do is hope that I made the right decision. Putting myself first has never felt so shitty, but at the end of this, I hope Preston's right. I hope it'll be us.

If not, I'll forever be grateful for the summer nights we spent together where he was mine.

47
Emma
one month later

"COULD YOU BRING THE OREOS TOO?" AUNT V ASKS ME FROM THE couch. She adjusts the sheet mask on her face, huffing when it continues to slip over her eyes and not stay on correctly.

I smile from the small, attached kitchen, busy cutting the tops of different candy bags open and pouring them into a large bowl. It's called a candy salad, and it's been Vanessa's and my favorite late-night snack in the month that I've been back home with her.

"I like the way you think, Aunt V." My eyes move from her perched on the couch to my phone that sits on a stand next to me on the counter. "The thing about girls' night is that you have to go big or go home. Junk food combined with skincare is peak girlhood," I tell my audience in the video I'm filming to post later.

"Preach!" Aunt V yells from the living room, her eyes trained on the TV.

We're having a celebratory girls' night because I've been nominated at an award show for breakout internet star. My management team begged me to fly to LA to attend the event, but I wasn't ready to step into the spotlight and have the media hound me with questions.

When I post to my own platform, I'm able to control the narrative. I have a team comb through the comments, so that isn't even something I have to worry about anymore. Anything I put out into the world, I control, and it's refreshing.

"Not another commercial break," Vanessa complains, shaking her head.

I laugh, continuing to pour the candy into the bowl. Our eyes were a little bigger than our stomachs with the amount of candy we picked out, but I love the variety of options we have for tonight.

"If you can't hear her in the background, my aunt Vanessa is impatiently waiting for the breakout internet portion. I, on the other hand, am so nervous. Whatever happens, I cannot believe you guys made me a finalist to begin with." I pause what I'm doing, looking at the camera as a wave of emotions passes through me. "I just appreciate you being here every step of the way on my very messy journey, and I need you to know how much I love every single one of you."

When I first came back to live with Aunt V, it was hard. All I wanted to do was call Preston and tell him I'd made a mistake. I wanted to find a way to be long distance and do anything to make it work. But then I'd see the Mambas' posts of him at practice or the paparazzi videos of him leaving the gym, and I realized he was staying true to his word.

He was devoting himself to his career, and he deserved that, to be the best version of himself as a quarterback and teammate. So, if he was going to hold up his end of the deal, I needed to hold up mine.

And while with each passing day, I feel a little more at peace with where my life's at, I know there's still more I want to figure out before jumping into things again. If Preston and I get back together, that'll be it for me because I still believe *he's* it for me. I just don't want to inevitably ruin things because I'm a mess, so I'll keep doing what I came here for.

I finish pouring the last bag of candy into the bowl, pushing thoughts of Preston to the back of my mind. I blink a few times, trying to stop my own sheet mask from slipping and falling into my eyes. I laugh at myself, knowing I'm going to have to keep that part in the video.

I've started to do more brand deals recently and have tried to diversify my content, but my favorite videos are still the ones where followers see the more authentic parts of my life. "Now that we have all the candy in here," I begin, telling my audience how to make a candy salad even though everyone is making them on the internet right now, "you just have to mix it all up and enjoy it."

I pick a sour gummy worm from the bowl and take a bite. I already know by the end of the night, my taste buds are going to feel like they're gone from all the sour candy I plan to consume, but I'm going to enjoy the candy anyway. It's not every day you're nominated for a huge award.

I stop the video and take my phone from the stand. There are a thousand texts from Winnie and Margo, who are watching together in Manhattan. I'm a little sad to not be there with them, but they both came to visit last week, and we spent a few days together.

Beck had to go out of town for work, and although he fought leaving Margo alone while Celeste is still so little, we were able to convince him that a girls' weekend would be a blast. Margo was all for it. I think she pretty much leapt off the private jet when I went to pick them up from the airport.

Beck, on the other hand, pouted the entire time he was saying goodbye, but I don't blame him. Celeste is almost six weeks and the most precious little bundle. Vanessa, Winnie, and I all fought over who got the baby snuggles while they were here.

It was great to show my best friends where I grew up. I think they knew I needed to see them but that I wasn't ready to return to Manhattan, and I'm forever grateful to have had the time with them.

"Are you coming or not? I need the candy and Oreos!" V calls from the living room. "Plus, these dang commercials should be done soon, and I don't want you to miss it."

I roll my eyes. While I've been here, I introduced Vanessa to streaming services, and now just the mention of a commercial makes her impatient.

"I'm coming," I tell her, grabbing the Oreos she so desperately wants in one hand and the giant bowl of candy in the other.

I take a seat on the couch next to her and put down the food. Vanessa immediately reaches for an Oreo and pops it into her mouth.

She blows a raspberry, pulling at the sheet mask on her face. "I'm pretty sure I just accidentally ate a chunk of this thing. I'm trying to be young and cool with you, but I think that's enough skin care for me tonight." She pulls the face mask off completely, folds it up, and places it on the side table next to her.

I repeat her motion, wanting to enjoy my food without accidentally taking a bite of the mask we were sent from a brand to try out. "You're always cool, V."

She immediately shushes me through her mouthful of cookie when the award show host pops up on the screen.

My phone buzzes in my pocket, and I look down at the texts rolling in. The first one is from Ophelia, my manager.

OPHELIA

> Yours is next! They were very adamant about getting your pre-recorded thank-you video from me in case you won. They don't typically do that unless you're the winner.

My heart races at her text. My hands shake with nerves as I type a text back.

EMMA

Maybe they're just extra prepared. Trying not to get my hopes up!

I look through my other texts while the host talks about a movie that just released. I'm trying to stay distracted up until the moment they present the award. If I think about it too much, I might throw up from nerves.

MARGO

Even Celeste wanted to party and watch Aunt Em win an award!

I smile at the photo she sends of Celeste. She's got a pair of pajamas on with little paintbrushes on it, and her eyes are wide open where she's snuggled in the crook of Margo's arm.

EMMA

Rub her belly for good luck for me!! Wish I was there giving her all the kisses!

Vanessa practically slapping my arm pulls my attention from my phone. "Oh my god, it's happening!" she screams as two influencers I recognize walk out to the stage.

I've talked with both of them online, and they even convinced me to attend a brand trip in Mexico with them next month. I'm excited to meet them in person and get out a little more, but I'm also really nervous.

No matter how many times I tell my management team I

think one day people are going to wake up and lose interest in me, they tell me it's the opposite. More brands want to work with me in different capacities, and I'm starting to believe that just maybe in admitting I was a mess to the world, I've found myself a career that I enjoy and find purpose in.

"Those girls seem so nice," Vanessa says from my side, her nails biting into my arm because of her nerves.

I place my hand over hers to try and stop my hands from shaking. I've spent days convincing myself that there's no way I was going to get this award. I didn't even know the award existed a few months ago. Besides, I haven't even been on the internet long enough to feel like I deserve to be nominated, but now that they're about to announce the winner, I'm realizing how badly I want it to be me.

"And the winner for this year's breakout internet star is..."

"I think I might throw up," I tell Vanessa, squeezing her hand hard.

"Shhhh," Vanessa responds, leaning forward.

The presenters open the envelope and share a knowing smile before both leaning into the microphone. "Emma Turner!" they yell excitedly.

The crowd breaks into a cheer while the world goes hazy around me in my childhood living room.

"Oh my!" Vanessa screams, jumping up from her spot on the couch and running a circle around the living room. "That's you, sweetie!" she shouts, looking at me with wide eyes.

I stay in place, trying to figure out if I heard that correctly. Suddenly, my prerecorded video pops up on the screen. I only recorded it a few days ago, and it took me and Vanessa hours to complete, even though I'd been given a script from my team.

I kept laughing and couldn't take it seriously because I never thought anyone would see it. It was my way of protecting myself if I were to lose—something I thought would happen.

I'm frozen for a few more seconds, not able to even hear what I'm saying on the screen because how is this happening? How is this my life? Six months ago, I had no idea what I was doing. I felt like a mess and a failure. Now, I'm winning an award.

This is unreal.

Vanessa runs over to me and throws her arms around my body, pulling me off the couch and into a hug. "Oh, my sweet girl, I always knew you'd do big things. Look at you!"

I hug her back, immediately breaking into tears. "This isn't happening," I mutter against her hair. The world still seems fuzzy. I can hear my phone vibrating against the cushion behind me, but all I can focus on is the fact that I *actually* won.

Vanessa grabs my face, tears welling in her eyes. "It happened, dear. You did it. I'm so proud of you."

A sob breaks free from my chest—a happy one. I hadn't realized how bad I needed to hear someone say they were proud of me until this moment. In fact, I don't think I would've believed anyone telling me they were proud of my accomplishments until this moment.

It's been a long time since I felt like I've done anything important with my life, but now, I finally feel like I have. It's the best I've felt about myself in a long time.

Vanessa pulls away before reaching down to grab my phone and hand it to me. "Now, celebrate with all your friends and fans!"

I take the phone from her, knowing I need to put something on my page thanking everyone. Before I can do that, a text on my screen catches my attention.

PRESTON

I've always known you were something special, rebel. Glad the rest of the world knows too. Counting down the days until February.

I read his text over and over again until I've committed it to memory. Notifications keep popping up, but I ignore every single one of them as I think about what to say back to Preston.

Do I even say anything at all?

We haven't spoken since I left his apartment. The way he barely looked at me as he left me in that elevator has been burned in my mind. I don't want him to think I'm ignoring him, so I type out a response and hit Send before throwing my phone and enjoying the moment with Aunt V.

EMMA

Your words mean the world to me. And me too, Rhodes.

48
Preston
two months later

MY CONDO FEELS EERILY QUIET EXCEPT FOR THE SOUND OF THE TV in my living room. I used to thrive in the quiet of an empty house. It left me alone with my thoughts, and being in my head used to be all about work. Now, my mind isn't as fun a place to be because it always drifts to Emma.

So, I no longer enjoy the silence. I leave the TVs on so I can pretend this condo doesn't feel empty without her.

"And the Mambas are already off to a great season, not having lost a game yet in the seven games they've played so far," Bill Silas, one of the nicest sportscasters I've met over the years, says on the TV.

"Something's got to give though, right? Preston Rhodes is playing lights out right now, but eventually, a defense is going to figure out how to stop him. Everyone thinks this will be their Cinderella season, but I'm not so sure," Roger Oleman responds.

I smirk at Roger's jab. The guy has never liked me—I don't know why—and even though he's supposed to remain unbiased, he'll use any chance he gets to have the Mambas losing against an opponent.

Bill clicks his tongue and shakes his head. "That's where I think you're wrong, Roger. I can't tell you the last team I've watched where I thought it was actually possible for them to go all the way to the Super Bowl without ever losing a game."

"No. I think the Portland Pirates have a great shot at taking them down next week. Austin Rickerd is playing out of his mind for it only being his third season. He's going to want to come out and prove to everyone that he's better than the seasoned vet that's Preston Rhodes."

I only pay half attention to the broadcast. I normally try to avoid all of the different sports stations during the season, not wanting any of their opinions to get in my head, but this season, things are different.

I've never been so focused in my life.

I don't care if Roger Oleman thinks I'm going to finally lose to Austin Rickerd. If anything, it fuels me even more to hear his opinion. I eat, breathe, and try to think about nothing but football. I tell myself it's because this is my last year in the league and I want to give it my all after I made a promise to Emma.

But deep down, I know the focus is because if I allow my mind to drift to anything besides football, it'll go to the woman I fell in love with—the one who wasn't ready for my love. And thinking about her—about what we could have been right now —hurts. Excelling and being the very best quarterback I've ever been doesn't hurt, so it's where all my focus goes.

The noise from the TV fades out as I look at the little black box in my lap. Inside it sits letters I've written to Emma that I haven't sent. I didn't write them for her to read, not yet at least. I wrote them because I needed to feel like I was still talking to her, even when I wasn't.

It's been a way for me to make sense of my feelings for her. One by one, I unfold the unsent letters and torture myself by reading over every one.

Rebel,

It's been two days since you left and I don't think I've ever felt pain like this. I know this is for the best. I know for us to work, which, god, that's all I want is for there to be an us at the end of this, that you have to go and find yourself on your own. I'm just really fucking missing you while you do it.

Yours,
Preston

Rebel,

I knew you leaving would hurt. That much was obvious. What I didn't know was how lonely I'd feel without you. From spending almost every second with you over the summer to not seeing you at all is like ripping off the most painful Band-Aid to ever exist. I want to come home and tell you how practice went. I miss walking through the doors and hearing you belting out lyrics to a boy band song I've never heard of. I just miss the little things with you.

Yours,
Preston

Rebel,

We had the season opener today. It was the best game I've ever played. I would've given anything to have you there to watch it. But sometimes when I really miss you, I go to your profile and watch your videos. You look happy. I want you to be happy. I hope you're falling in love with yourself a little more each day. That's how I fell in love with you. Little by little until you became the most important person in my life. You still are that person for me. You always will be, no matter what happens.

Yours,

Preston

Rebel,

I'm sorry people still ask you about me. I hate that the paparazzi followed you all the way to your aunt's house. I hate that I still can't shake the feeling that the opinions of others about us and you made you second-guess yourself. I hope I'm wrong. You're the most incredible person I've ever met, even as you're still figuring it out, and I hope the world sees that in you too. I know they will. It's hard not to.

Yours,

Preston

Rebel,

I know I shouldn't have texted you. You have no idea how many times I've typed out a text to you only to delete it before I hit Send. But after you won that award, I couldn't help myself. I've never watched award shows, and the ones I've attended I barely ever paid attention to. But last night, I was glued to the TV. I thought my heart was going to leap out of my chest waiting for them to announce the winner. I'm so happy it was you. Hearing from you, even if it was only a few words, gave me hope. I'll see you in February, Rebel.

Yours,
Preston

Rebel,

There was a moment today during the game where I got hit so hard that for a moment, I couldn't move. My teammates and coaches were huddled over me, their eyes wide with fear because they knew how hard that hit was. I couldn't hear a damn thing any of them were saying. Trainers were asking me questions, refs were trying to talk to my head coach, and the only thing I could think about was that time we walked out to the pier at midnight. The moon lit the path for us down the old, creaky boards. I remember it so vividly. The way you smelled, the baby-pink tank top you had on. We danced under the stars that night. And for some reason, as I

LAY THERE ON THE FIELD, I WANTED IT TO BE THAT NIGHT AGAIN. I WANTED TO BE BACK ON THAT BOARDWALK WITH YOU. I WAS PULLED OUT FOR CONCUSSION PROTOCOL, BUT WAS ABLE TO RETURN AFTER BEING CHECKED OUT. I TRIED TO FOCUS ON THE GAME—WE WON BY TWENTY-ONE—BUT IT WASN'T THE MOST FOCUSED I'D BEEN IN A GAME. ALL I COULD THINK ABOUT WAS WANTING TO BE BACK ON THAT BOARDWALK WITH YOU.

NEXT SUMMER I WANT TO DANCE WITH YOU ON THE BOARDWALK EVERY NIGHT.

ALWAYS YOURS,

PRESTON

REBEL,

I SAW THAT INTERVIEW YOU DID WITH RUBY ROBINSON. YOU'RE DOING BIG THINGS, EMMA TURNER. EVERY ANSWER YOU GAVE HER ABOUT YOUR LIFE AND YOUR EXPERIENCES WAS SO AUTHENTIC AND REAL. I LOVE WATCHING THE REST OF THE WORLD FALL IN LOVE WITH YOU, JUST THE WAY I HAVE. IT DOES STING A LITTLE, KNOWING YOU'RE HERE IN NEW YORK. YOU'RE SO CLOSE, BUT SO FAR. I MISS YOU.

YOURS,

PRESTON

I reread the latest one a few times, still feeling the tinge of pain knowing she's back here in New York. From what I understand, she's been all over the place recently. Mexico for a brand trip, LA for a shoot, and back here in New York for I don't know how long. It's probably a good thing I don't know where she's staying while she's here. She could be at Beck and Margo's, spending time with their new baby, or she could be with Winnie and Archer, or she could be staying somewhere on her own. I really don't know. It's better that I don't. If I did, I might not be able to control myself and go see her. But we've made it halfway to February. She really seems to be getting her life together. She knows how I feel. When she's ready—if she's ever ready—she knows where to find me.

So I'll continue to wait, even though waiting for her is the hardest thing I've ever done. It'll be worth it in the end, as long as she's mine.

49
Emma
three months later

I NEED TO BE ON A BEACH. OR AT LEAST SOMEWHERE THAT DOESN'T have freezing temperatures outside.

Like always, I forgot my gloves when running out to the little market a block away from my studio apartment. I'm always forgetting my dang gloves, and now I'm paying for it as I rush back to my apartment as quickly as I can. This is what I get for trying to be healthy and grabbing groceries to make myself dinner instead of just ordering out.

The wind whips at my exposed cheeks as I rush down the sidewalk back to my apartment. It's surprisingly busy for it being almost mid-February in New York. It's frigid outside, and if it wasn't for me trying to have a New Year's resolution of learning to cook for myself more, I wouldn't be out in the cold at all.

My plans for the night were to eat some dinner, look over some final details for an exciting announcement I'll be posting soon, and maybe torture myself by watching the Super Bowl event coverage in Miami.

I haven't told anyone, but I've secretly become a football fan throughout the duration of this season. Or maybe it's that I became a masochist. Either way, I've watched every one of Preston's games I've been able to.

Watching him win in overtime to make it to the Super Bowl

was probably the most thrilling—but exhausting—moment of my life. I couldn't be prouder that the Mambas are one game away from having a Cinderella season. Preston deserves to have his last season be so perfect, and I'm just a ball of nerves for the actual game tomorrow night.

And I just miss Preston.

With a sigh, I shake my head and close the distance to the entrance to my apartment building. The doorman opens the door for me, holding it as I rush inside with my groceries.

"Good evening," he says, his cheeks pink from the cold. I feel bad he's having to be out in it, but at least he's not out in it unless someone's wanting to get in.

"H-i-i—" I smile through my chattering teeth. I shake my body, trying to get the blood moving now that I'm in the warmth of the apartment building. My arms tremble with the weight of the grocery bags as I walk toward the elevator.

A figure standing by the elevators catches my attention. I stop, forgetting all about the heavy weight of the bags in my hands.

"*Gram?*"

She jumps, the shocked tone of my voice taking her by surprise as she turns to face me. It's definitely Gram, Preston and Peyton's grandmother, although I have no idea why she's here.

"Good lord, dear, how long were you going to make an old lady wait in the cold for you?"

My mouth hangs open as I take her in. She wears a massive parka in a dark shade of brown with a faux fur hat pulled over her gray hair. I let out a little sigh, just now realizing how much I missed the woman standing in front of me.

"Are you frozen? Take me up to your apartment so we can warm up."

"What are you doing here?" I ask. I want to give her a hug, but my hands are too full to do anything. I shuffle my feet awkwardly to the elevator, pressing the button with my elbow as I keep looking over at Gram to see if she's real or not.

Maybe I'm hallucinating. Can you do that when you're too cold? Am I hypothermic?

The elevator bell rings, but I'm too busy opening and shutting my eyes to check if I'm seeing things to get in.

Gram's eyebrows rise to her gray hairline. She waves her hands in the air. "Are you going to get in or just gawk at me?"

I jump, turning around and scurrying into the elevator before she can give me a lecture. The doors close. "Can you press floor sixteen?" I ask, my hands full and the button too low for me to get with my elbow.

Gram listens before crossing her arms over her chest. The elevator rises, and it's quiet for a moment as we wait for it to reach my floor. I stare at Gram, a little dumbfounded, wondering why she's here.

"Is everything okay?" I ask, my mind racing with the worst possibilities of why she'd come to visit me. I doubt this part of Manhattan is somewhere Gram visits frequently enough for her to just pop by. Now that I'm thinking about it, I don't know how she found out where I live to begin with. I just took over the lease a month ago, and I've agreed to only pay monthly as I figure out what I want to do next.

"We'll talk more when we get inside. I can barely see you over the bags of food. Are you feeding an army tonight?"

I laugh, looking down at the bags. I'd gone a little overboard with buying food, but it was one of those store visits when nothing sounded good, so actually, everything sounded like a good idea to put in the basket just in case. "No. No army tonight. Just me." And I guess maybe Gram, depending on the reason for her surprise visit.

Before I can ask any more questions, we're on my floor, and the elevator doors are opening.

"This way," I tell Gram, stepping out and walking down the hallway to my studio apartment at the very end. It's not the most luxurious space, but it's mine, and I'm proud of it. Aunt V and I spent a weekend together touring apartments a few weeks ago.

I was sad to come back to New York and leave her, but it was time.

As I stop in front of the door, trying to line up my pocket with the card reader on the door so it'll unlock, I can't help but hope Gram sees the potential for the space the same way I did. I want her to like it, even though I know I'm sure she's used to far nicer places here in the city.

I manage to get the door unlocked and open. Gram follows me into the space as I place both bags of food on the small island.

"Are you hungry at all?" I ask her, the both of us working on removing our coats.

She shakes her head, pulling her hat off and running her fingers through her short, gray hair. "No, dear. I would love to sit down and talk with you, though. You can put the groceries away first. I'll take a look around."

I smile, my eyes traveling over the space. There isn't a ton of room to look around since it's a studio apartment, but I don't mention anything about that. I rush to get the groceries sorted, my stomach in knots from whatever Gram wants to discuss. Once all the food is put away, I basically leap toward the small leather chair opposite hers in my tiny living space, ready to hear whatever she has to say.

"Is everything okay?" I ask again, my heart racing. What if something happened to Preston or Peyton? I hope nothing's wrong with the family.

Gram nods, spreading her arms wide and motioning for a hug. "Yes. I'll explain, Emma, I promise. First, give me a hug. It's been too long since I've seen you."

I gladly lean forward and pull her small frame into my arms. She smells exactly the same as she did over the summer. I didn't realize how much I missed it—how much I missed her.

"It's so good to see you, dear," Gram comments next to my ear. She pats my hair for a second before pulling away, a wide smile on her face. "It took me by surprise when Preston told the family the two of you went your separate ways. I thought I'd be seeing you at his games and over the holidays."

I nod, feeling incredibly guilty. It's not that I didn't want to be at his games or even spend the holidays with his family. I know all of that would've been the best time, but I needed the time and space to figure myself out and complete what I set out to do when I left for the Hamptons in the first place—find and fall in love with myself.

"It's good to see you too, Gram," I manage to get out through a clogged throat. "I missed you terribly."

Gram smiles before leaning back in the chair. Part of me wonders if I should've asked her if she wanted tea or something sophisticated. Unfortunately, my New Year's resolution doesn't include making my own coffee, so I have nothing besides water and energy drinks stocked in my apartment.

"Shall we get right to it?" Gram offers with a shrug.

I nod, my pulse spiking with anticipation. "Please tell me Preston's okay," I rush to get out. Last I saw, he was safe in Miami doing press for Super Bowl week. Did he get injured at practice? Oh god, what if he's hurt and can't play?

Gram clicks her tongue for a moment. "That's the exact reason I'm here, dear."

My stomach drops. What if something did happen? Before I can panic and ask her what happened, she holds her hands up to speak. "Physically, he's fine. He's focused on winning this game. But emotionally, lately, he's…"

"He's what?"

"He misses you, and I just wanted to come talk to you about what happened. I wouldn't be a grandmother if I didn't meddle a little bit in his personal life."

I swallow. I didn't know what to expect when I saw Gram waiting for me in my apartment lobby, but I wouldn't have guessed that she was here to meddle in Preston's and my relationship.

Apparently, I don't respond to her fast enough because she

keeps going. "Did you know that right after my late husband and I got married, I ran away for a week?"

My head cocks to the side. "No, I didn't." The only things I learned about Gram and Joseph were the things she shared with me and the small snippets of memories Preston told me about. But Gram's words take me by surprise because I wasn't expecting her to be the kind of person to run away.

"Well, I did. One morning, I woke up and realized I felt like I blinked and my entire life had changed. It didn't feel bad, but it felt sudden. I didn't feel like myself. So I left Joseph a note that I'd be back, and I caught the first bus out of the city."

I lean forward, entranced by Gram's words. "Where did you go? And *why* did you go?"

"I stopped at one little city after another. I couldn't tell you the names of most of them. Where I was didn't matter—it's that in that week to myself I embraced the changes of my life. I embraced the uncomfortableness of the unknown, and within that, I realized I'd never known myself more."

I mull over her words for a moment, a little shocked by the confession. "What happened when you got back home?"

"Joseph was waiting for me at the bus station. He pulled me off the bus and into his arms. I started crying from how much I missed him and how guilty I felt for feeling the need to leave in the first place. He didn't let me get the words out. I still remember it clear as day to this day, sweet girl. Joseph grabbed my face in his hands and looked me right in the eye when he told me he'd always give me all the time in the world, that he'd wait for me. I never wanted to be a wife, not really. I wanted to spend my days wrapped up in a book and pretend the real world didn't exist. I was scared by how much I loved him and was scared after we married so quickly. But I don't regret a thing. If I could go back, I would've married him sooner because that man loved me even when I was messy and indecisive. In fact, I think he loved me because of those things."

My eyes burn with unshed tears. I knew there was a reason

that the moment I met Gram, it felt like we connected. Now, I feel it even more because her journey and my journey are far more similar than I could've ever expected.

"Why are you telling me this?" I croak, wiping under my eyes. I still have a face full of makeup on from filming content earlier, so I'm sure there are black smudges under my eyes that I'm only making worse by wiping.

"Because I understand you, dear. I *was* you. And I know true love when I see it, and I can tell you my grandson loves you despite anything you don't love about yourself."

Tears stream down my face at this point. "You don't know that. I mean, he nev—"

Gram swats at the air between us dismissively. "I knew my boy was falling for you in the Hamptons, and still loves you to this day. The same way I knew that the story you two fed the family was bullshit. You two had just met and, for reasons I'm not sure of, were telling the world you'd been dating."

I stare at Gram with my mouth hanging wide open. I don't know if I'm more surprised she said the word "bullshit" or the fact she knew Preston and I were lying. "What?" I get out, pausing for a moment to think about how she could know. "I don't know what you're talking about," I lie.

Gram rolls her eyes. "Spare me the lies, darling. I could see right through your story."

"Why didn't you say anything?" I whisper. If she knew the entire time, she was really good at pretending she didn't. She seemed invested in getting to know the story behind me and Preston.

Gram folds her hands in her lap and smiles knowingly at me. "Because I could still see Preston was crazy about you, even from the very beginning. I'd never seen anyone bring him out of his shell the way you did. It didn't matter to me if you two had known each other for years or just met; all I knew was my boy was happy, and because of that, I minded my own business for once in my life."

All of the interactions I had with Gram that first week and even in the months after Peyton's wedding run through my mind. I feel a little silly about all the times we talked about our first dates and how we met in front of her, now knowing she saw right through all of it.

"Do you love him?" Gram asks, pulling me from my thoughts. I can barely keep up with her going from one subject to the next. I'm still recovering from her dropping the fact she knew about us, and the tiny tidbit she shared about believing Preston loved me, to even analyze my feelings.

Luckily, I've had plenty of time and space to think about how I feel about Preston. The answer I give her is easy and honest. "I do."

"Then why aren't the two of you together anymore?"

I look at the ceiling as I try to prevent more tears from falling. A lump forms in my throat as all of my fears and insecurities bubble to the surface. I can't even look at Gram as I answer her. "Because when I met Preston and fell for him, I didn't love how I felt about the mess that was my life. I pretended to, but at the end of the day, I didn't. My summer was supposed to be full of adventure and doing just that. I've realized in my time since the summer that it wasn't about getting my life perfectly together; it was about getting my life together enough to feel good about who *I* was. I needed to love myself and who I was becoming, the messy parts included. Instead, I let myself get lost in Preston. I fell in love with him before ever feeling that way about me. I knew, deep down, loving *him* before ever loving *me* and where I was at in my life on my own wasn't fair to either one of us if we wanted a relationship that'd last."

"What about now? How do you feel?"

I meet her gaze. My eyes sting from the tears forming, and at this point, there's no use in me fighting them. I let her see me cry. "Now, I feel good," I admit. "On some days, it's hard when I compare my life to others. I'm just finally starting to find a career I love, and one I hope I can do long-term. My friends already have established careers and families, and sometimes, on an off day, I find myself comparing my journey to theirs. But I quickly snap out of it and realize it's *okay* to be in a different place. I can appreciate the fact that I don't have my life together, and that's okay. I love that I don't take life seriously and can laugh at the embarrassing things I'll inevitably do. I've realized it's okay to feel a little lost in life. Most importantly, I've learned to love exactly where I'm at in life on the good days and the bad days."

Gram stares at me for a moment, her lips barely turning up with a smile. I shift in my seat under her stare, wondering if anything I just said made sense. "I think that's the bravest thing someone could do, dear. It's incredible you were aware enough to know you needed time by yourself first before loving somebody else. Be proud of the decisions you made. It was okay to put yourself first before jumping headfirst into falling in love."

I close my eyes as her words hit something deep inside me. I've always been someone who embraced not having my life together. I didn't mind being a mess. It was fun to joke about meeting a rich man and having him fall in love with me. I loved to make inappropriate jokes and to be spontaneous in following my friends from one end of the country to the next. But eventually, all the reasons I thought it was fun to be carefree became the things I started to dislike about myself. Since this summer, I've learned to embrace not having all of the answers. I've finally got to a place where I feel good where I'm at, even if I still have a lot of growing to do.

With a small gasp, I meet Gram's eyes as I push out of the chair. "I've got to get to Preston."

Gram smiles, her hands clapping together. *"Finally,"* she says dramatically.

"I've got to book a flight." My mind races, trying to remember where I'd stuffed my suitcase, and what I'll even pack to begin with to get to Miami in time to see Preston.

Gram lets out a huff, getting out of the chair slowly. "Nonsense. The charter plane is already booked and waiting for us at the airport."

"Really?"

Gram nods. "Now, let's go, darling. Get your bags packed, and let's go get your man!"

I laugh, shaking my head as I dart to my bedroom corner. Gram's right. I'm tired of thinking things need to be perfect or that I need to be perfect. I still have a lot to figure out, but one thing I'm confident about now is I don't want to do any of it without Preston anymore.

50
Preston

MY HEART POUNDS AS WE TAKE WHAT WILL MOST LIKELY BE THE final possession of the game. We're down by three. All we need is a field goal to tie it, but I don't want to tie. I want to end the game and win the Super Bowl.

I look around at the men standing in the huddle, all staring at me, waiting for me to make the call. They're tired—I can see it in their faces and by the way all of them gasp for air. The Portland Pirates had only been on the field for two minutes when they managed to get up by three points. We hadn't had much of a break, but a break won't be needed if we can just do one final drive and have the fairy-tale ending to our fairy-tale season.

I meet the eyes of the guys, suddenly feeling choked up about this possibly being the last drive of my football career. I want it to mean something, for us to go out on top as a team. Leaning forward, I make sure to yell so all of the men looking to me for guidance can hear me. "This game with all of you has been some of the best football I've seen in my life. It's been an honor to play these last four quarters with you, and I know we're tired, but we've got one more drive left. No one will be able to discredit the amazing things we've done this season if we just run down and score a touchdown."

The guys clap, nodding their heads and getting fired up. Their excitement has me moving forward with my speech. "They think we're going to run the ball to eat some of the clock, but we won't do that. Not yet. I'm going to throw it and make them wish they'd paid more attention to our game plan."

Everyone nods as I look over the play on my wrist. It's risky and could backfire on us. Their defense is the best we've played this year, so it won't be easy, but I'm ready for the challenge, and I know the group of guys around me are too. "One more fucking drive and the championship is ours." I swallow, suddenly feeling emotional knowing what I want to say next. "These will be the last plays of my career. I want to make them fucking count. We're going to win it."

"We'll win it for you," one of my receivers chimes in, hitting his chest to get even more hyped.

I smile, reaching across the circle and tapping his helmet. "We're going to win it for us. For our coaches. For the fans. Let's fucking go." The last part is yelled as I jump up and down. My muscles protest. They're tired and already ache. I've been beaten up on the field today, but all of that won't matter in the three minutes we have left of the game.

Everyone runs out to the line of scrimmage. I follow suit, my eyes traveling to the large jumbotron above our heads. It shows the suite I rented out for my family. It's crowded in there, making it hard to make out who's in there.

I know I see Peyton sitting front and center, her eyes glued to the field. Behind her, I swear I see a flash of blonde hair I'd recognize anywhere talking to Gram. I rip my eyes away, knowing it's my head playing tricks on me. No matter how badly I want Emma to be here for this moment, she isn't here, and that's okay. All that matters is the next three minutes of gameplay. After that, I can think about Emma all I want, but until then, I owe it to the men around me to stay focused.

I take my place behind my center. We both get into position, and just by the way the Pirates' defense is lined up across from us, they definitely think we're going to run the ball.

I smile, leaning forward and stomping my foot. "White eighty!" I yell, telling him I'm ready for the snap.

The next three minutes play out in a blur. It's the most perfect football that not only I've ever played, but the rest of my team as well. We work the clock perfectly until only four yards stand between us and winning the Super Bowl. It's fourth and goal, and the smart decision would be for us to kick a field goal to tie the game, but we opted out of that. We're not going into over-time. We've played great football up until this down, and we're going to win it with this one.

This defense is on to us. They know I've been throwing lights out and hitting every single one of my targets. We only started running the ball at the end so we didn't give them the opportunity to get the ball back if we did score a touchdown.

Everything around me slows down as my center snaps the ball beautifully, making it land right between my palms. I pretend to hand the ball off to my running back, trying to fake them out.

It works. They chase him while one of my other receivers gets double-teamed by two of their linemen. It leaves the perfect opening for me. Tucking the ball into my chest, I take off running toward the open goal line. One of the linemen notices me, and he starts running full speed right at me. My muscles protest as I try to beat him to the paint.

Knowing this is the last play I'll ever do in the league, I give it my all, no longer caring about what injury I could sustain from it. I leap, trying to go right over the lineman already coming at me at full force.

I can't hear anything as I soar over the goal line, the ball securely tucked into my chest. My shoulder hits the ground—hard—the same moment the full force of the lineman's weight falls onto me.

I wince, pain ricocheting through my body. I try to look to make sure I made it over the goal line, but I can't see anything. I hit my head on the way down, and things are fuzzy.

BRIGHT LIGHTS AND SUMMER NIGHTS   307

The only way I know we won is when my guys come rushing to me, pulling the lineman off me with the biggest smiles on their faces. I stay on the ground, trying to catch my breath from the run. I'm not a quarterback known for running or putting my body on the line, but I was willing to do anything to get this win.

"What a fucking play!" someone yells. I don't even know who it is. All I know is one moment I'm lying on the ground, and the next, I'm being lifted up by my teammates.

"Did we win?" I ask, looking around to see the reactions from others. The Pirates have already left the field as black and red confetti falls from the sky.

I don't need anyone to answer me. Suddenly, body after body is pulling me into a hug. Grown men around me fall to their knees and cry as I make my way across the field, completely stunned that we not only won but I'll never play another snap of football again.

My teammates hug me as family members and staff begin to rush the field. Cameras are in my face as different reporters try to get my reaction to winning. Someone hands me a Super Bowl hat, and I place it on my head, knowing going out on the very top is all I wanted.

I know people interview me about the win, but I have no idea what I tell them. I kind of black out, happiness completely overwhelming me. My eyes scan all of the bodies on the field, trying to look for my own family as players lift their kids in the air and embrace their loved ones around me.

And that's when I see her, my girl, rushing toward me in a small black skirt and wearing my jersey. I have to blink, wondering if seeing everyone else with their loved ones has me hallucinating. But something deep inside me knows the truth.

She's here. She's back. She's *mine*.

51
Emma

CHEERS ERUPT FROM ALL AROUND US, AND CAMERAS FLASH RIGHT next to us, but I don't pay attention to any of it. All I care about is getting to Preston and finally being in his arms after months apart.

I leap toward him, completely trusting that he'll catch me.

The moment his strong arms wrap around me, it feels like a weight has been lifted off my shoulders. I know I've missed him in our time apart, but I hadn't realized how deep missing him went until I found myself back in his arms. I missed him all the way down to my bones, and now that I feel him around me again, I know I can never let him go.

Preston's hand lifts to cradle the back of my head, keeping me pressed to him as he lines up his mouth next to my ear. "Tell me this is real," he says, his voice thick with emotion.

I nod, tears already welling up in my eyes. I don't mind these tears. They're the happy kind. "It's real. You just won the Super Bowl, Rhodes."

He laughs, holding me even tighter. People rush all around us, calling out our names as cameras flash in my peripheral. I barely notice them, too wrapped up in the moment with Preston to care. Something I've realized is this isn't about them; it's about us. That's what matters, and that's what I'll focus on. Preston runs his fingers through the hair at my neck as he lets out a content sigh. "No. Tell me *you're* real. Tell me you're here."

I pull away, wanting to be able to look at him with my next words. "I'm here and…" I bite my lip, knowing I could probably wait to tell him somewhere more private but not wanting to. "I love you."

His eyes go wide, and the smile he gives me is the most dazzling smile I've ever seen from him. It shines throughout his entire face, making my pulse spike with happiness. "You mean that, rebel? Because I'm so fucking in love with you that the thought of ever truly losing you rips me open inside."

I just stare at him for a moment, adjusting the hat on his head so it's backward. I press my forehead to his, soaking in the moment with him. "I think I'll always be a little lost. That's who I am. But I'm ready to be lost with you, Preston Rhodes. Now, tell me you love me again."

The hand not holding me against his body finds the side of my face. His thumb traces my cheekbone, and that small touch makes everything right in the world. I've missed even the smallest caresses from him and how he always has to be touching me. We've got a lot of time to make up for, and I cannot wait to start. "I love you, Emma. Everything about you. Even the things you might not love about yourself yet. And I'll spend every damn day proving to you that every single thing about you is worthy of love. Even the messy parts."

I cry, tucking my face into the crook of his neck. He allows me the moment, his arms wrapping around me and keeping me pinned to his body. I can hear people yelling our names, their microphones and cameras so close to us they've probably heard every word shared between us.

A freeing feeling washes over me as I realize I really don't care. All I care about is my love for this man, who has been nothing but patient and steadfast in his love for me. Now, I'm ready for the world to know how lucky I feel to call him mine.

I pull away. Our eyes meet, and it's hard not to let the biggest smile take over my face.

Preston leans in. He lowers his voice and talks next to my ear to try and make our conversation as private as possible. "I really want to kiss you right now, Em, but there's a thousand cameras on us, and I don't know if you want the spotlight on you like that or not."

I don't use my words to answer him. Instead, I grab his face and pull him in close to me. He smiles as our lips meet. It isn't the most passionate kiss we've ever had, but it's perfect. The clicks of cameras surround us as more and more people try to get our attention.

We savor the feeling of being the only two people in the world for a few more seconds before the kiss ends. Preston sets me down softly, his hand immediately finding mine.

Before we turn toward the flood of media personnel that want our attention, I reach up and press my free hand to Preston's cheek. He looks hot as hell in his football uniform and backward hat. He looks happy, and happy looks incredibly sexy on him. "Before we're overwhelmed by a thousand people congratulating you, I just wanted to be one of the first to say congratulations, Rhodes. You fucking did it. The man I love is a badass and the greatest in the league."

"I'll never get tired of hearing you say you love me."

I smile, spotting Preston's family waiting to talk to him. I'd been so excited that I ran ahead of them, my poor security detail trailing behind me, trying to keep up as I pushed and shoved my way through people to get to Preston as quickly as I could.

"Good. I plan on saying it a *lot* now."

"I like the sound of that."

"Good. Now, let's go celebrate."

The floodgates of media attention open, and I stand next to Preston the entire time, wanting the world to know how proud I am of him. One reporter after the next asks about us and the status of our relationship. Preston handles the questions beautifully, telling every one of them he's never been happier and that's all that matters.

I don't know how long we spend on that field talking to one person and then the next. When the Super Bowl MVP is announced, I'm not surprised it's Preston.

When he stands at the podium with the trophy in his hand and tears in his eyes, an overwhelming sense of happiness takes over me. He couldn't have had a better season for his last one. Just by the way his teammates and coaches look at him, I know he couldn't be respected more.

I let him soak in the moment with his teammates and family. He deserves the attention he's getting, and I'm just honored I get to share this moment with him. I smile when I realize that from now on, we'll share all our moments, the big ones and the small. And I cannot wait to experience every single moment life has to offer with the love of my life—Preston Rhodes. My forever. *Mine.*

Forever used to terrify me. The unknown was even scarier. But now, it's exciting. Whatever happens, I'll have Preston, and maybe a forever of unknowns with him is actually the perfect future. It's real, and it's ours. And nothing can beat that.

52
Preston

EXHAUSTION SEEPS INTO MY BONES AS WE FINALLY MAKE IT BACK TO the hotel room after a night filled with celebrating our Super Bowl win. Winning the last game of my career is a surreal feeling, but what made it feel even better was having Emma by my side throughout all of tonight.

When they handed me the trophy, I couldn't look at anyone but her. The smile on her face as she watched me give a speech will be burned in my mind forever. She seemed so happy and proud to watch me succeed, to experience it with me, and I'll forever be grateful that I got to share the moment with her. It made tonight all the better because I had the woman I love with me.

I look at Emma as she sits down at the end of the king-sized bed and begins to unzip one of her knee-high boots. I stand in the doorway for a moment, taking it in that she's really here.

She looks up at me with a sleepy smile. "What are you looking at, Rhodes?"

I fold my arms across my chest and lean against the doorframe. "You," I answer simply, still in awe that she's mine.

She shakes her head, pulling off one boot and then the other. Her eyes stay locked on mine as she reaches behind her and unzips the little black skirt she was wearing. My body heats and

I forget all about how tired I am just at the sight of her pulling the skirt down her thighs.

"Why don't you come sit? I don't know how you're still functioning after playing a game like that and celebrating for hours after." She pats the spot next to her on the bed.

I probably should feel more tired than I do at the moment, but seeing her undress in front of me, just being alone with her for the first time in months, gives me a second wind. We went straight from the stadium to the after-parties. We stayed out so late that the Miami sun will start to rise at any moment.

I close the distance and sit down next to her, appreciating the view of her in nothing but my jersey. "You look sexy as hell in my jersey, rebel."

She bites her lip, her fingers twisting in the fabric of the jersey as she lifts it slightly, showing the black pair of lace panties she's wearing. "I was hoping you'd say that."

I lean in and wrap my fingers around the base of her neck, pulling her in for a kiss. I don't know how many kisses I've stolen over the course of the night, but I can't help myself. All I want to do is make up for lost time with her. It's the reason I kiss her again, pulling her into my lap until she's straddling me.

Emma doesn't protest. She kisses me back with the same hungry passion. Her hips rock against me slightly as the kiss deepens. We kiss like that for I don't know how long, the two of us getting lost in each other. Part of me wants to strip her of every article of clothing she wears so I can bury myself inside her and get as close to her as possible.

The other part of me wants to savor this. We have the rest of our lives for one another. I can take my time. Right now, I'd rather get inside that beautiful mind of hers and find out what the past six months have looked like for her.

I'm the one to pull away. Because I can't help it, I feather kisses along her jaw and neck. I missed the beat of her pulse against my lips, and I have plans to kiss every single inch of her body now that I have her back.

"Tell me," I begin, continuing to press my lips to her skin.

The most breathtaking giggle escapes her as I nip at the tender spot behind her ear. "Tell you what?"

"Everything," I mutter. "I want to know how you've been, what you've been doing, and anything else you want to tell me."

Emma smiles. Her fingers absentmindedly trace circles on the back of my neck. "A lot has happened since I last saw you."

"Tell me all of it."

"What if I wanted to know about you?" she teases.

"All I did was focus on football. Now, tell me about you."

Emma rolls her eyes playfully. "When I first moved back in with Aunt V, things were hard. I missed you and was constantly questioning myself whether I'd made the right decision. Deep down, I knew I had. I knew if I didn't work on finding myself, eventually, I'd self-sabotage our relationship because I think it's hard to fully love someone before you love yourself. I could've gotten lost in you and lost myself even more, and while that might've worked for a short period of time, I wanted the forever kind of love with you, Preston. And I wanted the forever kind of love with myself. I needed to be alone for once in my life and be *okay* with that. So, I started working on embracing who I was. I hired a whole management team and decided I wanted to take social media seriously."

I keep her body pinned to mine as she recounts what her life has been like in the months we've been apart. I hang on every word, loving how confident she sounds. "I continued to keep it real with my followers. Like *really* real. Sometimes I was so honest and raw I questioned if I was doing the right thing, but it turns out when you tell your insecurities to millions of people on the internet, that a lot of them feel the same way too. I didn't feel so isolated. I accepted I wasn't the only one still trying to figure out what my passion was or who used dark humor to deflect how I felt about my life. After that, day by day, and little by little, I realized I was accepting myself for everything I was."

"I'm so proud of you," I tell her honestly. I loved her before, but I'm so happy she chose the path she did. While I missed her every second of every day, I love her even more for not rushing into things.

Emma smiles, her fingertips brushing over my jaw as she holds my face between her hands. "I'm proud of me too."

"So, what's next for you, Emma Turner? Besides being my girlfriend, of course."

She raises her eyebrows. "You haven't asked me to be your girlfriend."

My hands drift down her back until they're cupping her asscheeks. I pull her tighter to me, loving having our bodies flush against one another. "I was so excited to get you back that I'm already messing this up." I laugh, leaning in for one small kiss before continuing. I tilt my head back, wanting to be able to look into her eyes before asking the next question.

"Em, my love, my everything, will you be my girlfriend?"

She smiles, her entire face lighting up with her loud squeal. "Duh!" she rushes out excitedly, leaning in to kiss me. "Emma Turner, Preston Rhodes' girlfriend. Damn, that's hot."

I laugh, shaking my head at her. "Emma Turner, the most incredible woman to ever exist and the only one to ever hold my heart. Damn…that's hot."

We both laugh at my impression of her. "That's hot" definitely sounds a lot better coming from her mouth than it does mine.

"So there's one more thing I have to tell you," Emma begins before pulling her bottom lip between her teeth.

"And what's that, rebel?"

"I don't want this to overshadow your big day of winning the Super Bowl and retiring and all the things, so I can wait to tell you, but—"

I press my fingers to her lips. "We celebrate all of our wins together. One will never overshadow the other. Now, tell me what has you excited because I can see it written all over your face, and I want to celebrate it with you."

"Well…" Her body rocks up and down as she can barely contain her giddiness with whatever she wants to tell me. My heart already bursts with excitement for her, knowing how happy it's clearly making her, and she hasn't even told me what it is yet. "Your girlfriend will now be the host of a little podcast called *Quarter-life Crisis*, and there's already a bidding war between streaming platforms to be the one the podcast is exclusive to."

I stand up, my hands supporting her weight as I turn in excitement. "That's incredible." I keep her body pressed to mine, my mind reeling with amazement at her. I'm so taken aback by her and all that she's been able to accomplish in the months that we've been apart that for a moment, I can't even find words.

Emma gives me a wide grin, her eyes misting over with unshed tears. "I still can't fully wrap my head around people wanting to listen to me ramble even more about getting my shit together, but it's real. I'm already hoping my sports guy will be the first guest."

A lightness fills my chest at her words. "I'd be honored, rebel."

"I love you," she whispers, her features softening as her eyes track my face.

"I love you too," I respond, looking forward to a lifetime of "I love yous" with her.

"Thank you for being patient with me. For giving me the time I needed."

"You don't have to thank me for that. I'm happy you did because now I know that no matter what life throws at us, we'll handle it together."

She nods. "Together. Forever." The smile falls from her face as she licks her lips when her gaze falls to my own.

"Forever," I repeat. She wraps her thighs around my middle, and my fingertips inch underneath the fabric of her panties.

I sit down, my hands exploring her body. She does the same, her hands drifting underneath my shirt. When she lifts it up, I let her pull it off me. She throws it behind her, her lips kissing my throat until a small gasp leaves her.

My eyes find hers, catching her staring at the chain around my neck. More importantly, what's on the chain.

"Is that?" she asks, her voice quiet as she reaches out to grab the chain.

I nod. "It's been my lucky charm throughout the season. I wouldn't play a game without it."

Emma's bottom lip trembles as her eyes meet mine. "You kept the penny I found last summer?"

"I did." The moment she returned home, I found a jeweler that'd make the penny into a necklace charm for me. It allowed me to feel like she was still with me, even when she wasn't. All this time, she and her penny were my lucky charm; she just didn't know it. "I was never superstitious until this year and this penny. The chain broke in the middle of one of our games. We went into overtime, and I played like shit while I frantically waited for a team of trainers to put it back together. Finally, they did, and we pulled off a win, but I was nervous."

Emma looks at me in disbelief. "I thought you'd probably lost it the day I found it."

"Nope. I've kept it with me every day since. And it's not going anywhere now. It's my lucky charm. So are you."

"Hey, Preston?" Emma asks, rocking her hips up and down with a wide smile.

"Yes?"

She leans closer until our lips almost brush. "I know you're probably exhausted, but I need you. *Right now.*"

Her words are all I need to hear. I turn and set her gently on top of the bed. I thought I could wait until we got some sleep to have her, but I can't. And I fucking love that she can't either. "I need you too," I comment, pulling her panties down her thighs and appreciating the view of her truly in nothing but my jersey.

"Then come get me, *boyfriend.*"

I smile at the way she says boyfriend. God, I'll never get tired of hearing it.

"Whatever you want, *girlfriend*."

Emma laughs, but it gets cut off the moment I pull her to the edge of the bed and bury my face between her thighs.

Emma Turner. My fake girlfriend turned real one.

My life falls perfectly into place as I prepare to make love to the woman who owns my heart. Nothing for us was easy. We started out as something that was only supposed to be temporary. She's taught me everything I know about love and the sacrifices you make for a love like ours. But no matter what, through it all, we were able to find our forever between the bright lights and summer nights.

EPILOGUE
Preston
four months later

"Preston, I'm not so sure about this," Emma whispers from behind me. Her fingers tighten around mine as I lead her to the tall fence.

I turn around to look at her, only seeing part of her face through the darkness. The moon tries to illuminate the night, but the trees surrounding us make it hard. "Since when are you unsure about breaking and entering? If my memory serves me right, it was a year ago that I caught you hopping this same fence to crash Peyton's party."

Emma rolls her eyes, using her free hand to give me a playful shove. "At least then the club was open. It feels wrong for everything at Pembroke to be so dark."

I nod in agreement, leading her to a spot I think would work to hop the fence. My mind goes back to a year ago when I first laid eyes on her. Even that night, I knew something was special about Emma, and I've known every day since in the year we've met.

And what a year it's been. From the moment we won the Super Bowl, life has been full speed ahead for the both of us. Emma signed a major podcast deal. The podcast officially released last month and debuted at number one for all podcasts in its first week. I had the honor of being her first guest on the show, where we let it slip that we'd officially bought a house together in Manhattan—one right next to Beck and Margo.

"Right here looks good," I tell her, stopping at a spot in the fence that's slightly on a hill, making it a little less distance to climb.

"Babe, I just really don't think this is necessary." Emma's eyebrows pinch together with uncertainty.

Her reaction makes me smile. "Don't bail out on me now, rebel."

My heart leaps in my chest at the nickname I gave her a year ago to the date. Little did I know then that the woman who threw a heel in my direction would end up becoming the love of my life. She's made my life better in countless ways in the year since we met, and tonight, I wanted to return back to the place we met on the one-year anniversary.

"Imagine the headlines if we get arrested tonight," she quips, placing her hand against the fence. She supports her weight against it as she pulls both her shoes off.

I hold my hand out, taking the heels from her. "We're not going to get arrested."

One of the curled pieces of her hair falls in her face as she shakes her head at me. We'd gotten dressed up for a nice dinner at one of our favorite spots here in the Hamptons to celebrate the anniversary. I hadn't told her about my plan to break into the club until we were on our way here. Seeing the look on her face when I told her was priceless.

And she doesn't even know everything I have planned for the night.

"Are you going up first, or am I?" Emma asks, placing her hands on her hips.

I can't help but smile, loving how she's going along with my plan even though she thinks there's a chance we could get in trouble. "I'll go up first with your shoes. You come after so I can help you down."

She raises an eyebrow at me. "I don't seem to remember needing help last year."

This makes me laugh. "I wanted to help you, baby. But you came flying at me before I was able to finish counting down."

"You know I don't have patience."

I close the distance to her, pulling her body flush to mine. "It's one of the many things I love about you."

She rises to her tiptoes and plants a kiss against my lips. "Good. Now, stop procrastinating and climb the damn fence. I want to see what Pembroke looks like empty."

I lean in and give her one more kiss before backing away with a sigh. She was just saying she was unsure about breaking in, and now she's encouraging me to get to it. God, I love her.

"I'll let you know when I'm ready," I tell her, holding her shoes by the thin heels so I can still climb the fence.

"Sure thing, babe." She giggles, letting me know that as soon as my feet are on the ground on the other side, I need to be ready for her to hop over.

I make quick work of getting to the other side of the fence and landing smoothly. My eyes quickly scan my surroundings with a smirk before I train them on the top of the fence.

Just like I suspected, Emma's already impressively climbed the fence in a knee-length white dress and waits at the top. Unlike the first time we met, when I couldn't see her features because of the dark, tonight I can see all of her thanks to the full moon.

She waits for me with a smile on her face. She pulls her bottom lip between her teeth, and I know her well enough to know she's going to jump at any second, even though I haven't given her the green light yet.

"Okay, jump on one, two..."

"Three!" Emma yells, pushing her body from the top and falling right at me. Her heels drop to the ground as I make sure I catch her in my arms, not wanting her to get even a single scratch from my idea to break into the club.

"Do you ever listen?" I say, my chest rising and falling in quick succession from the rush of adrenaline.

Emma shrugs, backing out of my arms to grab her shoes. "You already know the answer to that, so I'm not even going to answer. You love me whether I listen or not, and that's all I care about."

I nod. She's right.

I cock my head toward the back door of the club, the one I know happens to be unlocked tonight. "Should we sneak in?"

She lets out a giddy squeal before enthusiastically nodding her head. She must realize how loud her sound of excitement was because she throws her hand over her mouth. "Yes," she whispers, all the fear of getting in trouble for breaking in seemingly gone.

I hold my hand out to her, hoping she doesn't feel how clammy it's gotten with nerves. I had one drive to win a Super Bowl in under three minutes, and I still didn't feel as nervous as I do at this moment. All I can do is hope she doesn't notice as I lead her toward the back door.

"It's so quiet," she mutters as we reach the building.

My heart hammers in my chest as my fingers wrap around the door handle. Emma doesn't seem to notice, thank god, and she begins to rattle on about the tennis match we have tomorrow with Jackson and Peyton.

"I think we have the win in the bag," she whispers as I pull the door open. "I'm ready to really kick their—"

She stops as I pull her into the hallway illuminated by hundreds of tiny candles.

"Preston." She looks back at me with wide eyes. "What is this?"

I can't help but smile. "Keep walking, baby."

Her fingers tighten against mine as she lets me lead her down the hallway. We follow the candles even as they continue into the room where I first started to fall for her a year ago. I press a kiss to her knuckles before dropping her hand.

She opens her mouth to say something, but the words she was about to utter get lost when her eyes land across the room.

"Oh my god." Her hands go to her mouth as she takes in the giant, illuminated letters that spell out 'Marry Me.'

When she turns back toward me, she finds me already on one knee with a ring box in my hand.

"Stop it." She lets out a loud, happy sob; her hands still covering her mouth in shock.

"Emma Turner," I begin, my mind suddenly forgetting the proposal I'd rehearsed in the mirror countless times.

"*Yes*," she cries excitedly.

I laugh, my hands shaking as I hold out the unopened ring box in front of me. "You have to let me ask first, Em. I've planned out this long speech to ask you to—"

"No matter what you say, it's already a yes," she says, grabbing my face in her hands.

I swallow, emotion clogged in my throat at how much I love this woman.

"God, I love you," I croak, grabbing her hand. It shakes against mine as I hold the box up.

"Emma, later tonight, when my mind isn't clouded from nerves, I'm going to recite to you the entire epic speech I had planned to ask you to be my wife. It was filled with all the reasons I love you and how you make me a better man each and every day. I've known since the moment you told me you loved me that I was going to marry you, and I don't want to wait any longer to make you my wife. I had all these other romantic things I was going to say with the proposal. It was filled with all the plans I have for us and how I cannot wait to be your partner in life for the rest of our lives, but fuck, all the poetic things I had in my mind are gone, so now..." I open the box, a rush of relief coursing through me at the way she gasps when she looks at the ring. "Will you marry me? I know I suck at words, but no one will ever love you like I do, and I promise to spend the rest of my life making sure you wake up each morning knowing how loved and cherished you are and…"

"Preston, yes." Tears stream down her face as she falls to her knees in front of me, her arms wrapping around my neck. "God, yes. A million times yes."

I wonder if she can feel the beat of my racing heart through the press of our chests. "You will?" I ask, needing her to say it one more time.

"Of course, I will." She kisses me, forgetting all about the ring still in its box that I need to slide onto her finger. I convinced Margo, Winnie, Pippa, and Emma's aunt to all come with me when ring shopping. I wanted all of their feedback to pick out the perfect ring for Emma, and I hope the large princess-cut diamond set on a platinum band of diamonds is everything she could've ever wanted in a ring.

I wrap my arms around her, holding her close to my body as I bury my face in her hair. "I love you," I get out, my voice shaking with how much I love her.

"I love you too," she responds immediately, leaning back so she can meet my eyes.

With a shaky hand, I slide the ring out of the box and place it on her finger. It's a perfect fit, and I love the sight of it on her. I've known she's mine for a while now, but I can't wait for everyone who sees her with this to know it, too.

"This is the most stunning ring I've ever seen," she says, her voice full of shock.

"Only the best for the most beautiful woman I've ever seen."

Suddenly, all of our friends and family pop out from behind the letters and run toward us. It's a frenzy of hugs and tears and congratulations. As everyone we love most shares in the excitement about our engagement, I pull Emma into my side and look down at her, marveling at the fact she's now my fiancée.

The smile she gives me as she meets my eyes is my new favorite one of hers.

It's one that promises forever.

And I can't fucking wait for a forever with her by my side.

THE END

WANT MORE BLACK TIE BILLIONAIRES?

The Black Tie Billionaires series is now complete. Read all books now!

BLACK TIE BILLIONAIRES:
Black Ties and White Lies: https://amzn.to/40POdqu
Pretty Rings and Broken Things: https://amzn.to/3Ponrlc
Bright Lights and Summer Nights : https://amzn.to/48d9Kgg

WANT MORE KAT?

To read the extended epilogue for Emma and Preston, make sure
to subscribe to Kat's newsletter. You can find it on
authorkatsingleton.com

ACKNOWLEDGMENTS

Can you hear me crying? This book tested me in ways I wasn't expecting. It's my favorite book I've ever written and I hope you loved the conclusion to this story as much as I do. Emma and Preston's story would not be what it is if it weren't for the amazing people I have in my life who support me every step of the way when writing and releasing a book.

First, to *you*, the reader. I'll never be able to thank you for how your love for this series and my words really changed my life. This book was written for every single one of you who begged for Emma's story. Your endless support means the world. It is you who is the lifeblood of this community. It is you that keeps me going even on the hard days. You're the reason I get to wake up every single day and work my dream job, and for that, I'm so freaking grateful. Thank you for choosing my words to read. Thank you for supporting me. You've given me the greatest gift by choosing *my* book to read. I love you so much.

To my husband, AKA Kat Singleton's husband. Thank you for everything you do behind the scenes to make sure all things Kat Singleton runs smoothly. You put so much time and care into all the behind the scenes things and I appreciate it beyond words. I love you and am so grateful that my forever is with you.

Kelsey, thank you for running my life. I don't even remember how I functioned before you (I did it miserably) but I'm so happy I never have to know that life again. Thank you for putting up with me even when I don't make things easy. Your friendship means to the world to me. I love you and everything you do for Team Kat.

Ashlee, thank you for creating the most stunning covers for the entire series. You brought to life exactly what I wanted, and even put up with me when my vision changed from one thing to another. I'm so lucky to call you a friend and I love you beyond words.

To my soul sisters who spend every day writing with me, encouraging me and cheering me on. I love you three with my entire heart.

To Salma and Sandra. Thank you for listening to me spiral about Emma and Preston's story and encouraging me when I'd panic about things feeling right. Your feedback is so important to me and I'm so grateful to work with the both of you. Thank you for helping making *Bright Lights and Summer Nights* ready to be released to readers.

To Meags, Chas, Cindy, and Katy, thank you all of your vital feedback that made this book what it is. You put up with my constant voice memos of new ideas and answered my million questions about the story. I wouldn't be able to do this without you and I appreciate your help in making Emma and Preston's story as perfect as possible. I love you forever.

To the content creators and people in this community that share my books. I'm so eternally grateful for you. I've connected with so many amazing people since I started this author adventure and it means the world to me to have all of you to connect with. I'm appreciative of the fact that you take the time to talk about my stories on your platform. I notice every single one of your posts, videos, pictures, etc. It means the world to me that you share about my characters and stories. You make this community such a special place. Thank you for everything you do.

To Valentine and everyone with VPR. Thank you for everything you do to keep me in check. It's not a secret that I'm a constant hot mess, and all of you are the reason I'm able to function. Thank you for making all things Kat Singleton run smoothly and amazing. I'm so thankful to call VPR home and for your help in getting *Bright Lights and Summer Nights* out to the world.

To the amazing humans on my own personal content team, thank you for making every release amazing. You babes are forever blowing my mind with the unique content you create based on my words and I'm so grateful to have all of you on this journey with me.

I have the privilege of having a growing group of people I can run to on Facebook for anything—Kat Singleton's Sweethearts. The members there are always there for me, and I'm so fortunate to have them in my corner. I owe all of them so much gratitude for being there on the hard days and on the good days. Sweethearts, y'all are my people.

Keep reading for the first chapter of Beck and Margo's story in
Black Ties and White Lies…

MARGO - 1

"Margo, Margo, Margo."

A familiar voice startles me from my computer screen. Spinning in my office chair I find my best friend, Emma, hunched over the wall of my cubicle. Her painted red lips form a teasing grin.

Pulling the pen I was chewing on out of my mouth, I narrow my eyes at her suspiciously. "What?"

She licks her teeth, flicking the head of the Nash Pierce bobblehead she bought me ages ago. "Who did you piss off this time?"

My stomach drops, and I don't even know what she's talking about. "Are you still drunk?" I accuse, thinking about the wine we consumed last night. We downed two bottles of cheap pinot grigio with our roommate and best friend, Winnie. Split between the three of us, there's no way she's still tipsy, but it's the best I could come up with.

She scoffs, her face scrunching in annoyance. "Obviously not. I was refilling my coffee in the lounge when *Darla* had asked if I'd seen you."

I stifle an eye roll. Darla knew I'd be at one of two places. I'm always either at my desk or huddled in front of the coffee maker trying to get the nectar of the gods to keep me awake.

Darla knew *exactly* where to find me.

She just didn't want to.

You accidentally put water in the coffee bean receptacle instead of the carafe and suddenly the office receptionist hates you. It's not like I meant to break it. It's not my fault it wasn't made clear on the machine what went where. I was just *trying* to help.

"I haven't heard from her," I comment, my eyes flicking to Darla's desk. She's not there, but her phone lights up with an incoming call. Darla rarely leaves her desk. It isn't a good sign that she's nowhere in sight. The sky could be falling, and I'm not sure Darla would leave her perch.

Emma rounds the wall of my cubicle, planting her ass on my desk like she's done a million times before, even though I've asked her not to just as many times.

"I'm working." Reaching out, I smack her black stiletto, forcing her foot off the armrest of my chair.

She laughs, playfully digging her heel into my thigh. "Well, Darla, that *amazing woman*, told me the boss wants to see you."

"I thought Marty was out for meetings all day today?"

Emma bites her lip, shaking her head at me. "No, like the *boss*, boss. The head honcho. Bossman. I think it's somebody new."

She opens her mouth to say something else, but I cut her off. "That can't be right."

"Margo!" Darla barks from the doors of our conference room. I almost jump out of my chair from the shrill tone of her voice.

Emma's eyes are wide as saucers as she looks from Darla back to me. "Seriously, Mar, what did you do?"

I slide my feet into my discarded heels underneath my desk. Standing up, I wipe my hands down the front of my skirt. I hate that my palms are already clammy from nerves. "I didn't do anything," I hiss, apparently forgetting how to walk in heels as I almost face-plant before I'm even out of the security of my cubicle.

She annoyingly clicks her tongue, giving me a look that tells me she doesn't believe me. "Obviously, I knew we had people higher up than Marty, they're just never *here*. I wonder what could be so *serious…*"

"You aren't helping."

There's no time for me to go back and forth with my best friend since college any longer. Darla has her arms crossed over her chest in a way that tells me if I don't haul ass across this office and meet her at the door in the next thirty seconds, she's going to make me regret it.

I come to a stop in front of the five-foot woman who scares me way more than I'd care to admit. She frowns, her jowls pronounced as she glares at me.

Despite the dirty look, I smile sweetly at her, knowing my mama told me to always kill them with kindness. "Good morning, Darla," I say, my voice sickeningly sweet.

Her frown lines get deeper. "I don't even want to know what you did to warrant his visit today," she clips.

Your guess is as good as mine, Darla.

"Who?" I try to look into the conference room behind her, but the door is shut.

Weird. That door is never closed.

"Why don't you find out for yourself?" Grabbing the handle, she opens the door. Her body partially blocks the doorway, making me squeeze past her to be able to get in.

Whoever this *he* is, doesn't grant me the luxury of showing me his face. He stands in front of the floor-to-ceiling windows, his hands in the pockets of the perfectly tailored suit that molds to his body effortlessly. I haven't even seen the guy's face but everything about him screams wealth. Even having only seen him from behind, I can tell that he exudes confidence. It's in his stance—the way he carries his shoulders, his feet slightly apart as he stares out the window. Everything about his posture screams *business*. I'm just terrified why *his* business is *my* business.

When they said boss, they really meant it. *Oh boy.*

What have I done?

Even the sound of the door shutting behind me doesn't elicit movement from him. It gives me time to look him up and down from the back. If I wasn't already terrified that I was in trouble for something I don't even remember doing, I'd take a moment to appreciate the view.

I mean *damn*. I didn't know that suit pants could fit an ass so perfectly.

I risk another step into the conference room. Looking around, I confirm it's just me and the mystery man with a nice ass in the empty space.

Shaking my head, I attempt to stop thinking of the way he fills the navy suit out flawlessly. From what I've been told, he's my boss. The thoughts running through my head are *anything* but work appropriate.

"Uh, hello?" I ask cautiously. My feet awkwardly stop on the other side of the large table from him. I don't know what to do. If I'm about to be fired, do I sit down first or just keep standing and get it over with?

I wonder if they'll give me a box to put my stuff in.

His back stiffens. Slowly, he turns around.

When I finally catch a glimpse of his face, I almost keel over in shock.

Because the man standing in front of me—my apparent boss —is also my ex-boyfriend's *very* attractive older brother.

ABOUT THE AUTHOR

Kat Singleton is an Amazon top 5 bestselling author best known for writing *Black Ties and White Lies*. She specializes in writing elite banter and angst mixed with a heavy dose of spice. Kat strives to write an authentically raw love story for her characters and feels that no book is complete without some emotional turmoil before a happily ever after.

She lives in Kansas with her husband, her two kids, and her two doodles. In her spare time, you can find her surviving off iced coffee and sneaking in a few pages of her current read.

ALSO BY KAT SINGLETON

BLACK TIE BILLIONAIRES:

Black Ties and White Lies: https://amzn.to/40POdqu

Pretty Rings and Broken Things: https://amzn.to/3Ponrlc

Bright Lights and Summer Nights : https://amzn.to/48d9Kgg

SUTTEN MOUNTAIN SERIES

Rewrite Our Story: https://amzn.to/3KNni8W

Tempt Our Fate: https://amzn.to/3W0K2XW

Chase Our Forever: https://amzn.to/3PIj85V

THE MIXTAPE SERIES

Founded on Goodbye

https://amzn.to/3nkbovl

Founded on Temptation

https://amzn.to/3HpSudl

Founded on Deception

https://amzn.to/3nbppvs

Founded on Rejection

https://amzn.to/44cYVKz

THE AFTERSHOCK SERIES

The Consequence of Loving Me

https://amzn.to/44d4jgK

The Road to Finding Us

https://amzn.to/44eIs8E

LINKS

PLAYLIST:
https://geni.us/BLSNplaylist

PINTEREST:
https://geni.us/BLSNpinterest

Printed in the USA
CPSIA information can be obtained
at www.ICGtesting.com
LVHW091126300624
784323LV00006B/155